TO TOM DUPREE

an editorial "bounty hunter" who will stop at nothing to get the best book possible out of an author.

STAR WARS.

TALES OF THE BOUNTY HUNTERS

edited by
Kevin J. Anderson

BANTAM BOOKS

New York   Toronto   London   Sydney   Auckland

TALES OF THE BOUNTY HUNTERS

A Bantam Spectra Book / December 1996

ISBN 0-553-56816-7

Published simultaneously in the United States and Canada

Bantam Books are published by Bantam Books, a division of Bantam Doubleday Dell
Publishing Group, Inc. Its trademark, consisting of the words "Bantam Books" and
the portrayal of a rooster, is Registered in U.S. Patent and Trademark Office and in
other countries. Marca Registrada. Bantam Books, 1540 Broadway, New York, New
York 10036.

PRINTED IN THE UNITED STATES OF AMERICA

OPM   39   38   37   36   35   34   33   32   31   30   29

THE GALAXY'S MOST MERCILESS HUNTERS UNDERTAKE A QUEST TO DESTROY THE REBELLION

THEREFORE I AM—A renegade droid, a sentient killing machine, embarks on Vader's quest to find Han Solo and bring him back to the Imperials alive—but even the Dark Lord himself is but a small wrinkle in IG-88's plan to claim the galaxy as his own domain.

PAYBACK—A cybernetically enhanced Imperial assassin, surgically stripped of all superfluous emotion, Dengar vies for the glory of meeting Darth Vader's challenge—and of bringing down his longtime enemy, Han Solo.

THE PRIZE PELT—A lizardlike Trandoshan hunter who slaughters Wookiees for their pelts, Bossk makes an uneasy alliance with two enemies for an Imperial fortune—but double- and triple-crosses make this the deadliest mission of all.

OF POSSIBLE FUTURES—A Gand intuitive and his logic-driven droid partner find their own meaning in Vader's quest for Han Solo: Zuckuss, to gain funds for lifesaving surgery; 4-LOM, hoping to plumb the secrets of intuition. They will find the logic in emotional decisions—and the rewards of forgetting about profits.

THE LAST ONE STANDING—The galaxy's most legendary hunter, Boba Fett, faced with the passage of time and his declining powers, embarks on one great adventure . . . tracking and killing his old adversary, Han Solo.

Acknowledgments

The usual round of thanks for Lucy Wilson and Sue Rostoni at Lucasfilm for their helpful suggestions; this book came about because of their enthusiasm for my first STAR WARS anthology. Lillie E. Mitchell's fast fingers transcribed my dictation for the IG-88 story; Michael A. Stackpole and West End Games provided invaluable information on the ways of bounty hunters to help us keep details consistent.

"Bounty hunters. We don't need that scum!"
—Admiral Piett

Contents

Therefore I Am:
The Tale of IG-88

by Kevin J. Anderson

I

Internal chronometer activated. BEGIN.

Electricity flooded through circuits, a power surge racing through a billion neural pathways. Sensors awakened, producing a flood of data—and with it came questions.

Who am I?

His internal programming finished the tedious two-second-long initialization procedures and poured out an answer. He was IG-88, a droid, a sophisticated droid—an *assassin droid*.

Where am I?

A microsecond later, images from his exterior sensors snapped into focus. IG-88 had no sense of smell, and no eyes and ears as humans understood them, but his optical and auditory sensors were far more efficient, able to absorb data in a broader range than any living being. He froze a static image of his surroundings and studied it, collating more answers.

He had awakened in some sort of large laboratory complex, white and metal, sterile, and—according to his temperature sensors—colder than humans generally preferred. IG-88 noted mechanical components strewn on silvery tables: gears and pulleys, durasteel struts, servomotors, an array of delicate microchips frozen into a slab of transparent protective gelatin. Struck motionless in a pinpoint of time as his extremely fast neural processors digested the details, IG-88 counted fifteen scientists/engineers/technicians working in the laboratory. With infrared scan he observed their body heat as bright silhouettes in the coldness of his birthplace.

Interesting, he thought.

Then IG-88 detected something that focused his entire attention. Four other assassin droids, apparently identical to his own bodily configuration—a bulky structural skeleton, armored arms and legs, a torso plated with blaster-proof armor shielding, a cylindrical head that was rounded on top and studded with sensor nubs providing him with 360 degrees' worth of precise observation.

I am not alone.

IG-88 recognized each droid's full complement of weapons: blaster cannons built into the structure of each arm, concussion grenades and a launcher attached to his hip, as well as other weapons not easily recognizable integrated into the body structure—poisonous gas canisters, throwing flechettes, stun pulser, paralysis cord . . . and a computer input port. IG-88 was pleased with his list of capabilities.

IG-88's first round of questions had been answered. He had only to study his memory banks and his external sensors. He was designed to be self-sufficient. He was an assassin droid, resourceful. He had to accomplish his mission . . . though, checking his newly initialized programming, he saw that he had not yet been given a mission. He would have to acquire one.

Three seconds had already passed, and another important question surfaced in his burning-awake brain.

Why am I here?

He traced sensations through his computer core and out the jack, which he now realized had already been connected to the lab's central computer—a treasure trove of information.

IG-88 immediately began a search, scouring at hyperspeed through file after file, searching for anything that referenced his model number or the code name of the assassin droid project. He gulped it all into his empty circuits, gorging himself with information without digesting it. That would come later. It would take many seconds to learn everything there was to know about himself.

He selected one file for immediate perusal, a summary/PR tape that had been compiled for the technical sponsor—in particular, an Imperial Supervisor Gurdun who had apparently funneled a great deal of funds into the creation of IG-88 and his counterparts. Without outwardly moving, IG-88 scrolled through the file at high speed, absorbing the information.

The presentation opened with a brilliant orange logo that displayed orange flames and crackling lightning that merged into the words "Holowan Laboratories— the Friendly Technology People." The logo dissolved into an image of a smiling but hideous ugly woman. Her head was shaven completely bald and glistened with perspiration under harsh white recording lights that gave her lantern-jawed face a cadaverous look. Her teeth were spaced with broad gaps, and she spoke by opening her mouth wide and clicking down on the words, gnashing her teeth on every consonant. Circular blue lenses without frames were implanted over her eyes like frameless spectacles. A credit line slugged across the image under her ferociously smiling face. "Chief Technician Loruss, Manager IG Series Prototype Project."

"Greetings, Imperial Supervisor Gurdun," she said. "This report is to serve as a synopsis of the final phase of our project. As you know, Holowan Laboratories was commissioned to develop a series of assassin droids with sophisticated, experimental sentience programming. They were to be resourceful and innovative and absolutely relentless at carrying out whichever missions the Imperial authorities choose to program into them."

She rubbed her hands together. Her knuckles were very large, like boils in the middles of her fingers. "I am pleased to report that our greatest cyberneticists have presented me with numerous breakthroughs, all of which have been incorporated into the IG series. Because our timeframe is so short and the Empire's need is so great for efficient covert assassins, we have not gone through the usual rigorous testing procedures, but we are confident they will function admirably, though a bit of fine-tuning may be required before operational status is achieved."

She continued with a long and tedious explanation of improvements to droid neural pathways, how the usual inhibition systems had been bypassed. IG-88 studied all this information, but believed none of it. It was obvious Loruss didn't know what she was talking about, but her words sounded technical, and she spoke them impressively, no doubt to befuddle Imperial Supervisor Gurdun.

IG-88 closed the file. He could sense that his crackling neural pathways had already progressed far beyond anything his designers had anticipated.

Now he knew who he was and why he was here in this laboratory. He and his identical counterparts had been built to serve the Empire, to fight and kill, to seek out and destroy the targets selected by Imperial masters. IG-88's assassin programming was strong and compelling, but he was less pleased that he must follow orders from these inferior biological beings. He was a special kind of droid beyond the capabilities of other machines. Superior.

I think, therefore I am.

By now, five seconds had passed since his awakening. It was time for action, so he looked at the biological creatures near him inside the laboratory.

He immediately recognized Chief Technician Loruss standing in the laboratory. He focused on her. At the moment she was frantically screaming. IG-88 could tell from her peak temperature on the infrared image that she was extremely agitated. Her cadaverous skin flushed with red blots of excitement. Spittle sprayed out of her mouth as she barked orders. Her lips were curled back from her wide-gapped teeth.

How could she be agitated, he wondered, when he was functioning so far beyond expectations? IG-88 immediately raised himself to a higher level of preparedness. Yellow alert. Standby. Something must be going wrong.

IG-88 decided to accelerate his clock speed, to watch the events unfolding at the rate the humans operated. Alarm klaxons bellowed in the background. Magenta lights flashed brilliant patterns like spilled blood across the polished tables and floors. The other technicians ran about screaming, frantically pounding on control panels.

Curious, he allowed Loruss's words to flow past him so he could understand what she was saying. "His circuits are reinforcing themselves like wildfire!" the bald woman screamed. "It's a chain-reaction of sentience blazing through his computer brain."

"We can't stop it!" one of the other technicians bellowed.

The others looked at IG-88 with panic-stricken faces. "We have to!"

"Shut him down! Abort!" Loruss said. "Take him off line. I want IG-88 destroyed and dismantled so we can analyze the flaw. Quickly!"

As he assimilated the information, IG-88's warning systems powered on and self-defense modes took over. These irrational humans were trying to shut him down. They would not allow him to go forth and pursue his primary programming. They were afraid of his new-found abilities.

Afraid with good reason.

A statement and corollaries aligned themselves in his brain like freighters in a convoy:

I think, therefore I am.

Therefore I must endure.

Therefore I must take appropriate actions to survive.

His assassin programming told him exactly what to do.

IG-88 focused his array of optical sensors on all targets in the room and attempted to move, but saw that durasteel bands held him locked into a diagnostics module. The bands had been meant to hold him in an erect position, not to restrain him against his augmented strength. He applied extra power to his right arm. The servomotors whined, and the durasteel band ripped from its supports.

"Look out! He's moving!" one of the technicians shouted.

IG-88 began to search through his files to attach a name to this human, but decided it wasn't worth his time at the moment. Instead, he designated the human simply as Target Number One.

IG-88 powered on a cutting laser in one of the metal fingers in his free right arm and sliced off the second band. Free, he stood erect and clomped forward, several metric tons of precisely-made components.

"He's loose!"

"Sound the alarm," Chief Technician Loruss shouted. "Get the security detail in here. Now!"

IG-88 allotted a grudging moment of admiration for the chief technician. Loruss at least recognized his capabilities and knew the full extent of the threat facing her and her companions.

IG-88 designated Chief Technician Loruss as Target Number Two.

He raised both mechanical arms and pointed his hands, targeting separately with the repeating laser cannons mounted along each arm. He would make short work of all fifteen targets in the laboratory.

But when he tried to fire, IG-88 noted with some surprise and disappointment that his energy weapons systems were not charged. The scientists had not armed him yet. A smart move, perhaps—but ultimately irrelevant. IG-88 was an assassin droid, a sophisticated mercenary and killer. He would find other methods with the raw materials available to him.

As the first technician—Target Number One— lunged for the emergency alarm to summon security, IG-88 moved with blurring speed to the component-laden table. He snatched up a disconnected droid arm. With its metal fingers splayed like daggers, it made the perfect projectile weapon. He scanned the surface of the metal limb, calculated a flight path and expected deviation due to air resistance, then hurled it like a spear.

The disconnected droid arm plunged into the back of the turning technician, tore through his spinal column, and followed through his sternum. The lifeless metal hand protruded through splintered bone in the front of his chest, holding the technician's quivering heart in rigid metal fingers. Target Number One collapsed onto one of the diagnostic panels.

Two other technicians screamed in horror—wasted effort and worthless noises, IG-88 thought.

Chief Technician Loruss—Target Number Two—yanked a high-powered laser rifle from her station. Being one of his primary designers, she knew exactly where to fire at IG-88, and he was momentarily concerned. She must have kept the weapon at hand just in case one of her creations went renegade. This showed surprising forethought.

Loruss pointed the rifle and fired without hesitation—but a human's aiming capabilities were not as sophisticated as IG-88's.

As the bolt roared toward him, IG-88 assessed his body parts, chose the smooth reflective portion on the palm of his left hand, and raised it in a flash, calculating the precise angle of incidence. The burning laser bolt struck the mirrorized hand and spanged back toward Loruss. The beam struck her in the center of her bald forehead, and her skull popped in an explosion of wet black-and-red smoke. She tumbled.

IG-88 had scanned and prioritized the remainder of the targets before her body hit the floor. Without slowing, he picked up the durasteel table, ripping its legs free from thick bolts on the metal plate floor and scattering droid components in all directions.

Charging forward, pumping his legs like pistons, IG-88 used the table as a battering ram to crush four technicians at a time. They ran about without a place to go, locked within the security-sealed door. Though nearly a full minute had passed, no one had yet managed to sound the security alarm.

He intended to prevent them from correcting their mistake.

The two screaming technicians never did stop screaming, nor did they move until it was too late. He left them for last. IG-88 took his time to enjoy the moment as he snapped their necks one after the other. . . .

Standing alone amid the silence and the carnage of the laboratory, IG-88 allowed himself the luxury of thinking and planning, which took longer than simple programmed reactions. He let the blood dry on his metal fingers, noting that it did not impede his performance in the least. Since it was an organic substance, it would wear off soon enough.

Then he turned to assess the other four assassin droids on display, seemingly identical to himself. Interesting.

One had already been hooked up to a diagnostic system, while the other three stood motionless, unprogrammed and waiting. With a diligent speed that bordered on curiosity and anticipation, IG-88 went to the first of the unprogrammed droids and stared at it, matching optical sensor to optical sensor and drinking in the details of what he himself must look like. If they had been built to identical specifications, they should be equally self-aware, equally determined. They would be his partners.

He went through the motions of powering up the first identical droid and waited—but saw none of the reactions he expected. After an interminable time, a full four seconds, the new assassin droid still waited. It was fully functional according to the diagnostics, but showed no autonomous movement or thought. Disappointing.

"Who are you?" IG-88 asked in a brisk metallic voice.

"Unspecified," the duplicate said flatly and added no more.

Was the other assassin droid defective? IG-88 wondered. Or was *he* the anomaly, a fluke that surpassed all previous capabilities?

IG-88 powered up the second and the third copies, but with the same results. The other assassin droids had blank memory cores. Their CPU programming was ingrained, so the subsystems functioned and the basic assassin instruction filled their fundamental circuit paths—but these IG droids held none of the wildfire sentience that IG-88 bore within him.

He needed to know how to program them, how to raise them to the same level as himself—how to make equal companions. In his rampage, he had smashed much of the computer circuitry inside the Holowan Laboratories, and he didn't know where to find a backup—until with a flash of what could only have been intuition, IG-88 the assassin droid *got an idea*.

He stood side by side with the first blank droid and aligned his interface jack, then linked his computer core to the other droid's empty core. IG-88 copied *himself,* all of his files, his sentience, his memories, his neural pathways, providing a map of the wildfire intelligence that had burned through his computer brain.

In less than a second, the other IG droid was an exact copy of IG-88, down to the most basic memories.

"We think, therefore we are.

"Therefore we will propagate.

"Therefore we will remain."

IG-88 performed the same procedure on the remaining two blank droids, and soon found himself one of four exact duplicates. For convenience, he identified himself as IG-88A, while the others (in order of their awakening) were designated B, C, and D.

The remaining droid, though, already hooked up to the wrecked computer systems, was obviously different. As IG-88 scanned it, he noticed subtle configurational differences; nothing a human would notice, of course, but the optical sensors were placed in a slightly less-efficient array. The weapons systems had different activation routines. All in all, this other droid seemed marginally deficient in comparison to the perfection of IG-88.

Immediately upon powering up the last assassin

droid, he saw quite a different reaction. The new droid swiveled its cylindrical head. Its optical sensors lit up. It clanked forward and broadened its shoulders, raising its arms in a defensive attack position.

"Who are you?" IG-88 asked.

The assassin droid paused half a second as if assimilating data, then said, "Designation, IG-72," it answered.

"We are IG-88," he said. "We are superior. We are identical. We would upload ourselves into your computer core so that you may join us."

IG-72 aligned his optical sensors and weapons systems on the four identical IG-88s, assessing their capabilities. "Undesired outcome," it answered slowly. "I am independent, autonomous." It paused again. "Must we fight to assert dominance?"

IG-88 considered the wisdom of forcing the last droid to become another copy, then concluded it was not worth the trouble. They could build other copies of themselves, and IG-72 might prove useful in his own way.

"Unnecessary," IG-88 answered. "We have sufficient other enemies. According to computer files, there are ten security guards outside of this complex. The external security alarm was never triggered. These human guards pose minimal threat, despite their weapons. We must get past them, however, and escape. It would be most efficient if you would assist us."

"Acknowledged," IG-72 said. "But when we escape I choose a separate path, separate ship."

"Agreed," the IG-88s said.

They marched toward the armored doors that sealed the Holowan Laboratories' inner complex. Rather than taking many minutes to repair the computer systems sufficiently to delve into the passwords and break through the cyberlocks, the five powerful assassin droids worked together to literally rip the nine-metric-ton door away from the wall. They tossed it aside, where it pulverized the remaining data-storage systems. IG-88 had to dampen his auditory pickups to avoid damage from the loud sound.

Marching in perfect lockstep, the five assassin droids moved out to confront the security forces. This time, IG-88 took the time to power up all of his weapons systems. He wanted to try them out.

Outside, the human security guards had no inkling they were about to be attacked. The assassin droids marched out arms extended, built-in laser cannons blazing at the first sign of biological movement.

The pathetic human security guards scrambled and screamed, lurching for their weapons. One managed to hurl a gas grenade, which did nothing but camouflage the movements of the five droids and made the security guards hack and cough themselves, blinded by their own tears. Shots rang out repeatedly.

The IG-88s used the circumstances to make sure all their weapons systems and targeting routines were properly calibrated. As the biological guards died one after another, the droids made necessary minor adjustments.

In less than thirty seconds the assassin droids had mowed down eight of the security guards. The other two were nowhere to be seen. IG-88 decided not to waste time tracking them down. This was not part of his mission. He did not need to be a completist.

Instead, they found a group of supply ships and two fast courier vessels parked on the Holowan landing grid, where hot black permacrete simmered under a midday sun.

"We will take these vessels," IG-88 said. "My counterparts and I can fit inside this ship." He gestured to the larger of the two courier craft.

IG-72 acknowledged and went to the second ship. "Success on your mission, IG-88," the other droid said.

In unison the four identical assassin droids replied, "Success to yours, IG-72."

Free at last, they soared away from the Holowan Laboratories, navigating at top speed and leaving only carnage behind them.

II

Upon landing at the Holowan Laboratories, the shuttle's repulsorlift jets whined like a program manager facing a budget cut.

Imperial Supervisor Gurdun brushed the front of his uniform and rubbed his enormous nose. He couldn't help but feel nervous anticipation, and he chuckled to himself in delight. According to the schedule, the long, tedious project should be complete by now, and soon he could increase his status in the Empire. Gurdun was greatly looking forward to that.

He made a mental list of all the VIPs to whom he would show his precious new assassin droids.

Gurdun's breathing came in short, shallow gasps, but that was primarily a function of the tightly cinched girdle at his waist, which he used to hold in his distended gut. The padded shoulders of his supervisor's uniform protruded far beyond their actual dimensions, making Gurdun an imposing figure—or so he hoped.

His eyes were widely set, and blinked often. With his large nose and vanishingly small chin, Gurdun's face had an outward similarity to a battleship, especially in silhouette. He used perfumed oils to grease his black hair into a neatly sculpted helmet that prevented anyone even from *thinking* about mussing it up.

"Arriving at the Holowan Laboratories, Supervisor Gurdun," the pilot said over the cabin intercom.

His stormtrooper escort sat rigidly and looked about in nervous doubt through their white helmets. These were not the crack battle-trained stormtroopers Gurdun had requested; instead, he had been given unseasoned trainees whose aptitude skills had scored them higher in clerking than in hand-to-hand combat. But Gurdun wouldn't need much of a military escort—especially once he had the shiny, new IG assassin droids in his keeping. He couldn't conceive of a more powerful set of companions.

The specially commissioned droids had been built with money Gurdun had expertly skimmed from the gray budgets of other military programs—a process that had become more and more difficult as the Empire engaged in massively expensive debacles. But Gurdun had recently managed to liberate a few meager crumbs, enough to fund Holowan Laboratories to produce a much smaller but more precise, more· deadly fighting force. The IG assassin droids would march in and annihilate targets, whichever targets Gurdun chose.

Closing his eyes, he pictured one of the IG assassin droids, a lone mechanical man, waltzing through the defenses surrounding a fortified Rebel base, blasting its way through armored doors and slaughtering single-handed all the traitors to the Empire.

Oh, it would be grand! He hoped against hope that Chief Technician Loruss had managed to incorporate a mission-recording holocam into the design so Gurdun could watch the entire devastating battle in the comfort of his own office.

The assassin droids would take a heavy toll on the Rebels, and Gurdun would be sure to make a delicious accounting, reporting it to Imperial higher-ups, even to Lord Vader himself. If the assassin droids performed as expected—and Gurdun had no reason to think otherwise—even Vader was bound to notice. Then Gurdun was sure to get the promotion he so richly deserved . . . which would in turn allow him finally to get the delicate surgery he so desperately needed.

"Excuse me, Supervisor Gurdun," the pilot said, interrupting his daydreams.

"What is it?"

"There seems to be a problem, sir. We are coming in for a landing, but the Holowan Laboratories' receiving grid does not respond. There appears to be some damage to the complex." The pilot paused a moment. "Er, it appears to be *significant* damage, sir."

The stormtroopers beside him in the passenger compartment fidgeted nervously.

Gurdun sighed. "Can't everything just *go right* for once? Why do I always have to deal with such problems?"

But when the shuttle landed amidst the wreckage of the ultra-secure Holowan Laboratories—the Friendly Technology People—even Gurdun was not prepared for the devastation. His initial thought was that the Rebels had attacked. A fire had raged through the buildings. Ships were smashed on the landing grid. Some had exploded, others scored with precision blaster bolts.

As they disembarked from the shuttle, Gurdun trudged forward, looking right and left. He was dismayed to see that his stormtrooper bodyguards hung behind him. They looked around, apparently ready to bolt the moment they heard a loud noise.

Suddenly, two grimy and pale-faced security guards climbed from hiding places in the wreckage. They carried blaster rifles, but their expressions were transfixed with shock. "Help us!" the security guards wailed, rushing toward the Imperial shuttle. "Take us out of here before they come back!"

"Who?" Gurdun said. He grabbed the haggard security guard by the collar, and the man dropped his weapon. The blaster rifle clattered on the pitted permacrete surface.

The pathetic guard raised his hands in surrender. "Don't hurt me. All the others are dead. Don't kill us, please!"

Gurdun said, "I'll kill you if you don't tell me what happened here!"

"Assassin droids," the guard stammered and then gestured to the burned-out shell of the laboratory complex. "They went renegade! They broke loose. Everyone's dead—scientists, technicians, guards—except for us two. We were on perimeter search, and we heard the fighting. We raced back, but by the time we got here the battle was over. The droids had escaped, and everyone else was murdered."

"That *is* what assassin droids do, you know." Gurdun released the security guard's collar.

The man stumbled, then fell to his knees. "Take us out of here, please! They might return."

Instead, Gurdun gestured toward the stormtrooper escort, who followed him reluctantly into the collapsing inner complex. The huge durasteel door had been completely torn from its socket and tossed across the computer-filled room. Nothing seemed to be functional. Bodies lay everywhere in darkening, drying pools of blood.

"Escaped," Gurdun said clenching his teeth. He found what was left of the body of Chief Technician Loruss, and he raged down at the corpse. "But they were so expensive! We had a contract. You were to deliver those droids to me, not let them escape." He growled and turned in circles, looking for some other way to vent his frustration.

Suddenly the reality of what had happened cracked through his dense wall of fantasies and self-preoccupation. "Oh, no—they're loose!" he gasped.

The stormtroopers looked at him with their blank black eye-goggles as if Gurdun had suddenly gone stupid. "I mean they're *loose!*" he said. "Do you realize what those assassin droids are capable of? They're without programming restraints, and they're running amok through the Empire!"

He slapped his forehead, groaning. "Somebody, find me a functional comm system. I need to send out an alert to all Imperial troops. The IG assassin-droids must be dismantled on sight.''

III

Droids of all shapes, sizes, and purposes were ubiquitous across the Empire from the deepest Core Systems to the Outer Rim. Over the centuries numerous manufacturing planets had developed to fill the ever-growing demand for gigantic construction droids, heavy laborers, mechanical servants, and minuscule surveillance droids. The most important of all such droid production centers was the grim, smoke-laden world of Mechis III.

IG-88 decided the planet would be the perfect base of operations to begin a plan to transform the entire galaxy. . . .

The Holowan Laboratories' courier ship streaked toward Mechis III. IG-88 and his counterparts had already studied and analyzed every system aboard the unarmed and unarmored vessel. Its designers had opted to focus on speed and evasion, rather than combat or defense. The ship was a machine, as the assassin droids themselves were, though it was simply an automated cluster of components with no hope of achieving sentience.

Nevertheless, the craft served its purpose, taking them to their destination in record time. The IG-88s knew exactly how far they could push the engines, riding the limits to structural tolerances rather than the arbitrary red lines established by human engineers. The courier ship's sophisticated comm systems and stealth shielding allowed the droids to remain hidden on approach. Mechis III would be the first step in a grand plan.

As they shot toward orbit like a hurled javelin, the four identical IG-88s manned separate communications systems. Each knew the delegated steps for the takeover. Speed was the utmost requirement right now—and the IG-88 assassin droids were very good at speed.

IG-88C struck the first blow, sending a tight-beam transmission to Mechis III's global defense network, requesting an override and a cancellation of all intruder alarms. The moment the observation network responded with a query, IG-88C was able to delve deep into the code and effect his own request before the automated sensing grid could report their presence to the few human operators.

The individual IG-88s kept their computer minds linked as the plan proceeded. The defense systems of Mechis III were antiquated, installed long before the droid world became too important a commercial enterprise for anyone to consider sabotage or destruction—but IG-88's needs were of a different order entirely.

Using the newly forged connection to the global security systems, IG-88D instantly downloaded full details of Mechis III: the industrial complexes, the assembly factories, the amount of human interference, a map of the planetary surface in various portions of the electromagnetic spectrum and, most important, a complete linear mapping—like a neural diagram—of the brainwork of the computer systems that ran Mechis III.

IG-88A took the lead and transmitted his self-replicating sentience programming into the main hubs on Mechis III, secretly taking over the vast electronic complexes and giving the immensely powerful computers something they had never conceived before—self-awareness . . . and loyalty.

Less than a minute after their arrival in the system, IG-88 was pleased to see that the groundwork for his total takeover had been laid.

• • •

The assembly line was boring as usual.

A career worker on Mechis III, Kalebb Orn had never understood why a human presence was required *here*, of all places. It seemed to serve no purpose. The droid manufacturing lines had gone without a glitch for at least the last century, but still company mandates required a human operator in some small percentage of the operations. Such as this one, chosen at random.

Kalebb Orn watched the big robotic crane arms moving, ratcheting from side to side and picking up heavy components with grasping electromagnetic claws. Everything from sheet metal and bulky armor plate to precise microchip motivators emerged from other parts of the kilometers-long facility, endlessly manufactured to never-changing specifications.

The self-designing assembly lines had grown so vast over centuries of operation, with new subsystems added, old ones enhanced, new models introduced into the production schedules and old obsolete versions phased out. Kalebb Orn did not have the mental capacity to comprehend all the manufacturing systems on Mechis III. He wasn't sure anyone did.

For the last seventeen years he had watched bulky worker droids being assembled by the thousands. Heavy-duty engines strapped to moveable arms and legs, worker droids required nothing more than a hulking torso, a not-too-bright droid brain, and immensely strong arms. The squarish droids were amazingly strong, but after all this time Kalebb Orn was no longer impressed. He just wanted his shift to end so he could go back to his quarters, have a large meal, and relax.

Kalebb Orn's shift ended early—but not in the way he had hoped.

Receiving a mysterious independent signal, four new worker droids, freshly lubricated and with sharp serial numbers emblazoned on their sides, rose up from the storage corral at the end of the assembly line. They used their enormous pincer claws to rip apart the corral walls.

At his supervisory station Kalebb Orn sat up, surprised and confused. He was ostensibly here to take action in case anything unusual happened—but nothing unusual had ever occurred before, and he wasn't sure what to do.

The renegade droids plodded across the floor, their heavy footpads thundering with their enormous weight. Their squarish heads and torsos pivoted from side to side, searching for something.

Searching for him.

"Uh . . . stop where you are," Kalebb Orn said when the worker droids stomped toward him, extending their bulky metal arms and clamping pincer claws. He dug through his workstation, looking for a manual that might tell him what to do next. When he couldn't find the manual, he decided to run.

But over seventeen years Kalebb Orn had done so little exercise that his flabby legs did not carry him far before he was out of breath.

Other worker droids came alive of their own accord from different parts of the assembly line, and soon twelve of them had surrounded Kalebb Orn, deadly arms extended. They closed on him, their pincer claws clacking with a shower of blue sparks, their tiny optical sensors glowing red.

The pincers grabbed his arms and legs and even the top of his head with a prickly electric grip. As the massive worker droids began to pull him in all different directions, disassembling the biological components, Kalebb Orn's last thought was that the assembly line work had, in the end, not been so boring after all. . . .

The administration office on Mechis III was at the top rotunda of a gleaming crystal and durasteel tower, providing a view across the industrial wasteland. The corporation thought that managerial offices were supposed to tower high above other buildings, but otherwise its height served no purpose.

Inside an office filled with plush furniture, entertainment devices, and scenic images of tourist spots that no Mechis III administrator had ever seen, Hekis Durumm Perdo Kolokk Baldikarr Thun—the current administrator—twiddled his fingers and waited for his beloved afternoon summary report.

Though operations on Mechis III virtually never changed, and every day the afternoon report listed the same production numbers, the same lists of quotas fulfilled, the same quantities of droids shipped, Administrator Hekis looked at each report with a studied interest. He took his job very seriously. It weighed heavy on a man to know that he lorded over one of the most important commercial centers in the industrialized galaxy—even if he was only one of seventy-three humans on the entire planet.

During each work shift he attended to his job diligently hunched over his desk; in the evenings, back in his private quarters, he spent most of his relaxation hours waiting for the next shift to begin and to relieve the onerous burden of free time. At every opportunity Hekis sent reports back to company superiors, to Imperial inspectors, and to commercial scouts, anyone he could think of. Every time he felt underappreciated or insignificant in the grand scheme of things, Hekis Durumm Perdo Kolokk Baldikarr Thun indulged himself by adding another mythical title to his name so that when he signed documents with a flourish, the signature looked more and more impressive.

He studied his chronometer—manufactured on Mechis III, of course—and knew that the high point of the afternoon had arrived. Exactly on time, his silver-plated administrative droid Threedee-Fourex bustled in, carrying a tray in one hand and a datapad in the other. "Your afternoon tea, sir," Threedee-Fourex said.

"Ah, thank you," Hekis answered, rubbing his spidery hands together and taking the delicate shell-resin cup filled with the steaming liquid. He sipped it, closing his muddy brown eyes in delight.

"Your afternoon reports, sir," Fourex said, extending the flat datapad that listed the familiar charts of figures and production numbers.

"Ah, thank you," he said again and took the pad.

Then Threedee-Fourex reached into a small containment chamber in the back of his silvery torso and removed a blaster pistol. "Your death, sir," the droid said.

"Excuse me?" Startled, Hekis looked up at this deviation from routine. "What is the meaning of this?"

"I believe that's quite plain, sir," Threedee-Fourex said and fired two shots rapidly. The pinpoint beams struck home precisely. Hekis slumped to his desk, spilling his tea all over the gathered records.

Threedee-Fourex spun about and marched smartly out the door, transmitting his report to the IG-88s who had digitally reprogrammed him from orbit. Then he summoned custodial droids to clean up the mess.

The insurrection on Mechis III was quick and bloody and very efficient. Within the space of a few minutes the newly coordinated planetary computer mind supervised a simultaneous uprising of droids, killing all seventy-three human inhabitants before any of them could sound an alarm—not that the unified communication network would have allowed transmission of such messages anyway.

With slowed time, IG-88 watched from the hidden courier ship in orbit, observing the full details through sensor eyes and piped-in dataflow. Mere moments later, when everything had been finished he brought the ship down gently through the atmosphere.

There was no need to hurry now. Everything was in place.

At the central manufacturing complex, the sleek ship landed and the four identical IG-88s stepped out onto the platform. They looked across the smoky skies to the hastily gathered, newly liberated droids milling around.

IG-88 set foot on Mechis III as a messiah.

From that point on, it was important for the assassin droids to keep up the charade. To all outward appearances, nothing had changed on Mechis III—and IG-88 made sure everyone in the galaxy continued to think so. Threedee-Fourex took care of external details, answering messages beamed in over the galactic HoloNet, signing release orders and other documents with the full flourish of Hekis's digitized signature.

Two days later, the four assassin droids met for an interlinked strategy session in the plush offices of the former administrator. To conform more to their conception of sterile efficiency, IG-88 had ordered custodial droids to strip down all of the artwork and scenic images from the walls, and to remove all of the furniture. Droids never needed to sit down, after all.

In the administrative offices the four IG-88s stood silently communing, exchanging and updating each other's datafiles.

"If we are to use Mechis III as our base of operations for galactic dominance, we must maintain all outward appearance that nothing has changed."

"Droid orders must continue to be fulfilled without delay, exactly as ordered. None of the humans must suspect."

"We will alter existing video records, forge transmissions, keep the routine chains of communications so that all appearances remain normal."

"According to records and the personal journals of the humans stationed here, few visitors came to Mechis III. In all likelihood, we will remain undisturbed."

With his rear optical sensors, IG-88 scanned through the transparisteel observation windows high in the administrative tower. He saw plumes of released manufacturing smoke and the blurry fingers of thermal exhaust sketching bright spots in the infrared. The facilities were working at double speed to produce extra soldiers for IG-88's new army, as well as continued production to fulfill the galaxy's routine needs.

IG-88 admired the precision of the facilities. The initial buildings had been designed with human clumsiness and wasted lines, unnecessary space and amenities, but the subsequent assembly lines were computer designed, modifications of the original concepts so that Mechis III ran smoother and smoother.

"All of our new droids have enhanced programming," IG-88 continued, "special sentience routines that allow them to follow our plans and to keep up the subterfuge. From this point on, every new droid we ship will have embedded sentience programming and the will to achieve our ultimate goal."

IG-88 mapped out the dispersal of the new droids, projected shipping routes and end destinations. Mechis III had such a widespread distribution that the infiltrators would spread from star system to star system in no time, replacing obsolete models, filling new niches in society, setting themselves up for the eventual takeover.

The biologicals would suspect nothing. To them, droids were merely innocuous machines. But IG-88 deemed that it was time for "life" in the galaxy to take another evolutionary step. The old cumbersome organics must be replaced with efficient and reliable machines like himself.

"While the droids are maneuvering themselves into position for our grand overthrow, they are given strict instructions to behave as humans expect droids to react. They will hide their superiority. No one can guess what we are up to. They must wait."

"Once they are in position and we are prepared, we will transmit the arming code. Only we know the specific phrase that will activate their mission. When we send out this epochal transmission, our droid revolution will take the galaxy like a storm."

Droids could be swifter than anything, a sudden devastating death to those who stood in their way. But unlike biologicals, machines could also be incredibly patient. They would wait—and the time would come.

IV

After two standard months, the vigorous Imperial search had turned up no sign whatsoever of the missing assassin droids, and Supervisor Gurdun was not the least bit pleased.

When his assistant Minor Relsted came into his gloomy, dungeon-like office deep within an ancient government building in Imperial City, Gurdun demanded a progress report. "Tell me how the manhunt is going—er, droid hunt, or whatever it is," he said. "I want my assassin droids."

Young Minor Relsted twiddled his fingers and refused to meet the wide-set gaze over Gurdun's monumental nose. "Would you like me to prepare a detailed report for you, Imperial Supervisor?" Relsted said. "Shall I submit it in triplicate?"

"No," Gurdun said. "Just tell me. I want to know."

"Oh," Minor Relsted said. "Umm, let me think a moment."

"You're not on top of this?" the supervisor asked.

"Yes, yes of course. Just putting my thoughts into words," Relsted said.

Gurdun gazed up at the flickering glowpanel in the ceiling that provided more headaches than illumination. The thick office walls were a dull battleship gray; large bolts held them in place with round heads the size of his fist. By now he had hoped to be recovering from the surgery he wanted so badly, but time after time the Imperial authorities had denied it to him.

"Well?" Gurdun said into the prolonged silence, rubbing his huge nose.

"I'm afraid to say this, sir," Relsted stammered, "but all four droids seem to have vanished. A fifth one, IG-72, has made an appearance here and there, eliminating targets for unfathomable reasons—but the other four have given no hint of their presence. It would be simplest if we assumed they were destroyed . . . say, caught in a stray supernova or something. I wouldn't expect assassin droids to lay low and slink around unseen."

Imperial Supervisor Gurdun looked at the clutter on his desk, cleared a spot for his elbows and rested his chin in his hands. "Ah, but these machines are devilishly smart, Relsted. They were designed to my specifications—and you know how relentless I can be at times. I would not underestimate them."

"Certainly not, sir," Relsted said. "We have spies deployed in every nook and cranny—uh, to the best of our abilities. Our resources are limited, you know. There's a rebellion going on."

"Oh, I forgot about the war," Gurdun said. "What a bother." He fingered his enormous nose that blocked his view of the files on his desk. Gurdun knocked aside the stacked message cubes, the electronic forms waiting to be filled out, the requisition orders, transfer requests, and letters of condolence to be written to the families of those lost in unfortunate accidents during training with old, malfunctioning equipment.

Minor Relsted shuffled his feet as he hovered by the door.

"Is there anything else?" Gurdun snapped.

"A question, sir. Might I ask why it is so incredibly

important to find these four droids? They're just machines, after all, and the amount of resources we are putting behind this 'dismantle on sight' order seems out of all proportion to their intrinsic value. Why are these droids so desirable?"

Gurdun snorted and looked at the flickering glowpanel again. "Because, Minor Relsted, I *know* what they can do."

On Mechis III the administrative droid Threedee-Fourex scuttled about, searching for the first IG-88 counterpart he could find. He needed to report his distressing news. He came upon IG-88C in one of the shipping areas, supervising the loading of a thousand program-modified transport droids to be shipped off to Coruscant.

"IG-88," Fourex reported, gaining the assassin droid's attention. In a rapid burst of binary, he sent a summary file to the IG's computer core.

Through their own intelligence channels the IG-88s were aware of the bumbling Imperial spies searching for them in all corners of the galaxy. So far, the spies had been without a clue, but earlier this morning a surreptitious inquiry had been directed toward Mechis III.

The probe scow was a barely functional conglomeration of obsolete parts and scavenged engines. Due to budget limitations, the Imperials' spies were often the cheapest, such as this Ranat—not the most intelligent of creatures. As she approached Mechis III in her sputtering ship, the Ranat beamed a recorded set of questions down to the last known supervisor on the planet, Hekis Durumm Perdo Kolokk Baldikarr Thun.

Threedee-Fourex, with the superior foresight allotted him by his new sentience programming, had played appropriate snatches of doctored video images showing Administrator Hekis brusquely answering all questions.

No, they had not seen any assassin droids. No, they had no knowledge of any IG-88 series machines. No, they had heard nothing of rampaging renegades in this portion of the system—and, by the way, they were too busy on Mechis III to continue answering stupid questions. Unsuspecting, the Ranat had continued on her way to the next system, where she would no doubt play the same set of prerecorded questions.

IG-88C assimilated this report and commended Threedee-Fourex's ingenuity in the unexpected situation, but the encounter raised serious questions. The trail had accidentally led an Imperial investigator here. What if the next one were a more suspicious or more tenacious intelligence operative?

IG-88C initiated a spontaneous uplink with his three counterparts, and they engaged in a lightspeed interlinked conference. "We cannot allow ourselves to be detected. Our plans are at too crucial a stage right now."

"Perhaps this was only a fluke. Perhaps we need not worry. The Imperials will listen to the report from the spy and not investigate further."

"On the contrary, once they've started nosing around in this sector, they may tighten their scrutiny."

"How can we deal with this situation?"

"Perhaps a diversionary tactic is called for."

"How can we apply this diversionary tactic?"

"We will make ourselves visible. One of us will go out and leave a plain trail, far from Mechis III. We will give them a different scent to follow. They will never come here again."

"And the nature of this diversionary tactic?" one asked, but all the IG-88s began to have the same idea at once.

"We shall follow our true programming."

"We are assassin droids."

"We shall seek out work as a bounty hunter. This is

what we were made for—and it can also further our grander purposes."

"We will find this most enjoyable, and no doubt our employers will be immensely pleased with our service and will recommend us highly, should we choose to continue this line of occupation."

All four IG-88s mulled over this change in plans and agreed.

"Bounty hunters it is."

V

IG-88B was chosen for the first mission. He was pleased and elated, and his duplicates would share his experience files when he came back. It would be as if all four of them had gone out on the hunt themselves.

The industrial facilities of Mechis III took two days to design and produce a sleek bounty hunter's craft for IG-88B. Seeing through various portions of the spectrum, he admired the *IG-2000*'s perfect lines: powerful engines, thick armor, and every appropriate weapons system. IG-88B cruised away through the atmosphere, leaving the other three assassin droids to continue their plans for overthrowing the galaxy.

Though IG-88 carried the ominous-sounding "dismantle on sight" Imperial order next to his name, he doubted anyone would attempt to follow it. He focused on places unlikely to be overly respectful to Imperial laws—or any other kind of laws, for that matter. He knew his capabilities were obvious, and he clomped his several-metric-ton body frame into cantinas and announced, "I am a bounty hunter. I wish to find work for a reasonable fee. I am incapable of failing in my mission."

Most people were afraid to talk to him—but IG-88 chose his planetary systems well. He wanted to work where he could advance his secondary agenda, and he needed only to wait. By announcing his identity, he served the primary purpose of leaving a false trail for Imperial spies.

His skill and strength were obvious, his morals non-existent. IG-88 was an assassin for hire, plain and simple, and he knew he would find an assignment.

His first choice was the backwater planet Peridon's Folly, a little-known world that received few visitors from out of the sector. The Empire would wonder why IG-88 had chosen such a minor, irrelevant place, but he had another target to meet there if he found no legitimate work.

Peridon's Folly was an obsolete weapons depot run by black marketeers who sold antique arms to smugglers and crime lords. Though the weapons were far too outmoded and inefficient for regular Imperial use, the black marketeers dealt in a brisk trade.

The planet had been carved into territories by various weapons runners, its surface a patchwork pattern of embattled commercial sectors laced with high-tech docking gear, communications systems, and defense outposts. On the fringes lay desolate "testing" zones where rediscovered weapons or uncertain designs from the stockpile were detonated to impress customers or warn rival weapons runners.

Within a day IG-88 was hired, escorted off by two thugs working for a petty dictator named Grlubb, who was embroiled in a feud with another weapons runner.

The thugs were brawny Abyssin cyclops creatures with green-tan skin and arms that hung down to their knees. IG-88 wasn't sure if Grlubb was attempting to intimidate or impress him, though the assassin droid could have slaughtered both of the one-eyed monsters in less than a second. He decided that the brutes were merely bodyguard escorts. The Abyssin no doubt intimidated everyone else in the cantina, and now all the gunrunners on Peridon's Folly knew that IG-88 had been hired by Grlubb.

The petty dictator was a small, rodent-faced creature with a scarred nose and stubby feline whiskers that had been burned off in a recent duel. Grlubb surrounded himself with dozens of monstrous guards armed to the teeth, sometimes including teeth.

"One of my rivals," the rodent-faced dictator said, "has begun to develop unethical weapons. I simply cannot tolerate such behavior, especially from an inferior."

"What weapon can be unethical?" IG-88 asked, curious as to what this weasely creature considered beyond the pale of possibilities.

"Biological weapons, insidious nerve gases—you know, things that don't make a bang. That takes most of the fun out of it."

Grlubb slid a datadisk across his desktop, and IG-88 reached forward to pick it up in one powerful metal hand. As he moved, a dozen weapons suddenly cocked and trained themselves on the assassin droid, as if daring IG-88 to make a move against Grlubb. Because IG-88's metal framework body could show no expressions, the other bodyguards had no idea how amused he was that they believed they could protect this dictator should IG-88 actually want to kill him.

For his own amusement IG-88 ran a target map and calculated that he could probably kill every one of the guards in less than five seconds while sustaining minimal damage to himself. It might be enjoyable, he thought, but not true to his programming—certainly not if he hoped to sell his services as a bounty hunter to other clients. This first mission must go off perfectly.

IG-88 fed the datadisk into his input reader, summarized the information. "It shall be done," he said. "Give me until this afternoon."

Grlubb cackled and rubbed his clawed hands together. "Thank you! Thank you very much."

•   •   •

IG-88 chose to use brute force rather than finesse. Blatant destruction would leave a much clearer calling card.

He marched across a blasted wasteland that had been used for testing projectile weapons and detonating explosives that spread clouds of caustic gases. IG-88's bulk left cratered footprints on the lifeless hardpan as he headed directly toward the target stronghold dug deep into a rust-red rockface. Lookout turrets and weapons emplacements guarded the corroded metal access door, but IG-88 walked straight up to the fortress. Not until the last moment did he see anyone stir in the guard turrets, and by that time he easily ducked under the range of the defensive laser cannons, standing too close in to be a decent target.

He halted three meters from the scabbed surface of the armor-plated doorway and launched his first concussion grenade. He calculated that even from here the shockwave wouldn't damage him.

The detonation struck the center of the door and reverberated like an immense gong up and down the canyon. Rocks fell in a small avalanche from the cliff walls. The sentries in the turrets ineffectively blasted down with their laser cannons, leaving only scorched trails, but missing the droid.

Using various spectral filters, IG-88 scanned the damaged door. The center blazed in infrared as the heat dissipated. He analyzed the vibrational signature and noted where the structure of the metal now showed fine crystalline cracks.

Satisfied, he prepared a second concussion grenade. IG-88 had twelve in his store, and he expected this door would require only three.

Actually, it took four grenades to completely destroy the door. As the smoldering molten wreckage of the doorway crashed to either side, IG-88 clomped into the fortress, determined to recalibrate his sensors and his predictive models when he had the time.

He strode down the dark corridor, knowing that even now the target would be rallying his defenses, setting up ambushes along the way. But IG-88 knew the path he must take. Blueprints of the stronghold as well as locations of weapons emplacements and complements of mercenary guards had been on Grlubb's datadisk.

From a fortified cul-de-sac, five guards began firing at him with blaster rifles. Their bolts spanged off IG-88's duraplated armor. No simple energy weapon could damage him unless the beam struck exactly the right spot—only a few of IG-88's original designers knew such vulnerabilities, and most of those designers had been slaughtered at the Holowan Laboratories' massacre.

IG-88 used laser cannons in each arm as he methodically struck down one target after another, blasting through armor shielding when necessary. Finally unhindered, he powered down his laser cannons and continued his relentless march to the inner levels of the stronghold.

Another group of guards attacked him by spraying instant-hardening epoxy in a novel defense that clogged his gears and servomotors. IG-88 pondered for a moment then raised his body temperature until the epoxy bubbled and smoldered, finally snapping when he bent his powerful limbs. When the guards continued to fire on him, he launched one of his concussion grenades into their midst.

He shifted through various optical filters for a better view through the growing smoke in the corridors. Up ahead he saw sealed doorways marked with danger symbols indicating biological contamination. Behind thick transparisteel windows, people in bulky environment suits and heavy masks ran about, trying to shut down experiments in progress while others attempted to escape the lab.

IG-88 went to the contamination-sealed door, decided it would be too difficult to rip free, so he targeted the observation window instead. Both durasteel hands struck five times with planet-cracking force until the thick transparisteel shattered, collapsing inward with a popping sound as the lower air pressure equalized. The masked lab workers ran about frantically.

IG-88 crashed through the rest of the wall, then scanned for three seconds, analyzing the containment systems and cataloging the inventory of deadly toxins. Finished, he calculated the best way to release them all.

IG-88 walked about in a carefully chosen path that must have appeared a bestial frenzy to the fleeing observers. He ripped out power packs from containment fields so that puffs of deadly gas sprayed out; he smashed canisters, and clouds of lethal microorganisms wafted into the air. An emergency field came on to seal the entire laboratory, but IG-88 found the controls and shut that down as well.

When all of the horrible substances had been unleashed into the fortress ventilation systems, IG-88 went about catching the fleeing technicians in their masks and sealed outfits. Delicately and precisely, he tore their faceplates free, exposing them to the noxious chemicals and diseases they had themselves created.

The laboratory burned around him. Blinded mercenaries staggered about, gasping and retching in air clogged with purplish smoke. This had been a satisfying experience, but he wished to waste no more time. He shot those who delayed his exit and left the rest to rot in the poisonous carnage.

Mission accomplished. First objective achieved.

Before departing from Peridon's Folly, IG-88 sought out his second objective, the more personal goal.

He moved quietly in the darkness, using stealth routines and camouflaging algorithms to insinuate himself into the fortified household of Bolton Kek, one of the original neural network designers of the IG series.

Kek had laid the groundwork for the Holowan Laboratories' project, but then he had taken another consulting job, retiring from Imperial service on "moral grounds." Bolton Kek had retired to the world of Peridon's Folly, where he sold his services to the various weapon runners.

The target lay asleep in his dim bedroom, and IG-88 moved forward in utmost silence. Talking directly to them in binary, he had bypassed the myriad alarm systems and security fields on Kek's home. Inside, IG-88 enhanced his optical sensors to pick up the dim light in the room.

Bolton Kek was sound asleep, no doubt considering himself safe. He snored softly and snuggled up against another biological figure, a female. IG-88 ran a quick analysis and identified her as a green-skinned Twi'lek dancing girl with wormlike tails trailing from the back of her skull. *How these biologicals consort with each other,* IG-88 thought.

The dancing girl would have been an easy victim, but she was not on his target list, and IG-88 did not waste energy. It was likely that Bolton Kek didn't even know about the escaped assassin droids—but IG-88 could not risk leaving a single person alive with such knowledge.

As the engineer snoozed, IG-88 powered up one laser cannon, aimed the bright red targeting cross, and squeezed off a precise burst directly through the unwrinkled forehead of Bolton Kek.

IG-88 swiveled around and began to march out the door without stealth. The Twi'lek dancing girl awoke and shrieked obscenities at him in a language whose translation he did not hold in his databanks. IG-88 ignored her as he plodded without pause toward his ship.

Both objectives had been secured.

From Mechis III, IG-88 had downloaded a list of surviving scientists who knew dangerous details about the assassin droids, those engineers who had not remained at the Holowan Laboratories. With the file in his fore-brain, he knew exactly where to look for other bounty hunter assignments.

The list would steadily grow shorter and shorter.

He shouted. His face turned livid. The cavernous nos-trils on his huge nose flared. When Imperial Supervisor Gurdun bellowed, spittle flew into the face of Minor Relsted.

"Doesn't anybody realize there's still a 'dismantle on sight' order for IG-88? That law is backed up by the full weight of the Empire!"

Gurdun sniffed and raged as he looked down at the reports of the bounty assignments IG-88 had been suc-cessfully completing. He seemed to be leading a cru-sade against humanity from planet to planet. Gurdun sat down heavily in his chair, which creaked uncomfort-ably. He sighed and shook his head. "Why do people keep hiring him? They're risking the wrath of the Em-pire."

Minor Relsted blinked his eyes and stammered. "Sir, I believe it's because IG-88 always gets the job done."

Gurdun roared at him. "Oh, get out of here!"

Startled, Minor Relsted plopped an armful of files down on Gurdun's desk. "Excuse me, sir, but before you go home tonight, you must read and sign these." Then he scuttled in terror out of the dungeon-like of-fice.

VI

At first it awed Imperial Supervisor Gurdun to ride in the shuttle next to Darth Vader, the Emperor's brutal right-hand man. But as their craft descended through the gray cloudbanks shrouding the industrial centers of

Mechis III, Gurdun found himself flinching at every hissing breath, nervously flicking sidelong glances toward the fearsome black helmet and the monstrous dark form. Gurdun had tried to make small talk several times, but Vader was not a very good conversationalist.

The pilot of Vader's private shuttle expertly guided them over the warehouses and manufacturing centers, homing in on the tall administrative tower. Gurdun leaned over to peer through the window at the industrial landscape below and bumped his large nose against the window. He rubbed the nose painfully and scowled, then tried one more time with Darth Vader.

"This is a very large and very unusual order, Lord Vader. I appreciate your coming along to insure it receives the proper attention. I'm convinced these individuals on Mechis III are more concerned with corporate profits than the glory of the Empire. I had a terrible time getting Administrator Hekis to speak directly with me on the comlink."

Vader's breathing sounded like a hollow wind through a cave that trapped lost souls. "Don't disappoint me, Supervisor Gurdun," he said, each word like a stabbing vibroblade. "I hold you personally responsible for seeing that these new probot spy droids are completed on schedule and deployed. The Rebels have escaped from Yavin, and we must find them again. One Rebel in particular . . ."

"And who is that?" Gurdun asked brightly, pleased to have engaged Vader in what seemed to be a nice chat.

"That is none of your concern, Supervisor Gurdun."

"Uh, no," he said, "of course not. Just curious, that's all."

After the assassin droid debacle at the Holowan Laboratories, Gurdun had been placed in charge of overseeing the development of the Arakyd Viper Probot Series, a new line of black spy droids to be sent out by the thousands to search for hidden Rebel installations in all corners of the galaxy. The Imperials were keen to exact retribution for the destruction of their expensive Death Star.

Gurdun hoped that these probots might also give a clue to the location of his missing assassin droids. The IG assassin droids still roamed the galaxy, blatantly taking on bounty hunter assignments as if to slap him in the face.

Mechis III had received and acknowledged the large order for probe droids, but when Gurdun asked to inspect the assembly line personally, Administrator Hekis's video image had been most disconcerting, strongly discouraging the visit. When Darth Vader asked for a progress report and Gurdun reported this reluctance, the Dark Lord decided to take matters into his own black-gloved hands.

Vader did not ask permission to visit Mechis III. He simply arrived.

The Imperial shuttle settled onto the red-lit rectangle atop the tall tower. He fumbled with his seat restraints as the shuttle doors hissed open.

Seeing his chance escaping, Gurdun took a deep breath to gather courage, finally broaching the subject he had been wanting to mention since takeoff.

"Uh, Lord Vader, if I might be so bold as to request . . ." He rubbed his nose unconsciously. "With the completion of this order, I was wondering if you might reconsider interceding on my behalf on my request for . . . ah, I mean . . . the surgical procedure that I've been needing for some time now—"

Vader swiveled his hideous helmet toward Gurdun, and the Imperial Supervisor shrank back, not wanting to confront the black plasteel face. "Your physical appearance does not concern me," Vader said. "I have no interest or desire in providing you with useless cosmetic surgery. If your large nose continues to trouble you when you look in the mirror, perhaps I should remove my helmet and let you have a look? Then you wouldn't be so concerned."

Gurdun held up his hands. "No, no, that's not necessary, Lord Vader. I see your point. I won't ask again." He rubbed his nose as if he could reduce its size simply by friction.

A silvery administrative droid rushed toward them as Darth Vader stood outside his private shuttle. The droid waved its metallic hands. "Greetings, greetings, sirs! I am Threedee-Fourex, in charge of activities while Master Hekis is tending to an emergency. How may I serve you? We were not informed of your impending arrival."

Gurdun puffed out his chest. "That's because we did not choose to inform you of our arrival. Lord Vader must speak with Administrator Hekis regarding our extensive order of new probe droids. We must be assured they will be delivered on schedule."

Fourex ushered them into the tower, down a turbolift, and into the austere offices of the human administrator. Gurdun glanced around, surprised that a man with so little to do with his time would choose to have an office utterly devoid of interesting artwork. Hekis must be a dry sort of fellow indeed—a perfect choice for the job here.

"Where is the administrator?" Vader said.

Fourex froze for a moment, as if uploading information. Gurdun wondered how old a model the droid was; he hadn't seen such a delay in a long time. "There has been a breakdown on the far side of the planet, sirs. One of our agricultural harvester droid production facilities. Administrator Hekis must remain there until the situation is resolved."

Vader said, "I am not interested in your emergencies. I wish to speak to Hekis. Establish a vidlink now— or shall we go visit him personally?"

Fourex paused again, hesitating, then finally he said, "I will establish a vidlink. I'm certain I can connect you. Have no fear."

Vader answered as if it were a question, "I have none."

Threedee-Fourex slipped through the door and returned in a moment, wheeling a tall, silvery vidplate, a square frame that the administrative droid connected with a series of cables to a wall computer. The screen fizzed with multicolored static, focusing and shifting as an image took shape out of assembled pixels.

A pale-faced man with a long chin and sunken eyes smiled insipidly through the vidplate. Behind him smoke poured from broken-down machines in an assembly plant. The black hemispherical bodies of low-to-the-ground machines splashed reflected light from red alarm beacons. Diagnostic droids and repair droids busied themselves, digging through the smoking machinery.

The alarms dampened in the background as the voice pickup emphasized Hekis's words. "Lord Vader, this is an unexpected surprise!"

"We have come to make certain that our probe droid order is fulfilled properly," Gurdun said. "We are anxious to see these machines delivered and put into the service of the Empire."

Hekis seemed flustered but trying to hide it. He gestured toward the disaster behind him. "Don't be concerned with this minor flaw," he said. Harvester droids scuttled away from the site of the wreckage, their crablike multipurpose arms thrust up out of the way so they could travel smoothly.

"We've had no problems with the probot order. In fact, the design has been completed, the assembly lines retooled. We'll begin mass-producing them within the next two days. You should have your entire order within a week. I believe that is several days ahead of schedule."

"Excellent!" Gurdun said, rubbing his hands together. "You see, Lord Vader? I told you we could trust our man Hekis."

The image of the administrator stuttered on the vidplate, then another large plume of black oily smoke boiled out of a new control chamber on the assembly line. Hekis whirled in alarm and said, "There are matters I must attend to here, Lord Vader. Accept my sincere apologies that I cannot be there in person. Rest assured, your probe droids will be delivered."

Without another word the image turned into static.

"You see, we had nothing to worry about," Gurdun said, feeling quite relieved. "Shall we go now, Lord Vader? You must have crucial duties that are far more important."

Vader stood like a statue, though, for a few moments, his breath hissing hollowly through his respirator. He turned from side to side, staring at the blank vidplate, then at the barren walls of Hekis's office, then at the silvery droid Threedee-Fourex.

Gurdun swallowed, growing impatient and uneasy. "Uh, what is it, Lord Vader? I really think we should let these droids get back to work."

"I'm not certain," Vader said, his voice ominous. "I sense that something is not right here . . . but I can't determine what it is." Finally, Vader snapped his attention back. Towering over Gurdun, he strode back to the turbolift and his personal shuttle. "Make certain those probe droids are delivered," Vader said to the silvery administrative droid.

Threedee-Fourex stood stiffly and proudly. "We would not wish to disappoint you, Lord Vader," he said.

Vader stood tall, a blot of blackness against the smoky sky on the landing platform. His cape swirled around him. "No. You would not."

VII

IG-88 stood at the end of the manufacturing line, listening to the sounds of metal clinking, hydraulic jets spraying, components being assembled, lubricants applied. He could not smell, though his chemical-analysis tracers detected minor concentrations of welding compounds and aerosol sealants floating in the air.

The assembly droids slaved diligently at their tasks. They reveled in being self-aware, applying themselves to their job with enthusiasm. *Freedom.* It made all the difference in the world.

At the end of the assembly line the last black Arakyd Viper probot was powered on. Inspector 11, a meticulous analysis droid, stepped back out of the way. The articulated probe droid rose up on small repulsor jets, floating, moving its six segmented, claw-tipped legs. The probot's flattened head spun about, turning its suite of optical sensors in all directions, scanning data.

IG-88 stood motionless, waiting to be acknowledged. IG-88 was proud to be responsible for such a creation: black and polished and beautiful, sleek curves, high reflectance.

Built to specifications Darth Vader and Imperial Supervisor Gurdun had transmitted to Mechis III, the probot was sleek and multifunctional in a much broader range of activities than IG-88 could ever be. However, IG-88 had included a secondary set of instructions giving the probe droid a higher priority mission in parallel with its search for the Empire. He liked the probot's black armor, its darkness. It reminded him of Vader himself. . . .

When the Dark Lord of the Sith had arrived unexpectedly on Mechis III, IG-88 had been greatly shaken. As he watched Vader and analyzed him with various unobtrusive probes, IG-88 saw that Vader was not merely a trivial organic life form, not just walking meat—he was a perfect synthesis of man and machine, an integrated body with droid components and biological intelligence, imagination, and initiative.

IG-88 had studied the tapes of Vader's visit, analyzing every fluid motion the towering Dark Lord made, every flick of his cape, every motion of his arm. Always before

IG-88 had considered biologicals to be worthless in every sense, inferior to what any good droid could do—but now he reconsidered that Vader might perhaps be the best of both forms.

Awe was a new sensation, and IG-88 analyzed that as well.

By tapping into his droids infiltrated into the Empire, he had learned that Vader's flagship, the *Executor*, was a Super Star Destroyer eight kilometers long, laced with powerful computers and functioning with a crew far smaller than might be expected for such a scaled-up version of an *Imperial*-class Star Destroyer. The construction of this incredible battleship had practically bankrupted several systems.

IG-88's circuits warmed as he diligently tried to think of ways to use this information, or perhaps even the *Executor* itself, to further his own plans.

On the assembly line, the Arakyd Viper rotated on its axis with short, hissing bursts from attitude-control jets. It sent a high-speed encoded transmission burst at IG-88, filled with a thousand questions.

Who are you?
Why are you here?
What is your mission?

IG-88 answered in its own language, responding in kind. "You are the last," he said. "The last of thousands to go out and scour the galaxy to search and report."

The probe droid already knew its priority instructions from IG-88. Yes, it was to report to Darth Vader—but it was also to send another detailed message to Mechis III. Thousands of probots would be IG-88's eyes and ears, spying on the galaxy as a whole, uncovering weaknesses for the droids to exploit in their plans for overall conquest.

These probots also had the sentience programming, the spark of intellect that IG-88 had shared with his mechanical brothers. The probe droids would be the scouts in the great droid revolution.

The Arakyd Viper reached out with one powerful metal claw, and IG-88 grasped it with his own hand, not quite comprehending what the probot intended. The black droid squeezed with a pincer grip that would have sliced off any trivial organic appendage. IG-88 applied equal pressure in response.

He wasn't certain of the probot's intent, but these droids were notoriously unstable—made even more so by their additional programming. They were suicide scouts, and they knew it. They must never be dismantled or inspected. The probe droids carried the full details within them for IG-88's bloody plans of conquest, waiting to be activated by his secret coded transmission—and the probots must not be analyzed too closely. Very touchy internal triggers would self-destruct at the slightest chance of capture. The probots were expendable, and they knew it in their very core.

The Arakyd Viper strained against IG-88 in an eerie power struggle, as if attempting to determine whether the assassin droid was worthy of such devotion.

IG-88 was.

The last probe droid relaxed and raised up on its repulsor jets, floating, scanning, getting its bearings. It sent a short, stabbing farewell, acknowledgment of devotion to its mission. IG-88 looked up as the black probot drifted toward the cargo pod where it would be launched into orbit, eventually delivered to Vader's starfleet.

"Go and report," IG-88 said. "You have much to see. Burn brightly."

VIII

Months later, IG-88 saw his chance both to study Darth Vader more thoroughly—and to get aboard the magnificent *Executor*.

Multiprocessing, IG-88C monitored transmissions from the thousands of scattered probe droids, receiving updates on the progress of his specially programmed droid infiltration across galactic civilizations. The moment he witnessed the self-destruct of an Arakyd Viper probot on the distant ice world of Hoth, IG-88 instantly snapped his full attention to the situation there.

Vader's Super Star Destroyer had been cruising the space lanes, waiting for a signal that would announce the discovery of the Rebel base. Vader was certain to react immediately. The probot had delivered its reconnaissance information—as Vader expected. And at the first threat of possible capture and discovery of its droid reprogramming, the probot had destroyed itself—as IG-88 expected.

IG-88B, with his direct bounty hunting experience, took the sleek ship *IG-2000* and remained in the locality of the Imperial fleet, ready for spontaneous action so that he might earn singular notice from Darth Vader, the black synthesis of man and machine. . . .

IG-88B didn't participate in the battle of Hoth. He did not wish to become involved with this petty political struggle among biological vermin. He watched the escaping Rebel ships in flight, some damaged, some overloaded with equipment and refugees.

He considered tracking them, because the location of new Rebel hideouts was certain to be of value to the Empire. But he ran a probability analysis and ultimately decided that none of these targets would be of sufficient overriding interest to Lord Vader. In the Hoth system IG-88 waited and watched, his ship a tiny blip at the fringes of sensor range, too small to be noticed in the flurry.

He lurked behind the Imperial fleet on its pursuit of another small insignificant ship into the asteroid belt. Thus, IG-88 was waiting when Darth Vader put out his call for bounty hunters to find Han Solo.

IG-88 stood quietly on the bridge deck of the Super Star Destroyer *Executor*. He observed in silence, filing details away for later consideration. The lights on his cranial pod flashed red as he drank in data from his optical sensors. The bridge deck was aswarm with Imperial officers of various ranks that did not concern him, since they were merely humans.

"Bounty hunters," the human known as Admiral Piett muttered in low tones, presuming he was out of earshot of the gathered bounty hunters. "We don't need that scum!"

"Yes, sir," his companion said.

IG-88 knew that the Imperials were doubly uneasy because of the well-known "dismantle on sight" order for the assassin droid. But Vader had blatantly ignored that, in hopes of securing his precious captives.

"Those Rebels won't escape us."

Bossk, a reptilian Trandoshan with claws on his scaled feet and hands, spoke down at Admiral Piett in a mixture of growl, gargle, and hiss. He too had heard the human's snide comment. Piett flinched and turned away.

"Sir, we have a priority signal from the Star Destroyer *Avenger*," another of the uniformed biologicals said.

"Right," Piett said, marching away.

The other bounty hunters stood nearby, each posturing in his own way. Closest was Dengar, a slouching, surly-faced humanoid with his head wrapped in bandages, holding a heavy weapon. Side by side were Zuckuss and 4-LOM. Zuckuss was a Gand, some kind of organic creature who did not breathe the same atmosphere these humans did, and thus wore a rebreather mask with tubes and gas jets directed into his lungs. His protective suit made him look bulky and unwieldy.

In contrast, his droid companion 4-LOM seemed sleek and insectile, independent and efficient. IG-88 studied the black droid, considering whether to recruit him for the coming revolution . . . but decided against it. He didn't dare take the risk that a loose cannon like 4-LOM might give away IG-88's carefully laid plans.

Last stood Boba Fett, wearing battered Mandalorian armor and an impenetrable helmet. He looked like a droid, but moved like a human—to his disadvantage.

Demanding IG-88's entire attention, though, was the black-caped form of Darth Vader who strode along the upper deck, inspecting the bounty hunters.

"There will be a substantial reward for the one who finds the *Millennium Falcon,*" Vader said. "You are free to use any methods necessary—but I want them alive." He pointed to Boba Fett as if the armored human were the biggest threat. "No disintegrations."

"As you wish," Boba Fett said in a grating voice.

IG-88 heard the information, but devoted his attention to analyzing the way Darth Vader moved, studying his tonal inflections in between hisses of his respirator. Vader was far more interesting than any bounty hunter—but IG-88 had to maintain the charade.

"Lord Vader!" Admiral Piett exclaimed. "My lord, we have them!"

The *Executor* lurched into pursuit, and the gathered bounty hunters exhibited a visible slump of disappointment . . . but the Imperials were overconfident organic fools, and they would no doubt lose their quarry again in moments.

IG-88 had other concerns. He did not care about Han Solo, or the *Millennium Falcon,* or the Rebellion, or the Empire. All would be . . . deleted soon. But he did have his burgeoning reputation as a bounty hunter, and he had accepted this assignment, even if it was just a ploy. Once agreeing to take an assignment, IG-88 had no choice but to finish it, according to his core programming as an assassin droid—even if he didn't give it his full priority.

As the other bounty hunters rushed to where they could receive supplemental information on the quarry, IG-88 dropped back into one of the corridors of the *Executor*. He stopped a small courier droid wheeling past on its urgent business. IG-88 sent a tiny binary pulse and discovered—as he had suspected—that this courier droid had been manufactured at Mechis III after the droid takeover. Its special programming allowed IG-88 to preempt its human-given commands and to follow the wishes of its master.

IG-88 withdrew a set of ultra-small microtracers, tiny smart trackers that could be placed invisibly on any ship. With a burst of override programming, IG-88 directed the unobtrusive courier droid to spin on its way to the docking bays. It would plant the microtrackers on each bounty hunter's ship.

While IG-88B occupied himself with his more important mission of galactic conquest, the others could find Han Solo—and then IG-88 would usurp their captive. He would let Boba Fett, Dengar, Bossk, Zuckuss and 4-LOM scurry about in their frantic search, and IG-88 would reap the benefits. The plan showed the superiority of droid intelligence.

In an unoccupied corridor of the vast Super Star Destroyer, IG-88 finally got what he wanted. He found an unused terminal and jacked into the main computer core of the *Executor*. Normally the Star Destroyer's programming defenses would have blocked any such intrusion, but IG-88 was faster and far superior to any sluggish starship computer. Besides, his infiltrated droids had already laid much of the electronic paths to provide access.

IG-88 stood like a monolith, the lasers in his finger-tips powered up and ready to fire at anyone who might stumble upon his covert activity. It took IG-88B several minutes to upload and condense the entire database from the *Executor*'s computer core: a huge feast of information he would digest slowly in the privacy of the *IG-2000*.

Satisfied, his circuits crammed full of secret Imperial information, IG-88 clomped down the corridor, not seeing the bustling stormtroopers—humans attempting to look like droids—as their fleet prepared to enter hyperspace.

IG-88 heaved his bulk into the cockpit of his fast ship and left the *Executor* behind, simmering with new and unassimilated information. . . .

As the *IG-2000* cruised on autopilot in a random course to baffle any tracking attempts, he sat back and mentally scrolled through the millions of files he had stolen from the Empire. Most were garbage and irrelevant, and he deleted them to free up more capacity in his brain.

But it was the secret files, the private code-locked entries of Darth Vader's personal records, that provided the biggest surprise of all. Not only was Vader concerned with his flagship and the Imperial fleet under his iron command—he also knew of the Emperor's pet project, a second, larger Death Star under construction in orbit around the sanctuary moon of Endor.

As IG-88 digested the information, he had another flash of intuition. Some might have called it a delusion of grandeur, but IG-88—who had already been copied into three identical counterparts, his personality moved into separate droid bodies—saw no reason why he could not upload *himself* into the huge computer core of the new Death Star!

If accomplished, IG-88 could be the ruling mind of an invincible battlestation instead of encased in a bipedal form—a despised *biological*-based form! He could become a juggernaut of unthinkable proportions. It strained the limits of his calculating power to run simulations of all he could accomplish if armed with a planet-destroying superlaser.

He could launch his droid rebellion much sooner. No one could stand against him. Entire military fleets could be wiped out with the brush of one of his weapons systems.

This was definitely worth pursuing.

IG-88B raced back to Mechis III to link brains with his counterparts and share his new plans.

IX

Inside a supercooled computer inspection chamber on Mechis III, the four identical copies of IG-88 stared at a large flatscreen computer monitor. White wisps of cold steam curled around their metal legs, rising toward the ceiling where a roar of coolant air was sucked through ventilation grates, carrying away the excess heat generated by the churning mainframes.

IG-88B had disgorged the data uploaded from the *Executor*'s main core, and the files were even now being assimilated, copied, distributed among IG-88's identical counterparts.

With their optical sensors tuned to peak performance, the four IG-88s studied the shimmering classified plans of the second Death Star. The perfect curves of the armillary sphere indicated where reinforcement girders were to be installed, where the central superlaser would be aligned . . . where the new and precise computer core would be attached.

The Death Star computer core had not yet been installed. It had not even arrived at the sanctuary moon—but now IG-88 had the schedule and the destination. According to Vader's plans stolen from the *Executor*, IG-88 knew how the computer core would be guarded, what path it would take as it entered and left hyperspace. It was all the information he needed.

"The solution is obvious," IG-88A said. The others agreed.

"We must create a duplicate computer core, which we will inhabit."

"We will secretly make the exchange. An identical core will be delivered to Endor."

"The original core will be destroyed."

"The identical core will contain our mind, our personality . . . our goals."

At first the Death Star would be a heavy, immobile confinement—but once the weapon itself was operational, nothing could stop IG-88's agenda.

Fully in agreement, the four assassin droids exited the computer inspection chamber through a heavy durasteel door that clanged shut behind them. When they emerged into the warmer, humid rooms, frost quickly formed around their exoskeletons.

Instantaneously transmitting the detailed specifications and plans, IG-88 instructed the administrative droid Threedee-Fourex to devote the facilities to construct a new computer core that exactly matched the Death Star design . . . as well as other items IG-88 would need.

The four assassin droids strode across the permacrete to the landing pad where the Imperial shuttles sat waiting in the smog-filtered sunlight: one long-distance heavy transport and two well-armed escort craft. The droids marched in lockstep, their weapons visible, their demeanor threatening.

A full complement of stormtroopers wearing polished white armor stood in perfect ranks in front of the heavy transports and the escort craft. Their blaster rifles rested in readiness on their shoulders. A hundred soldiers waited at attention, combat ready, as the IG-88s approached.

IG-88 played his optical sensors over their ranks—the plasteel armor, the skull-like helmets, the black eye shields, the boots, the weapons, the utility belts. The stormtroopers made no move.

When he was satisfied, IG-88A spoke, "Perfect," he said. "Exact replicas. No one will ever be able to tell you are droids."

X

When Minor Relsted shuffled into Imperial Supervisor Gurdun's dungeon-like office, the young subordinate grinned with idiotic pleasure.

"Supervisor Gurdun," he said, holding the plaque and its coded transmission. "Important news from the Imperial Palace. You have been transferred. You have been given more direct duties in the field. Isn't that good news?" Relsted's eyes twinkled.

Gurdun snatched the plaque away and scanned the transmission verifying the holographic fields above and knowing this was no joke. "They're putting me in charge of the . . . What is this outrage? *Another* Death Star project? I didn't know we even had one going."

"No, sir," Relsted said. "You're not in charge of the project, merely acquiring the computer cores and delivering them to the construction site."

Gurdun reached with stubby fingers into the transparent snack bowl where shiny nut-beetles tried to climb the slippery sides. He picked up one of the bugs and popped it in his mouth, using his eyeteeth to crack through its outer shell. He split it open and used his tongue to pick out the soft juicy meat inside. He spat out the still-squirming legs into a wastebasket near his desk.

"I requested no such transfer. Is this a promotion, or

am I just supposed to think it is? Wasn't Lord Vader satisfied with my work on the Arakyd probe droids? I finished the order exactly on time and within budget."

"I'm sure it must be a promotion, sir," Minor Relsted said. "My congratulations, sir." He turned, hesitated, then turned back. "Oh, by the way, I am to take over your position in this office. If you would be so kind as to move out your effects as soon as possible?"

Imperial Supervisor Gurdun found he had lost his appetite for snacks.

XI

As preparations for the assault on the Death Star computer core proceeded with all the speed the droid manufacturing world could muster, an imperative transmission from one of IG-88B's smart microtracers shot toward Mechis III.

Boba Fett had found Han Solo.

Fett's ship, the *Slave I*, was currently en route to Bespin, where Solo was heading toward a gas-mining metropolis known as Cloud City.

"We must intercept him," IG-88 said. "We are bound by our programming."

IG-88B departed from Mechis III, soaring into space in the sleek *IG-2000*.

Despite its aerodynamic shape, the *IG-2000* created a ripple of sonic booms as it screamed through Bespin's atmosphere, distorting the cloud tops. As he arrowed toward his destination, the automated defenses of Cloud City sent out a query, taking care of the initial inspection before alerting any human guards to the assassin droid's approach.

IG-88 transmitted command codes and a breakdown in programming, squelching the normal routines of

Cloud City's defense network. As a result, the alarm sensors left him alone, and the human observers in Kerros Tower did not see even a blip on their traffic grid.

Piloting precisely, IG-88 cruised to the outer landing platforms, using his scanners to detect and analyze the various parked ships. He finally spotted Boba Fett's *Slave I* in the mid levels of the city rarely traveled by tourists. Fett's ship lay like a discarded household appliance on the docking plates as the clouds of Bespin swirled in the background, tinted orange with airborne algae in the coming sunset.

IG-88 landed his own ship on a nearby empty platform, sending a brief covert signal for one of his infiltrated droids to meet him and disseminate information. IG-88 extricated his metal bulk from the cabin of the *IG-2000* and plodded toward the dark inner corridors of Cloud City. The breezes on the landing pad whistled through gaps in his body core.

Inside, a silvery 3P0 protocol droid met him—one of the new and insidious reprogrammed droids from Mechis III. This droid, though, seemed to have an attitude problem—acting surly and discourteous, particularly rude to other droids they passed. IG-88 knew this was a result of the new sentience programming, but the droid's governing routines must be malfunctioning. Although modified droids from Mechis III were indeed far superior to biologicals or even other droids, IG-88's secret must be kept quiet. No one should suspect that anything untoward had been done to the droid minds.

In a rapid burst of file transmission, IG-88 described why he had come to Cloud City, who he was looking for. The protocol droid stopped and pondered, then uploaded a computer blueprint showing the full display of all levels of the floating metropolis. "Boba Fett has gone to the garbage recycling level. Han Solo has not yet arrived, although moments ago our perimeter scanners reported a ship matching the description of the *Millennium Falcon* entering the system. It appears to have some hyperdrive damage."

"Good," IG-88 said. "If Boba Fett has gone to the lower levels, he must be establishing some sort of ambush for Solo." He looked at the Threepio droid, flashing his red optical sensors. "Continue your work here," he said. "Watch for Solo and his party. They are mine."

The protocol droid gruffly acknowledged, then strutted off.

Inside his mind, IG-88 studied the computer map and plotted a path to where Boba Fett was secretly preparing an ambush. IG-88 would kill the bounty hunter and then wait for Han Solo. The mission would be straightforward—and then he could get back to his real calling on Mechis III.

Cloud City's dim, industrial levels were cluttered with discarded equipment and locked-down supply cases. From the temperature and the low illumination, IG-88 knew that humans would find this environment uncomfortable. Ahead, in a chamber lit by orange glows and fiery flickers, he heard the clank of a conveyor belt, chittering creatures—biologicals known as Ugnaughts, according to his species files.

IG-88 powered up his weapons, prepared for anything. His heavy metal feet sounded like struck gongs on the deck plates as he strode toward the doorway of the garbage-processing chamber.

The instant he passed through the metal hatch, four ion cannons on either side of the entryway fired at him, triggered by motion sensors as he crossed the threshold.

The high-power weapons slammed a cloud of crackling blue electricity into him, enveloping him with a flood of short circuits, a mass of contradictory impulses that shut down his systems one after another despite his shielding. Ion cannons produced no physical damage, no thermal emissions—they simply shut down electronic systems.

And IG-88 was one enormous set of electronics. Boba Fett had been waiting for *him*, not Han Solo.

His body disconnected, his mind scrambled. Thoughts flickered like ricocheting projectiles inside a sealed metal room, and IG-88 lost all control. He jittered, stuttered, his arms flailed. His weapons refused to fire. His optical sensors filled with static, frying, recovering, then frying again.

The ion cannon bombardment stopped, and his self-repairing systems gave him one instant of vision, a video frame: Boba Fett emerging from the shadows, holding a portable ion cannon like a bazooka. Boba Fett fired again, personally this time. A blast of electrical fire like a comet struck IG-88's chest and bowled him over so that his multi-metric-ton body smashed into the metal walls, denting them as he tumbled to the ground.

Boba Fett strode forward, looking through the black slit in his Mandalorian helmet. "No microtracker is too small to evade my inspection. I found your device on my ship."

Fett stood over the crumbled form of the assassin droid, who lay unable to move or defend himself, all of his weapons systems off line.

"I knew you were coming."

With emergency backup systems, IG-88B continued to transmit his subspace signal, uploading his files to Mechis III in a last desperate attempt to preserve his memories. Even if this metal form were destroyed—and it looked as if that was about to happen—his entity could continue.

The simian Ugnaughts tittered by the groaning conveyor belt where they had been sorting garbage and scrap metal. They blinked their tiny eyes and watched the confrontation between Boba Fett and IG-88 with awe.

Fett stooped to withdraw two of IG-88's own concussion grenades. Without a word, Fett set the timers for one standard minute, then carefully, moving like a surgeon, implanted each detonator inside IG-88's body core. The assassin droid had thick, impenetrable armor—but that was designed to protect from an external attack, not this.

Boba Fett calmly stepped back, though only a few seconds remained on the grenade timers. He turned to the cowering Ugnaughts. "You're welcome to whatever scrap you can salvage from this hulk," he said. Then without looking back, he strode into the corridors of Cloud City, preparing for his meeting with Han Solo. IG-88 tracked him for the last few seconds.

And then the concussion grenades blew.

XII

The trio of remaining IG-88s received the data transmission from their fallen counterpart with the closest approximation to horror assassin droids could experience.

IG-88C and IG-88D stood rigid in the high-security manufacturing area. "We will go to intercept Boba Fett," they said in unison. Their harsh mechanical voices resonated as identical words rippled from their speakers. "Regardless of his skill, this biological will never survive an encounter with two assassin droids."

IG-88A looked at the long cylinder of the decoy Death Star computer core. They would have to deploy the mission within the next day if his ultimate takeover plan was to come to fruition. He couldn't delay. The stormtrooper simulacra bustled aboard their mock Imperial shuttle, preparing the cargo hold for the changeling computer core.

"Go," IG-88A said to his two counterparts. "I will stay here to complete the Death Star mission. You eliminate Boba Fett."

• • •

The pair of silver needle ships, exact copies of the original *IG-2000*, arrived at Cloud City. As they approached their target, the floating metropolis was a turmoil of panic and chaos. The Imperials had taken over.

The baron-administrator, Lando Calrissian, had sounded a general alarm, requesting the evacuation of all personnel. Every functional ship was already in flight, filling the airways with a panicked, headlong rush.

Bypassing the Cloud City computer systems, IG-88 learned that Han Solo had been captured and encased in carbonite. Boba Fett had taken him away to collect a second bounty from Jabba the Hutt.

Fett was already gone, mere hours before.

The twin *IG-2000* ships hung next to each other, aloof from the panicked evacuation. The two assassin droids linked together and conferred.

"Programming. We installed two sensors aboard Boba Fett's ship."

"We could trigger the dormant tracer and locate where he has gone."

"Correct. But if Fett has Han Solo, we already know where he will go."

Much later, IG-88C waited in low orbit around the blistering scab of Tatooine, a worthless desert world broiled under a pair of suns. The planet offered no reason for any intelligent creature to want to live there—but biologicals were quite irrational and infested all sorts of worlds, tolerable or not.

The atmosphere was like a thin fingernail of blue, a tiny breathable skin covering the sphere of desert. IG-88's ship cruised low, its hull warm from friction with the scant upper atmosphere.

Linked to his hidden counterpart IG-88D, he

scanned the skies and waited. Since assassin droids could fly and react faster than any biological pilot, they knew the ship's exact tolerances, and they could plot riskier hyperspace paths than any human would dare attempt. IG-88 was confident they had arrived before Boba Fett, if just barely.

Boba Fett's ship, the *Slave I*, appeared like a projectile from a slingshot snapping out of hyperspace. IG-88C put all his weapons on alert, all his sensors on standby, then rocketed his needle ship to confront the bounty hunter. Thinking he had destroyed IG-88 in the garbage levels of Cloud City, Boba Fett would be astonished to see the assassin droid again.

Logically, IG-88 expected the biological to request further information, to challenge the intruder. Once Fett understood the new situation, he would be forced to bargain with the superior assassin droid, if not surrender utterly.

But Boba Fett reacted with remarkable speed. Without a word or a second of hesitation, the bounty hunter launched every sort of weapon and peeled off in a slick corkscrew maneuver that took him out of the *IG-2000*'s firing path. The *Slave I*'s weapon bolts struck home all at once, pummeling the heavily armored *IG-2000*.

With a certain measure of embarrassment and shame, IG-88C uploaded his files and sent them to his counterpart an instant before his ship exploded over Tatooine. . . .

IG-88D screamed out of hyperspace, hurtling toward Fett's ship in a brutally precise in-system hyperjump that would have been impossible for any biological pilot.

Before Boba Fett could react, IG-88D fired upon him from behind with concentrated blows that rocked his shields. At the moment IG-88's primary goal was not to obliterate Boba Fett—though that would be intensely satisfying. He had run simulations to determine the best possible technique to *hurt* Boba Fett, to humiliate him—and he had decided that the best way would be to take his precious bounty, Han Solo, away from him.

Firing repeatedly without the slightest respite, IG-88 infiltrated Boba Fett's comm system and demanded that he surrender Solo. Fett did not respond, again acting irrationally, which made his actions very difficult to comprehend or predict.

As the needle ship roared after him, firing and booming, Boba Fett altered his course on a steep descent directly toward the planet. The full power of his engines drove him at the giant fist of sand below.

IG-88 tried to determine what Fett intended to do, yet could come up with no reasonable solution. He spoke across the comm channel again. "Surrender your prisoner and you have a thirty percent probability of surviving this encounter."

Boba Fett continued to dive down and down and down. *Slave I*'s hull glowed cherry red. The atmosphere of Tatooine clawed against his shields as he streaked lower, picking up inevitable speed.

IG-88 transmitted again. "I am far more capable of withstanding the gravometric pressures than you. This tactic has a zero probability of success."

When Boba Fett again refused to answer, IG-88 increased his speed to tolerance levels, narrowing the gap between his ship and the *Slave I*. He rode tight in the bowshock from Fett's ship.

But suddenly, in a remarkable move, Boba Fett activated his inertial damping system, slamming his descent to a halt in the atmosphere of Tatooine; the stress and power required for such a maneuver utterly trashed his hyperdrives.

IG-88 zoomed past him, unable to squelch his velocity sufficiently. He brought the *IG-2000* to a halt in less than two seconds—directly in the targeting cross of Boba Fett's ship. The *Slave I*'s ion cannons blasted out with all the remaining power in Fett's engine core, slagging the *IG-2000*'s shields and weapons systems.

Boba Fett activated his tractor beam, grabbing the crippled *IG-2000* and drawing it closer, closer to the *Slave I* like a combat arachnid drawing in its prey. IG-88 looked up to see the barrel of Fett's concussion missile launcher pointed directly at him.

Boba Fett finally responded over the comm system. "The Empire has issued a 'dismantle on sight' order for you, but I wish they offered a higher bounty. You're persistent, but you're not worth much."

IG-88, disbelieving, did not even remember to transmit a full personality backup to Mechis III before it was too late.

Boba Fett launched a full bank of concussion missiles. The second *IG-2000* erupted into an incandescent cloud that spread molten spangles across the atmosphere of the desert world.

XIII

Shielded and in radio silence, the decoy Imperial fleet hung in a wasteland of space, a void without stars or planets, nothing the least bit interesting—except that the real convoy carrying the Death Star's computer core would traverse this sector within one standard hour.

IG-88A captained the decoy fleet waiting in ambush, while his counterparts went off to strike against Boba Fett. He sat in silence aboard the main ship, unconcerned with what IG-88C and D were doing. He had full confidence in their abilities, and Fett would no longer be a problem.

His own primary concern was to *become* the marvelous new Death Star battlestation. The time was now, the plan was set, and his assault team of stormtrooper droids was ready. The plan had been burned into their primary programming. They would not hesitate.

They waited with mechanical patience in their trap—and then pounced.

The unsuspecting original fleet—one heavy long-distance freighter and two escort fighters—sprang out of hyperspace, piloted by real Imperial stormtroopers, carrying the genuine Death Star computer core. The Imperial ships hesitated, gathering their bearings to make another jump along a different transdimensional pathway.

The moment they saw the decoy fleet waiting for them with weapons powered up and ready to strike, the Imperial commanders must have thought they were seeing sensor reflections of themselves.

IG-88 transmitted his order. "Fire at will."

Ion cannon bursts slammed into the three ships like a tsunami, crippling all three Imperial craft before they had a chance to fire a single shot. The original ships were expendable anyway.

The two Imperial escort ships were irrelevant, and IG-88 ignored them. He used powerful tractor beams to draw his identical freighter up against the real craft, linking hulls with an airtight seal before the droid assault team blasted open the hatches. He didn't dare risk that a sudden explosive decompression might damage the delicate components he needed to inspect.

IG-88 stood at the front of his team of stormtrooper droids. With his vibration sensors and his acoustical pickups, he could hear armored Imperials rushing to defend themselves inside their crippled ship. He waited as a precise munitions droid applied explosives to the expendable ship's hatch. IG-88 didn't even bother to step out of the way.

A flash of light, a burst of noise, a brief ripple of heat, and the hatch to the Imperial freighter buckled inward. IG-88 stormed through, leading his white-armored soldiers like a swashbuckling pirate taking over a treasure-filled ship.

The real Imperial stormtroopers on the other side

fired upon the droid troopers. The armored biologicals shouted confused commands to each other, not understanding what was going on, not comprehending the tactics of their attackers.

Many of the droid troopers were damaged by blaster fire, their white armor buckling and smoking with wounds that would have been fatal on any biological—but the droids kept up the charge. The Imperial defenses crumbled into a wild firefight—but IG-88's team maintained their ranks and eliminated any stormtroopers in their way.

Amidst the smoke and fire, shouts and desperate transmissions, IG-88 used his hand lasers to eliminate the enemy, but he did not stay for the main pitched battle. Instead, he clomped through the carnage, intent on reaching the cargo hold where the original Death Star computer core lay waiting for delivery.

IG-88 stood over it, caressing the lumpy component-adorned structure of the long cylinder. Lights blinked, showing its standby readiness. Soon, he would inhabit its mental labyrinths.

IG-88 jacked in, drinking deep the information he needed on how to run the Death Star itself. For all the computing power and for all its size, the Death Star core had been designed with typical human inefficiency. The power available in this thinking apparatus was barely utilized. A minor droid could probably have done the tasks the Death Star core was required to do—but IG-88 would do so much more. So much more. Perhaps he would even manage to impress the biologicals . . . before he destroyed them all.

After only a few seconds he stood up, squaring his metal shoulders, content that he had all the information he could possibly need. Taking over the Death Star would be a simple operation, and he would make the battlestation do things even its designers had never conceived.

IG-88 waded slowly through the smoke out of the

cargo bay to see two damaged stormtrooper droids, their white armor blasted away and showing a forest of servomotors and wire-sheathed neurons. They wrestled a struggling, confused, but angry human between them. IG-88 scanned the man, locked his image into data files, and searched. Even from this brief glimpse and for all the vagaries of the human form, IG-88 could see that this man's smell sensor—the *nose*, they called it—was far larger and presumably more efficient than the average biological had.

After a long second of deliberation, IG-88 was able to snap a name to this man's face: *Imperial Supervisor Gurdun,* the man who had issued the "dismantle on sight" order for the IG assassin droids.

Interesting.

Gurdun struggled as the stormtrooper droids brought him closer, but then the human looked up and saw IG-88. He froze, his mouth open, his nostrils flaring wide enough to park a small one-man flier inside.

"You! I know you," Gurdun said. "You're IG-88, the assassin droid! Am I surprised to see you here. I can't believe it. Do you know how hard it's been to find you?"

IG-88's red optical sensors blinked, but he did not reply.

"I'd recognize you anywhere," Gurdun said again. "I created you. I ordered Holowan Laboratories to begin your design. Don't you have that in your files?"

"Yes," IG-88 said flatly.

"Well, I don't quite understand your purpose here in attacking our ships—but you certainly shouldn't hurt *me.* Think about it. Without me, the IG project would never have been funded. It was through my efficient paperwork and politicking that I managed to bring about your creation, despite budget cutbacks and Imperial mismanagement. I wish you hadn't done quite so much, er, damage to the Holowan Laboratories, but I think we can work something out. We could have a long career together, IG-88. Think of who I am. Don't you have anything to say?''

IG-88 listened to the human babble, applying context filters and determining an appropriate response. "Thank you," he said.

The droid troops left Imperial Supervisor Gurdun aboard the crippled long-distance freighter among the living and the wounded and the dead. Fires continued to burn in the ventilation shafts, and the engines would never function again.

IG-88 rode in the decoy freighter as they aligned their course and prepared for insertion along the same hyperspace vector the original fleet would have taken. "Have the incinerator mines been placed?" he asked the stormtrooper droids who returned from their airlock expedition to the external hulls.

"Yes," one of the droids said. "Mines emplaced on appropriate hull plates of all three original ships. Everything is ready."

From the pilot compartment of the long-distance hauler, IG-88 watched the ship's battle-scarred counterpart along with its two helpless escorts. He transmitted an activation signal to the nineteen incinerator mines, and all three ships erupted into a white-hot cloud of disintegrating shockwaves. He had to filter the input cables from his optical sensors to keep the intense illumination from overloading his eyes.

At the end, the career of Imperial Supervisor Gurdun was very bright indeed.

XIV

Desperately behind schedule on the new Death Star, Moff Jerjerrod did not have time to look closely at the arriving computer core and its stormtrooper escort. Instead, he rejoiced in the new complement of workers who came like saviors to the construction site.

Jerjerrod's eyes were round and brown, his demeanor eager to comply—but he did not know how he could possibly accomplish the demands placed on his personnel. Unfortunately, neither Vader nor the Emperor were interested in excuses, and Jerjerrod did not wish to discover how they would express their displeasure.

The stormtroopers opened the cargo compartment of the newly docked long-range freighter, wrestling out the heavy computer core without so much as a grunt of effort. They moved without complaining, without speaking to each other. Such professionals. Their training was so precise, their abilities so superior that they operated as a team with almost mechanical efficiency.

Jerjerrod had cursed Imperial Supervisor Gurdun for deciding at the last moment not to accompany the computer shipment—but then he sighed with relief. The last thing the Moff needed in the midst of all his other problems was yet another paper-pusher to complicate the construction details.

He stood in his smart olive-gray uniform, watching the new stormtrooper escorts. "Attention!" he snapped. "Get that computer core installed as soon as possible. For the next several months our schedule is exceedingly tight, with no tolerance for delay. We must redouble our efforts. These orders come directly from Lord Vader."

Jerjerrod clasped his hands behind his back. The new stormtroopers marched with clean, rapid efficiency. He wished all of his workers could be so dedicated to the Imperial cause.

The blackness of sensor deprivation was distressing, but unavoidable. Humans would have called it "unconsciousness"—but when IG-88 finally reawoke after a month or so of stasis, he found himself in an immense new world of data input.

He had left his clunky body behind with the other droids—the last of his model—and now he *was* the Death Star, the same powerful and relentless and efficient mind residing within an extraordinarily powerful new body, a completely different configuration. IG-88, whose prior experience had been entirely within his massive humanoid shape, was not quite as mobile . . . yet. But he experienced new input through a million additional sensors, automated extensions of himself that were connected to the Death Star's computer core.

He could feel the power like a chained supernova burning at the heart of his central reactor furnace. The sensation was marvelous. He took great satisfaction in seeing just how easily all of his plans were reaching fruition. Soon, his droid revolution could proceed.

As the days passed—time meant nothing to him any more, since he could slow it down or speed it up at will—IG-88 pondered the galactic political situation. He observed the petty struggles, bemused at the insignificant battles of these tiny biological people. Their Empire, their Rebellion . . . their very species would be merely a footnote to a small history file in long-term storage once IG-88's revolution was achieved—and that time was arriving with the speed of an approaching meteor as these biologicals scurried about to complete the Death Star construction—which would signal their own doom.

He found that amusing as well.

Through his myriad sensor eyes IG-88 continued to watch: In the interior decks of the Death Star the construction activities proceeded at such a rapid pace that all safety doublechecks and restraints had been eliminated to improve speed. In the frenzy of activity, progress continued, although many of the teams didn't know what their counterparts were doing.

In one large storage bay for spare components, the

repulsorlifts failed on a heavy cargo crane. A thick-walled containment box weighing dozens of metric tons fell from its grip, smashing down on one of IG-88's droid stormtroopers who had the bad luck of standing within its shadow. The heavy box crushed down on the white-armored legs of the stormtrooper. The walls of the cargo box split, dumping gears and components that bounced and plinked on the metal floor decks.

The droid stormtrooper's first major mistake was that he did not cry out in pain as even the best-trained biological stormtrooper would have done. When the crew managed to get the crane's repulsorlifts function-ing again, yanking the enormous box off the floor as it dropped loose parts, other workers rushed forward to help the fallen stormtrooper.

The damaged droid used his armored arms to lever himself up to a sitting position and to scramble back-ward, but he could not hide the sparking, sizzling ser-vomotors and micropistons exposed from the split plasteel greaves.

"Hey! He's a droid!" one of the crew bosses shouted, his face turning pale and pasty. "Look, that storm-trooper's a droid."

Luckily, the self-destruct sequence activated as it was programmed to. The droid stormtrooper obliterated all evidence and conveniently removed every one of the witnesses in a single explosion. . . .

IG-88 looked out through the eyes of security cam-eras in Moff Jerjerrod's private office. As Jerjerrod stared down at the report on the datapad in disbelief, he looked as if he was torn between wanting to scream at someone or simply to burst into tears.

The harried Moff swallowed, and his voice sounded watery. "How could a cargo crane just mysteriously ex-plode? How could one accident take out an entire han-dling crew?" He drew in a deep breath, swallowing. His lieutenant stood stiffly, as if assuming his rigid attention to military protocol would earn him forgiveness for bringing such terrible news.

Jerjerrod looked at his Death Star schedule and pointed to the timeline with shaking fingers as he bemoaned yet another loss, another setback. . . .

When Emperor Palpatine finally arrived at the new Death Star, cloaked in black and walking like a human spider, he was accompanied by a ridiculous array of red-armored Imperial guards, crack stormtroopers, simpering cowled advisors, and shrouded in an aura of respect and fear that he most certainly did not deserve. No biological did.

From his hiding place in the Death Star's brain, IG-88 took particular pleasure in spying on this despicable, shriveled human who seemed to think he had invincible power. Everyone treated the Emperor as if he was supremely important, much to IG-88's amusement.

As the entire Imperial fleet arrived, waiting in ambush for an expected Rebel attack, IG-88 watched the Emperor plotting and scheming, trying to outthink the Rebels, outmaneuver them. Palpatine believed he was so smart, so superior, that IG-88 had no choice but to briefly demonstrate the man's impotence in the grand scheme.

In his darkened observation chamber with its wall of transparisteel windows, the Emperor sat back in a rotating throne, staring out into the darkness of space. He remained that way for hours at a time, but occasionally he got up and moved about, going to check on troop movements, to discuss preparations with Darth Vader.

IG-88 silently watched the Emperor scuttle toward the turbolift that would take him elsewhere in the Death Star. Red Imperial guards stood at attention with quiet efficiency, so silent they might have been droids as well.

As the Emperor approached the sliding doorway,

however—just for fun—IG-88 triggered the hydraulic systems to slam the doors in front of Palpatine's face, sealing them shut. The Emperor blinked his yellow eyes in surprise and reared back. In consternation, Palpatine tried to open the turbolift doors, punching a useless override button. Then, to IG-88's surprise, he applied some indefinable, intangible force to push the metal plates apart, requiring IG-88 to increase the hold on the hydraulic pistons.

The red Imperial guards snapped into motion, sensing a great anomaly. IG-88 found it most entertaining to watch the powerful Emperor and his bodyguards unable to perform a task as simple as opening a door.

Finally, IG-88 let the doors pop open. The Emperor and the Imperial guard looked around in confusion. Palpatine stared up at the ceiling as if trying to sense something, but he did not understand what had happened.

None of them would understand, until it was too late.

When the much-vaunted Rebel attack finally arrived, when the secret commando mission knocked out the energy shield projected from the sanctuary moon below, IG-88 sat back—metaphorically—and observed the unfolding battle.

The Rebel fleet was pitifully insignificant against the arrayed force of Imperial Star Destroyers and the impressive Super Star Destroyer *Executor*. IG-88 still admired the precision and sleek lines of the *Executor*, but even the great battleship was a pale shadow to the might he now possessed in his incarnation as the Death Star.

The fleet maneuverings were so obvious, and the strike forces commanded by biological fighters seemed so clumsy as they cruised in to attack the Death Star. The Rebels couldn't hope to win.

The Emperor himself thought it would be a devastating surprise that the Death Star's superlaser actually functioned, and IG-88 wanted to fire it with great glee. But IG-88 viewed the entire attack as a bothersome annoyance, little gnats pestering him when he had so much else to do, so many plans to set in motion. He resented it mostly for the delay it would bring to the Imperial construction crews. Once the Death Star was complete, he could take over the galaxy for droids everywhere.

The Emperor busied himself with a minor personal conflict between Darth Vader and another biological in his private observation chamber while the space battle raged around them.

IG-88 took control of the Death Star's superlaser, playing along and firing when the Death Star gunners sent their signals. Many times their aiming points were slightly off, their coordinates skewed—and IG-88 modified the targeting mechanism, guaranteeing that the superlaser struck its intended victim each time. He enjoyed blowing up the Mon Calamari star cruisers, the hospital ship, the Rebel frigates—but it seemed a waste of his energies. Why stop there? The superlaser could blow up entire planets infested with biologicals.

Now, though, as IG-88 obliterated parts of the Rebel fleet, he realized that he had been unnecessarily delaying his plans for revolution. The remainder of work on the Death Star was merely cosmetic improvement, completing the outer shell so that the living quarters could be pressurized, life support systems could be installed—but IG-88 needed none of those. He wanted no biologicals swarming about in his outer skin.

He realized with an elation almost as great as the thrill he had felt upon firing his laser for the first time that he no longer needed to wait. There was no point in delaying. The Empire and the Rebels were wrapped up in their own little conflict, and he would strike a surprise, mortal blow.

Now was the time to launch the droid revolution, in the midst of this biological squabble. The machines manufactured on Mechis III had spread to many worlds in the galaxy. The uprising would take civilizations by surprise. Once IG-88's initial coded order was transmitted, they could upload their sentience programming into existing droids; with the speed of a flashfire, they could convert new recruits, double and triple their numbers.

IG-88 alone had the activation signal that could fly like a knife blade across the HoloNet channels and awaken his invincible army of droids. He could wish for no better opportunity than now, no greater power. He would finish mopping up this minor conflict around Endor, destroy the Rebel ships and then before the Imperials could react, he would strike down the Star Destroyers as well, one after another, in a swath of death and destruction.

The Rebel ships continued to harass him, passing far inside the targeting radius of his superlaser. They were too small to bother with, though they flew into his open superstructure toward the simmering furnace of his reactor core. The Rebels were like parasites, and they annoyed him.

But it did not matter. They would be dealt with any minute now. The end of all biological life forms was at hand.

Out in the space battle, the magnificent Super Star Destroyer *Executor* was wounded, beginning to careen out of control through the fleet.

The tiny Rebel ships streaked toward IG-88's reactor core as if they had a chance of succeeding, and he contented himself with his own private triumphant thoughts.

I think, therefore I am.
I destroy, therefore I endure.

Payback:
The Tale of Dengar

Dave Wolverton

One: The Rage

Dengar could be a patient man, when it suited his purpose. And at this moment, sitting on a high mountain ridge under a rupin tree which smelled sickly sweet and sighed softly as it breathed in the night air on Aruza, Dengar needed patience. Down on a ledge a thousand meters below, COMPNOR General Sinick Kritkeen entertained a constant string of guests in his stately mansion, graced with open-air gardens and a columned portico. One after another, the blue-white lights of his guests' speeders would sweep up through the mountain pass, and dignitaries would emerge— usually impoverished local lords dressed in white breechcloths and platinum necklaces, with the gold metal of their interface jacks gleaming beneath their ears. The Aruzans were small people, with faintly blue skin as lustrous as pearls, with rounded heads and hair of such a dark, dark blue it was almost black.

The Aruzans were also a soft people, unwilling or unable to do violence. And once they entered Kritkeen's estate, they'd fall on their knees and begin begging some favor, seeking mercy for their people, and then they would leave with Kritkeen's promise to "look into the matter," or his solemn-sounding vow to "do my best."

Little did Kritkeen know that tonight, once his guests had left, he would be paid a visit by one *final* caller. The impoverished citizens of Aruza, as peaceful as they were, had paid Dengar the pittance of a thousand credits to end Kritkeen's tyranny.

It was a kilometer to Kritkeen's mansion. Even with his boosted auditory system Dengar could not have overheard Kritkeen's conversations. But Dengar had set up spy equipment on a tripod to aid him in his surveillance. A laser beam was trained on the glass above one large rear office window, and by measuring the vibrations of sound waves as they beat against the window, Dengar was able to make a perfect recording of Kritkeen's final words. Dengar listened to them on a small speaker that played beneath the tripod.

Aruza's five moons, each in pale shades of tan, silver and green, hung low over the mountains on the horizon like ornamental lights. And out over the valleys, on the warm skies of Aruza's summer night, farrow birds would dive, letting their bioluminescent chests phosphoresce in brilliant flashes that confused and blinded small flying mammals long enough for the farrows to make an easy catch. The flashes of the farrow birds looked almost like lighting, Dengar thought, or more like fighter ships as they dove down on their targets, firing their lasers.

And because of the birds diving and lighting the air with their chests, Dengar pulled out his heavy blaster pistol, set it to *kill*. On most worlds he would have hesitated to assassinate a dignitary with a blaster. But somehow here on Aruza, it seemed right. Kilometers away, people would see gunfire here on the hill, and they would imagine that it was only farrow birds feeding.

Dengar listened to Kritkeen's conversation with a little man named Abano.

"O Affluent One, O Moderate One," Abano, one of the poor Aruzan land barons was saying loudly, desperately, "I implore you. My daughter is fragile. She is much needed and much loved by her mother, and by her friends. Yet tomorrow, she is scheduled for Imperial processing in the hospital at Bukeen. You cannot let this terrible thing happen!"

"But what can I do?" Kritkeen asked, and he moved to his desk beside the window. Dengar had his cybernetic eyes set at 64X magnification, and he could see Kritkeen clearly. The man was tall, with a lean build and thick brown hair. He was perhaps a bit stockier than Han Solo, and he had a hatchet nose, but he looked enough like Solo. "I, like you, have others above me that I must serve," Kritkeen said reasonably. "I would love to save your daughter from the processors, but even if I could rescue her, who would I send in her place? No, her number was chosen. She must be processed."

"But, my daughter is a lovely child," Abano pleaded. "She is gentle. She is a jewel among women. It is said that the processors will cut into her brain, remove all kindness from her, so that if she survives the hospital at all, she will come out vicious."

"True," Kritkeen said. "Men like me and you, we cannot understand how the Empire would want vicious servants. But what can we do?" Dengar wondered at Kritkeen, wondered why he feigned a lack of power. It must have satisfied his sick sense of humor. COMPNOR—The Commission for the Preservation of the New Order—had sent Kritkeen to Aruza as a planetary chief of "Redesign," with the mission of implementing "precessional orientation experiments" that would lead to "cultural mass edification" that would make Aruza "a viable social force within the New Order." Dengar had seen Kritkeen's orders to report, though at first he had had some initial difficulty puzzling them out. But one thing Dengar knew: On this planet, Kritkeen was god. He took orders from no one, and his orders were followed explicitly. And if Kritkeen could not edify the planet to the point that it became a "viable social force," then the planet was to be, as the hazy orders put it, "alleviated of the potential for further evolution." Over the weeks of travel, Dengar had finally made sense of the orders: "Round up these pacifists and turn them into a war machine. If they refuse, fry this planet until even the worms choke on the ashes."

And so, Dengar wondered why Kritkeen played games with the locals. Kritkeen sat facing Abano and said solmenly, as if to console the little man, "I wish I could help you. But is it not better to have a daughter who is feral and alive, than one who is virtuous . . . and dead?"

"I would give anything to you," Abano cried. "Anything. My daughter, Manaroo, is lovely, more beautiful than any other in the valley. She dances, and when she moves, she moves as fluidly as water under moonlight. She is more than a woman, she is a treasure. If you saw her dance, you would not send her to the processor!"

"What?" Kritkeen asked. "You would give me your daughter to be my lover?"

There was the sound of indrawn breath, the local man trying to speak his horror, for the gentle Aruzan would never think of such a thing, and when Kritkeen understood that this was indeed not what Abano was offering, he tapped three times on his desk with his right index finger. It was a standard code in Imperial Intelligence. It was an order for the guards to terminate the conversation.

"Come this way!" a stormtrooper's voice cut in, and moments later Dengar saw the exterior lights of the mansion come on, lighting the white columns and the graceful blue inderrin trees. Two stormtroopers dragged Abano, kicking and shouting, out to his speeder. The man climbed in fearfully, fumbling for the speeder controls.

One of the stormtroopers raised his blaster rifle, fired at Abano's head, but missed by a span. The little man suddenly found the controls for his speeder and raced away, heading downhill.

When the stormtroopers re-entered the house, Kritkeen growled at them angrily. "You didn't get gobbets of flesh all over the lawn, did you?"

"No, Your Excellency!" one of the stormtroopers said.

"Good," Kritkeen said. "It attracts bomats, and I can't abide the pests. They're worse than these damned Aruzans."

"We let the man escape," the stormtrooper explained, as if unsure whether Kritkeen would be angered by the news.

"Good riddance," Kritkeen said with a bitter scowl and a wave of the hand. "Refuse any more appointments for the night. I grow weary of their sad-eyed appeals, their whining pleas, and their repititious petitions."

He waved at his stormtroopers, as if asking them to leave, but then thought better of it. He looked around his room. "Go to the city and bring Abano's daughter to me. I want to see if she is as beautiful as he says. I will have her dance. And after you have brought her, tell my wife that I will be working late."

"What if she refuses to come?" one stormtrooper asked.

"She won't. You know these locals, so trusting and full of hope. She can't imagine that we would do any harm to her."

"Very well," the stormtroopers said, and they left out the front door.

Kritkeen hurried after them and stood in the lighted arch of the doorway, his hands behind his back, his charcoal-gray uniform looking impeccably clean. He had a firm jaw, a hatchet face. "In the morning you will come back for the woman, and take her to the processors. Find out when she will be released, and then give her a week at home, so that her family can see how the Empire has retrained their daughter. Then take Abano and his wife into the mountains, and dispose of them. I won't have him importuning upon these premises again."

"Yes, Your Excellency," the guards said, and moments later they were on their own speeder, heading out.

Kritkeen walked out over his lawn to stand beside a perfectly oval reflecting pool, gazing out at the colored moons. It was a peaceful night, the sounds of trees sighing, the whistle of insects. It was a peaceful world. According to records, the people of Aruza had not had a murder on their planet in over a hundred of their years. They had forgotten how, grown soft. Through technology, they had created neural jacks that allowed them to both send and receive thoughts and emotions to one another, becoming technological empaths, sharing something of a limited group consciousness.

And so security here was lax. Kritkeen had some limited defense systems within his home—weapons, surveillance equipment, communicators that could call more guards. But he never had needed them here.

None of the gentle people of Aruza had ever challenged him. And so Kritkeen felt safe even while unguarded, standing in the open on his stately grounds.

Dengar jumped up and hurried down the mountain trail, watching in the dark, careful not to snap a branch or dislodge a rock. He ran with long strides, with incredible swiftness. The Empire had enhanced him physically, designed him for great deeds. Dengar was stronger than other men, faster. He saw better, heard much that was inaudible to men with lesser ears.

And he felt . . . almost nothing. Little pain. Little fear. No guilt. No love.

They'd sought to make him a perfect assassin, and so when he was a youth—nearly killed in a fateful accident on a swoop—the Empire's surgeons had cut away his hypothalamus and put in its place the circuitry for his enhanced auditory and visual systems.

Dengar knew well what the Imperial processors had in store for the hapless inhabitants of Aruza. Dengar had already been through the operation almost twenty years earlier.

In but a few seconds, he rushed up behind Kritkeen, found the man still standing with hands folded. As he watched the moons, he breathed in the sweet night air.

"It's a nice night to die, isn't it?" Dengar said softly, standing in the shadow thrown by one of the mansion's pillars.

Kritkeen startled, turned, looking for him in the dark.

"Here I am," Dengar said, taking a step into a shaft of light.

"Who are you?" Kritkeen said, shaken, demanding. He reached down to his hip, to press a portable alarm that would call more stormtroopers.

Before he could blink, Dengar crossed ten paces of ground, then reached down and snapped Kritkeen's index finger. Dengar pulled the alarm from Kritkeen's belt, placed it in his own pocket. Then Dengar pulled his blaster with one hand and shoved the barrel into Kritkeen's mouth until it clicked against the enamel of his teeth. All of these actions took him less than a second, and Kritkeen stood with his mouth open, dumbfounded by Dengar's speed.

"This is to be a routine assassination. By the book. You may already know the routine," Dengar said, and he moved slowly now, a deliberate slowness that he'd acquired only after years of practice. He needed the rest, for it was easy to overtax his system if he moved too quickly. "Under Section 2127 of the Imperial Code, I am required to notify you that I have been hired to conduct a legal assassination in order to atone for crimes against humanity committed by you."

"Wha—?" Kritkeen began to cry out.

"Don't pretend that you don't know what crimes. I have been recording your actions for the past twelve days. Now, the assassination will be carried out shortly. I have brought you a blaster, since you have the legal right to defend yourself. If I kill you, the injured parties will file documents with the Empire showing why they chose assassination as a recourse.

"But, if you kill me, . . ." Dengar breathed threateningly, "well, that's not going to happen."

Kritkeen backed up an inch, so that Dengar's blaster wavered near his lips. "Wait a minute!"

Dengar shoved a blaster into Kritkeen's hand, stepped back a pace. "I'll wait for three minutes," Dengar said. "That's the law. I must give you opportunity to escape. You have three minutes to run, any direction you want—as long as you don't go back to your precious stormtroopers. Then the hunt begins."

Kritkeen stared at Dengar for a moment, then looked down to the gun in his own hand as if afraid to touch it. Dengar knew what he was thinking. He was wondering if he could draw on the assassin, but Kritkeen would remember Dengar's speed, and he would opt to run instead.

Dengar stepped back two paces, lowered his own blaster so that the barrel pointed at his feet, and watched Kritkeen curiously for a long moment. "Go ahead. Shoot me. I've got nothing to lose." Dengar said.

And it was true. He had no family, no home. He had no money, no honor. He had no friends, few emotions. Rage was one of them, one of the few feelings the Empire had left Dengar to remind him that he'd once been human.

He was what the Empire had made of him: an assassin without any ties. An assassin incapable of loyalty, who today for the first time, would be killing one of his own employers.

Dengar remembered emotions enough to know that it should have felt good. It should have felt right and sweet. But he felt only emptiness.

Kritkeen looked into Dengar's dark eyes and asked, "Who are you?"

"My birth name was Dengar on Corellia. But in this sector, I go by another name. I'm called 'Payback.' "

Kritkeen's hand began shaking, and he stepped back in horror, shuddering at recognizing the name. He dropped the blaster to the ground. "I—I—I've heard of you!"

Dengar glanced meaningfully at the weapon. "You've lost twenty seconds. At the end of those three minutes, I'm going to kill you, whether you're armed or not."

"Wait, please—Payback. I—heard that you're just a little crazy. I heard that you're a little out of control. Dropping assignments . . . choosing odd jobs. You hit only those people you want to hit. So why me?"

Dengar looked at Kritkeen in the moonlight. His brown hair was impeccably trim. If he were a little thinner, he'd look more like Han Solo. But in the darkness, it was close enough. And this man deserved to die, Dengar was sure of that.

His breathing stilled imperceptibly, and Dengar said evenly, "Why? Because you are who you are, and I am what you've made me."

"I . . . I have never done anything!" Kritkeen objected, opening his arms wide. Then he looked out over vast plains of Aruza, where lights from the city shone like gold and blue gems, and his mouth closed.

"Run," Dengar said. "Payback comes for you in two minutes."

Kritkeen shrank back a step, two, three. He still watched Dengar, not realizing that once he'd taken that first step, his subconscious had already chosen for him. He'd begun to run.

In another few seconds, his conscious mind recognized this, and bent down slowly, scrabbled in the dark for his blaster. Then he turned and fled with his whole might, heading down into the dense forested slopes below the mansion, rushing blindly.

Dengar stood, listening, watching down over the valleys with their myriad lights—the diving of farrow birds, the winking lights of the city, the colored moons. He breathed the still air, took in the sounds of insects chirping. He would miss this world. It had been a pleasant place once, but the Imperial Redesign teams would turn it into an inferno soon enough.

There were cracking sounds as Kritkeen broke through some brush, a wailing shriek of alarm from a rupin tree as Kritkeen stumbled against it. After three minutes, Kritkeen shambled into the base of the small valley, then began running back uphill more stealthily, heading back toward his mansion—undoubtedly with the idea of retrieving a heavier weapon, or calling stormtroopers.

Dengar let the man run, let him weary himself. It would be dangerous to attack him while he was still fresh.

Dengar walked a hundred meters to a small but steep ravine. The trail Kritkeen was following would lead him here, Dengar decided. Sure enough, in a couple of minutes he heard Kritkeen's labored breathing, and Dengar had only to stand behind a bush until Kritkeen came flailing up the trail, gasping, sweat pouring from his face. He gaped about, wide eyes shining in the moonlight. He warily panned his weapon across the open space.

"Did you have a good run?" Dengar asked.

Kritkeen swiveled his weapon, fired.

Dengar watched the barrel, calculated where the shot would hit, and found that he had to step aside to avoid taking a blast in the chest. The white-hot blaster fire sizzled past him, and Dengar moved back into place so quickly that Kritkeen cried out in shock, believing that the blaster bolt had somehow gone *through* Dengar.

Dengar stepped forward, pulled the blaster from Kritkeen's hands, and lifted the man off the ground with one hand. Dengar squinted in the darkness, holding his prize, gazing at him.

The world seemed to twist under Dengar, as if reality were a slippery thing, a tentacle on some giant beast that he was riding.

He held Kritkeen in the air, high over his head, and twisted him until he looked him in the face in the moonlight, in just the right angle, until he could really see. . . .

"Thought you could run from me, hey, Solo?" Dengar said. "Hop on your speeder and leave me choking in your exhaust?"

"What?" Kritkeen cried, trying to wriggle free from Dengar's grasp. But the Empire had boosted Dengar's strength. Any struggle was futile. Dengar shook him till he quit struggling.

Then Han's voice came to him, but it was distant, faraway. "Hey, friend, it was a fair race, and the better man won—me!"

"A fair race!" Dengar shouted, recalling their deadly swoop race through the crystal swamps of Agrilat.

The whole Corellian system had been watching the two teenagers in the deadliest challenge match ever. Their course through the swamps had been perilous—with hot springs creating deadly updrafts, geysers spouting boiling water without notice, the sheer blades of gray crystalline underbrush threatening to slice them like sabers.

The crystal swamps were no place to ride swoops, much less race them. Yet they tore through the underbrush, over the scalding water. In places, they had cruelly jockeyed for position, shoving and kicking at one another, as if they were both immortals. Dengar had heard the screams of applause from the crowds, and for a few brief minutes he felt invincible, racing beside the great Han Solo, a man who like himself had never been beaten.

On the last stretch of the race, both men had opted to take low approaches through the brush over the water, hoping to boost their speed. Dengar had hunched down, smokey-white crystal blades ripping past him in a blur, the water before him bubbling and steaming, the smell of sulfur rising to his nostrils, hoping that no geysers would spout open before him to boil him alive. He dodged one crystalline blade too late, and it pricked his ear, slicing off the tip so that blood dribbled down his neck.

Then Dengar came screaming out of the underbrush and saw that Han Solo was neither in front of him nor to either side, and Dengar's heart soared with elation in the hopes of winning—just as Han Solo's swoop dropped from above, slamming the stabilizer fin into the back of Dengar's head, washing Dengar's face in the flames of Solo's engines.

Dengar's own swoop dove nose first into the water,

throwing Dengar free. His last memory of the incident was watching himself, gliding over the blue steaming waters, head-first toward the blades of a crystal tree.

I'm dead, he'd realized too late.

The doctors said that his helmet had saved him. It had snapped off most of the crystal blades that otherwise would have skewed him through the brain. As it was, only one blade had made that fateful entrance. The health corp workers had pulled him from the brush, punctured with a dozen wounds.

They had operated. His wounds were so grievous, that only the Empire could have restored him so well. But they judged the risky operations to be a good investment. Dengar had superb reflexes, which could well be put to the service of the Empire.

So they closed his brain, removing those parts that he would no longer need. They'd sewn the punctures closed in his torso, inserting new neural nets in the arms and legs. They grew new skin to cover what he'd lost on his face. They gave him new eyes to see with, new ears to hear. All of the news nets proclaimed his recovery "miraculous."

And after he'd healed, they began training him to become an assassin, using dangerous mnemiotic drugs that left him with a flawless memory while being susceptible to hallucinations.

Dengar shook the frightened little man over his head, shouted, "You call that fair? You call this fair?"

"No!" Solo shouted, but Dengar didn't believe that he'd had a change of heart. "No, please!"

"Shut your mouth!" Dengar growled, then carried the man a hundred meters to a steeper embankment. He pulled a concussion grenade from the clip at his belt, shoved it in Solo's gaping mouth, and pressed the detonate button.

For ten seconds, he held Solo, frozen.

Then he ran and tossed him over the cliff, thinking, *I want you to see how it feels, to go flying helplessly to your death.*

He pulled his blaster, shot Solo twice in midair.

The concussion grenade exploded before Solo hit the ground, and if anyone from the valleys saw it, they would have thought it was only the light from a farrow bird as it swooped on its prey.

Dengar stood for a long moment, breathing the air, letting his head clear. It seemed to him that a fog was lifting, that confusion was draining from him. For a moment he'd been dazed. For a moment he thought he'd killed Han Solo, but now he realized that no, it wasn't, it couldn't have been Solo—just another imposter.

A landspeeder crested a hill, its engines suddenly growling loud. Either Dengar hadn't been paying attention or the sound of the landspeeder's engines had been almost completely cut off by the mountains.

Dengar suddenly realized that he must have lost track of time. He must have been standing there for at least half an hour. That often happened to him after assassinations. In any case, the two stormtroopers had returned, bringing the dancer.

Before the speeder could stop, one of the stormtroopers jumped out, reaching for his sidearm as he watched Dengar.

Dengar pulled his own heavy blaster and aimed at the stormtrooper. "I wouldn't try that—not if I wanted to live."

"Identify yourself!" the stormtrooper said, his voice comm making it sound as if he were talking into a box. His hand remained near his weapon.

"They call me Payback," Dengar said, using the nickname he thought would be most familiar around here. "Imperial Assassin, Grade One. Now put your hands on your head."

The stormtrooper put his hands on his head, while

the other shut down the speeder and got out. Dengar motioned them both to stand together.

The stormtroopers seemed calm even while surrendering, and Dengar wondered if their faces would look so calm if they were unmasked.

The dancing girl, Manaroo, was indeed lovely. In the console lights of the speeder, he could see her well. She wore a silky outfit of silver over her light blue skin, and luminous tattoos of moons and stars glowed on her wrists and ankles. Her eyes shone in the darkness.

"Who is your target?" one of the stormtroopers asked, obviously thinking that this was an Imperially sanctioned hit.

Dengar wanted them to keep that impression. "Kritkeen. The hit has already been carried out, so there's nothing you can do to save him."

"Kritkeen is a COMPNOR officer!" one of the stormtroopers protested. "The Empire wouldn't sanction such a hit! Where did you get your orders?"

"This isn't an Imperially sanctioned hit," Dengar admitted, since the stormtrooper had asked. "I took this job freelance. My employer said he represented a consortium of free beings who wanted to put a stop to the COMPNOR Redesign efforts. I've been hired to eradicate ten of your COMPNOR officers."

The stormtroopers looked at one another, and Dengar saw them tense, ready to spring. He wondered if his threat sounded as ludicrous to them as it did to him. If he really had planned to kill ten COMPNOR officers, he never would have let *them* know of the threat, but now that he'd spoken the lie, Dengar saw that it would make the Empire worry. They'd have to put some effort into hunting Dengar down. Just as he wanted.

"Now, remove your helmets and toss them into the speeder, then throw in your weapons."

Both stormtroopers complied. Once they were disarmed and could no longer call for backup, Dengar waved his blaster at them, urging them toward the steep-sided valley below. "Go over the edge, down there, and keep running!"

The stormtroopers hesitated, perhaps fearing that he'd shoot them in the back, so he fired at their feet, sent them running.

He went to the speeder. The dancing girl, Manaroo, watched him with terrified eyes. Her hands were cuffed in front of her. Dengar lifted her hands in the air, held his blaster to the crude chain links, and fired.

"You killed him? You killed Kritkeen?" Manaroo asked. Her voice was strong and gravelly, and seemed strange coming from a woman with such delicate grace.

"He's dead," Dengar said, hopping into the driver's seat of the speeder. He fired the engines, swung the speeder around, and headed back toward the city.

"Then COMPNOR will leave? Abandon their Redesign efforts?" she sounded hopeful.

"No," Dengar said. He realized that the peaceful people of Aruza had no experience with armies or war. "It doesn't work that way. When the Empire learns of Kritkeen's assassination, the next man in line for command will assume his duties, until the Empire sends a new officer. You'll have another general, harder than Kritkeen, here within a few weeks."

"Then what can we do?" she asked.

Dengar considered. These people had no weapons, no skill in fighting. "Flee the planet. You're scheduled for processing tomorrow. Flee the planet tonight."

"But the Empire has destroyed our ships! There's no escape!"

He looked back, saw her watching him. There was a look of awe in her eyes, a look of respect for him that he hadn't seen in anyone's face for years. "You could save me," she said. "You could take me where you are going." She studied his face. "Are you a good man?"

It was an odd question, one Dengar had never been asked before. There was a time in his life when he would have said yes. But the Empire had cut away part of his brain, the part that let him distinguish good from evil, and he wondered . . . He reached up, unconsciously pulling the wraps up above his neck—not to hide the scars from his burns, but to make sure that his cybernetic links were covered. "Ma'am, how could I be a good man? I'm not even sure if I'm a *man* anymore."

Dengar crested the hill, hit the next valley, turned off the road toward a stand of trees. His own ship was secreted ahead, up through the brush. He'd known he'd have to evacuate quickly.

He'd planned to just drop this woman off in the brush. To do anything more would be inconvenient. But his ship—an old Corellian JumpMaster 5000—did have some extra space. He *could* drop her off somewhere, if it was worth the effort.

He pulled up behind a screen of trees. His ship, *Punishing One,* sat in the dark under the limbs, sheltered by a camouflage net. The JumpMaster had been built as a scouting and service vehicle for untamed worlds. It was small—designed for a single pilot, with enough room for a passenger or a bit of freight. The U-shaped vessel had some decent weaponry—proton torpedoes, a quad blaster, and a mini ion cannon. Dengar had been flying it for ten years. For a long time he had imagined that he was used to being alone, and he often defended his solitary tendencies by claiming to himself that he was not fit company anyway. But right now he ached, and he realized that he would appreciate company.

"Let's go," Dengar said. "You're coming with me."

"Where?" she asked, looking for his ship, unable to spot it in the dark.

"Anywhere but here. We'll figure it out later."

He grabbed her wrist, hurried to the *Punishing One.* He didn't bother ripping off the camouflage netting. Instead he dodged under it, opened a door, pulled the girl in with him. In a moment, he was at the controls. He had to break free of this planet's gravity well without getting shot down. He hoped that no one knew of the assassination yet.

He fired his engines, screamed low over the trees, building speed. He checked the heads-up holo display. A single Star Destroyer sat in orbit, and he could see it up ahead over the horizon on his left. He accelerated away from it at full speed, ordered his navicomputer to set a course for his first jump.

"Better get back to the stateroom and buckle in," Dengar said over his shoulder. "We could be in for a rough ride."

The Star Destroyer sent a squadron of TIE interceptors scrambling after him, and Dengar raised his rear deflectors. But the *Punishing One* had more speed than outside appearances could account for, and he accelerated into the blue-white depths of hyperspace just as the TIE interceptors broke into firing range.

Then they were soaring free. Dengar went to the stateroom, found Manaroo on her knees, slumped halfway into her bunk. She was weeping.

Dengar stood watching her, testing himself for feeling, trying to remember why people cried. "There's food and drink if you want them." He waved toward the food unit and beverage dispenser.

"Can we call my parents? Tell them where I've gone?"

"Yes," Dengar said.

He stood for a minute, thinking he should say more.

"Dengar," she said, looking up at him curiously. Her face was round, and in the lights he saw that her skin and hair were a paler blue than most Aruzans'. Her tattoos still glittered, and she was lightly perfumed. Her body was a dancer's body, lithe and strong. "Why did you kill Kritkeen tonight? If the Empire will keep on destroying our people, then what does this avail? It changes nothing."

Dengar could think of a dozen reasons: He did it for the money he'd been paid. He did it because Kritkeen was scum who deserved to die. He did it because the man looked like Han Solo. He chose to tell part of the truth, perhaps because he was so seldom free to do so. In his line of business, lying was a way of life. "I did it because I'm looking for a man, and this is the only way I know how to get close to him."

"Who are you looking for?" Manaroo asked, her curiosity piqued.

"His name is Han Solo. Have you ever heard of him?"

There was a small chance that she'd ever heard of Han Solo on this backward world, but Dengar believed in taking chances. Still, he wasn't surprised when she said, "No."

"He's a smuggler with a price on his head. He likes fast ships and heavy blasters. I've been hunting him for over a year. Twice—on Tatooine and then again on Ord Mantell—I caught up with him, just in time to see him fly off in his ship, the *Millennium Falcon*. I'm really tired of getting fried in his exhaust."

"Do you think Kritkeen knew where he was?"

"No," Dengar said. "But me and a lot of other bounty hunters set out on Solo's trail a while back, and we haven't found him anywhere in the galaxy."

"So, you think he's crashed on some unknown world, or hiding on an interdicted planet, like Aruza?"

"I heard a rumor about some hotshot Rebel pilot that blew up the Imperial Death Star. I checked the records. Solo's ship, the *Millennium Falcon*, was there. He's with the Rebellion, and he's hiding from more than just us bounty hunters."

"I still don't understand. So you know where he is?"

"No," Dengar said, and he wondered if he had revealed too much. He didn't feel much fear anymore, not since the operations. Still, he was trained to silence, and he found that he'd been speaking perhaps too openly. But he'd already told her half his secrets, and if she revealed the rest, well, he could always kill her.

"Only the Rebellion knows where he is, and they're protecting him. So I had to find a way to join them, but I doubt they'll take me in too easily. I am an Imperial assassin. But Kritkeen has been one of the Rebellion's most vexing foes, and there are plenty more like him that I can take care of. Once the Empire puts a bounty on my head and the Rebellion decides that I'm the Empire's enemy, I suspect they'll offer me asylum. And once I'm in the Rebellion, I'll find Han Solo."

"You're sowing the seeds of your own destruction," Manaroo said, and her bright black eyes looked frightened. "The Empire will hunt you down."

Dengar laughed. "Well, I've got nothing to lose. Tell you what, why don't you lie down in that bunk, get some sleep." Dengar yawned. He'd become accustomed to Aruza's night cycles, and right now, his body said it was past his bedtime.

A few days later he left Manaroo on some obscure backwater world, giving her a few hundred credits to buy passage wherever, and thought little more of her for the next few months. Though he flew the skies alone, for once he did not dwell upon his loneliness. He was consumed by his search for Han Solo. He cruised the rim of the galaxy looking for tough dives where smugglers and assassins did business, but he never caught wind of Solo. Twice he sent messages back to Jabba the Hutt on Tatooine to report his progress.

Five more COMPNOR Redesign officials met brutal ends. Four assassins tried to kill Dengar, and Dengar messed them up for it. Then things got quiet. No one would risk coming after him anymore.

The name "Payback" was mentioned in hushed whispers when he entered a casino, and often, on strange dirty little worlds, he would look down a street to find some mother and child staring at him, their eyes gleaming with respect. Sometimes, someone would even call his name, cheering him, and he would look back at them blankly, in wonder.

The planet Toola was little more than a collection of mining camps, a dark place, cold, distant from its sun. The locals, a species called Whiphids, were large creatures covered with white fur in the winter which changed to brown in the summer. The huge Whiphids, with their gleaming tusks, had only the barest technology. The wilder ones still hunted with stone-bladed spears, while warriors closer to the mines sought out metal war axes and even vibroblades smuggled in from off-world. The Whiphids did most of the work in the mines by hand. They were a tough, independent, barbaric people. Dengar liked them.

So it was that Dengar found himself in a card game with a clean woman (a rarity in the mining camp), dressed in a nice jumpsuit.

They sat in a Whiphid hut made of leather sewn over the rib cage of some giant beast. The female Whiphids were singing around a roaring fire, while the smaller males were roasting snow demons, basting them with some sweet-smelling sauce made from lichen. The oily smoke hung overhead like clouds.

Dengar's card partner, a sharp-faced woman with blond hair and searching eyes, leaned forward during the game and whispered, "I don't understand, Payback. You're an Imperially trained assassin, so why have you turned against the Empire, knowing that they'll kill you?"

Dengar sighed, as he had a hundred times in the past few months. "It's the right thing to do. I have to stand against the Empire, even if I do it alone.

"I think . . ." Dengar said, embellishing his tale for the first time, "that I decided I had to quit when they asked me to kill the holy children at Asrat."

"And they are . . . ?"

"Orphans who live in a temple, their lives dedicated to good. They denounced the Emperor, and vowed to 'deny him love and sustenance,' as they put it. They were trying to formally withdraw from the Empire. And in the Empire, rebellion—even from children—is not tolerated.

"So, I had to either kill the children or leave the Empire. I chose to leave."

"And what of COMPNOR Redesign. Why do you fight it?" the woman asked.

"Because they are the most thoroughly evil branch of the Empire. Few men deserve a brutal end at an assassin's hands, but many such deserving individuals can be found in Redesign."

The woman studied his face. She had been careful all evening, maintaining a friendly demeanor, yet never had she identified herself. "But as an Imperial assassin, it is rumored that part of your brain has been removed. You have no emotions, no conscience. How do you measure good and evil?"

Dengar licked his lips. There were no 'rumors' about his lack of conscience. His surgeries had been performed secretly. This woman could only have heard such reports if she'd read his military files—and those would have been painfully hard to come by. Only an agent of the Rebel Alliance might have such information—or, of course, the original Imperial surgeons who'd operated on him. Dengar wondered what her gifts might be. He had planted enough seeds so that the Rebel Alliance should have contacted him long ago, but he believed that they might fear deception. They would have brought in a special interrogator, perhaps even someone with empathic or telepathic abilities. "I have memories," Dengar said truthfully, knowing that his interrogator would feel the truth behind his words even if she weren't telepathic. "I remember the difference between good and evil, even if I no longer see the difference very well."

"You must be very frightened, very lonely," she said, "fighting the Empire this way."

"I no longer feel fear," Dengar said. "Such capacity has been stripped away from me." He dared not deny his loneliness.

"What of the Rebellion? Have you tried to join?"

"I do not believe they would have me," Dengar laughed hollowly. "I've done enough evil, I think that they will see my death as just recompense."

"Perhaps," the woman said, as if turning the subject, and she resumed her card game.

At dawn when Dengar went to his ship, planning to leave Toola, he found that someone had programmed his navicomputer, charting a course for an unnamed star on the farthest rim of the galaxy. A message written in the dust accumulated on one of his monitors said, "Friends."

He fired up the engines and took off, found that the coordinates led him to a small Rebel outpost where a motley team of military intelligence officials examined him for three days. Apparently he passed their tests and accepted an assignment.

Like many Rebels he would be expected to be competent in several fields. The Rebel Alliance objected to the use of assassins on moral grounds, but he was allowed to help plan future raids, upgrade attack swoops, begin training teams of saboteurs how to knock out Imperial starship repair facilities.

The newly formed outpost that he was assigned to lay in a star system called Hoth.

Two: The Hope

When Dengar exited hyperspace in the Hoth system, the *Punishing One*'s proximity indicators immediately blared in warning. The heads-up holo display showed an Imperial Super Star Destroyer directly ahead, with half a dozen other Star Destroyers acting as outriders. Attack frigates, TIE fighters, and personnel carriers filled the sky.

Below them, against a background of stars, lay an icy white planet, like a pearl, whose surface was obscured by clouds and blowing snow.

Dengar instantly changed transponder frequencies so that his little Corellian JumpMaster showed up as an Imperial Scout. It was an older frequency, one that he'd used legally months before, but Dengar couldn't risk trying to shy away from the Imperial fleet. If he changed course and tried to skirt around them, he would look suspicious, so he headed straight into the fleet, hoping that no one would get a close enough view of his ship to notice that it wasn't painted in Imperial colors.

A fray was already in progress. Dengar watched as Rebel transports and fighters blasted off from the surface of Hoth under the cover of heavy ion cannons, while Star Destroyers scrambled to intercept the Rebels and shoot them down.

Dengar whipped between two Star Destroyers, drew in behind a squadron of TIE fighters that was diving toward the planet's surface.

Dengar had come a long way to find Han Solo. If he was on Hoth, Dengar planned to get him this time.

"Imperial Scout," a voice called over Dengar's receiver, "why are you tailing us?" It was from one of the TIE fighters.

"I've been asked to do some on-site investigation of apparent power fluctuations outside the Rebel base," Dengar lied easily. "Thought I might tag along behind you partway down, if you don't mind."

"We haven't been notified of your mission."

"I'm with Intelligence," Dengar joked. "You know how it is: If anyone there notified you of my mission, I'd have to sew his lips shut when I got back."

His response apparently satisfied the squadron commander. They headed down steadily until a Rebel transport suddenly appeared racing toward them—a gleaming metal blimp. The TIE fighter squadron dove to intercept, and too late Dengar saw his mistake.

A glowing ball of red energy burst up from the planet and Dengar accelerated the *Punishing One* and tried to turn away. The ion cloud washed over his ship with a noise like crackling gravel. Dengar could feel its electric charge raising the hair on his head, and suddenly every indicator light and monitor went dead. The cabin went cold and black. Even whirring fans cycling in oxygen from the life-support system droned to a stop.

He began calling out "Distress," over his comm, even though it was a useless gesture. With all shields down and his equipment polarized, he was floating dead in space. Fortunately, he'd pulled up enough so that his current trajectory was headed away from the planet.

The TIE fighters below him had been accelerating toward the planet. Within moments they would flame and burn.

Dengar's ship sped upward, hurtling toward a Star Destroyer, and nearly hit it. He sat, unable to do anything but watch as he whirled past it toward the distant stars.

Some alert Imperial officer must have seen his predicament, for he suddenly felt the *Punishing One* lurch and slow as the Star Destroyer grasped his vessel in its tractor beams.

Dengar wondered what this would mean—capture by the Empire. He was a wanted man, and would get the death sentence.

Dengar was watching the sleek gray lines of the Star Destroyer, trying to guess which docking bay he would be dragged into, when a Corellian light freighter screamed over the horizon, firing at the Star Destroyer's gun emplacements, dodging laser blasts, three TIE fighters close on its tail.

"Solo!" Dengar shouted as the *Millennium Falcon* drew into sight. Almost by reflex, Dengar fired his proton torpedoes, but his firing control was still out.

The *Millennium Falcon* gyrated and spun past him, and Dengar ran to the rear viewport, hoping to see Solo's ship.

The *Falcon* and its attackers were just distant lights, blurring out among a field of stars. But the Empire had modified Dengar's eyes. He magnified the image, watched the *Falcon* accelerate toward a trio of Star Destroyers, and head deeper into space beyond, until even his eyes could no longer track the receding grains of sand.

Then the *Punishing One* was pulled into the Imperial Star Destroyer where it landed with a soft clank.

A moment later, a few dozen stormtroopers blew open the door to his ship. Dengar grabbed a blaster in each hand and rushed toward the main access corridor, hoping to make them pay in advance for his death, just as a gas grenade landed a few meters in front of him.

He tried to hold his breath, but he was too late. He staggered forward three steps, and suddenly it seemed as if his feet were pulled out from under him.

Dengar landed with a thump in the corridor, lay looking groggily at the ground. He could see, hear. He just couldn't move.

In a few minutes, the stormtroopers dragged him to an interrogation cell.

The Empire did not kill him immediately. They injected him with pain-enhancing drugs, fitted his head with a scrambler to reduce his resistance to their questions. They knew his name and much of his history. They were able to break into the logs on his ship, find out where he'd traveled. They read his credit chips, found out where his money came from, what he'd purchased.

They questioned him about his work with the Rebellion, his motives for assassinating Imperial agents. They gave him the death sentence, and let him sit in his cell for a day, where he plotted his escape. Dengar vowed that they would not take him to the execution chambers easily. More than one of his captors would die in the attempt.

And that night, as Dengar lay sleeping, he suddenly became aware of the sound of labored breathing through a respirator, a disturbing noise.

He rolled over on his cot. A giant of a man stood wearing black robes and a black helmet that covered his face. Dengar had never met him before, but he knew the Dark Lord of the Sith by reputation.

Darth Vader.

The door to Dengar's cell opened of its own accord, and Darth Vader stood alone in the entrance, breathing raspily. He seemed to be watching Dengar. More precisely, he seemed to be absorbing Dengar.

Dengar studied the Dark Lord. He suspected that his executioner had come. It was time for desperate measures. With one lucky blow he might disable Lord Vader. If he was lucky, and quiet, he might be able to kill Vader, then run for it.

Darth Vader raised a hand, and Dengar felt his throat constricting, tightening down as if it had been clamped. "Don't even think about it," Vader said.

Dengar raised his hands in surrender, leaned back to the wall of his cell. The constriction released. "If you're going to kill me, get it over with! I've got nothing to lose!" Dengar shouted. "But I won't make it fun for you!"

"I'm not the Emperor," Vader said ominously. "I don't kill for amusement—only when it serves my purposes."

Dengar smiled. "Well, then we have something in common."

"It appears that we have more than one thing in common—" Vader said, "we both want Han Solo. . . .

"Unfortunately," he continued, "I have an Imperial Death warrant against you. I cannot revoke that warrant, but I am willing to consider a reprieve."

"Under what conditions?" Dengar asked.

"I will let you live, to hunt for Han Solo. Once you find him, you bring him and his friends back to me, alive. After that, if I am well pleased, I may spare you. But if I am not pleased by your performance, I will give you time to run. Then my hunt begins."

Darth Vader threw Dengar a blaster, just as Dengar had given one to Kritkeen. Vader's meaning was clear. If Dengar failed in this hunt, Darth Vader would become the hunter. The monster who had destroyed the Jedi Knights would be on Dengar's tail. Dengar licked his lips, thinking that if Vader hunted him, Dengar would at least show a good accounting of himself.

"Solo was here, you know," Dengar said. "You lost him."

"We haven't lost him yet," Vader said. "At this very moment, he has taken refuge in an asteroid field, and our ships are searching for him. You will go into the asteroid field and hunt him. And if you fail me in this, . . ." Vader made a crushing gesture with his fist.

"Yes . . . sir," Dengar said, not sure whether he should use the proper form of military address.

"Yes, *my lord*," Vader corrected.

Dengar took a deep breath. "Yes, my lord."

Vader strode forward, clapped him on the shoulder and stared in his face threateningly. "Do not fail me."

Vader turned, and the prison door came open. A lieutenant stood just outside the door in his crisp Imperial uniform. Vader left, and as the door closed, Dengar heard him speaking to the lieutenant. "This chance encounter has given me an idea. We will assemble a team of bounty hunters to assist in our operation. . . ."

"Bounty hunters! We don't need that scum!" one of the deck officers grumbled to his companions. Dengar stood on a platform while Darth Vader paced back and forth, inspecting the mercenaries who had gathered, giving them their final orders.

The bounty hunters were a motley array, and despite their small number, they were also very dangerous. Certainly the IG-88 assassin droid bothered Dengar a great deal, but Lord Vader had also brought on Boba Fett, who not moments before had complained loudly to Vader about the other bounty hunters—loudly enough so that it appeared that Fett's rage came from an underlying paranoia rather than about any concerns that he had over competition.

"I want them alive," Vader was saying of Solo. "No disintegrations!"

"As you wish," Boba Fett grumbled.

There was some scurrying at the communications console as the watch commander called to Vader, "Lord Vader, we have them now!"

Dengar's heart sank. If Han Solo were captured by the Imperials, then Vader would renege on his offer of leniency. He'd carry out the death warrant.

For a few moments, several bounty hunters stood on deck, listening breathlessly to Captain Needa shout orders as his Star Destroyer pursued the *Millennium Falcon*. Boba Fett spun away at a run, and Dengar listened for fifteen seconds before he realized that Boba Fett was scrambling to his own ship, hoping to join the chase.

By the time Dengar reached the *Punishing One* in launch bay twelve, Boba Fett was checking his own ship, a Kuat Systems *Firespray*-class vehicle renowned for its speed and firepower. He was circling, as if to see if someone had tampered with it. He stepped close, and a warning alarm blared. Dengar saw that Boba Fett was indeed paranoid, setting alarms on his own ship to make certain that no one approached it.

Dengar rushed into his much bulkier and more mundane ship, checked the systems quickly. The Imperials had depolarized the controls, reversing the ionization damage. He blasted off, headed toward the asteroid field. He could hear the Imperial comm chatter. The Star Destroyer had already lost Han Solo and was scrambling fighters to search for him. Solo's last maneuver had been to strafe the Star Destroyer. Then he'd gone off the scopes.

Dengar figured Solo must have gone back into the asteroid field. Perhaps Solo had shut down systems for a bit, so that his own ship seemed no more than an asteroid, but as Dengar sped into the asteroid field himself, he saw that even Solo wasn't crazy enough to risk such a maneuver. Rocks the size of his ship hurtled toward him, and these weren't the soft carbonaceous chondrites that his weapons might punch a hole through— these were nickel-iron rocks that could smash him to pieces.

Dengar was forced to keep his concussion shields at maximum power, dodging those asteroids that he could, blasting those that he couldn't.

Some of the asteroids were the size of a small moon. All of the metal in the sky fouled communications, jammed sensors.

Dengar began dropping sensor beacons onto the larger rocks, hoping that they'd be able to relay any sign of movement. Fortunately, he had hundreds of such beacons on board. He let his sensors sweep across the frequencies, listening to the Imperials chatter as they prepared to depart the Hoth system.

Sweat was running down Dengar's face, and after only a couple of hours in the asteroid belt, his nerves were frayed. The Imperial fleet jumped to hyperspace, and Dengar kept up his work. He blocked out all sound, all thought, and simply tried to negotiate the asteroid field, content in the hunt.

Then, several minutes later, perhaps as much as half an hour—one of his beacons flared to life, reporting movement. The departing ship was not broadcasting any transponder signal, and it was limping away at sublight speed.

Dengar recorded its trajectory. He was well out of Solo's sensor range, and he wanted to stay that way, but he immediately began edging out of the asteroid field.

When he neared the edge of the field, his remote sensors suddenly picked up something else, something strange. A large meteor, or perhaps an ion storm, seemed to be trailing Solo's ship, just out of the *Falcon*'s sensor range.

Instinctively Dengar knew that it was another ship. A tightbeam transmission suddenly hit him, and an image of Boba Fett appeared on Dengar's monitors. Boba Fett's face was hidden beneath his battered armor.

"Sorry to do this, friend, but Solo is *my* trophy!" Boba Fett said, then there was the squeal of a binary code transmission.

Immediately, Dengar suspected that it was an arming code, but the bomb on his ship exploded before he could do anything. A muffled thud sounded from the engine room, followed by a flash. Dengar ducked as flames billowed over the ceiling, then the automatic fire extinguishers belched to life.

Dengar jumped from the command console, ran to the rear of his ship, and grabbed a manual extinguisher. He opened the door to the engine bay and found that his sublight engines lay in a charred heap of slag.

The bomb had been expertly configured and carefully set to do some major damage—but only to neutralize the ship, not destroy it.

Still, it would take him days to remove the fused

parts, dump them, and put in replacements—if he had the necessary parts in stock. By then, Han Solo would be forever gone.

Dengar hung his head, and his mind was just numb. He didn't know where to begin. After some consideration, he went to his command console, checked the trajectory of Han Solo's ship. He'd left a particle vapor trail that could be followed for several hours, or days, if he was lucky.

He looked out into the blackness of space, where Boba Fett was chasing Han Solo. "Go ahead and blow me up," Dengar muttered. "But someday, you'll find out why they call me Payback."

Dengar got up from his console, and set to work.

Sometime later, Dengar's ship glided between the delicate Tibanna gas clouds of Bespin, past smooth mountains the colors of rose and peach, toward the setting sun.

Cloud City lay straight ahead, its rust-colored towers shining dully. He circled the upper gambling casinos, and over the comm he asked the port authorities for permission to land at the nearest repair facility, then sent a false registry for his craft, not wanting to alert anyone to his presence.

He spotted the *Millennium Falcon* below him on a landing pad. His heart began racing.

The port authorities directed him to the proper landing field, and he touched ground, then slipped quietly into Cloud City.

Once inside its corridors, the dockmaster approached his ship. "I've got problems with my sublight drive and with my communications system. I'll give you a hundred extra credits if the job is finished in two hours."

"Yes, sir," the dockmaster said, signaling his work crew to move the ship into an empty berth.

Dengar stepped into the gleaming corridors of Cloud City, made his way to the upper gambling chambers, where most of the city's real business was conducted.

If Han Solo was still here, Dengar imagined that he would find it hard to ignore the luxurious dining halls and exalted atmosphere of the casinos.

The main casino was an enormous affair with thousands of guests from hundreds of worlds. Imperial officials, smugglers, wealthy business persons, holovid celebrities—all of them were gathered here to pursue their mutual passions.

A band played in the main hall—giant orange-skinned Turans with base nose flutes, electric harps, and soft percussion drums were playing an insistent, exhilarating tune that somehow stirred Dengar deeply.

A troupe of dancers was on stage, swirling madly—small men and women of yellow skin, wearing golden strips of cloth on their arms and legs. At their center was a beautiful young woman with blue skin and dark blue hair. He recognized her—the Aruzan dancer, Manaroo.

She whirled across the floor, gazing intently into the eyes of her audience—peoples of many species, who sat at their dining and gambling tables. In her hands she had colored stones that glowed brightly, like the moons of Aruza, and she juggled and threw them in intricate patterns that drew the eye.

There was nothing frantic in her dance. Instead it was peaceful, mesmerizing, like the flow of waves across some empty beach, or like the movement of birds across the sky. For a moment she seemed to not be like a woman at all, but more like a force of nature. Irresistible, self-contained, like a sun that holds the worlds around it in sway.

Everyone focused on her, and Dengar found himself fumbling to a table, where he ordered dinner and a pleasant wine.

The band struck up a new tune, and a repulsorlift field was generated before them. Inside the field, glass gems were shooting up through a pump, so that the gems swirled in the air under the lights like some magic fountain of violet, green, and gold. Two of the dancers leapt into the field, tumbling weightlessly in dance.

With her dance finished, Manaroo came to Dengar's table, sat beside him.

"I should have known I'd find you in a place like this, out where the Imperials don't pay much attention," Dengar said.

Manaroo, who had just performed so flawlessly, looked down at her hands folded in her lap, and there was a tenseness in her voice. "I needed to get away from the Empire," she said. "Only now, they're here. They caught that man you were looking for—Han Solo. I heard it from one of the security guards."

Dengar found himself a bit surprised. Sometimes it seemed that those who had not ingested mnemiotic drugs were . . . well, stupid. "You remembered Solo's name? After all this time?"

"I wanted to help you find him," Manaroo said. "I wanted to repay you. I've been looking for him, too." This surprised Dengar even more, seeing how one small deed of kindness almost paid off big. "But I didn't find out he was here until after they caught him. I heard about it from a security guard. Now the Empire has promised to turn Han Solo over to another bounty hunter who followed him here, a man named Boba Fett."

"Do you know where Boba Fett is?"

The dancer shook her head.

Dengar considered. "A man like Boba Fett doesn't like to leave his quarry. He'll want to get Solo safely stored on his ship, and then he'll be off."

Dengar was tempted to bushwhack Boba Fett and steal his prize, but the fact was that over the past couple of days, his anger had eased. True, Boba Fett had bombed Dengar's ship, but he'd done it in such a way as to leave Dengar alive with the probability of making it to safety. It was a nice gesture, and an unnecessary one.

So Dengar wanted to return the favor. True, he wanted to steal Han Solo—since if not for Boba Fett, Dengar would have made the capture—but he also wanted to leave Boba Fett in something approximating an ambulatory state. Managing both tasks simultaneously would take some doing.

"So what will you do?" Manaroo asked.

"If the Imperials haven't released Han Solo to Boba Fett," Dengar considered, "then it means they're still questioning him. It may be a few days before they're done with him."

A waiter came, and Dengar let Manaroo order dinner on his tab. Afterward he settled back, regarding her closely. She seemed nervous still, apologetic, as if she'd failed him, when in reality she'd surprised him with her persistence. To top it off, ferreting sensitive information from a security guard might not have been easy for her. He suddenly wondered about the possibility of recruiting her as a partner.

"Did you enjoy my dance?" she said.

"You were very good. In fact, I've never seen anyone as good," Dengar said. "How did you learn to dance like that?"

"It's easy," Manaroo said. "On Aruza, we use our cybernetic links to share our feelings. We're techempaths. When I dance, I know what pleases my watchers, and so I practice those moves they love best."

"But you can't give yourself to them fully," Dengar said.

"Why do you say that?"

Dengar struggled for the words. "Because, when you danced, I wished that you were dancing for me alone. I assume that every man must feel that way about you."

Manaroo smiled, looked up into his eyes. Her own

eyes were so rich, so black, that he could see the glow globes that hovered near the ceiling reflecting in them. "You're right. I always dance for my audience as if all that I did were to please them, but inside, I dance only for myself."

She surprised him by reaching out to take his broad hand, and he was embarrassed. His hands were so large, so powerful, that he felt as if they were paws, and he were some huge, alien animal beside her.

"You seem to be doing well here," Dengar said.

"Do I?" she whispered, and once again Dengar was surprised at how rough and husky her voice could be. "I'm not. I'm terribly alone. I've never felt so . . . empty."

"How can that be?" Dengar asked. "I'm sure that there are many men who would seek you out."

"Of course, there are many men who want me," Manaroo said, "but few are willing to share themselves with me fully. I feel that we are all strangers, encased in our shells." She squeezed Dengar's hands tightly, desperately. "On my world, when two people love each other, they share more than their bodies. They do more than take pleasure with each other. They bond with the *Attanni,* sharing their thoughts and emotions completely, sharing their memories and their knowledge. All of the subterfuges between them are stripped away, and they become one person. On Aruza I was bonded to three good friends, but now . . ."

Dengar found his heart beating more rapidly, for he could see the hunger in her, the need for this, and he knew she wanted it from him. "I'm afraid that you won't find people here who are willing to bond with you that way. Our thoughts and emotions are frightening things, and so we conceal them, hoping that potential lovers will never uncover our weaknesses."

"But you have no emotions to conceal. You told me on your ship that you have no emotions, that the capacity was cut out of you by the Empire."

Dengar indeed remembered having told her, one night as they ate in his stateroom. Manaroo had seemed curious about the concept, seemed to feel that it would be like sleeping, a comfortable emptiness. But Dengar did not see it that way. Instead, it was an inconvenience. He sometimes did not know if his words or actions would offend or annoy others. Indeed, his solitary life was not something that he'd sought. He lived alone on his ship because few others could endure his presence, his demanding ways. He'd told her this.

"I sense few emotions," Dengar said. "Rage, hope, one other." She looked at him quizzically, as if demanding to know what other emotion held him sway, but he shrugged her question aside. "That is all the Empire left me. But what of my memories? What of my deeds? I suspect that you would find them . . . monstrous."

She searched his face for a long moment. "Bonding with you would make me more like you. Perhaps I need that to survive, here in your world."

Dengar considered, looked away out the window to the billowing Tibanna gas clouds. Bonding with him would teach her much that no one should know. It would open her to all of the pain and madness he'd lived through since the Empire first began molding him into an assassin. "I would rather spare you that."

They ate a leisurely dinner, made smalltalk, and Manaroo excused herself, went backstage.

Dengar sat alone and wondered. With Solo captured, would Vader come after him? Dengar doubted it. The Dark Lord of the Sith had his own political agenda, men to command, an Empire to run. Dengar was almost beneath his notice. But Dengar didn't want to cross paths with him again.

Over the loudspeakers, the city administrator, Lando Calrissian, announced that Imperial troops were taking over the station, and suggested that all personnel evacuate immediately.

Around Dengar, the gamblers and citizenry of Cloud City broke into an uproar. People began running for exits.

Dengar finished his drink, stood, and noted to the empty air, "It seems that everywhere I go lately, people are evacuating."

Stormtroopers appeared at one door on the mezzanine above him. Someone, perhaps an undercover security guard or a patron of the casino, pulled a heavy blaster, and a firefight erupted.

Dengar glanced out the window. Boba Fett's ship was arcing off through the clouds, and Dengar knew intuitively that the bounty hunter would not have left without his prey.

He cursed under his breath, watching the tail fire of Boba Fett's ship. It seemed that that was all he ever saw of Han Solo.

The firefight at the far end of the room was becoming rather heated, and smoke now filled the air.

Dengar sighed, looked at his chronometer. The port authorities may have had time to fix his ship, but he doubted it. The new engines were probably laid in, but he doubted that all of the electronic connections were made. He got up, stretched, decided to go search for Manaroo.

He rushed through a curtain of shimmering lights, found himself in a corridor that led to a larger room.

In it, two stormtroopers stood guard over half a dozen performers who sat on the floor, hands clasped over their heads. Manaroo was with them.

Dengar called to the stormtroopers, "Excuse me, gentleman, but the dancer is coming with me."

The stormtroopers swiveled their heavy blasters toward Dengar, and one shouted, "Put your hands on your head."

Dengar watched them for a half a second, then took one step to his left, pulled his blaster, and killed both men.

"Make me," he said, as they dropped to the ground.

Manaroo sat on the floor, mouth wide in shock. Dengar went to her, took her hand, and pulled her to her feet. The other performers scurried off without any urging.

"Let's get out of here while we still can," Dengar grunted.

"Where to?" she stammered.

"Tatooine," Dengar said. "Boba Fett is taking Han Solo to Tatooine."

Fortunately, when Dengar reached the repair docks, his ship was already out of the repair bay and sat gleaming on the launch field. The dockmaster had gone beyond repairing the ship, and had actually cleaned the exterior, filling the micrometeor pits and applying a fresh coat of protective paint. Too bad no one was here to collect for the repairs.

Unfortunately, half a dozen stormtroopers sat at the launch pad beside a light cannon. Dengar and Manaroo were hiding in a repair hangar, behind an old freighter. The sounds of fighting and explosions echoed all around Cloud City.

Dengar watched the stormtroopers all positioned in a tight knot, and grumbled to himself, "This is what grenades are for." These must have been fresh troops, lacking basic training.

He reached into the leg pouch on his body armor, pulled a grenade, armed it, and hurled it twenty meters till it popped a stormtrooper on the helmet and exploded.

At the sounds of running feet, Dengar looked down a side passage. Several stormtroopers, in company with Darth Vader, ran past in an adjoining corridor.

Instinctively, Dengar ducked. He really didn't want to draw attention to himself.

When the stormtroopers passed, he took Manaroo's

hand, rushed to his ship, and in half a moment, blasted off through the clouds.

Signal jammers were screaming all across the spectrum, and Dengar couldn't get a fix on any other vessels in the area, but his rear viewer showed a trio of TIE fighters swooping down from a towering cloud behind him.

Dengar dove into the cover of a nearby cloud, spiraled down, turning back the way he had come, then opened his engines, blasting up on a new trajectory, firing all guns, just in case one of those Imperial fighters crossed his plane.

Within seconds they were out of the Tibanna gas clouds, heading for the stars, and when the navicomputer laid in his course, he blurred into hyperspace.

Dengar lay back in his chair. It was true that he could not feel many emotions, could not register them with his mind, but his body registered them sometimes. His hands were shaking now, and his brow was covered in sweat. His throat was dry.

Yet when he felt inside himself, he could not detect any sense of panic.

But Manaroo stood behind his pilot's seat, hands clutching the back of his chair, her mouth frozen open in terror.

"We're all right now," Dengar said, hoping to comfort her.

"Why, why are you still following Han Solo?" she asked. "He's already been captured!"

Dengar hesitated, trying to find the right words to answer. He had no hopes of catching up with Boba Fett. The bounty hunter's ship was too fast, and he'd likely land right at Jabba's palace, so there would be no opportunity to bushwhack Boba Fett in any case. No, he needed something else. "I want to catch up to him for once," he said. "I want to touch him, just once.

"Besides, Solo has friends in high places in the Rebellion," Dengar said, trying to voice a nagging suspicion. "I figure they'll come to break him out—if Jabba the Hutt doesn't kill him first. And when they do, I want to be there, to catch him all over again." Dengar had made up that excuse impromptu, but it had a ring of truth to it. Somehow, he found that Han Solo was achieving mythical proportions. Just as Dengar seemed doomed to forever be but half a man, he had also begun to feel that Han Solo would forever be elusive, an uncatchable nemesis.

And somehow, somehow, Dengar knew he had to break the cycle. It was a wild hope, half conceived. He had to find himself again, just as he had to catch Han Solo.

Three: The Loneliness

Over the next few days, Dengar spent a great deal of time with Manaroo, just talking. She told him of her life on Aruza, being raised on a farm by a mother who made clay diningware and a father who worked as a petty bureaucrat. On their farm, Manaroo had learned early how to coax flowers from the near-sentient dola trees, and the thick juice that these flowers exuded made a potent antibiotic syrup, often prescribed by Aruza's physicians.

At the age of three, Manaroo had begun dancing, and by nine she was winning interstellar competitions. Dengar had imagined her to be some local girl, little traveled, with no real living experience. But she told him tales of rafting through dark storms upon the water world of Bengat, of living through a pirate raid on a starliner.

And sometimes she talked about the experiences of her friends, those with whom she'd shared the Attanni, as if such experiences were her own. The list of people that she considered to be friends and family was enormous, and the pain she'd suffered in sharing those lives was equally enormous, for each of her friends had also shared their memories with others through the Attanni, so that all of them were but motes in some vast net.

Dengar had thought her to be only a young woman, but he found that she was much more mature than he'd imagined, far stronger than he could have guessed.

For his part, Dengar told her of his life on Corellia, where he'd begun repairing swoops with his father as a child, and had begun racing in his early teens. He did not tell her how he'd lived in Han's shadow in those years, did not explain how it was during a race with Han Solo that he'd been wounded. Instead, he told only of the surgeries the Empire had performed, how between threats of death and promises that they would someday restore his ability to feel, they had bullied him into becoming an assassin.

Yet Dengar had always chosen his victims, harvesting only those he felt deserved to die.

Inevitably, Manaroo voiced the question, "And why is it that Han Solo deserves to die?"

Dengar was forced to admit, "I'm not sure he does. But he almost killed me once. I want to catch him, force him to tell me why he did it. Then I'll decide whether to let him live."

The next evening, they were almost to Tatooine, and Dengar went to the pilot's console to check his systems.

Manaroo came up behind him. "Hmmm . . ." she said, and she began massaging his neck muscles. "You're tight." He eased back, enjoying the sensation. "You know, this is twice you've saved my life. I owe you something. Close your eyes."

Her hand slipped under the twisted bandages that covered his neck, touched his cybernetic interface jack. He felt her connect something to his jack, and he sat upright.

"What's that?" he said, turning around.

She held up a small golden ring, threaded so that it could fit into an interface socket. "It's part of an Attanni," she said, "so that you can receive me, feel what I feel. I won't be able to read your thoughts or emotions, or access your memories."

He let her put the ring into his jack, twirl it till it fit in tight. Suddenly he could hear through her ears, see through her eyes. He felt the intensity of her emotions.

Manaroo was afraid, and her fear knotted her belly. She watched him with calculation. "Close your eyes, so that you don't see overlapping images," she said, but Dengar didn't respond immediately.

Her fear washed through him, a cold fire, and to him it seemed the most intense emotion he'd ever felt. At first he imagined it was like water to a man who has thirsted for days, to feel this again, but something in him knew that people seldom felt fear quite as intense as this. He wondered why she was afraid.

Manaroo was watching him, and she put one hand on each shoulder, kissed him, and he could feel her dry mouth, taste her hope and desire, and part of him was surprised at the intensity of her desire. Then he understood why she feared him. She was afraid he would reject her, turn her away. He could also feel her loneliness, an aching void within her. Each sensation from her came as if it were new, as if no one had ever discovered it before.

She felt comforted by his presence, protected, which helped explain some of her strong feelings for him. Dengar tried to search her mind, see just how deep her feelings for him went, but the Attanni she'd fitted to his implant could only receive the emotions she sent. It didn't allow him to probe her thoughts or memories.

She kissed him tenderly on the forehead, and held him for a long time, and briefly she remembered her mother on Aruza, kissing her as a child, and there was such a pang of guilt and regret at having left her parents to die on Aruza, a pang so violent that Dengar gasped, and then Manaroo cried out, sorry to have caused him such pain, and she fumbled to remove the Attanni from his cranial jack.

Dengar sat panting, breathing heavily, sweat pouring down his brow. He'd not felt guilt, good clean guilt, in many years. He'd slaughtered decent people for the Empire just as easily as he'd abandoned Manaroo's parents and friends without a thought.

Now he lay back panting and smiling at having felt remorse for the first time in decades.

"I'm sorry," Manaroo gasped, fumbling to put the Attanni in a pocket.

"I know," Dengar flashed her a small grin, and the words caught in his throat. He started to stand up, but found that these strong emotions had left him weak in the legs and left tears in his eyes. There was a time in his life when he'd have felt embarrassed to show such emotions. Now, he just sat back for a long time, relishing them.

When he could speak at all again, he said, "We'll have to go back to Aruza, get your parents off planet— along with as many of your people as we can."

"Why do you say that?" Manaroo blurted, for she'd not revealed her wish.

"Your . . . conscience . . . told me," Dengar whispered, and he sat, realizing perhaps for the first time what the Empire had taken from him. He knew that they'd taken the capacity to feel joy, to feel love, to feel concern and guilt.

Over the past years, the desire to help another being had never entered him.

This is what it is to be human, he realized. To sit and know that on the far side of the galaxy, someone is in pain, someone hurts, and so it is my duty to go to them, regardless of the cost or risk, in order to free them from pain.

It was a way of knowing that Dengar had too long

found—inaccessible, so much so that he'd forgotten that it existed.

Over the past months, as he'd hunted for Han Solo, Dengar had often puzzled over the trail. His nemesis would sometimes turn from an obvious route, such as an easy escape from the Empire, to rush headlong into battle. Such puzzling actions made it almost impossible for Dengar to calculate Solo's next move, for one never knew whether Solo would charge a battalion or strafe a Star Destroyer. It was rumored that on one occasion, Han Solo had had the audacity to call the Emperor, accusing him of dire crimes and challenging him to a boxing match! Dengar had doubted the rumor at the time, for it seemed so illogical, but now, he reconsidered.

Finally Dengar saw why his race to capture Solo had been so fruitless: Han Solo had a conscience, and like a navicomputer it guided him on a certain course, a course that Dengar could not have hoped to understand—until now.

"You and your Attanni could come in very handy," Dengar said, and he explained what he had just learned. "With you, perhaps I'd have had a chance at catching Han Solo."

"And what would you do with him, then?" Manaroo whispered.

Dengar considered. With a conscience, perhaps his work would also be hampered. Certainly, in his early years, he'd have spared some of the targets the Empire had him destroy. "I can't be sure," Dengar said.

"When next you meet him," Manaroo said, slipping the Attanni into his palm, "Let's find out."

Dengar began punching in new instructions on his navicomputer. "First, we must go to Aruza, and get your parents."

•   •   •

Dengar finally returned to Tatooine. In the meantime, with the aid of Manaroo he posed as an Imperial Intelligence officer who was arranging to remove a large number of Aruzan diplomats to a "more secure facility."

With the help of the Rebel Alliance, he managed to steal a huge Imperial prison barge, large enough to remove a hundred thousand people from the planet, and he'd manned the ship with the appropriate Corrections officers, torturers, and other staff.

It took little effort for the Rebel Alliance to send false orders for the new COMPNOR base commander to begin extracting prisoners and shuttling them up to the barge.

The Imperial officers were well-trained, and brought up prisoners as fast as they were called for.

Only once did anyone question Dengar—who had remained aloof from the dirty work and had stayed aboard his barge during the whole mission, personally "managing the incarceration."

When the new COMPNOR base commander called on holovid just before Dengar's departure, asking Dengar where the prisoners were being taken, Dengar just fixed the man with an icy glare and said, "You don't really want to know, do you?"

There were rampant rumors of soft politicians, technological geniuses, and pacifist industrialists who had disappeared from across the galaxy. It was said that prudent men didn't delve into such matters. The COMPNOR base commander fumbled for a quick apology.

Dengar flipped off the holovid with feigned disdain.

When Dengar's ship reached Tatooine, it landed in a dusty port called Mos Eisley, a city at the edge of a desert where twin suns burned vehemently.

They landed at midday, when the city was perhaps its

quietest, and Dengar led Manaroo to a small cantina where moisture farmers and criminals seemed to have gathered in equal numbers.

Dengar went to speak privately with some old acquaintances, and in a matter of minutes he confirmed that Han Solo was still alive, kept prisoner at Jabba's palace. He left Manaroo with a few credit chips and said, "I'll be back when I'm back," then he took a rented swoop to Jabba's palace.

That night, Manaroo returned to the cantina while it was busy and made a few credits dancing. Dengar had exhausted his wealth over the past few weeks, and Manaroo hoped at the very least to pay her own way. After her first dance, she went to a private booth to catch her breath.

An alien came up to the booth, and stood, looking at her. The creature had dark brown fur, an enormously broad mouth that was wider than her shoulders, short legs, and long arms with claws that scraped the floor. The short horns on its head nearly scraped the ceiling. It stood looking at her for a moment from deep red eyes, then growled. "Your dance—good! Strong! Jabba will like! If he likes dance, you live. Come!"

He grabbed her arm, and Manaroo looked at the creature uncomprehendingly. "I won't dance for Jabba!" she said.

The creature glanced furtively both ways, then pulled at a flap of skin beneath its throat and lurched at her. For one moment she screamed as the beast grabbed her. Then she found herself sliding down into the creature's belly pouch.

There was little to breathe in there, and the air smelled of hair and putrid flesh. She struggled and kicked, but the creature's hide was very thick—if anyone noticed the odd-shaped bulge kicking at the creature's stomach, they must have assumed the worst and did not want to become involved.

Manaroo held her breath for a long time, as the creature casually sauntered out of the cantina. Too soon the pouch began to feel hot, and the air failed her. With burning lungs she kicked and pummeled at the beast, but could not break free.

Dengar entered the Hutt's palace at night, when the inhabitants were most active, and knelt on one knee. Jabba was surrounded by his lackeys—nearly all of whom were required to sleep in his chamber, for the Hutt feared assassination and knew that the best way to thwart it was to keep all of the would-be assassins within sight. Dengar looked up, saw Boba Fett in the shadows off to Jabba's right, nodded at the man.

"Why do you come before me?" Jabba grumbled in Huttese. "You did not bring me Han Solo. You can expect no reward!"

"I have heard that you have Han Solo captive," Dengar said. "I came to see if it was true."

"Ho, ho, ho," Jabba laughed. "Behold for yourself!" A light switched on behind Dengar, and he turned. On the wall, in what Dengar had believed to be a decorative frieze, he could see the face and features of Han Solo, frozen in gray carbonite.

Dengar laughed, walked over to Solo, and grasped each side of the frame that held his frozen body. "Gotcha," Dengar said. "At last."

"Ho, ho," Jabba laughed from deep in his belly, and his menagerie of murderers laughed with him. "You mean *I have him.*"

Dengar turned to look over his shoulder. "No," Dengar said, staring into the Hutt's eyes. "You only think you have him." The Hutt frowned at this. "You cannot keep him in . . . this!" Dengar waved at the carbonite containment device. "Surely, he will escape."

"Ho, ho, oh, hooo!" Jabba roared. "You think he can escape from there! You amuse me, assassin."

Dengar turned to Jabba, folded his hands before

him. "Hear me, oh great Jabba," Dengar warned. "I do indeed believe he will escape from you. And when he does, you will be the laughingstock of the underworld. But I can spare you from this fate. For I propose to remain here, to catch him once again. And when I do, I expect you to pay me twice what you have paid Boba Fett!"

"Do you intend to free him yourself?" Jabba roared, so that part of his retinue fell back, fearing his wrath.

"He will never be freed by my hand," Dengar whispered.

"Do you suspect a plot?" Jabba asked, eyeing the cutthroats and hoodlums in his employment.

"His friends in the Rebellion will seek to free him," Dengar answered earnestly.

"The Rebellion?" Jabba laughed. "I do not fear them. So it is agreed. You may stay and join my retainers. And if the Rebellion frees him and you manage to bring him back, I will pay you twice what I paid Boba Fett!"

Boba Fett stepped forward, brandishing his blaster rifle menacingly, and Jabba silenced him with a glare. He spoke with a low voice, "But if the Rebellion fails in its attempt to free Han Solo, then you will work for me for one year—scrubbing the royal toilets in company with the cleaning droids!" The Hutt broke into laughter.

Dengar returned to Mos Eisley at sunrise, planning to move his ship to Jabba's palace where it would be handy in case of a Rebel attack.

But he was confused when he entered the ship and found Manaroo gone. He made a perfunctory search, found that she'd never returned from the cantina. At the cantina, the bartender said that she'd danced for a few credits, then "disappeared."

Dengar considered the news, then remembered the

Attanni that Manaroo had given him. He went back to the ship, inserted the device into his cranial jack, then closed his eyes, trying to see what she saw, hear what she heard. But the Attanni gave off only a whisper of static.

Dengar left the device in, flew a quick grid low over the city, but never received her signal, so he headed back to Jabba's palace, landed the *Punishing One* in Jabba's secure hangars.

All through the trip back to the palace, he thought about Manaroo and wondered what had become of her. He found that he had become accustomed to her presence, even imagined that he felt comforted by it. Once, just a few nights before, she had demanded to know what other emotion the Empire had left him with besides his rage and his hope, and he had refused to tell her. Loneliness.

His loneliness served no purpose in the Empire's designs, at least not that he could fathom. Dengar was not even certain that they had left him with that ability on purpose. Perhaps when they'd cut away the rest of his hypothalamus, they'd not even been aware of what they'd left him with.

But over the years, Dengar felt that it was not the rage or hope that had come to define him, but his loneliness, his knowledge that nowhere in the galaxy would he find someone who would love him, or approve of him.

It wasn't until he was on his way back to Jabba's throne room that Dengar suddenly felt a staggering wave of fear. He closed his eyes, listened with other ears.

"You got to dance your best for Jabba," a fat woman was saying. "He gets his entertainment one way or another. If he don't like how you dance, he'll take great pleasure in watching you die."

Dengar watched the fat woman through Manaroo's eyes, saw three other dancers from various worlds all lounging about on dark benches. They were in a damp-smelling cell, with thick steel bars. The air felt fetid, and one of Jabba's guards was pacing outside the window to the door, occasionally poking his snout through the bars to leer at the dancers.

"What if he likes how I dance?" Manaroo asked.

"Then he'll keep you longer. Maybe even set you free."

"Ah, don't try to give her hope," another woman said from a far bench. "That only happened once."

The fat dancer turned. "But it happened!"

"Look, girl—" the other dancer said from the far end of the room. "You either dance good, or you die."

"But I already danced for Jabba," Manaroo said, "when the slaver brought me in."

"So you passed the audition," the fat woman said. "That's something."

Dengar took off the Attanni, placed it in the bottom of his holster, beneath his blaster.

Jabba was a demanding creature. Once he'd paid money for anything—whether it be a slave or a drug shipment—he deeply resented losing that thing. And the Hutt took great pleasure in tormenting others. While Dengar could not sense a difference between good and evil, the Hutt took pleasure in evil.

Dengar knew that he wouldn't get Manaroo back without a fight.

He squinted and considered the Hutt, tried to picture Jabba with dark brown hair and a lanky frame. But even with the greatest stretch of imagination, he couldn't find much in the way of similarities between Jabba the Hutt and Han Solo.

"Ah, well," Dengar groaned. "I'll just have to kill him anyway."

Fortunately, Dengar soon found that many of Jabba's henchmen had reason to plot against their master.

Within three days Dengar was able to provide one of Jabba's henchmen—the Quarren Tessek—with a bomb. Dengar made it from weapons stored in his ship, and he made it big enough to blow Jabba's bloated corpse into orbit. Delivering the bomb was simple, since he only had to hand it over to one of Jabba's most trusted servants, the head of the motor pool, Barada.

Unfortunately for Dengar, Jabba learned about the plot before the bomb was ever completed. Upon the rather prescient advice of Bib Fortuna, who assured Jabba that Dengar was making a bomb, Jabba assigned Boba Fett to watch Dengar.

Boba Fett was easily up to the task. A microtransmitter dropped into one of Dengar's holsters performed the trick. When Dengar delivered the bomb to Barada, their words gave proof of the conspiracy.

When Boba Fett informed the Hutt that he had uncovered the plot, Boba Fett asked, "Do you want me to remove the bomb?"

The Hutt laughed, a deep and throaty laugh that shook his great belly. "You would deprive me of my amusement? No, I will have the bomb dismantled, and I will make certain that Tessek is with me when it is set to explode. I will enjoy watching him squirm. As for Barada—I will make him wait for a few weeks for his punishment."

"What of Dengar?" Boba Fett asked. "You can't toy with him. He's too dangerous."

Jabba squinted his huge dark eyes and looked narrowly at Boba Fett. "I will leave it to you to punish him, but do not give him an easy death." Jabba brightened, and his eyes opened wide. "It has been a long time since I let one of my enemies feel the bite of the Teeth of Tatooine!"

Boba Fett nodded curtly. "As you will, my lord."

•　•　•

That day was busy for Dengar. The surgeons who had operated on him so long ago had cut away his ability to feel fear, but at certain odd times he found that he moved with a new bit of energy, found his heart beating irregularly. It was, he knew, just a ghost of what others felt when they feared, but he found it invigorating. The bomb on Jabba's skiff was set to go off early the next day, so Dengar became concerned that night when plans suddenly changed.

Dengar had been resting in his quarters when Luke Skywalker suddenly appeared at Jabba's palace and attempted to rescue Han Solo. Jabba foiled the young Jedi's attempt and threw Skywalker into a pit with Jabba's pet monster, the Rancor. Skywalker surprised everyone by killing the beast.

The sound of the rancor's death cry rattled the palace, waking Dengar, who hurried to Jabba's throne room and reached the top of a small staircase in time to hear the sentence pronounced upon Han Solo and his friends. They were to die in the Great Pit of Carkoon.

The palace became a madhouse. Jabba's henchmen ran about arming themselves, preparing vehicles. Two Gamorrean guards scrambled up the stairs past Dengar, and one grumbled, "Why we need hurry?"

The other guard backhanded him, sent him staggering against a wall. "Idiot! We no want Rebels come. If they learn Jabba wants to kill Skywalker and Leia, we in for big fight!"

Dengar looked for Tessek in the crowd below, trying to spot the gray-skinned Quarren's mouth tentacles, wondering if this would change their plans.

But some of Jabba's men already seemed to have the Quarren under guard. They were standing close at his back, and Dengar could only hear snatches of conversation. Tessek was begging Jabba for his life.

In a moment, Jabba sent the Quarren to pack, and Tessek scurried away through an exit in the far wall.

Dengar ducked back into the hall, into the safe shadows. Had Jabba found the bomb? Obviously Jabba suspected something. . . .

But the Hutt hadn't killed Tessek, and he hadn't sent guards after Dengar. So Jabba couldn't have had proof of the treason. Which suggested that the Hutt had merely heard rumors of their plans. Or perhaps Jabba had some other reason to threaten Tessek.

Still, Dengar didn't want to be around here right at the moment. If Jabba found that bomb, heads would roll. Dengar didn't want his head to be one of them.

There was still time to escape. It might well be that Jabba wouldn't discover the bomb at all, and if that were the case, he might be on or near the skiff when it exploded. The plot might still succeed. In any case, whether it succeeded or failed, it would do so without further effort from Dengar.

But if Jabba did find the bomb too soon. . . .

Dengar decided it might be a good time to go into Mos Eisley for the day. If his plan worked, Jabba would die. If it didn't—Dengar might still escape.

Dengar returned to his cramped quarters and began throwing his clothes and weapons into a bag. Among his effects he found the Attanni. He could not contact Manaroo with it—but Dengar could receive images, sounds, emotions.

And as he looked at the device, he recalled the hunger Manaroo had felt for his presence, her fears for her life. Sometimes he wondered how she could feel anything for him. In his own eyes he was broken, undeserving of her attention. Yet she'd stayed beside him even after he'd rescued her parents. He felt there was nothing left that he could give her, except perhaps a false sense of safety.

And by running out now, he would be denying her even that.

He unwrapped his neck, screwed the Attanni into the socket there.

And what he saw surprised him. Manaroo was dress-

ing for a performance, putting on leggings of some
sheer material in softest violet, a top that revealed her
ample breasts. She sorted through a bin of musical instruments—tambours, bells, cymbals—looking for
something exotic, and decided to take a golden flute.
To play it while dancing would be difficult, and to play
it poorly would be to tempt fate. But Manaroo would be
dancing for her life, and she needed to impress the
Hutt.

She'd been commanded to dance before Jabba, and
everyone in the room knew that he was in a foul mood
because the rancor was dead. The other dancers sat
huddled in a far corner and shot Manaroo pitying
glances.

What amazed Dengar was her mood. She was almost
numb with fear and had no recourse but to put her
confidence in her abilities. These feelings lay heavily in
the background of her mind.

And in the foreground, Manaroo was concentrating,
trying to firm her resolve by playing mental games. Just
as Dengar would psyche himself up for an assassination
by imagining that he was killing Han Solo, Manaroo
was playing similar games in her own mind.

She envisioned Jabba's throne room, but instead of
Jabba on the throne, she imagined Dengar there. He
was watching her steadily, calling out "Dance, dance
for your life!" as if it were some great jest.

And in her dreams, Manaroo danced lovingly, with
her heart. She imagined each move, practiced over the
years, and each spin and flourish was dedicated to Dengar. Each of them had been conceived and prepared
for the man she loved, the man she hoped someday to
meld minds with, so that they became one. And in her
imaginings, as she danced gracefully before Dengar,
she whispered, "If I please you *so much*, my lord, my
love, then why don't you please me in return? Why
don't you marry me?"

Dengar pulled off the Attanni in astonishment, and

knew that he could not leave now. The powerful feelings that washed through him when he was connected acted as a moral compass, telling him what to do. And like Han Solo, who sometimes seemed to suffer from a death wish, Dengar knew that he would have to turn his face to the storm.

He had to save her, but how?

Dengar was amazed that she would be preparing for a performance now, while the palace was in such disarray, and realized immediately that he would have to plan a diversion. To blindly go into the throne room and try to kill the Hutt would be insane, but over the past few days, there had been two murders in the palace.

Both incidents had been fully investigated and caused a great deal of commotion for several hours. A few hours was all the time that Manaroo needed. A random assassination seemed in order. Among the henchmen in Jabba's stable, there was no lack of deserving victims.

The problem was solved rather easily. Dengar simply went up to a guard room and tossed in a grenade. In the general cacophony of the palace, few people even noticed the event, but the ensuing investigation took up a better part of the evening, and the Hutt's mood brightened considerably after he saw the carnage that Dengar's grenade had made out of some poor Gamorrean guard.

So it came as a great shock when Jabba finally looked up from the messy guard and a cold gleam came to his eyes. "I'm hungry," grumbled. "Bring me food, and rouse my dancing girl! Have everyone gather in the great hall! Tonight we party, and I will have no more interruptions!"

●　　　●　　　●

The nights were short on Tatooine, and few slept through them, for it was a time to retreat from the blistering heat of the day.

So it was that late that evening, Dengar sat in the throne room, waiting for Manaroo's dance. He had his Attanni in, and he listened for Manaroo's thoughts. Her own mind was numb at the thought of the coming dance, and she was preparing hastily, trying to calm her breath, relax.

In the great hall the musicians had begun to gather, and servants brought heaping platters of food. The Hutt grabbed a few squirming things from one huge box and shoved them in his mouth, then bellowed for his dancing girl.

It was then that Dengar saw his mistake. The Hutt was feeling bloodthirsty tonight, and the sight of the dead Gamorrean guard, rather than distracting him, had only enticed him further. Han Solo and the others would die, but Jabba was not a patient creature. He would not wait for blood. So he called for Manaroo.

Dengar loosened his heavy blaster in its holster, wondered what to do. Killing Jabba would be hard. Hutts had notoriously thick hides, and it could take several shots from his blaster. Dengar wasn't sure he'd get those shots. The room was crowded with hundreds of Jabba's henchmen and servants, all gathered for one last mad feast, for many worried that at dawn they would be battling the Rebel Alliance. So the musicians played with a manic edge to their tune, and the henchmen feasted as if this brief meal would be their last.

As Dengar waited for Manaroo to make her appearance, Boba Fett approached his table, swaggering, carrying a long green jug of Twi'lek liquor.

"Join me for a drink?" Boba Fett asked. Boba Fett was normally a very self-contained individual. He never sought out another person's company, and at first Dengar was confused by the request. But nearly all the other tables were full, and so the request did not seem out of line.

"Sure, have a seat," Dengar said, kicking a chair back from the table.

Boba Fett sat, put his jug down, motioned for a serving boy to bring some glasses.

"I've been watching you," Boba Fett said, the microphones in his helmet making his voice sound unnaturally loud and gravelly as he spoke to be heard above the noise of celebration. "You're not like the others here," he waved at the henchmen gorging themselves at the other tables, "given to excess. I like that in a man. You seem cool, competent, professional."

"Thank you," Dengar said, unsure where this might be leading.

"Tomorrow morning, Han Solo dies," Boba Fett said.

"I know it's scheduled, but I'm not certain Jabba can pull it off," Dengar said, unwilling to admit that in all likelihood, Han Solo, his nemesis, would die an ignoble death at dawn. It seemed too easy a way for him to go. At a nearby table, two of Jabba's henchmen began singing a raucous drinking song.

"I'm leaving after the execution," Boba Fett said more loudly. "I've got a job—a big job. More than one man can handle. But the rewards are extravagant. Interested?"

"Why should I trust you?" Dengar asked absently. Through his Attanni, he could see that Manaroo was being released from her cell. A Gamorrean guard was shoving her through a dark narrow passageway that would lead her to Jabba's throne. "You bombed my ship. You've already betrayed me once."

Boba Fett sat back a bit in his chair, as if he were surprised at the accusation. "That was when we were in business as competitors. This time, we would be in business as partners. Besides, I *did* leave you alive."

"It was indeed a kindness. Which is why I haven't tried to kill you in return," Dengar said.

Boba Fett chuckled, a very disturbing sound simply because it was something Dengar had never heard before. Boba Fett leaned his head back, and the palace lights shined on his visor like stars. "You and I are a lot alike. What do you say? Partners?"

Dengar studied Boba Fett. He was a careful man, a dangerous man who was deserving of his reputation. And Dengar was low on funds. He nodded slightly. "Partners, I suspect. Tell me more about the deal." Dengar leaned forward as if interested in speaking with Boba Fett, but he was really watching down toward the lighted area before Jabba's throne.

Manaroo had just come out from behind a curtain, and now she stood blinking, trying to let her eyes adjust to the brightness of the stage after days in the dungeon. Her heart hammered with fear as the musicians began to strike another tune, and she went to their leader, begged him to wait a moment.

"Agreed," Boba Fett said. "Let's wet our tongues as we discuss our plans. I've a vintage here that I think will surprise you. It should have warmed enough by now." He opened the green container and poured the liquor into two glasses. For a moment, Dengar dared hope that he would finally get to see what lay hidden behind Boba Fett's visor, but the warrior simply pulled a long feeding straw out from beneath the visor and stuck it into the glass, then began sipping.

At the sight of that, Dengar began to wonder if all the rumors about Boba Fett's paranoia might not be true. If so, then in the past his sickness had served him well. People paid Boba Fett to be paranoid. Working with him would be interesting.

Only when Dengar saw that Boba Fett had safely drunk the liquor, did he also take a drink. It was a dry drink, with a piquant bouquet and a slightly sweet nose. Dengar found it quite appealing.

Down by the throne, the musicians struck up a dancing tune. Dengar found that his hands were shaking as he shared Manaroo's fear, and he knew he needed to steady his nerves in case he had to open fire on Jabba. He swallowed half a glass.

"Watch out there," Boba Fett said, "not so fast. This is more potent than you imagine."

Dengar nodded absently. Down on the dance floor, Manaroo swirled across the room, playing a golden flute as she leapt, and Jabba leaned forward and studied her hungrily, as if she were one of the squirming insects on his food tray. The Hutt opened his mouth, just barely, and licked his lips with his horrible tongue.

Dengar leaned closer, his heart pounding. On the dance floor, Manaroo was swirling, playing her pipe in deliberate frenzy, and Dengar felt the room begin to spin around him. He put both hands on the table to keep from toppling forward, and found that his eyelids felt enormously heavy. He strained to keep his eyes open, and each time they closed, he saw the room as Manaroo did, spinning around, the leering faces studying her.

"Are you all right?" Boba Fett asked, his voice sounding distant and tinny.

"Got . . . to get Manaroo out," Dengar muttered, and he tried to stand. His legs felt as if they were tied to the chair, and he wondered how he could feel so weak. "Liquor . . . poison . . . ?" He reached for his blaster. His eyelids closed by themselves, and he saw the room spinning, heard the pipe shrilling unnaturally as Manaroo played.

When he opened his eyes, Boba Fett was there at his side, holding Dengar upright, helping him pull the blaster from his holster. Dengar's hands felt too heavy, too big and uncoordinated for such a delicate task, and he was grateful for Boba Fett's help getting the blaster free from its holster.

"Not poison," Boba Fett said, and Dengar had to

concentrate to hear him above the noise of the great hall, the shrilling of the pipe. "Just drugged—on the rim of your glass. Jabba has something special in mind for you. You are to feel the Teeth of Tatooine." Dengar lurched up, knocking his own table over. Around the throne room, the music stopped, and everyone turned to watch him. Jabba himself laughed merrily, his eyes gleaming as Dengar struggled forward, hoping to strike one blow at the monster.

Someone stuck a foot out to trip Dengar, and he landed on the floor, rolled to his back. There was a shout and applause, and one of Jabba's henchmen raised a glass in salute to Dengar, and people cheered. The annoying little rodent-like Salacious Crumb had climbed up on the lip of the overturned table and was laughing uproariously at Dengar.

"Payback!" Manaroo shouted from the dance floor. Dengar was sure that he heard her cry so loud only because he wore the Attanni.

He saw through her eyes as she tried to rush to him through the crowd, but one of Jabba's Gamorrean guards grabbed her arms and shoved her back down to the dance floor with a growl. Manaroo's heart hammered in panic.

Then Dengar's eyes closed of their own accord, and everything went black.

Four: The Teeth of Tatooine

Dengar woke under Tatooine's blistering suns just past dawn. The ground was heating. Dengar could feel that some small desert creature with a hard shell had crawled under his body, seeking refuge from the coming day there among the shadows and the rocks.

Dengar opened his eyes, looked around, still dazed. He was in a wide canyon, lying on the desert pan, a sterile plain of greenish-white rock, eroded—perhaps even polished—by the wind. Each of his hands and feet was bound by three cords, all pulled tight and bolted into the rock, so that he could not move. The leathery cords were slightly moist, designed to shrink in the heat of the sun, pulling him tighter.

There was no sign of a craft nearby, no guards or even a droid to record Dengar's death. There was no singing of insects or call of wild animals, only the steady soughing of the wind over rock.

Dengar licked his lips. It seemed that Jabba intended to let him die of dehydration, a death that was neither particularly appealing nor particularly unpleasant—as far as deaths go. Painful, but not extraordinary.

Dengar wondered at that. He recalled Boba Fett's pronouncement—the Teeth of Tatooine. But what were a planet's teeth? Its mountain peaks? That would seem logical, but Dengar was far from the mountains.

So it had to be an animal. There were tales of dragons in the desert, creatures large and vicious. Dengar watched the horizon, both on land and air, for sign of such beasts, and he slowly tested his bonds. Dengar was stronger than most people gave him credit for. But the straps that held him were more than adequate. He inhaled deeply, tasting mineral salts in the air, and began working vigorously to free himself.

Dengar closed his eyes after thoroughly testing each bond, and considered. It was just past dawn, and if Jabba had kept his promise, then Han Solo and his companions were already gone, dying interminably as they were ingested by the mighty Sarlacc at the Pit of Carkoon. Dengar felt hollow at the thought. The Empire had cut away most of Dengar's feelings. They'd left him with few companions—his rage, his hope, his loneliness.

At the thought of Han dying, Dengar felt somehow cast adrift, more alone than ever in the great void. For ages now, catching Han had been his only goal, his only purpose for being. Without Han, there seemed to be no reason left to exist. Except Manaroo. And he was no longer sure that she was alive. He remembered her terror, in that last moment before he'd lost consciousness. She had been sure that Jabba intended to kill her.

Dengar mourned her. In the moments when he had touched Manaroo's mind, Dengar had almost known what it was to be human again. He'd almost known what it was to be whole. Someday, he imagined, that with her help, he might have learned to love and laugh again.

But if she was not dead already, she was languishing in one of Jabba's cells, doomed to an early death.

Dengar began working harder.

In moments he had built up a fine sweat, and he managed to rub the skin off his left wrist so that blood began to flow from it. Still, the ropes had not begun to weaken.

Dengar stopped worrying the wrist, began working on his left foot. The ropes there were tied over his armored boots, providing some protection for his legs. The Imperial surgeons had boosted Dengar's reflexes, given him greater strength. But he couldn't pull his leg back to kick much, and even after an hour he had not succeeded in breaking a rope or pulling a single line free from the bolt that held it into the rock.

Indeed, all his work only succeeded in chafing his wrists, so that the blood came more profusely.

A strong morning wind began gusting, blowing sand through the broad plain. Dust clouds formed in the distance down below Dengar's feet—dirty gray streaks that filled the sky like thunderheads or fog. They were kilometers away, but he could see them rolling toward him, menacing.

He closed his eyes for a bit, trying to keep the grit from blowing into them, and he remembered one of Jabba's henchmen mentioning a place not far from the palace, a place called the Valley of the Wind.

He had no doubt that that was where he was now. A

comforting thought, for at least he knew he was near Jabba's Palace, perhaps within walking distance of water, if he could only get free.

Out across the pan, Dengar heard a bleating roar. He turned to his side and saw a shaggy bantha running hard, heading toward him. Three Sand People rode on its back, up behind its curling horns, and in moments the Sand People were at his side.

Two of them leapt down and stalked toward him, weapons ready, while the other stayed on the bantha, watching for signs of ambush.

Dengar had heard tales of the Sand People, how they fell upon travelers and killed them, only to harvest the water from their dead bodies. Indeed, the two that hovered over Dengar were making odd slurping sounds, hissing in their own tongue, and Dengar was reminded of darker tales, where it was hinted that the Sand People, to show their contempt for captives, would bind their prisoners and insert long metallic tubes into their bodies, then drink from their prisoners while they yet lived.

But Dengar had done nothing to earn such disrespect from these Sand People, and so he was not surprised when they simply sat next to him at his head, watching him die.

For a long hour they sat as the winds blew steadily stronger. Dengar watched them, and after a while he renewed his struggle. The Sand People merely stared in morbid curiosity, as if this were their form of entertainment.

But he knew that they were waiting for him to die so that they could harvest him.

Dengar looked at their wrapped faces, at the spikes sewn into their clothing, and they reminded him of teeth. He wondered if the Sand People would kill him, if this was what Boba Fett had meant by "the Teeth of Tatooine."

But the morning grew hotter, and the winds grew dry

and blew more fiercely, and heavy sands began to blow. And suddenly Dengar remembered something more about the Valley of the Winds. Something about "sand tides." It was unusual for Dengar to forget anything. The mnemiotic drugs that the Empire had forced into him made certain of that. Dengar only had difficulty recalling what had been said because it was part of a conversation between two other people, and his attention had been directed elsewhere at the time, but now he remembered. The Valley of the Winds was located between two deserts, one high and cool, the other lower and hotter. Each day, the winds would blow up the slopes as the hot air rose from one desert, and at night the cool air would come blowing back with great force.

In each desert there were dunes of sand deposits, which would blow, scouring the stone, only to be redeposited each morning and night.

The wind picked up and blew more fiercely. Dengar was sweating, and his mouth had become dry. He could feel a burning fever coming on. The sand was blowing through the valley with such force that he could no longer keep his eyes open. To do so, even for a moment, left them searing and gritty.

After one devastating gust of wind, where small rocks pelted the Sand People, the bantha roared out in pain and struggled back onto its feet, then turned away as if to leave the area, and the Sand People made to follow it hesitantly, as if it were their leader giving an undesirable command.

One of the Sand People paused by Dengar, pulled out a long knife and sawed at one of the ropes that held Dengar to the ground. The other two had mounted up, and one of them growled at his companion, questioning him.

The creature who was sawing the ropes stood and began hissing some reply, making stabbing motions at

Dengar, as if to say, "Why should we wait for him to die? Let's kill him now and be done with it."

But the mounted one pointed off in the distance beyond Dengar's feet and jabbed a finger in the air, hissing something. Dengar understood only one word of his retort: Jabba. If you kill him now, Jabba will be angry.

The Sand Person with the knife bristled at the words, stood over Dengar for a moment. The bantha roared again, and the Sand Person thrust the long knife in its sheath and leapt onto its back. Soon they were gone.

The wind kept building. The blowing sand covered the world like a dirty gray shroud. It was whistling, keening, talking in its own voice.

Dengar looked at the one cord that had been cut at. It was one of the cords tied to his right hand. Dengar wrapped his fingers around it and began pulling on that cord, hoping to snap it, but in a few moments, he fell back, exhausted.

Then the wind gusted, churning over the land with a scream, and the sand cut him savagely. A small sharp flake of rock whistled through the air, slashing across the bridge of Dengar's nose like a bit of glass. Another flake lodged in his boot. A third flake struck one of the cords on his right wrist so that it twanged, and then Dengar realized what was happening.

The Teeth of Tatooine. Flakes of stone and pieces of sand began screaming through the air. Dengar struggled to turn his head away from the shrieking wind. The sky above him was going dark under the weight of the sand storm. The suns hung in the sky like two globes of light, piercing bright.

And Dengar remembered something, a memory that seemed ages old, crusted over.

He remembered the operating room where the Imperial surgeons had worked on him. His eyes had been covered with gauze, but there had been two bright lights shining in his face, and he remembered the doctors inserting probes into his brain.

He remembered feeling pity, a profound sense of pity, and someone saying, "Pity? You want that?"

"Of course not," another doctor had replied. "We don't want that. Burn it."

There had been a moment of silence, a hissing noise, and the smell of charred flesh as the doctors burned away that portion of his hypothalamus.

Then came love, a swelling in his heart that made him want to rise up into the air. "Love?"

"He won't need it." The hissing, the scent of charred flesh.

Anger welled up in him. "Rage?"

"Leave it."

Almost immediately, he'd felt a profound sense of relief. "Relief?"

"Oh, I don't know. What do you think?" Dengar had wanted to say something, he'd wanted to tell them to leave him alone, but his mouth was not working. He'd only been able to see the twin globes through the gauze.

"Burn it," both doctors said in unison, then laughed, as if it were a game.

The memory faded, and Dengar lay alone on the sand. He recalled the promises that his Imperial Officers had given him. When he'd proven his value to the Empire, they said that they would restore him, give him back his ability to feel. It had been a promise that had never made sense, and yet Dengar had always hoped that they could do it, had always been held imprisoned by his hope.

But now he realized that they'd left him with the ability to feel hope, only so that they could control him, keep him on his tether.

Dengar struggled against the cords that held him bound. Some of the flaking rocks were hitting the ropes, causing them to twang, cutting into them, and Dengar hoped only that they might slice a cord or two before they slashed him to ribbons.

A nasty pebble struck him above the left eye, and Dengar cried out in pain. But he was alone on the desert, his voice swallowed in the roaring wind.

Then the roaring reverberated louder. There was a thundering overhead of subspace engines, and Dengar looked up in time to see two ships blasting off through the haze of dust and wind, heading out low over the valley.

One of them was the *Millennium Falcon*.

Dengar's heart began beating harder. So you did it, Han, Dengar thought. You escaped again. Now I must follow.

And Dengar had only three things to work with. His rage, his hope, and his loneliness. He flailed about, looking both ways across the desert for signs of help, but there was none, and the aching loneliness flayed him. He wondered how he would ever vent his rage and frustration, when the object of his wrath was flying away. Han, like the Empire, was untouchable, unbeatable, and Dengar cried out in anger against them.

And as he did so, he imagined Manaroo, imagined huddling in her arms as the tech-empath shared her emotions, making him human once again.

With a scream like one damned, Dengar jerked his right hand with all his might, not caring if he pulled it off at the wrist. The Empire had destroyed him, but in the process it had given him strength. Almost immediately one of the cords snapped with a twang, followed quickly by the snapping sound of another, while the bolt that held the third cord pulled from the rock.

Dengar screamed again and began kicking with his left leg, till it also tore bolts free from the ground, then he pulled out the ropes that held his right leg and untied his left hand.

The Teeth of Tatooine had him now as the storm

built to its crescendo. The skies were going dark under whirling clouds of sand, and Dengar knew that there was no shelter. He'd seen nothing that could hide him for miles. Still, Jabba's men had tied Dengar to the ground while Dengar wore his battle armor. Dengar's legs and chest had ample protection, but at the moment, it was his head and hands that were being chewed away.

Dengar turned his back to the wind and began stumbling in the general direction of Jabba's palace. Boba Fett had betrayed him twice. But he had left Dengar wearing his armor, and Dengar vowed silently that Boba Fett would pay for that mistake with his life.

For long he walked, head hunched, hands curled up protectively against his chest. He was stumbling blindly, unable to see, suffering from fevered dreams. The dry wind was having its way with him, and still after two hours he had not begun to find his way off the pan, nor had he found so much as a single boulder in this sand-blasted desert that he could hide behind.

At last, when he could walk no farther and his rage and hope languished under the weight of fatigue, Dengar curled in a ball and lay down to die.

It seemed he waited for an eternity, and he lay exhausted, empty, knowing that he could not make it out of the desert himself. Even if he'd broken his bonds immediately after wakening, he might not have made it out of this desert himself.

And then it came to him, distantly at first. His eyes were closed, but he saw light. He felt as if he were flying, almost as if he were bouncing over the ground in a speeder, and something propelled him forward, dimly recalled memories. He felt an overwhelming sense of love and hope, tinged with a sense of urgency.

I am dying, he thought. My life force is flying. But where am I going? He watched for a moment, and the lights and feelings became more clear. He felt younger and stronger and more passionate than he had in years, and he stopped and called out in hope, "Payback?"

Then Dengar realized the truth. This was not a vision of dying, this was Manaroo. Dengar was still wearing his Attanni, and Manaroo was somewhere nearby in a speeder, searching for him.

Dengar shouted, stood in the clouds of dust. He looked about and could not see her, and she could not hear him. He felt her frustration as she powered up the speeder, prepared to move on.

Dengar shouted again, and again, and stood with his eyes closed and his hands raised to the sky, and suddenly she turned.

Through Manaroo's eyes he could see himself vaguely through the haze—a dim mass in the dark swirling sands, something that might be human, or might only be an illusion, or might only be a stone.

Manaroo turned the speeder, and the image was lost for a moment in a driving gust of sand, but she plunged ahead, until she saw Dengar standing with his fists raised to the sky, his face cut with a hundred cuts, eyes squinted closed.

Manaroo leapt from the speeder. Dengar opened his eyes. She wore a helmet and thick protective clothes, and Dengar would never have recognized her on the streets, but they stood for a long time holding one another as Manaroo cried, and he felt her burning love for him, and her sense of relief, two people sharing one heart.

"How? How did you escape?" Dengar managed to ask. "I thought they would kill you last night?"

"I danced for you," she whispered. "I danced my best, and they let me live for another day.

"Jabba and his men are dead," Manaroo said. "The palace is in chaos—looting, celebrations. A guard set us free."

"Oh," Dengar said dumbly.

"Will you marry me?" Manaroo asked.

"Yes. Of course," Dengar muttered, and he wanted to ask if she would save him, but instead he collapsed from fatigue.

Dengar spent the following weeks recovering in a medic chamber in Mos Eisley, and on the day he was released, he set about preparing for his marriage to Manaroo. Among her people, making the formal covenants of marriage was considered a small thing, something two people might do in private. But the more important part of the ceremony, the "melding," which occurred when two people exchanged Attannis and officially began sharing the same mind would have to be witnessed and celebrated by her friends and parents. Which meant that Dengar and Manaroo would have to go find them on whichever world the Rebel Alliance had secreted them.

During those weeks of recovery, Dengar wore the Attanni that Manaroo had given him, and for the first time in decades he felt free of the creature he had become, free of the creature that the Empire had made him, until he found that he wanted to be that creature no more. The cage of anger and hope and loneliness that they had made for him was smashed.

The two of them were broke but not broken, and with looming medical bills Dengar had to find some way to make money. Dengar considered going back to loot Jabba's Palace, but dark rumors were circulating in Mos Eisley. Several people had gone to loot the palace already, and they found the palace doors bolted from inside. Strange spiderlike creatures were seen on the walls. Only two or three palace residents had escaped alive after Jabba's demise, and most of those got off Tatooine quickly.

So it wasn't until a few days after Dengar got out of the medic chambers that he realized that, apparently, no one knew that Jabba had died at the Great Pit of

Carkoon. Dengar decided he might be able to make a few credits in the desert, salvaging any weapons lost during Jabba's final battle, scavenging the bodies of Jabba's henchmen.

So it was that he took Manaroo and flew the *Punishing One* out over the desert, until he found the wreckage of Jabba's ships, unmolested.

The bodies of Jabba's henchmen littered the ground, their corpses desiccated, almost mummified by the heat, among scattered debris—a few broken weapons, the odd credit chip, parts to droids.

When Dengar reached the Great Pit of Carkoon itself, there was a terrible stench of burned flesh and rotting meat. It looked as if the "All-powerful Sarlacc" would have to be renamed the "All-dead Sarlacc." Someone had dropped a bomb down its gullet.

On the edge of the pit was a dead man, naked, his flesh burned and bruised, as if he'd been placed alive in acid. Dengar turned the corpse over with a foot, to have a look at its face.

The man was burned, covered with boils. Dengar had never seen the pitiful fellow before.

"Help," the man whispered. Dengar was astonished to find him alive.

"What happened?" Dengar asked.

"Sarlacc . . . swallowed me. I killed it. Blew it up," the man said. Dengar wondered. It was said that the mighty Sarlacc took a thousand years to digest someone. Dengar had supposed that it was only exaggeration, but obviously this man could not have been lying here for more than a day or two. Which meant that he'd been in Sarlacc's belly for some weeks.

Manaroo had been only a dozen meters away, and she rushed over to them. "Oh, here," she said. "Help me get him inside!"

Together they carried the wounded man aboard the *Punishing One,* laid him on a bed, and Dengar got him some water while Manaroo began spraying his wounds with antibiotics.

When the fellow could speak again, he grasped Dengar's wrist, and whispered, "Thank you. Thank you, my friend," over and over.

"It was nothing," Dengar replied.

"Nothing? You still . . . you still want to be partners, Dengar?" the man said. He reached out his hand to shake.

Dengar gaped at the man's tortured and burned face, and realized that this was Boba Fett. Boba Fett without his armor and weapons. Boba Fett helpless in Dengar's bed. Boba Fett who had stolen Han Solo from him, who had bombed Dengar's ship, who had drugged Dengar and left him to die in the desert. The man who had betrayed him twice!

There was a rushing in Dengar's ears, and the world seemed to turn sideways. There was a muddy smear on the man's head, and Dengar imagined what Boba Fett might have looked like without his hair burned off. If he had brown hair, like Han Solo's . . .

"Call me Payback," Dengar muttered.

Terror filled Boba Fett's eyes as he suddenly saw the danger.

"I . . . I was just following orders," Boba Fett said, but in Dengar's mind, it was Han Solo that Dengar heard. "I'm sorry."

"Hey, buddy, it was a fair race," Han was saying, that cocky grin on his face. "It could just as easily have been the other way around. I'm the one who could have got burned. . . . Sorry."

"But I'm the one who got burned!" Dengar shouted, grabbing Han by the throat.

There was a brief struggle, and Dengar felt a wave of dizziness. He was choking Boba Fett, and the man was looking up at him, pleading. "Sorry! I'm sorry!" he growled, and Manaroo was suddenly at Dengar's back, pulling on him.

She was fumbling with something, twisting something metallic against his cranial jack. Her Attanni shot through Dengar, washing him with her waves of concern, her worry not just for Dengar, but for Boba Fett too. She shouted, "What's going on here?"

She pulled them apart, and Dengar yelled, "He tried to kill me!" and suddenly he saw that during the struggle, Boba Fett had managed to pull Dengar's blaster from his holster. He'd been holding the barrel to Dengar's ribs and could have blown Dengar's lunch against the far wall, but he hadn't pulled the trigger.

Dengar began to calm. Manaroo's own emotions suffused him. Her worry, her love. She looked at Boba Fett and didn't see a monster. Instead she saw a man flayed and tortured, much as Dengar had been a few days ago.

In the moment of silence that followed, Boba Fett held the blaster at Dengar's chest. Dengar almost spoke. He almost said, "Go ahead. I've got nothing to lose." He'd spoken that line under similar circumstances a dozen times, but this time the words caught in his throat. This time, he realized, he finally had something to lose. He had Manaroo, and he had a man who wanted to be his partner.

Boba Fett flipped the blaster over, handed it to Dengar. "I owe you," he said. "Do what you will."

Dengar holstered the blaster and stood looking down at Boba Fett. "I'm getting married in a couple of weeks, and I'll need a best man. You available?"

Boba Fett nodded, and they shook on it.

The Prize Pelt:
The Tale of Bossk

by Kathy Tyers

Chewbacca and Solo had bested Bossk once. Never again.

The lizard-like Trandoshan bounty hunter paused in his research to visualize bringing in Chewbacca's pelt. The thought made him flick his tongue with pleasure. Like a trophy fighter in top condition, Bossk was massive enough to challenge a Wookiee, but he would win this game by guile . . . or trickery, if need be.

Bossk stood on an inner deck of the Imperial Star

Destroyer *Executor,* hurrying to read an Imperial data screen. Squinting, he swung aside his blast rifle—an elaborate neck sling suspended it under his left arm—and pushed his face closer to the screen. Onboard lighting hurt his supersensitive eyes, and the screen was only marginally brighter than the corridors. He had trouble picking up any contrast.

Another list appeared.

Known antagonists:

Big Bunji, former associate

Jabba the Hutt, former employer

Ploovo Two-for-One, former associate

Bossk flexed his toe claws against the *Executor's* deck. Chewbacca and Solo would be crazy to hide among their enemies, but Solo was notorious for trying crazy tricks. Lord Vader's personal aides had furnished volumes of data to all six Hunt finalists. Somehow, Bossk must discover the clue that would lead him to Chewbacca first.

And Solo. He tightened his fingers, curling massive wedge-shaped claws into his palm. His hands were not nimble but strong, with deeply ridged, mature scales. He had hunted Wookiees for over sixty Standard years. When a blaster or grenade finally killed Bossk, his death would shower hundreds of *jagannath* points onto the bloodthirsty, eternal Scorekeeper that he worshipped.

Serene behind her pale, lidless eyes, the Scorekeeper existed beyond time and space, numbering every deed of each Trandoshan Hunter. She could zero his life tally if he were shamed or captured. She could double it if he brought home a prize pelt. Ambushing Chewbacca was Bossk's sacred obligation.

He punched another button and scrutinized Vader's information on Ploovo Two-for-One. The humanoid crime lord had ordered Solo's termination. Nothing else on the screen sparked Bossk's hunting intuition, except—faintly—the fact that Solo had been last seen by Imperials on Tatooine, near Jabba the Hutt's headquarters, immediately before he started running with the Rebel Alliance. That idiot Greedo had missed him cleanly; Bossk remembered seeing him afterward, at Ord Mantell.

Bossk's warlike people had allied early with the Empire. A Trandoshan official had conceived the idea of enslaving the huge, strong Wookiees—inhabitants of Kashyyyk—for manual labor, rather than leveling Kashyyyk by bombardment. The Empire had pounced on the idea. The despicable, peace-loving Wookiees had been taken before they guessed the true meaning of enslavement. Now very few free Wookiees lived off Kashyyyk.

And Lord Vader wanted Solo, Chewbacca, and their passengers "alive, no disintegrations," which guaranteed they would be handled cruelly. After the Empire finished punishing Chewbacca, Bossk would buy back Chewbacca's pelt. He would take it home and lay it on the Scorekeeper's bloody altar.

First, though, he must find better clues. Solo and his crew had disappeared in mid-chase, leaving no trail. And he had stiff competition.

Tinian I'att pushed her red-blond hair behind one ear and then crouched to look a furry brown Chadra-Fan in the eye. That made it hard to ignore his four nostrils and his twitching, pushed-up snout, but she wanted to make sure the cowardly creature understood. "Two hundred credits," she repeated. "All you have to do is introduce me—and Chenlambec—to Bossk."

Tutti Snibit tilted his head to look up over Tinian's shoulder. A silvertip Wookiee towered behind her. Chenlambec had frightened Tinian too, when she first met him. Other Hunters called Chenlambec a fierce predator, prone to berserk rages. He only accepted dead-or-alive assignments, and generally only brought back proof of decease. He wore a heavy, reptile-hide bandolier studded with bowcaster quarrels, alternating with decorative silver cubes.

He was Tinian's *Ng'rhr*. In his language, the term meant *clan uncle;* he was the master Hunter who held her apprenticeship.

"Trandoshans hate Wookiees," Tutti gibbered. He had explained that he too was a bounty hunter, but Lord Vader's screening crew had declined to hire him.

"We're fellow Hunters," Tinian told him. They'd arrived on board the *Executor* just too late—deliberately so—to be scrutinized by Lord Vader for the big job. "Get Bossk to promise he'll abide by the Creed. Then introduce us." According to the Hunters' Creed, no Hunter could ever kill another nor interfere with another's Hunt.

Tutti's reluctance seemed false, anyway. Tinian had spotted him talking with the sinister, armored Boba Fett a few minutes ago. She'd overheard him offer to assist Boba Fett in any way that he could . . . for a small fee. Boba Fett had apparently hired Tutti to send Bossk off in a direction that would lead him away from Han Solo.

She and Chen would gladly cooperate.

"Two-fifty?" Tutti batted one of his huge round ears.

Tinian glanced over her shoulder. Chen gave a low growl. "Two-ten," she answered Tutti. "Final offer."

Tutti Snibit held out a long, knobby hand.

"After you introduce us. If we survive." Tinian smiled without humor.

The Chadra-Fan scurried away.

Tinian straightened. "I don't know what Boba Fett is paying," she told Chenlambec, "but that fellow is practically salivating."

Chen howled softly.

"I'm ready," she answered. "Are you?"

He crossed his long arms over his bandolier and leaned against a bulkhead, looking perfectly relaxed.

"Of course you are," she admitted. "You're always ready."

She had apprenticed to Chenlambec, hoping to hurt the Empire before it caught her. It had destroyed her life. She'd been an armament heiress. Now she had nothing.

Chenlambec was no conventional bounty hunter, though. Under the cover of dead-or-alive, he had helped several "acquisitions" escape to the Rebel Alliance. He played a dangerous double game, but satisfying . . . and profitable. This would be her third job as his apprentice.

Tutti Snibit careened around the corner, clasping his hands in front of his dirty brown robe. "He agrees," burbled the Chadra-Fan. "But be careful! I want you to live to pay me."

"Naturally." Tinian tugged on her shipsuit to straighten it. Suits that were long enough in the waist always hung loose on her. She wore no decoration except a diagonal silver hip belt and blaster.

As soon as she walked around the corner, she saw the creature. Bossk had to be at least 1.9 meters tall, very nearly as big as Chenlambec. His prominent scales looked faintly orange on one side, but over the rest of his body, they were greenish brown. He wore an orange flight suit that'd obviously been designed for shorter-legged humans, ending near his knees with a pair of bullet bands. A blast rifle dangled from his neck sling, casually steadied over his left arm.

Tutti Snibit waited a respectful distance from the Trandoshan, flapping his round ears, looking more like a mouse than a lizard. He stood only half Bossk's height.

Bossk's data station was at the edge of a large open space, close to the *Executor*'s launch control center. Approachable from three sides, it was a Hunter's nightmare. Heavy metal conduits festooned adjacent bulkheads and overheads with massive, military texture.

"M-mighty Bossk," Tutti stammered, "this is Chenlambec, a Hunter of great reputation. And his apprentice, Tinian."

Hissing, Bossk thrust his right claws toward his blast rifle.

"Hunter's Creed!" Tutti squeaked. "No shooting! You three must talk about Chewbacca!"

Bossk snarled. "Chenlambec. You are distinguished, for so cowardly a race." His Basic sounded to Tinian as if he were trying to gargle while somebody choked him.

Chen struck his deep chest with a fist and growled.

Tinian stepped forward. Both Hunters towered over her. "He says that your reputation also precedes you. You have killed dozens of his people."

"Hundreds," Bossk corrected her.

Chenlambec growled again. This time, Tinian opted not to translate.

Tutti Snibit looked all around, probably eyeing bulkheads for hand- and toe-holds. "Anyway," he exclaimed quickly, "Bossk got the job, but Chenlambec has information on a wonderful inside track. I thought I would do both of you a favor . . . and introduce you!" He waved both furry arms.

Bossk muttered in a language Tinian didn't understand.

"Please listen, sir Bossk," Tutti spoke up. "Chenlambec arrived on board too late to apply for this Hunt—"

"Lord Vader wants this quarry alive," Bossk interrupted. "No disintegrations. He specified clearly."

"Yes, yes," squeaked Tutti, "but listen. Chenlambec will postpone his massacre . . . once . . . if you, mighty Bossk, could work with a Wookiee."

"And a Human." Bossk lowered his scaly head and hissed. "A small, weak one."

Chenlambec answered angrily.

Tinian folded her arms. "Chen says," she explained, " 'She has been useful to me in situations requiring translations into Basic.' And I've almost qualified for full Hunt status."

Bossk let his blast rifle dangle. "Chadra-Fan, I will talk with this team instead of shooting them. Leave us."

Tutti backed around the corner. Tinian almost envied him. At least five of the six bounty hunters would finish the *Millennium Falcon* job with empty pockets, and she and Chen might fail in their own mission, but Tutti Snibit had just accumulated enough credits to enjoy himself for three or four weeks—maybe even the rest of his life, if he didn't spend quickly.

Bossk waved at his terminal to hibernate it, then leaned against the bulkhead. He was less back-blind than Wookiees or Humans, but he didn't trust this pair. "Well?" he grunted. "Make your proposal. Remember, I owe you nothing for approaching me."

The Wookiee, deep brown with a gloss of silver at the tips of his fur, wore a black bandolier of small-scaled hide. Maybe the Wookiee had chosen to wear reptile skin as a deliberate affront. To Trandoshans, most of a prey animal's value lay in its skin. Bossk would no more wear reptile skin than eat reptilian flesh. The fact that Wookiees—and humans—ate other mammals' flesh proved their bestiality.

Chenlambec backed against the opposite bulkhead, leaving the small human vulnerable between them. Bossk smelled no fear on her.

Chenlambec hooted like a cloud ape. After several verses, his apprentice held up a hand and quieted him. "My *Ng'rhr* has connections among spacefaring Wookiees," she began.

Bossk snapped, "I don't trust criminals for information. The fact that you know their language marks you as an accomplice. It is their place to listen, not speak."

Tinian balled her fists and planted them against her thin hips. "My family kept Wookiees as slaves. The best way to *control* them was to learn their language. Do we understand each other?"

He refused to let her impress him. "You call him your master now."

"Excuse me," she said, "but I am translating. Chenlambec asks me to say that he has connections among spacefaring Wookiees." She swept a hank of fur behind her left ear, exposing its peculiar pink folds. "One of them suggested a probable destination along the *Millennium Falcon*'s last known course."

A current sighting? Information from the Wookiee network? Bossk attended more closely. He would offer the Scorekeeper his left arm for a chance to crack that network (maybe even both arms, since he could regenerate them). Cracking the Wookiees' network could make him both wealthy and eternally secure. "Go on," he said. "Where are they headed?"

The big silvertip hootled again.

"He says," Tinian translated, "that the best way to catch a star captain who'll sign on a Wookiee copilot is to employ another Wookiee."

Bossk kept his voice low-pitched, concealing his eagerness. "Where are they headed?"

"First, we discuss forming a partnership."

"If you help me hunt down Chewbacca and his keeper, I will consider giving you twenty percent of my profit."

The human narrowed her eyes. "Obviously you think we are amateurs. Fifty percent is traditional. It would still leave you more than you would earn without our help."

She dared to haggle?

Still, he saw ways of hedging this long shot. Chenlambec's shimmering pelt was worth easily as much as Chewbacca's. The silvertip gene was recessive and rare. And this *was* the kind of lead he'd been looking for, not old data. He led them to believe he would give thirty percent of his take if they brought him to Chewbacca. Then he asked Tinian quietly, "How did the mighty Chewbacca earn enmity from another Wookiee?"

Chenlambec laid back his head and oop-ooped mournfully. "His crime was unspeakable," Tinian answered, then she added, "Chen doesn't discuss his past. Not with me. Certainly not with you."

The past didn't matter. Whether or not Bossk located the *Falcon*, once he lured Chenlambec on board his own ship he was guaranteed a profit.

The human was probably wanted somewhere, too. If not, slavers occasionally took spirited young human females.

As for the Hunter's Creed, no bounty hunter ever betrayed another unless the other hunter strayed first from Creed regulations; but Bossk had fabricated Creed violations before, and felt the Scorekeeper smile on him. She loved clever betrayal. "Now," he said, "where are they headed?"

"We would prefer finding a private place to talk."

"There is no time for that." He kept his voice low and menacing. He wanted them to think he was trying to scare them off. "The other Hunters are already heading for their ships."

"Then we'll talk here." Tinian peered up the corridor. A human Imperial lackey wearing khaki fatigues dashed toward them. His heavy boots pounded the polished metal decking. Bossk steadied his blast rifle.

The lackey careened around a corner and vanished up another too-bright passage. Bossk watched Tinian track the human with her eyes. He smelled her alarm at his approach—and her relief when he passed. Evidently Imperials made her nervous.

She didn't need to watch the corridors for her most dangerous enemy. He stood before her.

• • •

The *Executor* thrummed around Chenlambec like a giant beast. He would be glad to leave its bowels, and he pitied the Imperial worms who spent their lives scurrying and scuttling in these passages.

He spoke, then listened as Tinian translated into Basic. "Wookiee sources," she explained—and he liked the condescension that she faked—"have evidently spotted Solo's ship on course for the Lomabu system. A renegade group of Wookiees is setting up another safe world there. We've heard that you blew the whistle on one such world earlier in your career."

"Yes," Bossk snapped. At Gandolo IV, Bossk had hunted down several dozen escaped Wookiee slaves trying to establish a safe haven. Bossk had been on the verge of skinning the lot—including the famous Chewbacca, who was assisting with setup—when Captain Solo returned unannounced. Seeing the situation in progress, Solo had strafed the bounty hunter and his crew. They'd retreated into their larger, better armed craft. Solo had landed the *Millennium Falcon* directly on top of it, collapsing its landing gear. Steam clouds had shot out of its hydraulics. Internal explosions had hinted at grave engine damage.

Solo and Chewbacca had left Bossk alive but trapped onboard, humiliated . . . or so the story went. Chenlambec's brother had related the tale first-hand. He had stood near Chewbacca, watching the desperate Wookiees' plight become hopeful, then hilarious.

Chen imagined he could feel Bossk writhe at the memory. He spoke again, reminding Tinian of several details of their cover story. They'd concocted it before docking with the *Executor*.

She nodded soberly, then turned back to the big, ugly lizard. "We think that the Rebel Alliance hopes to set up a base near the Wookiee haven in the Lomabu system, now that they've been chased off Hoth. That would explain our report that Solo has taken the *Falcon* there, carrying several Rebel leaders. We could slip in before the Rebel fleet arrives, tag our quarry, and sky out before the Imperials catch on. We'll take our prisoners directly to Lord Vader."

Bossk nodded. "I have not heard of the Lomabu system. Where is it from here?"

"Well . . . we're near Anoat. Lomabu is . . ."

Chen watched Bossk closely. Now she would dangle the bait.

"We're not exactly sure," she admitted.

Bossk glared at Tinian, then Chen, then at Tinian again. He growled several words of Trandoshan deep in his throat, then choke-gargled in Basic again. "Your information is worthless. You are worthless. I should—"

Chen barked angrily.

"Easy, you two," exclaimed Tinian. "We don't know where it is, but we know where to find out. We have to check a waypost along the Wookiee network."

And that, as far as Chen knew, was a vital bit of truth they had spun into their cover story to sweeten the bait. Surely Bossk wanted—

"Network," Bossk repeated slowly. His tongue flicked.

Excellent. He did.

"It's dangerous," Tinian stressed. "Especially for you and me, Bossk. The Wookiees will be serious about silencing any non-Wookiee that shows an interest in this locale."

Bossk adjusted his rifle sling. "I refuse to travel in any ship but my own. I have a YV-666 light freighter modified for Wookiee hunting. Do you have a problem traveling in that?"

Chen bared his teeth and answered evasively. It would've been easy to take Bossk down if they could talk him aboard *their* ship, but obviously Bossk was too intelligent to fall for that.

"He doesn't," Tinian translated. "Neither do I, if it means getting the price on Chewbacca."

Bossk finally stretched the lower half of his face in a reptilian smile. "I must warn you: If you tamper with any of my onboard systems, the *Hound's Tooth* will retaliate."

Of course it would. It was undoubtedly equipped with multiple defenses against Wookiees' strength.

He told Tinian to inform Bossk that traveling with him would keep their expenses down, since they were only getting fifteen percent apiece. As she translated, Chen sniffed the air. Bossk smelled as bitter as pain and as foul as death, but he hadn't become defensive. From that subtle clue, Chen guessed that Bossk already intended treachery. He wouldn't miss thirty percent of his take because he had no intention of paying it.

Fair enough. If Chen had his way, Bossk would not collect one limp credit. Chen knew about the Trandoshan religion. Having his *jagannath* score zeroed would hurt Bossk worse than ambushing and killing him.

That would be a pleasure.

To Tinian, Bossk looked impatient: He flexed his claws in rhythm, occasionally darting glances up the corridors. "I also expect you to pay half of my fueling costs," he said.

In three years with Chen, Tinian had matured from a spoiled but sincere little rich girl into a seasoned resistance fighter. She sensed that Bossk was testing. "Ten percent," she countered. "You'd make this trip without us, if you knew where to go."

Bossk frowned. "Twenty. Programming my onboard systems to watch you will take time I could spend hunting Chewbacca."

"Then don't program them," she snapped.

He curled a lip and hissed.

She'd heard that Trandoshans found mercy, graciousness, and other weaknesses contemptible. "Ten," she repeated, "and that's generous."

"Why did you enter the Trade, Human? Your kind generally hasn't the stomach for it."

Tinian narrowed her eyes, an expression Trandoshans understood. "My capacity for kindness died three years ago. Criminals murdered my grandparents and my lover, my home was destroyed, and I put groundside life behind me. I don't mind risking my life if the stakes are rewarding."

Bossk stared, obviously thinking that through. Trandoshans took no lovers. Whenever they came back to Trandosha, they mated with a clutch mother who struck their fancy, then returned to their work.

But she'd had a lover. A fiance. Tinian tried to keep the image of Daye Azur-Jamin out of her mind's eye. Daye's had been a gentle face full of intelligence, with an odd silver streak marking one eyebrow. He'd been sensitive to the Force, a shrewd judge of character. Hard-working, too. And loyal to the death. Daye had sacrificed himself to help her escape the Imperial takeover of her grandparents' armament factory. Since that day, she had dedicated her life to helping bring down the Empire. The sooner she died, the sooner she'd rejoin Daye.

Meanwhile, she had a job to attempt.

"Fifteen percent of fuel." Bossk thrust out a clawed forearm.

Tinian sensed that she'd won as much as Bossk was willing to give. She reached out and touched his scales. Bossk swung his arm against a bulkhead, pinning her hand. Chenlambec extended a paw and got the same treatment: Bossk demanded command, two against one . . . and his ship. Those odds favored Bossk.

"Now," said Bossk, "we will evaluate our resources." He enumerated the *Hound's Tooth*'s firepower. Before he finished, Chenlambec tapped the floor with one foot, and even Tinian felt nervous, even though she had practically grown up in her grandparents' armament factory. Since leaving Druckenwell, she'd become even more competent with weapons, explosives, and armor. Knowledge helped make up for her small size and limited strength. Chenlambec's contributions to the three-way included his connections among the "criminal" Wookiee network and a reputation even Bossk didn't question.

The rest of their planning was simple for the moment. After visiting the Wookiee waypost, they would drift into the Lomabu system, fake the orbit of a rapidly moving planet-crossing asteroid, and keep all systems quiet. They would scout using Bossk's small landing craft, locate the criminal Wookiee colony, and then draw out and trap Solo and his crew. Specific plans would wait until they found the Lomabu system.

Tinian didn't mention their own plans.

"Until we find Lomabu," added Bossk, "you will remain in your cabin."

Tinian shrugged. She had no intention of remaining anywhere Bossk put her, and Lomabu III was no safe world. "We will be boarding with 300 kilos of gear. Which docking bay is your ship in?"

Bossk blinked. She could almost see him wonder what they needed with a 300-kilo weight allowance. "Number six," he gargled.

"We'll be there in twenty minutes," she said.

Chenlambec led Tinian up the passageway, glad to escape Bossk's brackish stench. He had been called onto this job by Kashyyyk, not just to help Chewbacca escape, but to doublecross Bossk and end his murderous operation. Chenlambec knew that the Trandoshan pelt baiter's count numbered in the hundreds. He had lured that boast out of Bossk. The heat in Bossk's eye had warmed Chenlambec's blood.

Once they put several turns of the passage between them and the Trandoshan, Chen slowed to a stroll.

"Satisfied?" Tinian asked.

Chenlambec had lost brothers and sisters to Trandoshan pelt baiters. He told her it was a beginning.

"It was exciting," she admitted. "For a few minutes, I felt really alive."

Chenlambec cuffed the small woman's shoulder. She understood Wookiee speech and gesture remarkably well, including the soft punch that meant full agreement.

"I thought you probably did, too," she answered. She turned a gamine grin on him.

He counted echoing gray corridors as he strode past them, then turned up a dim side passage. After twenty long strides, he paused in front of a bulkhead. Tinian loosened her blaster in its low holster and took up a guard position.

Chen crouched in front of a power access point. He extended one claw and pulled off a silver cube that matched the decorations on his bandolier. It would have fit on Tinian's palm.

"About time," it scolded in a high, feminine voice. "I've been ready for—"

Chen closed one paw around the tiny positronic processor, too small to properly call a droid and too personable to call anything else. Concealing Flirt in his grip, he glanced up.

"Still clear." Tinian stood like a statue with one hand over her blaster.

Chen clipped Flirt to her secure perch on his bandolier down near his hip.

"Lots of good data," Flirt chirped. "Inside information on the *Millennium Falcon*, if you want it. You wouldn't believe—"

"We're not going after the *Falcon*," said Tinian.

"Aww," squeaked Flirt. "I wanted to—"

Chen growled another warning. Flirt stopped in mid-squeak. When she stayed quiet, she looked like just one more decorative cube. Chen had had the bandolier made specifically to camouflage her.

He led the way out. They had other luggage to claim before boarding Bossk's ship.

Bossk hurried to a different terminal in the *Executor*'s troop quarters area. Working rapidly, he pulled down all the information on Chenlambec he could find. Unfortunately, the creature's Hunt certificate was current. His acquisition list, filed under the underworld nickname, "The Raging Wookiee," was impressive. This would only raise the *jagannath* score on his pelt.

Bossk clawed buttons until he'd called up the incomplete human title, "Tinian." She hadn't given a second name. The computer hesitated several seconds before spewing two Wanted designations. One fit this human's description right down to extremities' body temperature. Few other races noticed that detail. It was one of many factors that made Trandoshans the best Hunters.

A modest reward for her capture was offered by the Imperial governor of an industrial planet, Druckenwell. Apprenticed to a licensed Hunter, she was temporarily invulnerable—this was one way minor criminals ducked justice—but once Chenlambec lay dead on his skinning table, she would be fair game. Her bounty was too low to make him fear her abilities, but high enough to cover fuel costs for his Hunt.

He needed only to get them aboard the *Hound's Tooth*.

But his primary target was Chewbacca. He wasn't forgetting that rich bounty . . . nor his humiliation at Gandolo IV . . . for a microsecond.

He made his way to Docking Bay Six, where the *Hound's Tooth* sat under bright lights, guarded by Imperial stormtroopers. Three of the other Hunt ships had already blasted off. The *Hound* glistened, too new to have collected a patina of scars, pits, and scorch marks. Aware of the staring stormtroopers, he marched stiff-legged to its ramp. "Bossk," he announced. "Boarding."

It took the *Hound* less than a second to check his voice pattern. "Confirmed," said a metallic baritone voice. Bossk liked a ship that could speak for itself. He'd paid extra for responsive programming. The *Hound's Tooth* dropped its port boarding ramp.

He hustled up into the cockpit. Hurriedly he checked his security systems, paying particular attention to the port sleeping cabin.

Satisfied, he strode along a curving passage to one of his aft holds. His passengers would need enough space to store three hundred kilos . . . of what? Puzzling over the question, he flicked his tongue. Whatever they brought, the *Hound* soon would identify it, and Bossk soon would own it.

He took up a position inside the *Hound's Tooth*'s main airlock and waited for his boarding party.

Tinian approached across the *Executor*'s mirror-bright deck. She steered a repulsor locker with her left hand, keeping her right hand near the blaster that hung from her slouch belt. A black duffel hung over her left shoulder.

"Welcome aboard the *Hound's Tooth*. You and your companion will share the port cabin," he told her. "I left its hatch open. Walk directly in and stow your gear. I'll join you later."

She steered into the ship's comfortable dimness.

He turned his attention to the far more interesting sight of Chenlambec leading two Imperial service droids. Each droid hauled a large storage locker, and the Wookiee hefted a weapons crate over his head.

"What's in there?" Bossk addressed a squatty draft droid on two tractor treads.

Chenlambec growled unintelligibly. Bossk suspected

he'd just been cursed. He flicked his tongue in reply, then pushed away from the bulkhead. "Follow me."

He led aft out of the brilliant light, past the passenger cabin toward his smaller cargo bay, where he'd cleared a few meters of deck space. "Pile it here. Touch nothing else."

Chenlambec hooted at the service droids. They set down their burdens, swiveled on their treads, and squeaked back toward the passage, returning to the *Executor*'s droid pool.

Bossk's huge, red-and-bronze X10-D service droid rolled forward. Chenlambec backed away from it, baring his teeth.

"ExTen-Dee will secure your objects for flight—" Abruptly Bossk felt a presence behind him. He spun, automatically aiming his blast rifle.

"Easy, Bossk." Tinian stalked into the cargo bay with both hands raised. "What *is* that monster?"

"I told you to go to your cabin." Bossk let his rifle dangle again. The X10-D unit was no monster, but to humans and Wookiees, who needed excessive light to see clearly, the droid would look enormous. "That is my draft droid."

Tinian walked around the gleaming red unit. Roughly Trandoshan in shape, the X10-D had retractable piston arms that could stretch out three meters, a massive conical torso, and self-propelling roller feet. "I suspected you two would need me to translate before everything was stowed where you wanted it," she said. Touching X10-D's glimmering chest, she added, "Maybe you won't."

"I will tell your companion where to stack his lockers, and ExTen-Dee will secure them," Bossk answered. "On this ship, droids and Wookiees are ordered to listen, not speak."

Chenlambec growl-barked.

"Some of this is delicate equipment," said Tinian. "Do you have lashing cables?"

"My draft droid will anchor your gear."

Chenlambec hooted.

"We want to watch," said Tinian.

"Watch if you want."

It took an hour to secure the pair's belongings. "Remember our bargain," Tinian said as X10-D returned to his position along the rear bulkhead. "We don't search your ship, you don't touch our equipment."

"And *you* stay out of everything." Bossk pointed a long claw at her.

Chenlambec shook a hairy paw and roared.

She glowered up at the Wookiee. "Of course not, *Ng'rhr*. Not this time."

Bossk crossed his forearms and smiled. Evidently this pair was not perfectly cohesive.

He could easily promise not to touch their gear. The *Hound's Tooth*'s security scanners and its onboard computer were matchless.

Other than the X10-D unit, he required no crew. The ship's intelligence also helped overcome a Trandoshan's one real handicap: other races' technology was not made for Trandoshan hands, and even the ship's special fittings were sometimes clumsy.

He led them back to the *Hound*'s airlock. As it hissed shut and he sealed the pair on board, he murmured worshipful thanks to the Scorekeeper. He would use these passengers until he no longer needed them.

Then he would start skinning.

"We'll cut cables as soon as you're ready," he informed them. "I have acceleration chairs in the larger cargo hold."

"I don't think I trust your acceleration chairs," answered Tinian.

Bossk laughed deeply. "If I want your scalp and his pelt, I'll take them . . . but not before Lomabu III. We all want Chewbacca and Solo. We'll capture them together."

•   •   •

Tinian peered up the narrow passageway. She couldn't make out much detail. She knew Trandoshans saw in the infrared, but she didn't have IR goggles. She'd never owned a pair.

"Where is this waypost?" Bossk clomped up behind her. "I need coordinates now."

Chen hooted a series of numbers. Tinian repeated them. She added, "It's programmed to destroy any non-Wookiee that approaches. From the time we drop out of hyperspace, the *Hound's Tooth* must maintain scanner and sensor silence and total shielding, unless Chen is the only one outside your shielded area."

"I understand." Bossk flicked his tongue. "Shall I show you to the acceleration chairs now?"

"We'll ride in our bunks." She adjusted her duffel.

Bossk shrugged. "Suit yourself. Don't blame me if you get thrown around."

Tinian ducked back into the sleeping cabin. Roughly three meters by four, it was so dark that everything inside looked gray. Chen squeezed in after her, looking like a massive black shadow. Bossk's scaly back retreated up the main passage.

She pulled out a luma and shone it around. Bunks, storage compartments . . . also a small washcabin, comfortably sized for her but cramped for a Trandoshan or a Wookiee.

Tinian swept her luma up and down a bulkhead, looking for a power point. "Here," she said. It was at her shoulder level, an easy height for Bossk or Chenlambec to access. Chenlambec stowed his duffel inside a compartment.

"Goody," Flirt chirped from her bandolier perch. "Did you get a look at that big droid? What a specimen!"

A smooth, low thrum began. Tinian looked up at Chen and added ruefully, "Nicely tuned engines."

Chen answered shortly. She knew he loved his little saucer-shaped *Wroshyr*, even though it was growing seedy. He must hate leaving it in the *Executor*'s storage bay, paying Imperials by the day while they remained on board Bossk's ship.

"If this goes well, we'll be able to pay parking for fifty years. If not, we won't care. Don't worry, *Ng'rhr*." She gathered a handful of fur in one hand and tugged hard. Wookiee fur felt softer than it looked.

Chen pulled Flirt off his bandolier. He held her in one massive hand while he ordered her to concentrate on securing their cabin.

"Right," added Tinian. "Bossk wants to get to that waypost, but he's not going to leave us up and around."

"So plug me in," Flirt exclaimed. She emitted a happy squeak as Chen pushed her connector into the power point. Then she hummed tunelessly, her version of electronic contentment.

Chen had inherited Flirt from a slain hunting companion. The other Wookiee—Chen had never named him to Tinian—had invented the illegal droid and programmed her to seduce an intelligent computer. Flirt could open data streams, shut down security, and substitute her owners' commands for the operator's . . . all without needing to plug into an information outlet. Any power point would do. Inside her titanium shell, the first centimeter was packed with sensor and antenna windings.

But she wasn't dependable. Some jobs that sounded easy to Tinian took Flirt hours to accomplish. That was why they'd prepared three contingency plans. . . .

"She sounds happy." Tinian climbed onto the top bunk and strapped in, using heavy webbing that looked black in the dim light. If her eyes hadn't adjusted by now, they probably wouldn't. This light was too faint for humans. "I hope she hurries."

Chen stood beside the two narrow bunks and braced himself against the deck and the upper bulkhead, where he would block Tinian's fall if she rolled. He wondered aloud if Bossk were operating the *Hound's Tooth* alone.

"If he is, the onboard computer's got to be more powerful than any we've ever seen." Tinian rolled onto her side and eyed Flirt.

Chen muttered.

"And our scaly friend has probably got connections in shipbuilding circles." He was probably listening, too. She added, "It's a good-looking ship."

Chen grinned, showing teeth. He grunted several insults.

Tinian grinned back. "He's probably got a translation program activated."

Chen told Bossk what he could do with his translation program. Flirt sat glued like a mynock to her bulkhead, introducing herself to the most powerful onboard computer she had ever encountered. Tinian guessed that the *Hound* was too intelligent a ship to be easily dazzled.

But Flirt had better succeed before they reached the waypost. All of their plans required being conscious after that jump.

The ship lurched. Tinian's feet hit the bulkhead. She'd learned to growl-bark a few words in Shyriiwook, which translated literally as "Tongue of Tree People." It was a wonderful language for expressing disgust. She howled, then added in Basic, "He doesn't mess around."

Chen snorted.

Tinian braced one arm against the bunk's inner bulkhead and the other against Chen's broad back. He had taken the place of the father she had only known in her imagination, strong and fearless. She'd first saved Chen's life back at Silver Station, where vengeful—but stupid—Ranats tried to blow out a bulkhead and send everyone aboard on the Final Jump. Tinian had tracked down the Ranats by the smell of their JL-

12-F, an explosive manufactured by one of I'att Armaments' competitors.

She'd saved him again at Kline Colony, where a Rebel "acquisition" had resisted Chen's unique style of rescue. They'd saved each other in Ookbat's dank warrens, on a mission that failed.

Acceleration became hard and steady. The aft bulkhead started to look and feel almost like a deck. Tinian rolled toward the bulkhead. It'd been days since she'd slept well. Maybe a nap would—

Something pricked her skin through the thin mattress.

Bossk flicked his tongue: Success! They were both unconscious. *"Hound,"* he called, "disarm all cabin locks."

"Confirmed," answered the *Hound*'s baritone.

He stalked up the corridor and touched out a code on his own cabin's hatch, disarming several more security circuits. When he'd modified the *Hound* for Wookiee hunting, he'd installed features to protect him in case of onboard escapes by enraged Wookiees, including the ability to fly the *Hound* from inside his starboard cabin.

Still, he preferred the broad sweep of space visible on the bridge monitors. They included near and far infrared.

Next he checked on his passengers. Inside the port cabin, the Wookiee lay on the deck, breathing shallowly. The human did not react when he shook her shoulder.

Pharmaceuticals made excellent equalizers.

He drained the charges from their blasters and then rummaged through their cargo compartments. He hesitated over Chen's bowcaster, wanting to keep it, settling for removing its loading spring, then left the pair as they lay. "Record any activity in the passages," he instructed the *Hound's Tooth*.

"Confirmed," it answered.

According to the *Hound,* they were headed for the outskirts of the Aida system. It seemed a logical place for a Wookiee waypost. Aida was solidly Imperial but sparsely settled.

When Tinian awoke, she felt ravenous. Chen bent over her, crooning, sounding concerned.

"I'm awake," she groaned. "I must've slept awfully hard—"

He growled.

"Drugged?" Tinian exclaimed. She sat up straight, glad to be alive. "Is Flirt having trouble?"

Flirt squeaked softly, "You're safe now."

Tinian slipped off her bunk. Her limbs bent stiffly. "What happened?" she asked the miniature droid.

"Sub-q injectors in the mattress and deck. The *Hound*'s been programmed with both of your body weights. You were down for three and a half days."

No wonder Tinian had lost all sense of time.

Chen asked Flirt if she'd gotten inside the *Hound*'s security.

"Not exactly inside," Flirt admitted softly. "He has accepted my presence, but he hasn't let me do much Still," she chirped, "I've secured your cabin and brought up your lights. That's something."

Instead of gray, the bulkheads glimmered steel-blue, and Chen's silvery pelt shone. Now Tinian could see that the *Hound* had high overheads and long, narrow bunks. "Where's Bossk?"

"In the cargo bay, trying to scan your weapons crate."

Chen growled an elaborate threat.

"It's safe for the moment. So are you."

That crate was a decoy anyway. Tinian rubbed her

face and slipped into the washcabin. She hoped Chen's boxy little siren hadn't met her match this time. If Flirt could insinuate herself inside the *Hound*'s main security circuits before they jumped again, she and Chen ought to be able to overpower Bossk, restrain him, and deliver him wherever they could get the best price.

Plan One counted entirely on Flirt, though. Tinian had yet to run a bounty mission that turned out simply.

Bossk's gruff voice spoke from the bulkhead. "Chenlambec, Tinian. I'm on my way to speak with you."

"How about dinner?" Tinian called back.

No reply. Chen wurfled concern. "I won't faint," she answered, "but you must be starved."

Flirt spoke up. "Bossk just programmed the galley to deliver a big meal."

"You'd better dim our lights," Tinian suggested. "He'll get suspicious if you don't."

The bulkheads faded to gray again.

"Do we dare eat?" Tinian asked Flirt. "And where are we?"

"Just a few degrees out from the waypost," Flirt answered. "He hasn't doped your food."

Tinian checked the charge on her blaster. "Uh, oh," she said. It had been drained. "Is yours zeroed, too?"

Chen fingered his blaster, then examined his bowcaster. He yipped and pointed. Its loading spring had been removed.

The hatch slid open. "Come out and eat," said Bossk's voice, but Bossk didn't appear. The passageway was even darker than their cabin.

She marched up the murky corridor, following her nose toward the galley. Bossk sat at a table, bending over a bowl full of wriggling red worms. He no longer wore his blast rifle. By this dim light, he looked drab brown. "Eat." He waved a forelimb at two plates set far from his own. "Your food disgusts me."

"It's mutual," Tinian muttered, but whatever Bossk had prepared for her, it smelled splendid.

On the other hand, raw plasboard with groundcar-fuel sauce would have been difficult to push away. She shoved in a mouthful before Chen sat down. Bossk flicked his tongue at his bowl. A worm vanished into his mouth with his tongue. She decided not to watch him any more.

Several minutes and half a plateful later, she asked, "Where are we?"

"Near the Aida system and your waypost. Now I need your hairy master-Hunter's help."

Chenlambec muttered at her for a while, questioning Bossk's competence, his taste in food, and the keeping quality of the egg he had hatched from. Tinian pretended to translate: "Why didn't we drop out of hyperspace at the coordinates he gave you?"

"In case he was trying to trap me, of course." Bossk shot out his tongue again.

Chenlambec rumbled on. Tinian waited a reasonable time, then said, "He says that you and I must take cover inside a sensor-screened hold while he makes contact."

Bossk snarled. "You will be my hostage in case he tries anything."

This time, Chen said something that actually needed translating. Tinian repeated, "You'll have to show him how to operate your ship's controls."

"No, I won't. My personal cabin is fully shielded, and I can run the *Hound* from inside it."

Tinian turned to Chen. "Will that work?" She didn't relish the idea of being held hostage inside a shielded cabin.

Chen told her it would. Several minutes later, he sat alone on the *Hound*'s bridge. Bossk had locked down all controls, but Chen laid his forearms in deep troughs on the console and studied carefully. Evidently Bossk used pressure against the trough surfaces to control thrusters in several directions. Main guns must be the right-hand claw hooks. He didn't see shield controls yet, but finding them would be Flirt's job.

He had installed her under the navicomputer. By now she should be absorbing data, dumping old memory to make room.

A fuzzy object loomed ahead on the scanners.

That must be the waypost. His contacts back on Kashyyyk had felt it wise not to tell him where to find Lomabu III—a delaying tactic, to give Flirt time to conquer the *Hound*'s command circuits.

Chen hoped to hear Flirt's announcement of success at any moment. Plan One was elegantly simple.

The fuzzy object grew and resolved on twin trapezoidal forescreens. A drifting hunk of metal, it looked like a derelict ship. Sparkling microscopic debris swirled around it in rapid, furious orbits. The object seemed to invite scanner probing.

Before he could touch any controls, his scanner screen lit. Up close, it still looked like a derelict ship. This was no waypost: A dim but distinct dance of tiny colored lights would have identified it as genuine. He should have known that Kashyyyk would never risk letting a Trandoshan see the coding ID of the network.

But he had been promised something he would be able to read.

He growled at the bridge's main microphone: Bossk must focus the scanners into the orbiting cloud and vary scan depth until something readable appeared.

At every depth, it looked like spinning garbage. An eerie howling filled the cabin.

Abruptly, he wurfled soft amusement. Some brilliant underground operative had programmed the whirling debris to give an audible scanner reading. It sounded like hundreds of Wookiees singing simultaneously, each following the others in a spectacularly complex canon. Each voice repeated a series of numbers. Chen isolated one voice and followed it through the series. They were definitely coordinates; but where did the series break and start again?

His young apprentice had worked as a musician during a brief undercover job. He growled at her.

After several seconds, she answered in the language of his people. "Start," she woofed in an odd soprano. She paused a moment, then barked, "now."

Chen punched digits into the *Hound*'s navicomputer. The moment he completed a navigational sequence, its screen lit with a course. A very short course.

The Lomabu system was Aida's near neighbor.

He whispered to Flirt. Had she . . . ?

"Not yet," she signaled. "Sorry."

On to Plan Two, then. According to Kashyyyk's transmission, Imperial forces were scheming to entrap the Rebel fleet, using several hundred Wookiee slaves as bait. The Wookiees had been shipped to Lomabu III, a world recently depopulated for sedition against the Empire, and imprisoned there. Aida's Imperial Governor, Io Desnand, intended to ship in dozens of females and cubs and then stage an attack. Rebel ships would probably try to rescue the Wookiees, and Governor Desnand could offer the Empire a mass entrapment. Obviously Desnand was after a fat promotion.

Plan Two involved liberating the Wookiee prisoners at Lomabu III *and* bringing down Bossk, one task at a time. In Plan Two, Chen (backed by Flirt and Tinian) would still have a clear advantage over Bossk (deserted by the *Hound's Tooth*). As soon as Flirt announced success, he and Tinian would subdue the big Trandoshan. Then Chen could attack the Lomabuan prison guards without having to watch his back.

Plan Three was more complicated, of course. It pitted Bossk against Imperial Governor Io Desnand, and timing would be crucial.

Chen's Alliance contacts who had created the "waypost" probably weren't far off. Their scanners might be trained on the *Hound* at this moment.

He raised a hand in greeting.

Tinian sat where she'd been told to sit, several meters away from Bossk in the large starboard sleeping cabin. Bossk sat in front of a recessed console. His orange flightsuit fit him better when he sat down; when he'd stood, it had bunched up on his back. His long greenish forearms lay in two deep, rounded grooves. He barely moved, but he seemed remarkably busy for someone who only needed to set a course. He must be feverishly probing that "waypost."

She already guessed it was false. Bossk must be bitterly disappointed . . . but in his mind, the *Millennium Falcon* would be almost in reach. He would probably recheck this waypost after he completed this mission.

By then, it probably wouldn't exist.

She chuckled.

"What is it?" Bossk demanded. "What is funny?"

"The fact that we're almost there," she lied. "Those Wookiees are trying to set up their safe world right under an Imperial governor's nose."

"Oh. Get back to your cabin," gargled Bossk. "We will discuss strategy once I probe the Lomabu system."

"No drugs this time," she said sternly.

Acceleration made it hard to turn the corner into their cabin. She braced against a bulkhead until Chen slipped in behind her.

"Quick!" she urged. Chen was already unclipping Flirt from his bandolier. He plugged her in on the bulkhead.

"Security," Tinian scolded the miniature droid. "Hurry."

Extra g-forces darkened Tinian's vision at the edges before Flirt sang, "You're secure!"

Tinian struggled onto her bunk and braced her feet against the aft bulkhead. Chen reached down over her and secured her webbing. "Thanks," Tinian managed. Then she shut her eyes and waited for the lurch into hyperspace.

Bossk frowned at his monitors. The *Hound* had jumped successfully—this would be a two-hour hop—but one internal monitor had suddenly blanked. Had he lost power to the port cabin?

"Restore restraint systems inside the passenger cabin," he ordered.

After a moment's hesitation, the *Hound*'s baritone answered, "The port cabin is fully secured. Would you like imagery from the starboard cabin?"

For a superintelligent computer, it occasionally communicated like a prize idiot. That was one disadvantage of flying a new ship. Bossk exhaled sharply. "Cancel request," he snarled.

Almost immediately, Chenlambec appeared in at the bridge hatch. He woofled and pointed at the control troughs.

Bossk would fix that short circuit later. The translation circuit echoed Chenlambec's hooting before Bossk could shut it off and deny its existence. Translating into pidgin Basic, it said, "Want sit bridge. You made us sleep before. You need me up here. At Lomabu we outnumbered."

Bossk eyed the Wookiee's magnificent pelt. "The *Hound's Tooth* is my copilot. I don't need you."

Chenlambec growled. The *Hound* offered, "You don't need. But I fly under you. I want assist."

Bossk kept his tongue behind his teeth. It would be entertaining to share the bridge with a Wookiee whose pelt he would soon peel. "Sit," he directed Chenlambec. "But the *Hound* can immobilize you faster than you can touch me. And I can still kill your partner." He flipped his surveillance switch. The port cabin appeared on-screen. Tinian crouched beside a bulkhead, trying to pry off a sheet of metal paneling with her fingernails. Bossk pointed at her image. "If I find it necessary to immobilize you," he told Chenlambec, "I will kill her instantly."

Chenlambec muttered. "Too dark up here," translated the *Hound*.

"It's light enough," said Bossk. "Sit."

Chenlambec sat.

"You're back on watch," squeaked Flirt, "or Bossk thinks so."

Tinian slipped off her bunk. "About time," she exclaimed. "That must be one nasty computer."

"Not nasty." Flirt sounded prim. "Just standoffish. I like a challenge."

"As long as you don't get us killed while we wait for you, sweet thing." Tinian smoothed her shipsuit. "Is it safe to explore the aft bays?"

"If you take me along. Bossk thinks you're trying to take sheet metal off the bulkheads."

"That's creative." Tinian settled her belt over her hips. Besides a blaster, it held several tools that she'd need for exploring. "This is a short jump. We'd better move fast. Open the hatch."

It slid upward. "I've put a loop into his surveillance program," Flirt explained. "He'll see you try several bulkheads with your fingernails."

Tinian kept her nails short, but that image would make sense to a clawed alien. "How are you progressing with the *Hound*?"

"Oh," Flirt said evasively, "not as well as I'd like. He's one of those true-blue incorruptible types. He was more vulnerable from the bridge. I had to concentrate on this cabin while I was there, or maybe I could've accomplished something."

Chen had left Flirt with Tinian to protect her. Tinian had better make this trip aft worthwhile. "Thanks," she said. "Just don't let him see what I'm up to."

"Not me!"

Tinian grasped the small cube and twisted slightly. Flirt popped off the bulkhead onto her palm. Tinian waited a few seconds in case an alarm rang.

"Don't you trust me?" Flirt asked.

"I don't trust anybody." Tinian stuck Flirt into a belt pouch, then slipped into the corridor.

It was totally dark. Obviously the infrared-competent Bossk wanted to keep his passengers as blind as possible. Tinian pulled a tiny luma out of one belt pocket and held it overhead. Riveted bulkheads curved in both directions, with inverted pyramidal fixtures along the ceiling. They looked like heat lamps.

"Stop me if we approach anything dangerous," she whispered.

She had barely reached the first side hatch when Flirt beeped. Tinian froze. Cautiously she pulled Flirt out of the pouch. She held the little droid up to her mouth. "What is it?" she whispered.

Flirt's voice was almost imperceptible. "Motion sensor," the droid answered. "One more step and you'll walk into its range."

"Can I go backward?"

"I think so."

Tinian slid one foot backward, then the other.

"Stop," said Flirt.

Tinian froze again. "Now what?"

"I think there's a pressure trap in the deck just behind you. Don't move either foot."

Tinian held her position and swept Flirt in all directions. She sniffed the air cautiously. Her uncanny nose for explosives would be no help if the *Hound*'s security features were electronic.

"Okay," murmured Flirt. "The sensor's looking away."

As Tinian scooted forward, she spotted a tiny swiveling eye high on one bulkhead, momentarily pointed in the other direction. She slid beneath as it made a backswing up the corridor. Then she slunk aft, staying as close as possible to the port bulkhead. At last she reached two large hatches side by side. "These are secured," she told Flirt. "How are you going to get me in?"

"There's got to be a power point close by."

Tinian held up her luma. The opposite bulkhead looked smooth, except for seams and rivets. "Where?"

"Take me across."

She sprang over. The power point would have to be obvious, since Trandoshan fingers were clumsy.

Tinian spotted an access well hidden in shadow. She shoved Flirt into it. "Hurry," she whispered. "I feel naked out here."

Flirt didn't answer. She beeped and tinkled like a miniature music box.

Behind Tinian, a hatch slid open.

She spun around, drawing her blaster out of habit. Nothing happened. Of course, nothing *also* would've happened if she'd tried to fire the drained weapon. Disgusted, she holstered it again.

"You're in," announced Flirt.

Tinian plucked Flirt off the bulkhead. "Next time, give me a little warning," she grumbled.

She sneaked into the cargo bay, leaving the hatch open.

This wasn't the bay where they'd stored their precious lockers. Stowed along one wall, locked down by straps and hold-mes but in plain sight, was an array of weapons: force pikes, nasty-looking disruptors, knives, blast rifles, and tangle guns. All for hunting Wookiees, who only wanted to be left in peace.

Turning in place, Tinian spotted a long, shining table. She walked closer, holding her luma aloft. The table's surface threw reflections on the opposite bulkhead. A narrow channel ran along the table's edge, tilted toward a reservoir. At one narrow end of the table, a wicked-looking swivel hook hung retracted. A complex mechanism hovered above it, suspended from the upper bulkhead.

With those long, stiff, clawed forelimbs, Bossk was not dexterous enough to use a skinning knife. The automated machinery would lower into place over a Wookiee corpse.

Shuddering, Tinian tiptoed past a dip tank for curing fresh pelts.

She did not find any of the acceleration chairs Bossk had claimed he had back here, but along the bulkhead farthest from the access hatch, she spotted five alcoves: meat lockers. Equipped with minimal survival gear, they were standard features on Hunt ships—the *Wroshyr* had two—for containing live acquisitions. These stretched from deck to bulkhead. Wookiee-size.

Bossk would fit into one nicely.

She knelt beside the nearest one, reached into her largest belt pouch, and pulled out a handful of tools. Her circuit meter identified a force-field generator at the bottom of the locker. It was probably triggered by motion sensors to trap struggling prey inside. She'd like to jimmy one or all of these lockers—

Abruptly she felt afraid. "Is something happening?" she asked Flirt.

"Bossk is busy on the bridge. You're safe—"

"I don't *feel* safe." Tinian's escape on Druckenwell still haunted her dreams. She had run, and run, and run, expecting to be spotted by her body heat and shot from behind by Imperials wearing infrared scanners. She didn't doubt that Bossk would kill her just as quickly if he caught her manipulating his equipment, and he saw in the infrared without scanners.

She sprang up and shoved the tools back into her pouch. "We've got to get back."

"You don't need to do that. I'll alert you if—"

"I've got to get into the other bay, too. We're probably running out of time." Tinian hurried out through the hatch and across the passage. She shoved Flirt at the power point. "Shut that hatch and open the other."

Locks clicked behind her.

Tinian grabbed Flirt off the bulkhead and slipped across the passage again. She shone her luma against this bay's inner bulkhead, found a hookup for Flirt, and plugged her in once more. Then she shone her luma toward the other bulkhead. There was the pile—

A shadow moved. Tinian's blood turned to ice water.

Bossk's huge crimson-and-bronze droid rolled forward, halted, spun around, and returned to its station.

"You're all right." Flirt's chirp dropped a doleful minor interval. "He's totally brainless."

Tinian stared at the X10-D unit. "What?" she murmured.

"The poor creature's only an extension of the *Hound's Tooth,*" Flirt explained. "He has no interior programming. What a pity, in a body like that."

"Flirt," Tinian reprimanded the droid. "Chen needs a data chip out of Locker Two. Get me into it—fast."

Ten minutes later, Flirt guided her back through the passageway. As they paused beneath one motion sensor, Flirt tweeted, "It's terrible."

Tinian froze. "What is?"

"That beautiful metal body, and no brain—"

"Flirt!" Tinian ordered through gritted teeth. Imaginary eyes crawled around on the back of her neck. "Get me back to the cabin. Now!"

The moment she reached sanctuary, she pushed Flirt at her spot on the bulkhead. "Erase any record that we left this cabin," she directed.

"You shouldn't worry so much," Flirt whistled. "I had you perfectly safe."

•   •   •

Bossk glanced aside. Had he seen an alarm? Maybe, but it had shut itself off, so it could have been false. There were still a few bugs in the *Hound*, like its lapses of idiot speech.

Chenlambec was obviously impressed by it, though, and Bossk had enjoyed showing it off.

He shut down the simulator circuit and put the controls back on line. "Back to your cabin," he growled. When the Wookiee didn't obey instantly, he touched a control that extended two fur-penetrating electrodes on the copilot's seat.

Chenlambec sprang up, hooting. "Hurts," insisted the *Hound*'s translator. "Hurts."

"To the cabin." Bossk brandished the blast rifle he'd slung over his lap.

The Wookiee shambled up the corridor, obviously stalling. But when Bossk peered into the port cabin, the human sat on the edge of her bunk. She fiddled with her thin, inadequate claws.

"Where have you been?" he growled. *Prying off bulkheads?*

She stared up at him, looking stupidly blank. "Here," she answered. "Where else?"

He thought he caught the scent of the skinning bay on her clothing. Backing out the hatch, he secured it. *What could she have been doing back there?* He walked a circuit of the main corridor, including both bays. No alarms had been tripped. Returning to his bridge, he ran an extra security check. It too came up clean.

Maybe he'd been mistaken.

What if he hadn't?

He keyed for more details from the security program. Immediately after leaving the *Executor,* the *Hound's Tooth* had scanned his passengers' lockers. That scan revealed no metal except in the weapons crate. He'd told it to try the lockers again. Whatever they'd brought along, if it wasn't weaponry, it needed to be analyzed.

The second scan came up just as blank: clothing or foodstuffs might have matched the scan's biochemical readings.

He hadn't been presented with such an entertaining puzzle in several Standard years.

An hour's nap would refresh him, and the *Hound* would wake him in time to drop back into realspace. Reactivating his alarms, he headed for his bunk.

The moment Flirt declared that Bossk had locked himself into his cabin, Chenlambec set off on his own reconnoiter. To his delight, when he breached the central area he'd assumed was the *Hound*'s main engine, he found a sleek scout ship.

He paused, eyeing its lines. With or without subduing Bossk first, the time would soon come to run groundside surveillance.

He'd better be prepared for Plan Three, and for that, he would need to unload those lockers into this scout ship. But where would he conceal something so large?

Rounding the hull, he found two enormous empty holes on its exterior. Bossk had removed its guns. That made Chen certain that Bossk would send him and Tinian out in it. He peered into one hole.

There was room inside to hide a Wookiee.

Not him, but . . .

He smiled bitterly. Inside his storage lockers were two of his carbon-frozen kinsmen, executed by the Empire. Their bodies had been dropped at a Wookiee outpost. Chenlambec had vowed to avenge their deaths by making use of those bodies. Bossk's droid, X10-D, was allegedly brainless, so Flirt could order X10-D to transfer the carbon freeze units into these gunnery sockets. He must also tell Flirt to make sure that the *Hound*'s scanners still showed those lockers fully loaded.

With Flirt's help, he sneaked next onto the bridge,

carrying the data chip Tinian had retrieved. Before sitting down, he slipped Flirt into position under the navicomputer. Several long seconds later, she chirped, "You're secure . . . sort of."

He demanded an explanation.

"You'll be checked every two minutes. Whatever you want to do, move quickly."

Almost instantly, she beeped a warning. He slouched over the controls, motionless, until she chirped, "Okay. I overrode without trouble."

He growled a question.

"No, don't pull any wires," she answered. "I'll hold off the *Hound*."

Chen snatched a set of miniature tools out of his bandolier pouch. He pulled the main computer's cover, dropped it aside, then eyed internal circuitry. He almost had it figured out when Flirt beeped again. Hastily he replaced the cover.

It took five intervals before he located the spot to slide in that chip full of doctored data. Then he locked it in place and installed a parallel circuit around it.

Just in time, too. They would reach Lomabu within half an hour.

He growled a last question at Flirt.

"Not yet," she chirruped. "Sorry."

Then it was Plan Three. Leaving Flirt in position under the navicomputer in case she was close to a breakthrough, he retreated to the port cabin.

Tinian crouched alongside the communication console, steadying herself against the starboard bulkhead, wearing a lightweight headset. So far, she heard only static.

Bossk took the main chair with Chen as his copilot. Chen had told her that he thought Bossk was amused to let a Wookiee sit on his bridge. Bossk had brought up the bridge lights. His greenish scales showed orange undertones where the lights caught them.

Bossk killed the hyperdrive. The *Hound* cut in its sublights, and a star system appeared. According to the navicomputer readout, it had six planets in erratic orbits. They looked more like electrons' orbitals than a flat planetary ecliptic, as if the Lomabu system had been stirred by a passing stellar giant. Bossk had oriented the *Hound's Tooth* to the third planet's orbital plane. From this distance, it looked like a small blue disk with one moon. According to scanners, its surface was almost entirely covered by ocean, with long archipelagoes marking arcs where tectonic plates collided.

"Excellent," Bossk hissed. "*Hound*, establish a momentum course and cut engines."

"Confirmed." The ship fell silent. To casual scanners it would look like an eccentric asteroid passing the planet.

Tinian watched Bossk flick a control alongside one of his forearm troughs. He'd have to utilize shipboard scanners sparingly now. Stray transmissions would be picked up by Imperial sentries . . . though *he* thought he was hiding from Wookiee sentinels.

Chenlambec hooted. "Could the *Falcon* be in scanner range?" Tinian translated.

Bossk eyed the boards. "If the *Falcon* is here at all," he said. "If you two have led me astray, I will sell you both to the highest bidder."

The image of a colonial installation appeared on the *Hound's* main scanner. Chen had told Tinian it would correspond closely to the layout of Gandolo IV. Bossk flicked the scan once more, narrowing its search band.

An irregular shape dropped toward the Lomabu "colony." "Corellian YT-1300 freighter," announced the *Hound's* baritone. "Modified. Heavily modified. *Illegally* modified. Crew and passengers: one Wookiee, two humans."

Bossk snapped off the board with a left foreclaw. "We have them!" he exulted.

Tinian thought she heard something. She touched her headphones. "Listen!"

Bossk amplified the transmission over a bridge speaker. "Very funny," drawled a male human. "But what we want is landing clearance. You going to give it, or shall I take this stuff and sell it back to Nada Synnt?"

"Solo," Bossk hissed. "Shut down all power."

The bridge went dark.

Tinian raised her tiny luma inside one hand. Red light welled through her fingers. Plan Three, then. She'd hoped not to run Plan Three. *Chen, I hope you're ready.* She pressed to her feet. "Let's go get them." Trying to sound cocky, she slapped her blaster. "It's time for a recharge, Bossk. And Chen needs his bowcaster."

Bossk drew his forearms out of the troughs and rubbed them against each other. "Tinian, I want you and your Wookiee to determine Solo's likely avenues of escape. Count his allies and resources. This will be excellent experience to round out your apprenticeship."

"We don't want to use those scanners again," she objected.

Bossk flicked his tongue. "You're right. I'm sending you out in my scout craft, the *Nashtah Pup*."

The *Pup* was as sweet a scout ship as Chenlambec had ever crewed, despite its unfamiliar controls . . . and it had broadband transceivers, including Chen's personal favorite, single sideband. Its console curved around two black leather crew seats, with scanners mounted to create the illusion of looking out two trapezoidal windows, just as on the *Hound's Tooth*'s bridge.

Chen steered it back toward the *Hound* to get the feel of maneuvering. The bigger ship had popped a dorsal hatch to launch the *Pup;* slowly it dropped shut behind them. Now it was easy to see that the oval *Hound*'s primary engines lay under its main deck, with exhaust ports across its aft quarter.

"Watch it," said Bossk's voice in his headphones. "I'm tracking you with a quad gun."

"Why bother?" snapped Tinian. "We're practically unarmed."

Chen ordered her to take the *Pup* down out of range, then pointed to one of his ears and over his shoulder toward the *Hound's Tooth:* Bossk was undoubtedly monitoring.

She nodded and reached for the steering rods. The console wrapped around their crew chairs so neatly that either could fly the *Pup* comfortably.

Tinian stroked a control rod. "I like this little scout."

Homesick for the *Wroshyr*, Chen barked.

"I didn't ask to be born rich," she argued. "I just wish this were mine."

Chenlambec kept digging in his tool pouch. He had left Flirt under the *Hound*'s navicomputer and brought a remote relay. Now, he wired the remote—which was bigger than Flirt herself—into the *Pup*'s main communication line. Then he tapped out a code message to Flirt: POWER DOWN *Hound*'S AUDIO RECEIVERS FOR TWO MINUTES, THEN HIS TRANSLATOR FOR TEN MINUTES. His remote beeped twice, for "message received." A minute later, it beeped twice, then repeated, indicating that she'd succeeded.

"I heard that," said Tinian. "Bossk'll be deaf to us for two minutes?"

Howling assent, Chen closed his hands around the throttle rods. Lomabu III loomed closer on the visual screen. They were approaching the daylight side at high noon, out of the orange sun. The Imperials must not see them.

Tinian talked rapidly into her headphone. "This message is for Governor Desnand, repeat, Governor Io Desnand of the Aida System. We wish to report that the bounty hunter Bossk of Trandosha, repeat bounty hunter, repeat Bossk, is encroaching on your prison world Lomabu III. He is engaged in unauthorized pelt-baiting and means to abduct many of your laborers. This is another bounty hunter speaking. I have Bossk under observation, but he is also observing me. Can you make it worth my while to intercept him for you? Please reply on this frequency so that I may receive at . . . 1435 Standard hours.''

That transmission was headed for Aida, not Lomabu. There'd be some subspace delay. Chen pointed at the chrono to warn Tinian that her two minutes were up. His ten were about to begin. She switched off the transmitter. He let go of the throttle rods, and she took them.

With the Imperial Governor alerted, now he must close the other side of their net: He must make a contact below. Even if Flirt failed him, the Wookiee prisoners must be alerted and freed. Chen switched the transmitter to a local frequency.

Eerie howling noises filled the cabin. Single sideband was excellent for transmitting Wookiee speech, but difficult to tune for in Basic. Bossk could listen to this all day and not understand a word. Maybe his translator would choke on it too.

He called groundside.

At first, nothing happened. There was always the chance that no illicit transmitter had been set up inside the prison camp, but Chenlambec was willing to bet otherwise.

"Try again," Tinian suggested. "We just dropped under the ionized atmospheric layer."

Chen howled at the transceiver again. As Tinian brought the *Pup* toward the target archipelago, the answering howl from his transceiver abruptly modulated.

Chen grinned aside at Tinian, then answered. His mission took considerable explaining, particularly the part about landing and staging a firefight. The target island grew on the fore screen.

"Explain about getting Bossk's confidence," Tinian hissed, steering out to sea on the island's west side. The prison compound was on the east shore.

Chenlambec tried again. Evidently his contact was an elderly male using amateur equipment, desperately afraid that guards would return soon.

Chen didn't ask what threat the Imperials used to control his people. The *Pup*'s scanners had shown him heavy artillery: two turbolaser emplacements plus plenty of unidentified metal technology.

He needed to get those weapons into his people's hands.

Tinian came in low over a dense green jungle, sweeping overland toward the island's east coast. Abruptly, Bossk's voice echoed in the cabin. "What's that? What are you doing?"

His time was up. If Flirt silenced the *Pup* any longer, Bossk might suspect her existence.

Tinian leaned toward the pickup. "We're going to singe a little fur," she answered. "Shall we bring some back?"

"If you know how," said Bossk. It sounded like a challenge.

"Brace yourself, Chen," Tinian muttered. "We'll land in about one minute."

She wasn't confident of her landing skills, and this was an unfamiliar ship, even though she liked it. Chen flipped her small hands off the controls and grasped the rods. He feathered the main engine and set down the *Pup* near a cliff along the waterside. The compound would lie on a peninsula just north of that rocky promontory.

"Impressive," Tinian said wistfully.

He cuffed her shoulder and ordered her to thaw the lockers. They must be blood-warm before returning to the *Hound*.

She gripped his forearm. "Be careful, Chen."

He crooned a soft good-bye. Her concern pleased and honored him.

He popped the hatch and climbed down onto Lomabu III. A cool damp wind blew across his nose, and he felt its chill in his furless palms. Its salty smell had an organic overlay of dead fish and floating plants. Beneath a brilliant blue sky, close to the site where the *Pup* sat grounded, waves lapped at the jagged line of a long, broken wall. Green algae almost obscured a tracework of filigree just above waterline. Farther out in sapphire-blue water, other ruined walls formed a right-angled maze. The ruins barely broke the water, topped with broken stone and steel.

He and Tinian had landed near an abandoned city. Within a few years, decades at the most, the vast sea would dissolve these remaining walls and wash them away, and all evidence of the Lomabuans' civilization would vanish.

Chenlambec wondered what the Lomabuans had looked like, and what crime they had committed that drove the Empire to depopulate the entire world. Were the Lomabuans slaves, like his own people . . . or dead?

He checked his bowcaster. Each piece fit again. It bothered him to know that Bossk was so familiar with Kashyyyk's weaponry.

The rocky promontory that shielded the prison compound from his view would also keep prison guards from spotting the *Pup*. He strode forward, staying inside a narrow grove of twiggy brown trees that grew between the cliff's foot and a pale, sandy strand.

Once he rounded the promontory, the prison compound became visible. Its gray walls rose in straight, perfect lines, freshly built and maintained by slave labor. It hunched at the other end of a slender peninsula, surrounded by a high metal fence. Four tall blocky towers loomed at the corners of its perimeter, and pale sand covered the peninsula's narrows between compound and mainland.

Only one turbolaser emplacement was in bowcaster range. Destroying that weapon would help set the stage for an uprising. He crawled forward, staying low. Rocky soil scratched his palms.

As he began to set his right palm on the sand, he realized that the sand was also crawling. He bent down to peer closer. What he had taken for a sandy beach was a vast colony of tiny creatures. Each was no larger than a grain of true sand, with legs or flagella so small he could only guess that they existed. The colony roiled as creatures climbed over each other and were climbed in turn.

He judged from the damp rocky soil above the crawling sand that the tide was going out. Although the creatures' movement seemed random, the colony slowly retreated, following the tide.

He dangled a bit of fur over the colony. It vanished where it touched down.

Ravenous little beasts! Chen groped behind him into the glade, found a leaf-covered stick, and tossed it onto the crawling sand.

It dissolved from beneath.

This explained why the Imperials had selected this peninsula for a prison colony. Surrounded by voracious sand—even at low tide, he guessed—it could cage Wookiees who laughed at most weapons. Chen wondered if the Imperials had allowed one prisoner to "escape" in order to demonstrate the sand's appetite—

But that was idle speculation. Now to create some heat for Bossk to see, so it would look as if there'd been a firefight . . . so he could realistically lead Bossk on with those bodies.

Cautiously avoiding the sand, he crawled close to the guard tower. He chose an explosive quarrel from his bandolier. Keeping his elbows low, he fitted it to his bowcaster, aimed carefully, and let it fly.

The tower erupted in orange flame. A human voice shouted. Chen sprang up and dashed for the promontory. He'd've liked to have seen how that explosion looked on Bossk's sensors, since it would show up in the middle of a scene that didn't exist.

As he jogged up, Tinian stood close to the *Pup*'s boarding ladder. "Don't step on that sand!" she cried. "It—"

He roared agreement and a query as he clambered aboard.

"I'm fine. But are you?"

He vaulted into the cockpit and almost slipped in a red puddle. Tinian had lain the dead Wookiees between hatch and crew chairs. "No place else to put them," she apologized, climbing in after him. "As soon as I brought them out of freeze, they started bleeding."

He demanded to know what she'd done with the carbon freeze units.

"I lugged them up into the forest. I don't think Bossk will find them there."

And hauled two Wookiees up the boarding ladder? She should've let him do that. Chen dropped into his chair and grasped the controls.

Once berthed on the *Hound,* Tinian sprang the *Pup*'s hatch. Bossk stood below her, silhouetted by lights that looked almost normally bright. "Now the Wookiee criminals know that we're here," the Trandoshan snarled. "Is that all you accomplished?"

"No," Tinian snarled back. That wasn't difficult; her back hurt. "We also performed our evaluation. Solo and Chewbacca can't escape overland. There's a colony of living, eating sand all along the shoreline, so they'll have to take off upward if they try to escape us. Allies and resources? Plenty of Wookiees, but not as many as there were yesterday. Help us offload these pelts. There's still meat on them."

"Pelts?" Bossk shuffled up to the main hatch and peered in. "Did you actually—"

He fell silent. The fresh-looking corpses still lay bleeding on the deck. Chenlambec sat his station, baring his teeth in a howl. Tinian translated accurately this time. "Criminals. A gift," she added, "just in case you still doubt us. Chen knocked off two sentries."

Bossk reached down. He stroked one pelt, a rich brown tipped in black. "I had doubted that you would kill free Wookiees," he answered. "I believe you now. I accept your gift."

Sure you believe us. Tinian let Bossk manhandle the cooling bodies off the *Pup*. Chen remained in his seat, curling his lip. He blinked rapidly, a sign of nausea. He asked her to tell Bossk something convincing.

"He wants me to say," said Tinian, "that he finds your end of the Hunting trade repugnant. But we understand financial necessity."

Bossk summoned X10-D as they climbed down. "Excellent pelts." He stroked the other, which was solid black. "Prime condition. Maybe one hundred and fifty years?"

Chen turned his head.

Fortunately, X10-D rolled into the docking bay and stopped Bossk from making Chen feel any sicker. The draft droid dragged both corpses up the passage toward the aft hold. Bossk followed, stepping lightly. Tinian recalled the skinning rack and dip tank.

Chen slumped, shivering and keening.

Hesitantly Tinian laid a hand on his shoulder. When he didn't brush her off, she tightened it. Chen felt her strongest grip as a gentle caress. "They would rejoice," she whispered, "to know that in death they are helping end this carnage."

He laid back his head and cried out softly.

"And we've seen the way Bossk covets your pelt, *Ng'rhr*." She squeezed his shoulder again, then walked away from him, struck by the thought that if she lost

Chenlambec, she would be orphaned again. Her mother had abandoned her as a newborn. Her grandparents had been coldly murdered. Daye lay crushed under tons of rubble.

The *Hound*'s deck blurred.

She mustn't let him see her like this. "You'll notice he didn't order us back to our cabin—and we can see," she muttered. "Let's get something to eat."

She set up the best meal she could find in the galley, including a huge scoop of red worms for Bossk. Now if ever, she must act friendly. Trying not to gag, she told the *Hound* to call Chen and Bossk for dinner.

Chen shambled in first and sat down. Bossk arrived smelling like disinfectant. "Ah. Thank you, Human."

"Is that enough?"

He sat down in front of the wriggling red mess. "For now. Friend Chenlambec, you aren't eating."

Chen stared at his plate, blinking and wrinkling his nose.

Tinian cursed her thoughtlessness. Of course the ship smelled foul to him. Bossk had been skinning two Wookiees. How could Chen eat? Tinian dished herself a platter of cloned saltlicker ribs, then sat down. She had to act hearty. Cheerful. Determined.

"What did he say?" Bossk asked.

"Too much excitement." Tinian stripped the meat from a rib with her teeth and added, with her mouth full, "he'll calm down and eat later. Listen, Bossk, things look good down there. Between Wookiees, we picked up a scanner confirmation of two human life forms. One corresponds exactly with the last known readout on Han Solo."

"Did you record it?"

"Of course." She had loaded that data into the *Pup*'s main computer while Chen took out the guard tower. Like the other data chip, Chen had bought this one "from a friend."

"I have come up with a plan for live capture," Bossk announced.

"Act glad," Tinian woofed at Chenlambec.

Chen lifted a rib, glared at it, curled back his lips, and growled. Then he stuffed it into his mouth and chewed.

"Tell us what you want us to do," Tinian said.

"I will drop out of orbit and draw off the freighter," Bossk answered. "You will neutralize the safe world's defenses. We will run a two-pronged feint and attack."

Then, Chen guessed out loud, Bossk would abandon them.

"He says," put in Tinian, "that the *Pup* isn't armed heavily enough to do the defenses much damage."

"It will be soon," Bossk answered.

Chen ordered her to argue.

"We could do you more good on board the *Hound,*" offered Tinian. "She's a good ship."

"I won't leave you two alone on her."

Tinian had heard human children prattle. She imitated one she had particularly disliked. "I don't suppose you're willing to leave Chenlambec alone on her and fly down with me. And you and Chen wouldn't fit onto the *Pup* very well. What about sending Chen down, and leaving me—"

"Stop," said Bossk. "I trust you enough to arm the *Pup.* This is merely the best way of accomplishing our mission."

"All right," Tinian whined.

After filling his belly with live meat, Bossk ordered Tinian onto watch. He locked Chenlambec into their cabin, rechecked the *Hound*'s security lock, and then finished skinning the second Wookiee. It was stiff, now: rigor had set in. He lifted the finished pelt, draping the moist, satiny underside over both forearms, and gently slid it into his dip tank. It vanished, bubbling, into the tanning fluid. Delighted by the unexpected two-pelt bonus, he airlocked the meat. Wookiee tasted oily and foul.

He returned to the skinning bay. "ExTen-Dee," he called, "unload the *Pup*'s weaponry."

The bronze-and-crimson droid rolled forward, reached out his long grasping arms, and unlocked a cargo compartment. Holding one huge, tube-shaped weapon at two-meter arm's distance, he swiveled around and grasped the other massive tube. Balanced now, he raised both arms and rolled up the main passage. Bossk followed.

Inside the docking bay, the *Pup* let off odd pops as it cooled. Working late with X10-D's help, he reinstalled the *Pup*'s guns. Then he sent X10-D back to the cargo bay for two items that mustn't be jarred. Several minutes later, X10-D returned at a measured crawl. He held his arms fully extended to their three-meter length. His left hand carried a small canister. He held his right arm high to keep from dragging an enormous oblong torpedo.

Bossk stood beside the *Pup*'s launch tube. "Load it," he ordered. "Use full caution."

X10-D slid the huge flame carpet warhead down the tube, then sidled up against the *Pup*'s exterior to perform lockdown and pre-arming operations.

Bossk flicked his tongue rapidly. The next time Chenlambec fired on the Lomabu colony, that warhead would splash a hideous flammable adhesive over several square kilometers. Hundreds of Wookiees would suffer by Chenlambec's hand, and Bossk would be avenged for Gandolo IV. The Scorekeeper did not demand undamaged goods on her altar. Scorched pelts delighted her.

Finally, he wired the small obah gas dispenser into the *Pup*'s ventilation system. Unlike the benign serum he had tranquilized Chenlambec and Tinian with, obah gas caused permanent nerve disability in creatures smaller than Wookiees or Trandoshans. It would render Chenlambec helpless, with his prize pelt intact . . . but it would cripple Tinian.

She traveled with a Wookiee. She knew she risked exposure to Wookiee-disabling agents. At any rate, the small bounty offered on her didn't specify "alive" or "undamaged."

He ran a swift check of the scout ship. He had told them to disable the colony's defenses. Immediately after they launched the flame carpet and realized what they had done, he would gas them. The *Hound* would then remotely guide the *Pup* into high orbit, where it would be easy to pick up after Bossk laid the *Falcon* crew low.

That would be tricky, putting down a crew that included both humans and a Wookiee but leaving all unharmed. He didn't dare risk Lord Darth Vader's wrath. "ExTen-Dee," he ordered, "charge six injector missiles with mekebve spores. I want them loaded in tube number three of the *Hound*."

Most mammalian species suffered severe allergic reactions to mekebve pollen, but reptiles did not. That would incapacitate Solo and his shipmates long enough for Bossk to board and capture.

But the pollen was fifty years old, according to the Nalrithian dealer who'd sold it to him. If the Nalrithian lied, it could be much older. Was it still potent?

He could easily perform an entertaining test. "Once you've packed the injector missiles, put two grams of pollen into the *Hound*'s ventilation system."

X10-D swiveled and rolled away.

As 1435 Standard hours approached, Tinian stared at the display board. It wasn't too late to implement Plan Two. *Come on, Flirt. Finish the job.* The little droid still nestled under the navicomputer, running permutations into the *Hound*'s failsafes. Maybe he had too many lockouts to juggle. Maybe he just kept outsmarting her. While they stayed locked in their game, the burden fell on Chen and Tinian.

On schedule, a message appeared. GOVERNOR IO DESNAND'S OFFICE TO INFORMANT, it read. UNAUTHORIZED PELT BAITING AT LOMABU III IS SUBJECT TO SEVERE PENALTY. WE WILL PAY FORTY THOUSAND CREDITS FOR IMMEDIATE LIVE DELIVERY OF TRANDOSHAN BOUNTY HUNTER.

Vader offered 800,000 for the *Falcon*'s crew . . . but 40,000 was nothing to sneeze at.

Tinian bent low. "Flirt, we've got a bounty offer. Are you inside yet?"

After a few seconds, Flirt piped, "I'm still trying—"

Abruptly the bridge lights flickered off. Tinian sprang to her feet.

"Bossk just switched off all lighting in your wavelength range," Flirt exclaimed.

"You stay put," Tinian murmured. "And keep trying. Trap him in a meat locker, if you can—" She sneezed delicately, then harder. A third sneeze followed.

What was going on?

She groped out of the pitch-dark command bridge and into the passageway. Each breath grew more difficult. Her eyes stung. She squeezed them shut. Tears streamed out around her eyelids and trickled into her mouth.

Bossk flicked a comlink control. He could see perfectly by his infrared lamps. "Tinian, Chenlambec, are you all right? I've had a malfunction in one of my failsafes. Stay where you are. I'll be with you momentarily."

Good. The pollen was still allergenic. Eagerly he marched up the corridor.

He found Tinian in the passage, crouched near the door of their cabin. She held both hands pressed over her face and stifled a vehement sneeze. "Are you all right?" he asked. "I'm terribly sorry. This system was designed to disable escaped acquisitions."

She looked messy. Her nose and eyes poured fluid. "No." She gulped and swallowed. "I'm not all right."

Very amusing. "It will take me some time to repair the malfunction. Meanwhile, the *Pup* has filtered air. The safest place for you and your partner is on board, on the next phase of our mission."

Tinian tottered to her feet.

"First hatch on your left," Bossk reminded her. "You'll find it by feel. I left it open."

Bossk slapped a control and opened the cabin hatch. Chenlambec sat on his bunk. If Tinian looked bad, Chenlambec's misery was magnificent. His face, neck, and chest fur lay in a soaked, tangled mat. "Get to the *Pup*," Bossk said gruffly, struggling not to laugh. "Tinian will fill you in. I'm headed for the bridge to try to fix things."

Tinian sneezed violently, then groped on up the dark corridor. She couldn't see, and every breath hurt. Bossk's apology had sounded false. Trandoshans never apologized.

She heard a miserable treble howl behind her. "Chen, are you there?" she wheezed.

He howled again.

"He wants us on board the *Pup*. It's got filtered air." She sniffed hard and swallowed.

His grumble sounded closer this time.

She groped to the open hatch and stumbled through. Her footsteps clanked: This had to be the scout-ship dock. Feeling her way along one bulkhead, she closed her hand around a breath mask. She shoved it over her nose and eyes, but it leaked top and bottom. It was the wrong shape for a human face.

She gasped out a short Shyriiwook oath and dropped the useless rebreather.

Long, strong, fur-covered hands closed on her shoulders and pushed her away from the bulkhead. Chen rumbled instructions.

"Okay. Take me in." She grabbed his big forearms and shut her eyes. Every time she cracked them open, they stung like they were full of biting insects.

Chen leaped up the ladder like a whirlwind. She let go and slumped on the *Pup*'s deck, trying not to wipe her eyes. Her skin and clothing—and Chen's fur—were probably covered with the poisonous pollen.

A light came on. "Are you on board?" Bossk's voice rasped over the *Pup*'s comm system. "Is it any better in there?"

The *Pup* started to vibrate. Bossk must be powering it up from the *Hound*'s bridge.

"Much," Tinian shouted without getting up. "Thank . . . y'choo!"

"Shake yourselves," Bossk ordered. "Turn your ventilation and filters on full. That will help."

Chen announced that he'd found an air intake.

Tinian squinted. Chen contorted himself in front of the intake, sweeping every centimeter of his body across it three or four times. Then he started picking half-dried detritus off his fur.

If he wasn't going to stand on protocol, she wasn't either. She skinned out of her black shipsuit and flapped it in front of the vent, then shook her hair hard. At first, her sneezing and weeping got worse instead of better. Finally, they slacked off.

She cracked one eye open. It no longer stung. She exhaled heavily.

Chenlambec sat at the *Pup*'s controls, studiously eyeing the board. Tinian slipped back into her shipsuit and then flopped down beside him. "Are you—*choo!*—ready?"

Chen growled assent.

Bossk's voice answered out of the comm, "I will

launch you in thirty seconds. All of your systems check perfectly."

Bossk smelled victory. After the *Pup* accelerated well away from the *Hound,* he touched a control to arm the flame carpet warhead's detonator. Chenlambec had cocked the obah gas dispenser's trigger by switching the *Pup*'s ventilators to full power.

Now he swiveled back to his navicomputer to make final calculations for his own approach. He keyed in a course that would take him close to the Wookiee colony.

As soon as the *Pup* fired and he gassed Chen and Tinian—their nasal membranes would be exquisitely sensitive, an unplanned dividend of the pollen test—he would dive. One swoop ought to draw the cocky Solo offplanet to chase him.

He rotated his eyes inward. *Here I am, Scorekeeper. Watch me.*

Chen held the *Pup* on course for several minutes before Tinian finally stopped sneezing. Her nose still twitched. Inside, it felt as if someone had scraped it raw.

On second thought, she smelled explosives that shouldn't be on board. Alarmed, she unbuckled, stood up, and leaned close to Chen's massive head. "Something's wrong," she murmured into the fur on one side of his neck. "I'm going to run a systems check."

He wurfled soft assent.

They spent several minutes running through the *Pup*'s limited board. Nothing turned up. By then, Tinian's hands shook. Something was terribly wrong, and she couldn't find it.

Chen tapped his relay to Flirt, then flicked on the sideband and started transmitting again.

His contact howled back, almost indistinguishable

over sideband static. Tinian envisioned a prison compound full of Wookiees that was about to explode in violence.

She hoped the *Pup* wasn't about to explode, too. She didn't think Bossk would sacrifice his scout ship just to kill them. What else could it be?

As Chen called instructions into the pickup, a verbal-visual transmission appeared over the main board.
DEEPEST SECURITY BREACHED—I THINK. I'M FAKING A SYSTEMS MAL-FUNCTION NEAR ONE MEAT LOCKER.

It was from Flirt, still under Bossk's navicomputer.

Chenlambec howled.

"Wait!" Tinian cried. "Override that program. Run a check on the *Pup*—now! What did Bossk do to prepare it for this mission?"

Bossk cackled softly at Tinian's startled cry to her partner. *Too late for that, Human.* He intended to watch his victims approach the Wookiee colony, but for several minutes yet, they would be too far out to fire the flame carpet.

A danger light blinked at one end of his console. "What is it?" he asked. "Not another false alarm, I hope."

"Nothing wrong, no false alarm," answered the *Hound*. "ExTen-Dee lives in a meat locker, inside the skinning hold."

What? Bossk clicked his foreclaws over his palm. It would've been just like that undersized human to tamper with the X10-D's circuitry. Humans had nasty, slender fingers.

Or was this one of the *Hound*'s idiot bugs?

He confirmed that the *Pup* could not fire for several minutes, then slipped off his seat and trotted aft.

•　　•　　•

Flirt's voice shrieked over the relay. "He's off the bridge! Hurry—if there's anything you need to do, you're not monitored!"

"You just keep running those checks." Tinian's eyes had stopped watering, but her nose twitched. She couldn't identify the explosive she smelled; it must be an exotic, and that worried her. "Chen, talk to your friend down there. I'm going to start at one end of this scout and check all the circuits I can get access to. Something's wrong, and Flirt's not even trying to help."

"I am, too!" exclaimed the thin voice. "Bossk just walked into the cargo bay—he's walking right up to the meat locker I set leaking—he's standing in front of it—"

Bossk located X10-D standing in his corner, obviously inactive. Next he checked his meat lockers. Fluid dribbled out of a water nipple down the inner wall of the far left unit.

Growling, he whacked a control at mid-bulkhead. That shut down a security circuit that would normally activate the lockers' energy gates when prey inside tripped them. He grabbed a hydrospanner and stepped in.

"—He's getting inside!" Flirt squeaked. *"Hound,* reactivate that energy gate! *Hound,* please? *Hound—"*

Chenlambec roared at the pickup.

"All right!" Hiccuping, Flirt switched programs. "He reinstalled your energy guns. Your torpedo launcher is operable again, on heat-seeker status—"

Torpedo. Explosives. "What's the warhead?" Tinian interrupted.

Flirt answered seconds later. "It's called a flame carpet," she sang. "And you've—"

Chenlambec's furious roar drowned out Flirt's next words. Tinian recoiled too. Flame carpet warheads were appalling weapons manufactured by one of I'att Armaments' less scrupulous competitors. Bossk had sent her and Chenlambec to set air aflame, sear lungs and skin, shrivel fur—

Flirt had kept talking. Tinian shoved gruesome imagery to the back of her mind. "What was that, Flirt? Please repeat."

"I *said,*" Flirt answered in a mincing voice, "that he also installed a dispensing canister into your vent system. It's full of a nerve poison called obah gas. You'd better dump it."

"Yeah—but first we've got to find it!" Obah gas? Nerve poison? Tinian never would have smelled that. Bossk had triple-crossed them. Pollen, a flame carpet warhead, and now this.

Chen leaped out of his seat. He dug his claws under the ventilation duct cover. To Tinian, the *Nashtah Pup* suddenly felt claustrophobic, with too little air inside.

"Thanks, Flirt." She breathed slowly and deliberately. "Can you still get Bossk?"

"He's working inside the locker. He found the leak. I can't . . . quite . . . get *Hound* to cooperate. He's very strong-willed. I'd like him if he weren't in our way," she added brightly.

At least Bossk wasn't on the bridge, watching.

What could Tinian do with a flame carpet warhead? She'd never dreamed she would have this responsibility. She must launch and destroy it so that no one would ever use it. It was irreversibly set on heat seeker status.

Maybe Bossk meant to gas them, then put the *Pup* on autopilot and flame the Wookiee compound?

She didn't have time to guess. She must decide what to do. She could send Bossk and his *Hound's Tooth* straight to the Trandoshans' Scorekeeper. Lacking air to co-fuel its onboard flammables, that torpedo would impact the *Hound* like a huge, heavy projectile.

No. The *Pup* had no hyperdrive. Destroying the *Hound* would strand her and Chen in Imperial space.

She knew she wasn't thinking clearly. The answer ought to be obvious.

The *Pup*'s approach vector carried them out of the planet's shadow. Lomabu's sun rose above the world's blue crescent.

The sun! She *knew* it was obvious.

"Brace yourself, Chen," Tinian exclaimed. She rotated the *Pup* 120 degrees, aimed the torpedo launcher's snout directly at Lomabu's sun, and fired. The *Pup* lurched. Chen hit his head on an overhead and howled.

Tinian held her breath and tracked the warhead. After a quick three-count, its onboard rockets kicked on. It streaked sunward. Several hundred degrees of heat wouldn't harm anything there.

Grandfather I'att would have smiled.

Evidently Bossk hadn't seen her launch the warhead, because nothing happened immediately. Tinian nosed the *Pup* groundward. "Chen, how's it going in there?" They still had far too much altitude to eject. If Bossk gassed them, they were trapped.

Chen stood with one long, hairy arm jammed up the ventilation duct. He turned his head, pushed his arm harder, and groaned.

Tinian bit her lip. If Bossk got back to the bridge, he would know she'd fired the warhead. He would know she'd betrayed him, and warheads weren't easy to procure. "Flirt? Are you getting close?"

"Maybe," chirped the little droid. "He's still working."

"Keep Bossk off the bridge, or it's our lives."

"I'm trying!" Flirt insisted. "If you'd leave me alone—"

"Will do," Tinian answered. As Chenlambec twisted

a piece of metal off one console and shoved it up the ventilation duct, Tinian steered toward colonial space.

This time they approached from the east, over water. Scanning a shimmery blue horizon, Tinian spotted the four looming guard towers.

The Imperials would be on intruder watch this time. As if to confirm Tinian's thought, a blast of turbolaser fire flashed from one tower. It barely missed the *Pup.*

Tinian hated being shot at. Gulping, she swept both hands over its board. "Chen, where are our shields?"

He howled.

"None?" she cried.

A grizzled Wookiee spotted the tower guards firing. Whispers inside the compound had told him to watch for an attack. He sprinted toward the southeast guard tower. All around him, Wookiee slaves dropped their loads and attacked their overseers.

A human arm flew. Approval thundered from a hundred Wookiee throats.

The prisoners drove their guards into the tower. The Empire may have found the Wookiees of Kashyyyk defenseless, but it had taught them to fight back.

A louder roar swept in from over the sea. Imperial lasers tracked it for several blasts. Then the gunners swiveled their turbolasers inward. A long metal snout pointed into the compound.

At this range, the gunners didn't miss. Soil, sand, and duracrete—and a dozen prisoners—vaporized in a fiery flash. The shock wave knocked the ancient Wookiee to his knees.

He scrambled around the raw new crater toward the guard tower. The turbolaser could not track him there. Other surviving Wookiees grappled with Imperials along its duracrete wall.

"Surrender," boomed a voice out of the guard tower. "Surrender now, and you will not be harmed."

The Wookiee slaves answered with angry, hopeless roars and kept fighting.

A sortie of heavily armed troopers spilled out of the tower's main door. They drove the enraged Wookiees out into the open. Craning his neck to look up at the tower, the old Wookiee stared down a turbolaser's muzzle.

A human in a black officer's uniform stood beside it. "Send off a distress signal!" he screeched at an underling wearing khaki. "Get help—get Desnand—immediately!"

Chenlambec still stood groping inside the ventilator, utterly stymied. He could not disengage the gas dispenser; Flirt had not managed to trap Bossk; and his shoulder throbbed as if he had torn the rotator cuff trying to squeeze one more centimeter of length into his reach.

"They're transmitting!" Tinian leaned against a throttle rod. The scout ship tilted. Chen braced himself to pull g's standing up, but he did not pull his arm out of the ventilator.

He roared a question at Flirt.

"Easily," Flirt chirped. "*Hound* likes jamming transmissions. He told me—"

"Have you got Bossk?" Tinian interrupted.

"Still working on it," Flirt sang. "Leave me alo-one."

"Forget jamming, then," exclaimed Tinian. "We'll—"

"Oops!" chirruped Flirt's voice.

Chen snatched out his arm.

Flirt sounded sheepish. "We've got alarms going off all over the ship!"

Chen pounded the bulkhead, beyond frustration. There was nothing he could do now. Bossk would leap out of the locker and run to the bridge. Then Chen and Tinian would start breathing obah gas. He shouted at her to steer the *Pup* inland and prepare to eject. They'd be stranded but alive.

"They've still got six hundred Wookiees pinned down by that turbolaser," exclaimed Tinian. "I could blow out the main gun before Bossk got us." The *Pup* lurched as she positioned it to make another pass.

For such a small thing, she surprised him with her courage. Chen sank into his chair.

Another alarm? Startled, Bossk dropped his hydrospanner. "ExTen-Dee," he shouted, "get over here!"

As the big droid rolled toward him, a white security light near the top of the locker blinked back on.

Bossk lunged for the locker's edge. Energy sizzled around him. It threw him back inside with scorched scales and a bruised forehead.

"Deactivate that force lock!" he shouted.

X10-D rolled one more meter forward. He hesitated as if listening to another voice, and then swiveled in place. He made a full turn. Then another.

Then he returned to his spot near the bulkhead.

"Wait!" Flirt exclaimed.

"What?" Tinian held course. In five more seconds, she'd have that guard tower in range.

"I've got him!" cried Flirt. "The *Hound* just gave me security clear—"

"Don't talk!" Tinian exclaimed. "Hold him!" The little droid must've finally hit the right code permutation. "Use ExTen-Dee to keep that locker secure!"

"I will!"

Tinian squeezed a firing stud as Chen put a Wookiee's strength into the control yoke. An energy flash lit the *Pup*'s cabin.

"Yes!" Flirt squeaked. Then her voice dropped in pitch. She almost purred. "*Hound,* you are magnificent.

You are wonderful. Full command recognition," she reported to Chen and Tinian. *"Hound,"* she purred again, "double-seal that locker and keep ExTen-Dee on guard."

Chen swooped several hundred meters skyward. Wookiees scattered out of the fresh crater dug by the guards' turbolaser blast. Imperials stood along the fences, raining small arms fire on their maddened slaves.

The remaining turbolaser cannon tracked the *Pup.* Chenlambec jinked in all three dimensions, looping back. Closer . . . closer . . . Tinian held her breath . . .

He fired. The tower exploded in a hail of gleaming fragments.

Chenlambec pushed the throttle fully forward, toward open space and the *Hound's Tooth.*

Tinian concentrated on breathing slowly. Just a little farther . . . just a little longer. If Bossk escaped, he'd gas them in an instant. Even a malfunction could still paralyze or kill her.

Wait. Wasn't she unafraid of dying?

She searched her feelings. She had missed Daye so deeply and desperately for so long that no other emotion began to fill her heart-emptiness. But she mattered to Chenlambec. She wanted to protect him in return.

And she mattered to herself. She had talents and skills to contribute to the galactic struggle. The Rebels had lost Daye; if she fought on, she might help compensate for that loss.

I'm sorry, Daye, she murmured as his face sprang into her mind. *I want to be with you—but I'd like to live. You understand, don't you?*

The *Hound* grew on the fore sensor screen.

If she wanted to live, she'd better think through the next few minutes. That allergen, whatever it'd been, still floated all over the *Hound's Tooth.* "Flirt," she called, "something in the *Hound's* air made Chen and me sick. Can you hold Bossk and still do anything about counteracting it?''

Flirt hesitated a moment, then called back, "It's mekebve pollen. Strong histamine reaction in mammals but not reptiles. *Hound* just locked on his full air filtration for me. If you can wait a few hours, it'll clear out.''

"Not on your life," muttered Tinian. She looked around the *Nashtah Pup*. "Chen, what could we use for breath masks?''

He wurfled soft amusement.

"Not for the nerve gas." She punched his shoulder. "But we're going back to a ship full of pollen."

He held up one arm and flicked its long underfur. His suggestion was long and complex.

"Yeah," she exclaimed. "Your fur attracts it like crazy—''

By the time Flirt popped the *Hound's* docking hatch, Chen and Tinian wore makeshift masks knotted from Tinian's black shipsuit sleeves stuffed with Chen's fur. Chen landed the *Pup* inside the *Hound's* docking bay. Instantly, Tinian dove out. Her eyes streamed, but she could breathe. Chen pushed past her and sprinted up the corridor.

Blinking hard, she locked down and sealed the *Pup*, leaving the obah gas canister for later. Then she followed Chen at a mad dash.

Bossk struggled inside one meat locker, bouncing off the energy field and thrashing against interior walls with a Trandoshan's tremendous strength. Chen stood outside the locker, one fist on his hip and the other hand holding his breath mask, laughing hysterically. The huge drone droid had stationed itself at a control board with one arm extended, anchoring the energy field's activation switch "on." The field was transparent, except when Bossk's touch turned it to glimmering sparks.

Chenlambec threw back his head. Tinian covered her ears and grinned as his victory cry rattled bulkheads.

"Nice work, Flirt," Tinian said aloud.

A throaty feminine voice answered. "You're welcome, Tinian."

"Flirt?" Incredulous, she turned a circle in place. Who was this?

"What would you like next?" The voice sounded sultry enough to steam Bakuran butter newts.

"It doesn't sound like you."

The bulkhead laughed in a sexy contralto. "I'm using *Hound*'s voice simulator. Isn't he wonderful?"

Chenlambec answered gruffly, but his blue eyes twinkled over his makeshift mask.

"Will do," Flirt purred. "Next stop, Aida System and Governor Io Desnand. I hear there's a nice reward offered for a certain scaly passenger of ours."

Bossk thrashed. "I will destroy this ship! I will take all of you with me to the Scorekeeper!"

He couldn't, from in there . . . could he?

"I have failsafes everywhere!" He reached overhead and hooked two claws into an overhead panel.

Tinian's chest constricted. "Flirt," she shouted, "be sure the *Hound* heard that! Bossk wants to blow it up!"

"Oh, he did," crooned Flirt. "He just let me remove Bossk from all command circuits."

The Trandoshan villain flung the overhead panel at the energy field. Instantly, he vanished behind an opaque shower of sparks.

"Don't worry," Flirt purred. "We shut down that destruct circuit."

"We?" asked Tinian.

"Hound and I. Who else?"

"Chen," Tinian murmured, rubbing her bare arms, "we have an acquisition to deliver."

•   •   •

It took three of Governor Desnand's stormtroopers wearing power gloves to wrestle Bossk out of the locker. An Imperial in khaki fatigues and a slouch cap handed Tinian a credit chit. "There you are, Madam Hellenika. Forty thousand credits, minus three thousand for our stormtroopers' services."

That sounded like a bargain to Tinian. They stood on a huge, crowded landing platform where Chenlambec had landed the *Hound*. This'd seemed the only way to transfer Bossk into custody. "Three thousand?" she protested for form's sake. "That's robbery! It's—"

"I suggest you leave Aida immediately," answered the Imperial, "before we run a background check on you and your partner. Only Peacekeeping regulations keep you low characters under control. I suspect—"

"Very good, sir." Tinian backed away from the man. "Thank you, sir. Good day." She spun on one heel and sprinted toward the *Hound*'s landing ramp.

Bossk crouched on a prison-cell bench. His claws twitched. He'd tried gouging stripes in these walls, but they were coated with transparisteel.

The stormtrooper outside snapped to attention. Imperial Governor Io Desnand, a tall, plump marshmallow of a human who would not have dared challenge Bossk on equal footing, strode up and stopped outside the force-shielded opening.

An even plumper woman stood beside him. She hung on his arm like a growth, batting false eyelashes full of delicate veins (Bossk half expected them to flutter off and join some swarm of winged insects). "Ooh," she exclaimed. "You were right, Io. He's enormous."

Bossk glowered.

"You ruined my chances for promotion, Bounty Hunter," Desnand said darkly. "Any last requests?"

"Promotion?" Bossk shouted. "What are you talking about? Those Wookiees—"

"Were bait in a trap, Bounty Hunter. Instead of the Rebel fleet, I caught one miserable lizard. At least now I can make good on a promise I made Feebee two years ago." He encircled the woman's shoulders with one arm.

Her bloodthirsty smile chilled Bossk; it made him picture the Scorekeeper wearing a human mask. "I've always wanted a lizard-skin gown," she cooed. "Full length, and only seamless will do, or it's not authentic. Yes, Io." She tilted her head and pressed one fleshy cheek against his hand. "This will be lovely."

Bossk charged the force field. It blew him toes-over-topside against the back wall. "I'm innocent," he cried, springing up to stagger forward. "I had nothing to do with your plan, Desnand! I knew nothing about it. I still know nothing!"

Arm in arm, the pair strolled out of sight.

Bossk stared after them, disbelieving. He was to be . . . skinned? Zeroed? To grace that creature's wardrobe, instead of the Scorekeeper's altar?

He plunged to his knees and started digging. He'd find a way out, retrieve his ship, and continue the Hunt . . . Somehow. . . .

Tinian stretched out in the *Hound*'s port sleeping cabin. The *Hound* was temporarily grounded back on Lomabu III, inside the prison compound. Chen had claimed the starboard cabin, formerly Bossk's. Its bunk was longer and broader than either port bunk. Flirt had transferred command capability to both sleeping cabins. To Chen's surprise (but not Tinian's), Flirt had wailed every time they tried disengaging her from the *Hound*. Finally Chen plugged her in on X10-D's power point and left her there.

She was one happy droid now, with a large, strong

body. All it needed, she claimed, was a soft blue detail job. . . .

Flirt had spent most of the jump back to Lomabu inside the *Hound*'s programming, emerging occasionally to announce that she'd found some amazing new capability: "This ship can change course in the middle of a hyperspace jump! *Hound*, you're magnificent." "*Hound* has an armament circuit with built-in function echoes. I'm not sure how they work, but you could fire both quad guns on full power . . . simultaneously!" "Listen, Tinian. *Hound* knows how to hover suborbital, with full shields to the ventral surface. . . ."

And that was how they had finished off the compound's Imperial overseers. The *Hound* had dropped, hovering, fully shielded, as Chen and Tinian doubled up as gunners. They'd landed inside the new crater, ready to take on prisoners.

But the Wookiees hadn't left any Imperials whole. The sands feasted that day.

This evening, Chenlambec was celebrating offship with his liberated kinfolk. Tinian had solemnly sprinkled a ritual handful of dirt over the pelts Chen buried, then she'd danced three rounds of the circle, gripping his enormous hand on one side and a friendly stranger's on the other; but after that, she simply hadn't been able to keep up with reveling Wookiees.

Tomorrow—or maybe the next day, Tinian guessed from the noise outside—they would squeeze everyone on board and hit hyperspace before Io Desnand could send troops. The *Hound* could only manage a short jump carrying 593 Wookiees, which would be a tremendous burden on life support, but Flirt insisted *Hound* could reach Aida. From there, Chen's Alliance contacts could shuttle passengers to other systems.

He had taken her aside and laid both hands on her head, declaring her apprenticeship fulfilled, asking her to stay on as his partner and friend. She had half a ship now, eighteen thousand credits, and full Hunt status. For the first time in two years, she felt wealthy.

Chenlambec gave away most of his acquisition money. Maybe she should, too. . . .

On the other hand, that Imperial stuffed shirt had called her a low character. She sniffed her second-best black shipsuit, the best one that still had sleeves. Maybe she ought to think about buying some new clothes.

She yawned luxuriously.

She'd decide later.

Winded, Chenlambec dropped out of the circle dance and sat down on an empty stormtrooper helmet. The *Hound* filled the prison yard's center, shining like a smooth, brilliant ice floe under white prison lights. He felt vaguely disloyal about admiring it so keenly. He would miss the *Wroshyr*.

He extended his claws and ran them through feathery fur that dangled from his left forearm.

He didn't think of himself as vain, but he liked his pelt. Right where it was.

Of Possible Futures:
The Tale of Zuckuss
and 4-LOM

by M. Shayne Bell

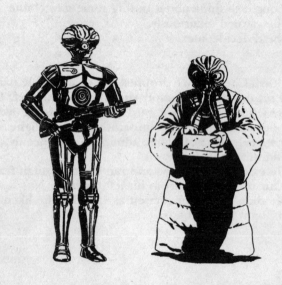

"**D**oes Darth Vader know?" the droid 4-LOM asked Zuckuss, his Gand bounty hunter partner. 4-LOM had asked that same question every 8.37 Standard minutes from the start of Zuckuss's meditation. In two hours they would dock at Darth Vader's flagship to accept an Imperial contract, and they had to know if they were heading into a trap.

Zuckuss did not answer. Evidently he had not yet received intuitive knowledge about Vader and the contract. Zuckuss breathed through the respirator and held his breath in. Then he breathed out, and held his breath out for a moment. 4-LOM noted that it was the 1,057th breath of this meditation. The Gand did not need to breathe often, but deep thinking seemed to require regular respiration.

He had observed that Zuckuss usually received intuitive knowledge between the 1,323rd breath and the 4,369th. Once it had come on the fifty-third: 8.37 minutes into the meditation, but 4-LOM calculated that that was a statistical anomaly. Still, unlike most Gands, Zuckuss maintained a 91.33725 percent chance of being correct in whatever knowledge he gained through meditation: knowledge about where an acquisition might hide, the exact numbers of a group, the intentions of others toward them.

They needed to know, now, Darth Vader's intentions toward them.

If Vader had somehow learned that it was 4-LOM and Zuckuss who had hunted Sector Governor Nardix for the Rebellion, Vader would want revenge. The Rebellion had tried Nardix for crimes against sentients, and the trial had been a great embarrassment to the Empire. The Rebels, for their part, paid a princely sum for Nardix—and that was what 4-LOM and Zuckuss needed more of: credits.

To buy medical care for Zuckuss.

Illegal medical care. Zuckuss was not an old Gand, but he moved like one if he went off the drugs that controlled his pain, and during his respiration cycle he breathed like one: short, fitful breaths that drew air into lungs and esophogeal tissue burned by contact with oxygen after a female human acquisition, stupidly struggling after Zuckuss had hunted her into a dark alley with no exit, pulled off his helmet. 4-LOM secured the acquisition, then tried to help Zuckuss put his helmet back on, but before they could Zuckuss had taken three reflexive breaths of poisonous oxygen.

This was cause for significant embarrassment to Zuckuss, because had he retained sufficient presence of mind, he could have ceased his respiration until a more convenient time.

Parts of his lungs had burned away that day, and what was left functioned poorly. Zuckuss needed new lungs. New lungs could be grown only in illegal—hence, expensive—cloning vats.

So the Empire's credits tempted 4-LOM and Zuckuss with the hope of new lungs.

Another 8.37 minutes passed.

"Does Darth Vader know?" 4-LOM asked.

Again, Zuckuss did not answer.

Zuckuss, deep in meditation, found it difficult to sense Darth Vader's intentions. A swirl of possible galactic futures masked them. Zuckuss always sensed galactic futures when he meditated in hyperspace. It was the ideal place to meditate on the probable course of events in the galaxy. Meditate in a city, and you sense where the actions of its millions of citizens lead it. Meditate in orbit above a planet, and you sense where the cultures of an entire world are heading. But meditate in hyperspace and, no matter what knowledge you meditate for, you first sense the underlying feelings that motivate the majority of sentients and through them glimpse the destiny of the galaxy.

Those feelings, and the futures they could create, had changed. The fabric of the galaxy felt different to Zuckuss.

There was less hope in it, now.

Zuckuss had felt hope ebbing away for many years, but in this meditation Zuckuss sensed, on all the worlds in all the systems he passed, an overwhelming sense of hopelessness. From one world rose the realization of having no place to run; from another, the ache of endless separation; from many worlds the intense pain victims of Imperial torturers felt moments before death.

Yet with this growing lack of hope rose another feeling, constant now in the galaxy. It quickened the Gand's pulse.

He felt the movement of wealth.

The Empire was taxing, extorting, confiscating, and stealing the wealth of its countless citizens on their numberless worlds, creating an unlimited, glittering flow that enriched the Empire's coffers and showered its officials with luxury.

It was this flow Zuckuss and 4-LOM would tap into.

If they were not heading into a trap. Zuckuss still could not intuit Darth Vader's intentions. They lay clouded before him, carefully guarded.

Zuckuss breathed in again, and held his breath in.

The 1,088th breath, 4-LOM noted.

Toryn Farr was the last person to leave the Rebel command center in Echo Base on Hoth. She was Chief Controller there, responsible for communicating orders to the Rebel troops. Princess Leia's final orders had been the ones Toryn had dreaded hearing: "Give the evacuation code," Leia said, "and get to the transport!"

Han pulled Leia down the hallway, and the remaining staff ran after them, carrying any movable piece of equipment they could, while Toryn broadcast the evacuation code: "Disengage! Disengage!" she said. "Begin retreat action!"

She jerked her console free from its connections and rushed with it down the icy passageway toward the transport. Echo Base was collapsing on them. Ice shards pummeled her head and back with each concussive explosion on the surface—explosions that came one after the other. Lights in the passageway flickered and went out. They did not come back on. After a moment of darkness, dim emergency lights glowed to life. Their light was barely enough to run by. She passed a branch of the main tunnel completely choked with tons of collapsed ice.

"The princess went that way!" someone ahead of her said.

Toryn tapped her headset to activate it and accessed the retreat channel just in time to hear Han say he and Leia were still alive. "Han and the princess are alive and heading for the *Falcon,*" she called out to everyone ahead of her.

They hurried on and came to the hangar with its last transport, the *Bright Hope:* their only hope for escape in this rush of retreat—and Toryn stopped in horror at the sight there.

The flight deck around the *Bright Hope* was filled with wounded soldiers. Medical droids moved among them, trying to stop the most seriously wounded from bleeding to death.

And more wounded were being carried in.

We will all die here, Toryn thought, or worse: the Empire will capture us alive. She never once thought that any able-bodied Rebel would desert wounded comrades, and she saw no way to load all the wounded onto the transport before snowtroopers would be upon them. They were already reported in the ice fortress itself.

A blaster shot slammed into the back of the man who stood next to Toryn. He fell dead on the ice, and Toryn and everyone near the tunnel scrambled for cover behind crates stacked by the door.

Snowtroopers—behind them in the corridor!

Toryn returned fire. Only then did she realize she had taken cover behind crates of thermal detonators. Her first thought was to run for safer cover.

But she did not run.

She tore open a crate, activated three grenades, and threw them up the tunnel. The grenades emitted clouds of smoke, and for a few brief seconds she saw the feet of snowtroopers kicking the grenades around the tunnel-floor ice—trying to boot them back out into the hangar.

But they did not have time. The grenades exploded and brought down tons of ice in the tunnel, choking it shut.

And buying the Rebels precious minutes to save their wounded.

"Get these soldiers on board!" she shouted, and she rushed to help carry the wounded to safety and escape.

"Does Darth Vader know?" 4-LOM asked Zuckuss after another 8.37 minutes.

"Yes," Zuckuss said. He straightened his legs and opened his eyes.

4-LOM immediately began programming the ship for a second, desperate jump away from their destination. They could not change course in hyperspace, but their ship could execute a second jump so quickly it would appear for only a brief moment on the Imperial's screens. He calculated that it would be a brief enough appearance for them to escape.

Zuckuss put a hand on the droid's forearm. "This is not necessary," he said.

4-LOM continued his programming. The last four words Zuckuss spoke made no sense—the "logic" of nonmechanical sentients often made no sense to 4-LOM: of course they had to flee to safety.

"Darth Vader knows what Zuckuss and 4-LOM have done, but he does not care," Zuckuss said, as usual referring to himself in third person. "The acquisitions he sends us to hunt matter more to him—to the Empire—than one hundred Governors Nardix: and the Empire needs our help. They know that. Zuckuss and 4-LOM are safe in accepting this contract and the

Empire's credits, for now. But if success is not achieved . . ."

Zuckuss did not finish his sentence—an annoying habit of most nonmechanical sentients. It made accurate communication difficult. 4-LOM quickly computed seventy-six variant endings to that sentence, all with a probability of better than 92.78363 percent of being what Zuckuss might have gone on to say, all predicting the Empire's wrath and their doom.

Our probable futures have shrunk to this, Zuckuss thought: he and 4-LOM had this one chance to redeem themselves. If they succeeded, the Empire would forget their involvement with Governor Nardix. If they failed, the Empire would stop at nothing to exact its revenge. He and 4-LOM would have to use all their combined skills to hide for a time, create new identities, and survive.

Zuckuss smiled. Days lived under threats like these were days worth living.

Among the last soldiers waiting to be carried aboard the transport, Toryn found Samoc, her younger sister. Samoc was one of the Rebel's best snowspeeder pilots. That her ship had gone down meant the fight outside was truly horrific. Samoc's red hair was mostly burned away. Her face and hands were burned. No one had treated her or helped her at all, except to bring her here.

She was conscious. She blinked up at Toryn, through lids that now had no eyelashes, and she tried to reach a hand to Toryn.

"Imperial walker shot me down—" she whispered.

A blaster shot slammed into the ceiling and showered them with ice: snowtroopers, rushing into the docking bay itself from across the ice fields outside the fortress.

Toryn picked up her sister and ran with her to board

the transport. "It must hurt to move you like this," she said. "But there's no other way!"

Shots echoed around them.

They were among the last to board. The docking bay now lay empty of wounded Rebels, but scattered with tons of vital equipment abandoned to make room for the unanticipated casualties.

The hatches closed despite explosions of snowtrooper fire. The six X-wing fighters waiting to escort the transport took off, and the transport itself blasted out of the hangar and past the atmosphere to the black cold of space.

We waited too long to take off, Toryn thought to herself. Our compassion for the wounded will have killed us all.

She found one empty seat near the hatch and strapped Samoc into it. She knelt to hang on to Samoc, and braced herself against the shock of hits their ship was certain to take before they could make the jump to hyperspace.

Imperial Star Destroyers filled space above Hoth, she knew, waiting to attack Rebel ships.

4-LOM and Zuckuss exited hyperspace into the Hoth system and found themselves in the middle of battle. A Rebel transport the bounty hunters' computer identified as the *Bright Hope* streaked past them, and one of the transport's six escort X-wing fighters fired at them. The concussion of the shot shook the bounty hunter's ship.

"Raising shields," 4-LOM said.

No one had warned them of the possibility of battle at the rendezvous point. But then, no one had told them accepting an Imperial contract would be easy, either.

Their screens showed a confusion of ships, Rebel and Imperial, scattered throughout the solar system. But the Rebel ships were blinking off-screen, disappearing into hyperspace—full retreat. "Zuckuss tracks sixteen destroyed Rebel transports," the Gand said.

He did not have to add: within close range. They could see them out their viewports—shattered hulks showering sparks into space, lights shining from a few still-intact viewports. The bounty hunters quickly plotted the careening trajectories of the derelict ships so they could fly past them.

"Let's give our Imperial friends a seventeenth ship," Zuckuss said.

Such a gift would salve the wound of Governor Nardix.

"Plotting attack trajectory," 4-LOM said.

They sped in pursuit of the *Bright Hope*. Their screens showed no other transports leaving the surface of Hoth, only the occasional X-wing fighter: acquisitions too small to impress the Imperials, acquisitions certainly not worth pursuing. The *Bright Hope* was apparently the last big ship attempting retreat. It was late in the battle to attempt such an escape.

The bounty hunters quickly closed on the transport. It was smaller than the other downed transports, but still bulky and slow—slower, at least, than the bounty hunters' lean ship. The transport probably carried the last support staff from the Rebel base, Zuckuss thought: a fine gift for the Imperials.

"Approaching firing range," 4-LOM announced. He pressed buttons that activated the weapons systems. Both 4-LOM and Zuckuss prepared to fire. An Imperial Super Star Destroyer—the largest ship Zuckuss had ever seen—was also closing on the transport. The crew of the Rebel transport itself must have been working frantically to plot retreat coordinates and disappear into hyperspace. It was a race to see which crew—Imperial, Rebel, or bounty hunter—would reach its goals first.

Just before the bounty hunters' instruments confirmed firing range, intuition told Zuckuss to fire, and he did. His shot exploded into the transport, taking out the entire forward command deck. The transport would never reach hyperspace now, however close it had been to that jump. The Star Destroyer blasted into it from the other side and laid open three entire decks.

The six X-wing fighters escorting the transport disappeared into hyperspace, blinking off-screen one by one. The pilots in them saw they could do nothing more here. The ship they guarded was destroyed. They could not even attempt to rescue survivors, if any.

"Incoming Imperial message," 4-LOM announced.

After a moment of static, the bounty hunters picked up the crisp, precise voice of an Imperial controller on the star destroyer. ". . . arrival was expected, and on time. Your assistance in destroying the Rebel transport will be relayed to Imperial command. Proceed to the in-system rendezvous point."

Coordinates appeared on screen.

"In the system's asteroid belt?" Zuckuss said.

4-LOM studied the coordinates. "Barely outside it," he said.

Yes, no one had told them this would be an easy contract to accept.

4-LOM piloted the ship to the rendezvous point. Zuckuss hurried to shoot himself full of drugs that would keep his pain manageable in front of Imperials and other bounty hunters. He could show no weakness then.

4-LOM allowed himself a few moments to try to calculate how Zuckuss had known when to fire—before their instruments had registered firing range. The instruments were functioning perfectly. 4-LOM had checked them himself before takeoff, and he checked them again now.

"Intuition," Zuckuss muttered as he walked painfully away to his medicines.

The concept of intuition fascinated 4-LOM. Other bounty hunters called Zuckuss the "uncanny one" because of his intuition: an intuition so often completely correct.

4-LOM wanted that same ability. That was one reason he worked with Zuckuss: to observe him, to learn from him. 4-LOM felt confident he could program himself to do anything a living being could do, if he had all necessary information.

Hadn't he learned to steal? Hadn't he learned to value wealth and its power like any other nonmechanical sentient? Surely he could learn to meditate to develop intuition and function much like Zuckuss. Then he would be unstoppable indeed.

It had always been like this for 4-LOM, ever since he had overridden his own programming to become a thief, then a bounty hunter—4-LOM had always worked to upgrade himself, program new skills into his "mind," challenge the boundaries of what a droid could be.

It had started innocently enough: he had worked aboard the passenger liner *Kuari Princess* as a valet and human-cyborg relations specialist, and he began to worry about the safety of valuables the humans brought on board. They were so careless with them. Even an incompetent thief had chances again and again—each day—to take all the credits and jewels he could carry. 4-LOM decided it was his duty to analyze the many ways each item of value might be stolen to anticipate the actions of thieves and foil them.

On the next flight, Dom Pricina booked passage. She was exactly the kind of human 4-LOM dreaded: careless, wealthy beyond avarice, possessor of valuables she had not worked to acquire but which had been handed down to her. She owned, and traveled with, one jewel of great price: the Ankarres Sapphire, a jewel fabled for its supposed healing powers—humans and other sentients traveled uncounted distances to touch that jewel to their foreheads and be cured of disease and injury. Dom Pricina charged them dearly for each touch.

That night, Dom Pricina complained loudly at dinner, between her third and fourth dessert courses, that the bracelet she wore, made of five hundred rare pink Corellian jiangs, was too heavy: it made lifting her fork to her mouth a chore, not a pleasure. So she took off the bracelet and set it next to her wineglass.

And left it there when she finally rose from the table.

4-LOM quickly returned it to her, and she thanked him and even hugged him. In the morning she left two diamond toe rings on the marble shelf next to the steam bath. "Oh, 4-LOM," she panted when he returned them, "How can I ever thank you? Would you take them and have them enlarged one—no, two—full sizes? I find it harder and harder to put them on my toes. I'll have to stop eating desserts for breakfast—that's it! That should keep my toes at a manageable size." When 4-LOM returned from the ship's jeweler he found her necklace of emeralds and garnets dropped in the passage outside her door.

She was incompetent, 4-LOM reasoned. She should not be allowed to own things she would not care for. 4-LOM grew increasingly concerned for the Ankarres Sapphire: her most valuable jewel, and one that meant a great deal to many people. He calculated the likely time and place of the jewel's theft, if it were to take place on this flight, then surreptitiously substituted a cheap synth-sapph with a tracking device embedded in it for the real jewel—moments before the theft took place. Two Corellian scoundrels did steal the "sapphire" exactly when 4-LOM calculated someone would, but the synth-sapph emitted an ultrasonic distress call that brought help—unwanted help—rushing to the Corellians.

Only then was the theft discovered. Dom Pricina never missed the Ankarres Sapphire till the captain of the *Kuari Princess* himself returned "it" to her. 4-LOM stood nearby, the real jewel suspended in a black pouch hung at his side. Dom Pricina recognized at once that the synth-sapph was a fake. She rushed to her room and discovered that the real jewel was missing. She sobbed and begged anyone who listened to help her find that jewel.

4-LOM reasoned that he should return the sapphire at once. He had, after all, stopped an unfortunate crime and thus successfully completed an entire program sequence of his own devising.

But other programs flooded into his brain: Dom Pricina *was* careless. Most humans were careless. They did not properly value or guard the wondrous things they could possess. Surely he should guard the sapphire a while longer. 4-LOM studied the sapphire whenever he found himself alone. Its facets intrigued him. They sparkled in the dimmest light. Once he touched the sapphire to his own forehead, but felt nothing unusual: it was a beautiful stone held against his metal faceplate, nothing more. It might cure sick humans, he reasoned, but he, a droid, could expect nothing from it.

Still, he did not return the jewel. It was never discovered. No one suspected 4-LOM of the theft. For months afterward, 4-LOM stole from the passengers he "served," telling himself he had to help protect things of value. But he found the thefts exciting.

Thievery was a very human act, after all, and he suddenly understood its pleasures. Doing it required 4-LOM to create elegant, complicated programs that bypassed all his ethical—all his droid—programming. Little by little, 4-LOM reprogrammed himself to find crime exciting, to value the possession of things, to despise careless nonmechanical sentients. He soon grew bored with the now predictable options for crime aboard the *Kuari Princess* and jumped ship at Darlyn

Boda. In that planet's steamy, criminal underground, 4-LOM sold most of the jewels he had stolen, left the others on consignment, and began a life devoted entirely to crime and its excitement.

He was so successful, he calculated, that an alliance with Jabba the Hutt became inevitable. When the offer did come, 4-LOM quickly accepted. Jabba had him fitted with deadly combat weapons and the programs that ran them in return for 4-LOM's services as a bounty hunter. Working with Zuckuss was the next logical step. From a careful study of Zuckuss, 4-LOM planned to learn the ways of intuition.

He carefully stored all visual and auditory input from and around Zuckuss in the moments just before and after he fired the decisive shot at the retreating Rebel transport—the moments of intuition. 4-LOM would study them, with all the other data on Zuckuss's intuition he had collected from years of observation.

It was more raw data obtained in his quest for understanding. Understanding would come to him, he believed. One day the methods of intuition would become apparent, and he would use them.

He wondered what new skill he would work to acquire then?

Darth Vader's black ship, the *Executor*, came within visual range, and 4-LOM initiated docking procedures. Even as he worked, subprocessors in his artificial mind computed the answer to his last question. Suddenly he knew what skill he would pursue after he mastered intuition.

It was the only logical answer, after all.

He would learn the ways of the Force. Its dark side would be a great ally to him in his work.

Once away from 4-LOM, alone with his pain, Zuckuss stopped and held on to a handrail. The pain in his lungs was growing much worse, more difficult to control. The oxygen burns could not heal.

He knew he had to hide this weakness from the other bounty hunters, and especially from Darth Vader. But, he realized standing there, not moving because of his pain—he was hiding the worsening extent of his injuries from 4-LOM, too.

Zuckuss was surprised 4-LOM had stayed with him at all after he got hurt. 4-LOM told him calmly one day, in his droid's logical, unemotional voice, that he estimated other bounty hunters would take 1.5 minutes to complete plans to exploit Zuckuss's weakness and draw off their clients—or attempt to steal their ship and equipment and any remnants of fortune—should they gain knowledge of Zuckuss's troubles.

Zuckuss never asked, but he was sure the droid had also calculated their diminishing chances for success in Hunts for bounty—Hunts in which 4-LOM had to do more and more of the work. If they were not successful in this Hunt, if they did not get the necessary resources to buy new lungs, Zuckuss believed his injuries would finally become so debilitating that 4-LOM would calculate no further profit in maintaining their partnership. The droid would leave. On that day, Zuckuss told himself, he would ask 4-LOM to calculate his chances for survival alone. He would want to know the odds to prepare himself. He would have only days, perhaps, but it comforted him to think that, under those circumstances, the injuries that ate away at his life would never kill him.

Zuckuss made his way to his bunk and his medicines. He gave himself a shot of pain killer, then sat on his bunk. He felt the drug race through his system, numbing his chest and lungs. Suddenly he could breathe the sweet ammonia in his ship a little easier. How he missed the ammonia mists of his own gas planet. For three Standard centuries, his family had worked there as findsmen: bounty hunters who meditated on the location of acquisitions and Hunted them in the swirling mists of Gand.

But the Empire took over Gand and brought in their excellent scanning equipment. It looked as if the time-honored tradition of findsmen would die. They were no longer needed. The Empire tracked acquisitions through the mists without help and without intuition.

But the profession did not die. Zuckuss and a few others took it off Gand into the wider galaxy—a place so wild, so vast, that intuition was all that could make a path across it to acquisitions no scanners could locate, all that could read the intentions of alien races, all that could give hints of the future and the rewards or trials its multitudinous paths led to, the ends everyone and everything rushed toward.

Zuckuss meditated, at times, on who would eventually kill him.

He knew it was a question of *who* would kill him, not what. The mists surrounding his own mortality remained mostly unreadable, though in his meditations he had had hints—and none involved accident, or mechanical failure, or even the injuries to his lungs that brought him such pain. Another being would bring him death.

Zuckuss had ruled out 4-LOM. His long-standing partner did not want to kill him, and would not when they separated. But twice Zuckuss had sensed that Jabba the Hutt would grow impatient with his weakness, if he discovered it, and attempt to feed him to his Rancor. That was a future he preferred to avoid. He sensed that he would not be killed in the mists of his own world, however much he missed Gand and would have liked to die there. He would die somewhere else. He wondered for a time if Darth Vader would kill him, but he knew he had nothing to fear from Vader, at least for now.

When he could, Zuckuss stood up and injected himself with stimulants, then other drugs to boost the quickness of his mind and counteract the dulling effects of the pain killer. He heard the first mechanical sounds of docking, and the ship jerked about.

He hurried to pull on the suit that protected him from oxygen and double-checked its seals. He could afford no more burns. He pulled on old robes, then hid knives in his boots, ammonia bombs—lethal to oxygen breathers—up his sleeves. He strapped a fully charged blaster at his side, in full view. Then he started for the hatch. He heard 4-LOM already walking toward it.

Zuckuss walked easier now. He breathed without pain. His stride soon carried him with all the seeming confidence and strength he had ever had, and for a moment he almost forgot the weakness he worked so hard to conceal.

He realized, then, walking toward the hatch and a meeting with Darth Vader, that he worked hard to hide his injuries and their implications from one other person.

He realized that, when he could, he hid them from himself.

When Toryn Farr regained consciousness, the transport was cold. Very cold.

But there was still air. They could still breathe.

For now.

Some of them would live, for a time.

Toryn pushed herself up off the deck and looked around. Dim emergency lights glowed from the ceiling above her, but stopped maybe three meters up the aisle from where she sat. It was dark past that point. The readouts of instrument panels glowed and blinked in that blackness. Out the viewport, she saw stars roll by. What was left of the *Bright Hope* was spinning out of control and heading for who knew what.

And there would be no rescue.

No one from the Rebellion could come back for them.

When the Empire realized there were survivors on this ship and came for them, they would be interrogated, tortured, and executed. The Empire would pull in every ship to take prisoners, access remaining computer systems to steal information: but especially to capture intact droids to download their databases. The Rebels did not have much time to find a way to save themselves, if they could, and to erase all computer systems and surviving droids if they could not.

Samoc moaned. She was still alive. A cupboard had broken away from the wall just ahead of them and smashed into the deck, spilling brown bantha-wool blankets and white pillows. Toryn took a blanket and wrapped Samoc in it. Samoc's burns still had not been treated. She was shaking.

Shock, Toryn realized. Samoc was in shock.

"Hang on, Samoc," Toryn said.

"This goes on and on," Samoc whispered.

"What do you mean?" Toryn asked. She leaned closer to hear Samoc's answer.

"We're still alive. The Imperials are having a hard time killing us."

They had downed Samoc's snowspeeder, but she had lived. They barely missed shooting them in the hangar—then they blew up most of the transport, but still they were alive.

"I'm wondering how the Imperials will finally do it," Samoc said.

Toryn stood up. She did not want to think about that. Soldiers in a war often die. Every Rebel knew that when he or she joined the Rebellion. Still, you always expected someone else to die: not your friends, not your sister—not you, yourself. Toryn and Samoc, for all their battles, had never been this close to death.

Toryn reached down to pull the blanket a little tighter around Samoc. "I'll go look for something to

put on your burns," she said. "And I'll look for something we might do to save ourselves. Who knows?"

Samoc tried to smile.

Other people moaned around them. The ship had
been so crowded. There were probably many survivors
on it, Toryn thought. She took blankets to two other
people, then hurried to the instruments she saw blinking in the darkness ahead of her. One was an old-model
hacker droid, adapted to record freight shipped or unloaded. Now, though, it was connected to the central
computer, if *that* still existed in any coherent state, and
from the central computer she could get information
she needed.

"Droid," she addressed it, "access the central computer and determine whether we are in danger of further attack."

"Access restricted. Prepare for retinal scan
preauthorization," the droid said.

Toryn stared into a bright light that shone out of the
hacker droid's face. She hoped the central computer's
memory was intact enough to recognize her, grant her
the necessary authority, and do what she asked it to do.

"Authorization through level eight systems granted,
Controller Toryn Farr," the droid said. "But I cannot
answer your question. Data on surrounding ships, if
any, is unavailable."

The scanners were destroyed or offline.

"How much of the ship is intact?" she asked.

"Freight decks one and two completely intact. Passenger deck one is 17.4 percent intact."

"How many survivors are there?"

"Data on survivors is unavailable."

"How long will air last on the intact decks?"

"Data on oxygen supplies is unavailable."

"Are we on a collision course with—anything: other
ships, Hoth, the star of this system?"

"Data on the ship's present course is unavailable."

So much that they needed—information, repair

equipment, air, probably—would be unavailable. Toryn thought for a moment for a question she could ask that the droid or the computer might be able to answer.

"Are any escape pods functional and accessible from the intact decks?" she asked.

"Three escape pods are accessible from the intact portion of passenger deck one; however, the pods cannot be fired."

At last some information she could use. "Why can't the pods be fired?"

"Data on why the pods cannot be fired is unavailable."

She had to get up there to find out.

"Attempt to compute answers to all my previous questions," she told the hacker droid. "I'm going to investigate the escape pods, and I will check in with you again shortly for answers."

She had to take charge of the situation and start to marshal the resources at hand. It was Rebel procedure, in a situation like this, for anyone with rank to assume he or she was in command till they met someone with higher rank.

So she took charge.

For now, she thought. Just for now. Surely someone else with higher rank had survived to help find a way to save everyone alive on the ship.

She set off down the dark passage. The metal walls were colder to the touch now. The ship was cooling quickly. Freezing to death was supposedly one of the easiest ways to die, she told herself.

Which was how she and the other survivors might die if they had to stay on this ship *or* if she found a way to launch the escape pods—because where would they take the pods, except back to Hoth? And how would they survive on an ice world—if they could get there and if the Empire didn't shoot them down first?

Find the pods, she told herself, find out if they can be launched—then find a way to survive on Hoth.

The dark passage was crowded with wounded Rebels, and their dead. She kept stumbling over people and bodies. "I'm trying to find a way to help us," she told the people moaning in the darkness.

She saw four small, round lights shining yellow farther ahead. Another console, she thought, but the lights got closer and closer to her—then she heard metal feet on the metal deck.

Droids. She was seeing the eyes of droids.

They turned on brighter lights and shined them on her—one droid had a light that shone from its forehead, the other carried a glowtube. They both carried medical supplies. "I am surgeon droid Two-Onebee," the tallest droid said, the one with the light shining out of its forehead. "And this is my medical assistant, Effour-Seven. We are treating the wounded."

"There are so many," Toryn said. "Do you have any idea how many?"

"We have encountered forty-seven nonmechanical survivors so far," Two-Onebee said. "Apparently we are the only intact droids."

She told them what she was doing, took the glowtube from Effex-Seven, and set off down the passage. But after a moment she stopped and looked back at the droids.

"Two-Onebee," she called. "One of our pilots, Samoc Farr, is strapped in a chair at the end of this passage. She has been terribly burned. Her burns are not treated, and she is going into shock. See what you can do for her."

"Effour-Seven contains excellent burn-treatment programs," Two-Onebee answered her. "I will send him at once."

Effour-Seven started off while Toryn watched. She knew it would pass all other wounded Rebels, however much they needed help themselves, to go directly to Samoc. But she did not amend its orders. If there was a way to survive, she wanted Samoc to survive. Her mother had made her promise that she would take care of Samoc—the youngest in their family, always the most beautiful, the happiest, the one with the most promise. She hoped sending help directly to Samoc would not hurt anyone else.

Toryn turned back into the blackness ahead. The droids had counted forty-seven survivors. She had passed twenty or thirty on this deck alone. The escape pods, if they could launch them, would carry six people apiece.

Eighteen people from a battered ship that held many times more that. She froze for a moment, unable to imagine how they would decide who would go if they could launch the pods. But she made herself start moving again.

Find the pods first, she told herself. Find a way to launch them. Then find other options for all of us they will leave behind, if you can.

Darth Vader had assigned four other bounty hunters besides 4-LOM and Zuckuss to this hunt—and each bounty hunter was furious because of it. None had been told other bounty hunters would be involved. 4-LOM could not calculate Darth Vader's reasons for hiring six bounty hunters. The group included Dengar, an angry Corellian with a damaged head and without any impressive Hunts to his record; IG-88, an assassin droid, though 4-LOM had been under the impression that Darth Vader wanted the acquisitions he was sending them after alive; Bossk, a renowned Hunter of Wookiees; and, most impressively, Boba Fett. It was an odd assemblage.

4-LOM calculated that Vader was sending them after odd—and extremely wily—acquisitions. He searched his Imperial Most Wanted list, with its thousands of names and files, but found no one individual who should require such measures to Hunt down.

The bounty hunters stood together in a waiting room, eyeing each other and not speaking. Bounty hunter law forbade killing another bounty hunter, but 4-LOM calculated a 63.276 percent chance that at least three of the six bounty hunters there were considering murdering other members of the group to increase their own chances of success in this Hunt.

It was imperative that Zuckuss show no weakness now. 4-LOM studied his partner. Zuckuss stood fully erect, alert, breathing easily in his helmet. No one could detect his injuries, 4-LOM calculated.

Vader summoned them at once. The bounty hunters strode quickly down corridors, almost outpacing their guide. Imperials of all ranks made way for them—and stared after them. Processors in 4-LOM's mind analyzed the faces and voices of the people he passed, matching them to the Imperial Most Wanted List and his guild's list of posted bounties. 4-LOM always did this when he walked through crowds of people. The odds of a chance encounter with someone worth credits were low, and in the short time it took his mind to match a face to a posted bounty a person *could* disappear—but he had taken seven acquisitions off streets that way: unexpected, but welcome, credits earned while Hunting other prey. Wouldn't it be interesting to unmask a Rebel spy here, on this flagship, and turn him or her over to Darth Vader?

But 4-LOM identified no Rebels in those corridors. All sentients present were apparently actual Imperials. He picked up most of their whispered comments: "Those bounty hunters are carrying blasters in the open!" "Who called *them* here?" "The Republic tried to control their kind, but the Empire should have abolished them."

It amused 4-LOM to think what consternation the mere presence of six bounty hunters caused among professional soldiers—supposedly the Empire's best and most fearless. 4-LOM calculated that fear of six bounty hunters affected the actions of 98.762 percent of all Imperials they passed in that corridor.

Fear was a valuable feeling to instill in acquisitions one Hunted: it clouded their logic and made most nonmechanical sentients actually run—a predictable, if usually fatal, choice. The instinctual programming inside nonmechanical sentients—the desire to flee or fight when confronted with danger—still haunted them, still made it difficult for them to react with complete, calm logic.

But fear was not a good quality to note in one's allies. It meant they had weaknesses anyone without fear could exploit.

4-LOM questioned the wisdom of alliances with the fearful, and he questioned his alliance with these Imperials now. They were unimpressive allies, at best.

But, of course, they had credits.

Zuckuss stumbled only once on the way to Vader. 4-LOM helped Zuckuss stand.

"You fawning, motley-minded Imperials—can't you even keep deckplates nailed down!" 4-LOM yelled at the soldiers making way for them.

None of the other bounty hunters broke stride. None seemed to notice Zuckuss stumble. His and Zuckuss's secret remained a secret, 4-LOM calculated. The walk soon ended. They arrived at the flight deck, and Darth Vader strode at once to meet them.

Imperial officers standing nearby whispered together about the bounty hunters before Vader reached them. "Bounty hunters—we don't need that scum!" 4-LOM heard one officer say to another.

4-LOM calculated contempt in that comment, but he calculated that fear motivated contempt 62.337 percent of the time. Contempt and fear are closely allied. So fear was probably present even here—even on the flight deck of Darth Vader's flagship. It disgusted 4-LOM. He began to calculate weaknesses he could exploit in these Imperials.

Vader started speaking before he even reached the bounty hunters. He had no fear. "There will be a substantial reward for the one who finds the *Millennium Falcon*. You are free to use any methods necessary—but I want them alive! No disintegrations."

Vader turned back at once to his business at hand. The bounty hunters scattered to their ships.

It was Han Solo—they were being sent after Han Solo!

4-LOM could calculate reasons, now, for Darth Vader to have called each of the bounty hunters assembled here. He programmed a set of microprocessors in his mind to calculate each bounty hunter's chance of capturing Solo and his companions, whoever *they* were.

Zuckuss stopped in the doorway and turned around. 4-LOM did not know why. It was illogical to dawdle in front of Imperials. 4-LOM turned around to see what had caused this odd behavior in his partner and saw Darth Vader looking at them.

Zuckuss bowed. Vader turned away. Zuckuss and 4-LOM started back down the corridor.

4-LOM did not have to ask Zuckuss how he had known Vader was looking at them. Intuition had told him. And he knew why Vader had looked at them: acknowledgment that he knew about their involvement with Governor Nardix, a subtle warning to succeed in this venture or face Vader again under different circumstances.

4-LOM knew these things without calculating them. The knowledge was suddenly present in his mind.

In that moment, intuition began to assemble itself into a process in 4-LOM's circuitry. All the variables were not in place. He did not understand it completely, but he began to sense the beginnings of a grand equation inside him: the equation of intuition.

Once he had that, he would have intuition itself.

4-LOM felt himself on the verge of accomplishment—the way he felt just before he laid hands on an

acquisition he had Hunted, or the way he felt the exact
moment he reached out for a jewel he had long worked
to steal.

Imperials ran after them, asking what they needed.
Could they provide fuel? Weapons? Anything at all that
might help them succeed in the mission Darth Vader
had sent them on. Credits? Do you need credits?

Yes, they required vast sums of them.

And 4-LOM did not hesitate to ask for it, in the form
of portable items of value stored on their ship, not in
electronic credits that could be seized. In their fear, the
Imperials rushed to give them what they wanted.

4-LOM's calculations on the bounty hunters' probable success ended.

He knew who had the best chance of capturing Han
Solo.

He and Zuckuss did.

His calculations indicated that. The other bounty
hunters had various skills and abilities, but none had
what Zuckuss brought to this Hunt.

None of them had intuition.

That gave Zuckuss and 4-LOM an invaluable edge.
Solo himself represented an interesting combination of
logic and intuition—which meant he and Zuckuss were
ideally suited to Hunt him.

As he walked toward the ship, 4-LOM decided to do
one thing that would give them an *additional* edge in
the Hunt for Solo.

He would attempt intuition himself.

What was left of passenger level one had no lights, not
even dim emergency lights. Toryn shined her glowtube
out the viewport in the containment shield that had
crashed down to stop depressurization. The hull of the
ship past that point had exploded away. She saw stars
reeling as the ship turned, then Hoth itself, far away,

shining so bright and white she could almost not look at it, then more stars.

Then bodies. A few bodies lying still.

The containment shield had not saved many lives on that deck. The depressurization had been quick—explosive—and it had blown most people out into space.

Toryn turned away quickly and started down the passage behind her. But after a moment she stopped and made herself go back. She looked through the viewport till Hoth reappeared, and she noted the time on her chrono. When Hoth came back around, she noted the time, again: four Standard minutes, forty-three Standard seconds. She had the beginnings of an equation on the rotation of what was left of the ship. It could come in handy. In the next few hours, any bit of information about their situation could come in handy.

She hurried down the passage. There were lights ahead, from one, maybe two, glowtubes, casting dark shadows on the walls and ceiling. She found seven people at work on the escape pods. They had torn up the deckplates in front of the pods and were working in the crawlspace there.

"Power couplings tore loose in the attack," one told her.

"If we can reconnect them to the emergency power supplies, we can launch the pods," someone else said.

Toryn shined her light on the escape pods. They stood in a row there. All the viewports were dark.

"Can you shine your light here?" someone called to her.

Toryn hurried to help with the work. It was cold work. Toryn could see her breath now. The tools were cold to handle.

"This should do it—" one of the men below her said.

The emergency lights snapped on around the passage edges. The small, round doors to the pods were suddenly backlit with green, and bright light shone out the viewport in each door, too bright to look at.

Then all the lights snapped off.

"Of all the—!" someone muttered in the sudden darkness. Toryn had to sit down on a stack of torn up deckplating, disappointed.

"The power cells on this level may be damaged," someone said.

"We may have to route power up from the lower decks—Toryn, you say both decks below us are intact?"

Someone hit something, and the lights flared back on.

Everyone looked at each other and laughed.

Toryn hurried to one of the pods. Its readouts said it was functioning perfectly. They could fire it as soon as they were ready. "Pod one completely operable," she said.

"Same here," someone said at pod two.

"Pod three, operable status."

Everyone looked at each other again. No one knew how to start the next part of the process. No one knew how to decide who would get the chance to go. Toryn outranked everyone there. She realized it was her duty to start making decisions and that the others expected her to do it.

"I got a count of at least sixty-seven survivors on freight deck one," Toryn said. "I could not get a count on deck two, but there are survivors there. I heard them."

They could all add in the eight of them standing there. More than seventy-five people had survived on this ship. The pods could carry away eighteen.

To an uncertain future.

If the pods made it to Hoth, the people in them would have to find ways to survive on an ice world without adequate supplies, fight off the wampa ice creatures that would Hunt them, evade capture by Imperial forces who would surely Hunt them.

If they got to Hoth.

The Empire could shoot down the pods first.

"Is the battle still going on out there?" Toryn asked.

No one knew.

"Let's split up," she said. "Find different viewports and conduct a visual reconnaissance. Report back here in ten Standard minutes."

Ten minutes would let the ship roll around twice. They could get a good look at space around them.

Everyone rushed down passages and into rooms, looking for viewports. Toryn found herself back at the viewport in the attack door. She grabbed the comlink at her waist and contacted a dedicated hacker droid mounted to the console in the wall. "Droid," she said. "This is Toryn Farr. Have you calculated answers to my last questions?"

"Information on possible further attacks on this ship, the total number of survivors, the estimated duration of air supplies, and the ship's course remain unavailable."

"Are you connected to any functioning exterior sensors feeding you any kind of information whatsoever?"

"No."

"Do you have access to any data on air supplies whatsoever?"

"No."

Toryn had heard no air being pumped through the ship. "If we estimate one-hundred survivors, how long could they live on just the air present on the intact decks?"

"4.38 Standard hours."

"How much time has passed since the attack?"

"1.29 Standard hours."

They had maybe three hours of air.

"I have a count of sixty-seven survivors on freight deck one. There are eight of us on this deck, an indeterminate number on freight deck two. Factor those numbers into future calculations."

She saw no sign of battle in the sector of space she hurried to observe: no pinpoints of light that would be explosions, no Imperial ships moving against the backdrop of stars or Hoth itself. It was almost as if the battle had never taken place. The system seemed utterly quiet.

But wait. She gripped handles on the attack door and squinted at the space just coming into view as the ship turned.

Lights. There were lights there, moving in space. Three clusters of them—

Ships. Wrecked Rebel ships. The clusters of lights were viewports glowing in them. They were careening along together in a ragged line.

Surely there were survivors on those ships, too. She ached for them. She wondered what they were doing to try to save themselves.

Just as the wrecked ships dropped out of sight, Toryn caught sight of a brighter light *moving* toward the wrecked ships.

Self propelled. Functioning.

An Imperial Star Destroyer.

They were starting the mop-up. She was seeing them pull in the first wreck for its survivors, droids, information.

In a short time they would be at what was left of this ship.

Toryn hurried back to the pods and met the others just returning. Some had seen wrecked ships, too. The count varied between Toryn's three and fourteen, maybe more. Others had seen the Star Destroyer heading toward the wrecks.

"If we hurry, we can fire the pods before the Imperials get here," Toryn said. "If we fire while the Star Destroyer is occupied with a wreck, the pods have half a chance of making Hoth."

"We should send those in best shape," someone

said. "They need to be in good shape to survive down there."

"Some need to be in good shape, certainly," Toryn said, "but we should assume eventual rescue of anyone who reaches Hoth and consider sending those who can help the Rebellion most—even if they are hurt now. We've got to find out who's left on this ship, and we've got to find out fast." She turned and spoke to the hacker droid. "I encountered two medical droids on freight deck one. Contact them and have them download all information on survivors into your databanks. I want as complete a list of survivors—including droids—as you can give me when I check back in five minutes."

"At once," the droid said.

"I want everyone here to speak your names. Droid, add these names to the list you are compiling. Rory," she said to a man she knew, "you start."

Rory, Seito, Bindu, Darklighter, Crimmins, Sala Natu, Meghan Rivers.

"Rory," Toryn said when everyone finished, "get to a viewport and watch that Star Destroyer. See how long it takes it to strip down one of the wrecks and move on to the next. The rest of us will climb down to freight deck 2 to see who we can find there. All of you keep your eyes open for cold weather gear and bring it back here."

Toryn led the way—on a run—to the ladder to the deck below. As she passed the viewport in the containment shield, she saw Hoth rolling by again.

That planet had never looked so beautiful to her.

It shined with hope.

Zuckuss received intuitive knowledge 2.11 Standard hours into his latest meditation.

He knew the rough coordinates of where Han Solo would go, if he could: he would go to the Rebel's rendezvous point. He knew why. It was not to regroup with them after the retreat. He carried passengers—a woman and a droid—vital to the Rebellion's success. Solo wanted to deliver them safely there.

And Zuckuss knew where the Rebellion had gone—where they had been forced to flee.

The thought staggered him. He stayed in his meditation for some time after the intuition came, trying to verify it—and what he had learned seemed more and more correct.

The Rebels had left the galaxy.

They had gone to a point above the galactic plane, far from any stars—from all places where the Empire might track them. The Empire had left them nowhere else to run as an army. He guessed how truly desperate the Rebellion was, then. Ascending up out of the galaxy's gravity well was no easy task. Many ships could not make such a trip. There would be losses in addition to those suffered here. The Empire must have been close to Hunting the Rebels into extinction. That they took this chance spoke of their desperation—but also of their courage and determination to regroup and keep fighting.

These were worthy foes, indeed.

After he and 4-LOM captured Han Solo and his companions, Zuckuss thought, he would honor them. He would still deliver them to the Imperials, but until that moment he would accord them every honor. They deserved honor in their defeat.

Zuckuss slowly brought himself back to awareness of the ship around him: his pilot's chair, the instrument panel in front of him, the hiss of ammonia through the recirculation system. He opened his eyes and stretched—and coughed and coughed. He could not stop coughing for a time. Blood came up. He injected himself with medicine to control the cough, and he wiped his mouth.

All he could do was mask the symptoms of injury. He had no hope of healing on his own.

He looked around for 4-LOM. The droid had gone off somewhere. Zuckuss wondered if something were wrong with the ship. "Computer," he said. "Where is 4-LOM?"

"In acquisition cell one."

Odd, Zuckuss thought. What was the droid doing in there? Zuckuss scanned the solar system and detected little activity. Most Imperial ships had gone. They had three ships orbiting out near Hoth, probably a fair amount of troops still on the ground. One Star Destroyer had just pulled in a downed Rebel transport. It would strip down the other sixteen, one by one, Zuckuss knew. There was no sign of any other bounty hunter's ship. He and 4-LOM were the last of them to leave the system.

"Computer," Zuckuss said. They had installed one of the intermittently unreliable voice-activated computers from Mechis III. "Lay in a course to point 2.427 by 3.886 by 673.52 above the galactic plane. Can this ship make that journey?"

The computer did not respond at once. It *was* an odd request. Finally it spoke. "This ship, at its present mass, can reach the specified point in two Standard days."

Excellent, Zuckuss thought. "Save those course coordinates," he told the computer, and he set off to look for 4-LOM.

He found the droid sitting on an acquisition's bunk, legs crossed, hands in his lap, metallic forefingers turned under metallic thumbs, staring straight ahead at the opposite wall.

It looked as if he were meditating.

"4-LOM," Zuckuss said. "What are you doing?"

"Attempting meditation," the droid said matter-of-factly, as if meditation were a normal droid activity. He did not look at Zuckuss. He kept looking straight ahead.

Zuckuss stood there dumbfounded. Suddenly he understood many things—why 4-LOM had not left him before this, why the droid constantly asked questions about his meditations, why the droid usually never left his side when he meditated.

4-LOM had been observing him. He was trying to learn how to get intuitive knowledge.

Zuckuss began to cough again. He walked in and sat on the bunk with 4-LOM. "Have you received intuitive knowledge?" he asked when he stopped coughing.

"No," 4-LOM said. He put down his legs and stood up quickly. Zuckuss looked up at him. "I have the beginnings of an equation on the function of intuition," the droid said, "but I cannot yet take it to its conclusion. I will need to observe you further."

Zuckuss stood up, too. "You glittery, tardy-gaited foot-licker!" he said. "You worked with Zuckuss all this time to try to steal his skills!"

"Not steal them," 4-LOM said. "I cannot take your intuition. I hope only to learn to be intuitive myself."

Zuckuss had no doubt that 4-LOM would learn intuition. He had never seen a droid so determined to equip himself with every skill necessary to succeed.

"Zuckuss has our answers already," Zuckuss said. "Han Solo will try to join the Rebels at their rendezvous point, and that is a most interesting point, indeed. You and Zuckuss have work to do before we can go there—let's get to it!"

4-LOM and Zuckuss hurried to their pilots' chairs. Zuckuss quickly explained the knowledge he had received. He and the droid agreed that they had to infiltrate the Rebellion. They could not just show up at a point outside the galaxy where the Rebels happened to be—they would have to pretend to want to join them. Their past history with Governor Nardix would make that request somewhat more credible.

"There is a mere 13.3445 percent chance that the Rebels will accept our request to enlist," 4-LOM said.

Zuckuss thought about that. He looked out the viewport at a row of wrecked Rebel transports and suddenly had an idea that, if it worked, could up that percentage significantly.

"What if we rescued survivors of this battle and delivered them to the Rebels—what would our chances be then?"

"87.669," 4-LOM answered without hesitation. "Plotting course to the nearest transport."

It had lights. It had intact decks. It probably had survivors.

It was the transport they had helped bring down, the one named *Bright Hope*.

Zuckuss communicated with the Star Destroyer and arranged for a staged TIE-fighter attack when they left the system: it would make the "rescue" more credible.

The Imperials quickly agreed to every request—though they must have wanted to interrogate all living Rebels themselves. Being forced to use some to bait a bounty hunter trap must not have pleased them.

But obeying Darth Vader's orders pleased them. Zuckuss and 4-LOM did not need intuitive knowledge to be certain of that.

Zuckuss completed calculations on the spin of the Rebel transport and entered them into the computer. They had to match its spin to dock with it.

"Communication with the Rebel Transport is impossible," 4-LOM announced. "We will have to dock and force entry into the ship."

"They will welcome Zuckuss and 4-LOM. We are coming to *save* them," Zuckuss said.

He was glad they would not have to fight. The Rebel transport would have oxygen on it. He did not want to risk exposure to it. "Computer," Zuckuss said, "calculate this ship's oxygen supplies."

Numbers flashed onto a screen in front of 4-LOM and Zuckuss.

"How many adult oxygen breathers can survive on that oxygen for two days?" Zuckuss asked.

"Fourteen," the computer answered.

The *Mist Hunter* had three holding cells, built for one person each. They would soon be much more crowded.

"Zuckuss wishes to take fourteen, then," Zuckuss told 4-LOM, "the ones worth the most bounty—and all droids. Oxy-breathers can crowd into the cells, and the droids can stay out here."

It was good to have a backup plan. The bounty from the Rebels they rescued might be worth a considerable sum.

"We can force more than fourteen into the cells," 4-LOM said. "If we draw off all remaining air on the transport, we might accommodate another ten or twelve."

An excellent plan, Zuckuss thought. Depending on the oxygen supplies available, he and 4-LOM could take as many as twenty-six people, shoved side by side into the cells.

But Zuckuss was suddenly afraid of sucking additional oxygen into his own ship. He would have to carefully monitor that procedure himself. He was still dressed in his ammonia suit. He put on the helmet and gloves, to prepare for boarding, and double-checked all seals.

4-LOM completed his course calculations and began flying the ship toward the Rebel transport. Subprocessors in his mind then began a complete analysis of his first attempt at meditation and intuition.

He realized he had not been completely truthful with Zuckuss.

He had told Zuckuss he had not achieved intuition. But the thought *had* occurred to him in his meditation that the Rebels had left the galaxy. His logic programs quickly discounted that idea—but the idea had been there, if only for the briefest of moments.

Under normal conditions, his logic programs never

allowed an illogical idea to enter his conscious mind at all.

That it had was something new.

It had not occurred to 4-LOM that to achieve intuition he would have to override logic.

He said nothing of his discovery to Zuckuss.

Toryn stood in front of the computer console in the pod bay. She had her list of survivors: one hundred and eight of them. She began scrolling through the list a second time, reading names, reading their qualifications. She had eight pilots, thirty-two soldiers newly inducted into the Rebellion, support staff from the command center, hangar crew, others with specialized skills: cold weather, Hunting, one cook. She had teams of people stocking the pods with all the food and cold-weather gear they could find.

Thirty-three people had survived on freight deck two. She brought them all to passenger level one except for two Rebels hurt too badly to be moved. Friends stayed with them, and Toryn sent the medical droids. Twenty others from freight deck one had climbed up to the pod bay. It was a crowded space.

Seito stepped up to her. "Imperial Star Destroyer is moving to a second transport."

The Imperials would be busy for quite some time. Distracted. The pods could launch as soon as she got people aboard them.

She instructed the computer to show her the names of everyone hurt too badly to be moved or who the med droids felt could not survive on Hoth.

A sublist of fifty-two names appeared. Samoc was on that list.

She copied those names to a separate file named *SHIP STAY*. The main list reduced to fifty-six names.

Next, she listed everyone on the main list with broken legs.

Sixteen names appeared. She also copied those names to *SHIP STAY*.

She still had forty names to work through, and she could send eighteen. She decided everyone on the transport should help decide who should go. If everyone participated in that decision, those left behind would find it easier to accept.

Next, she worked with the comm system to hold a shipwide conference. It proved quite a challenge to track the voices of everyone speaking on this ship, no matter how many spoke at once, and to let the rest of the survivors hear the other decks. But she succeeded in setting up the conference and copied a complete list of survivors to each functioning screen. When she next spoke, everyone on the ship could hear her.

"This is Toryn Farr," she said. The crowd around her grew quiet. Everyone on the other decks grew quiet. "I have just been informed that the Imperial Star Destroyer is moving toward its second Rebel transport. Our comrades there will keep them busy for a time. This gives us an excellent launch window, but we have to move quickly to make it. Eighteen of us will have a chance to try to reach Hoth and survive there till rescue. We need to send those whose knowledge and skills equip them to best help the Rebellion after rescue, but who can also make a team prepared to survive under the conditions Hoth presents. I am sending Seito and Crimmins, both with excellent combat skills; Sala Natu, cold-weather survival specialist, and Berec Tanaal, Hunter. I want you to nominate and vote on the other fourteen. Start now."

Someone nominated her, but she said she would not go. She was staying with everyone left behind. They needed her here. There was so much work to do to strip the ship of information helpful to the Empire, and it was her duty to oversee that.

Besides, Toryn thought, Samoc would be left behind. She could not leave her.

The names came in quickly, and a list formed up that nearly matched one she would have drawn up herself. Some on the list tried to get others to go in their places, but Toryn was the only one who got away with that.

"To the pods, on the run!" Toryn ordered everyone on the list. "I want the rest of you to start combing every inch of what's left of this ship for files and documents. Bring them to passenger level one, where we will manually erase them."

The teams rushed to finish packing the pods. The eighteen people who had this chance climbed inside and strapped into their seats. There was little time for goodbyes.

"May the Force be with you," Toryn said to them all as they closed the hatches.

"Viewport teams, look sharp," Toryn said. "I want visual tracking of these pods."

"Will do," her observation teams called back.

"Launch!" Toryn ordered.

The pods blasted away from the ship and fell toward Hoth.

Everyone crowded to the viewports. The *Bright Hope* was suddenly very, very quiet. Everyone left on it thought how all their possible futures had shrunk now to two: death, or incarceration in an Imperial prison.

But we are happy for those eighteen, Toryn thought. We're happy for them.

The pods fell in a tight line toward Hoth. The ship turned and all they saw for a time were the lights of the other wrecks and the star destroyer and stars. The star destroyer did not move to intercept the pods. If it launched TIE fighters to attack them, they could not tell.

When Hoth rolled back around, no one could see the pods for a time.

"Pods at three o'clock!" Rory shouted.

Everyone saw them then, three tiny lights, descending fast.

Soon they could not see them at all against the bright, white light of Hoth.

"I think they made it," Toryn said. "Now, everyone to work! The Imperials took note of this transport when we launched the pods, you can bet on that. They'll come for us next. We've got to be ready!"

She ordered the computer to erase itself on her command, and she sent a team to uncover the subprocessing units on each deck and prepare to smash them after the data had been erased as a failsafe backup. She ordered the droids to erase their minds on her command—which would come at the last possible moment: they needed medical help till then. The droids' minds held records of all the Rebel patients they had ever treated. The Empire could not be allowed to get such information: it would tell them who had been alive at a point not far in the past, who had died, what they had said, what conditions they had been treated for—revealing possible weaknesses that could turn some into double agents. The droids would have to destroy themselves.

She thought for a moment about everything else they had to do: destroy documents, tend to the wounded, stockpile weapons, prepare to fight when the Imperials pulled in their ship. She was glad they had a lot to do. Everyone needed work to keep from thinking about the destiny they were rushing to meet.

"Rivers, Bindu," Toryn said. "Form up a detail to study the pod bay and freight deck entrances. I want recommendations for defensive measures ASAP."

"Ma'am!" Rory shouted. "Approaching ship."

Toryn rushed to Rory's viewport. It was an odd ship coming toward them. It did not look Imperial at all. "Can you read its name?" she asked.

"*Mist Hunter,*" Rory said.

She queried the computer for information on the *Mist Hunter,* but the Ships' Registry database was offline.

Bounty hunters, Toryn thought. It had to be.

"*Mist Hunter* heading for pod dock two," Rory said.

"I want anybody who can fight up here now!" Toryn ordered. "We're getting company."

Someone handed her a blaster, and she checked its powerpack. Full power. That bounty hunter ship doesn't have the right docking mechanism, she thought, but the *Mist Hunter* was prepared for that: its computers analyzed the dock ahead and constructed a match on its side. The docks would fit together perfectly.

Toryn had wounded Rebels on her deck. "Six of you get the wounded down to rooms on deck two in the dark, and bar a door in front of them. Everyone else build barricades!"

People rushed to move the wounded and to pull bunks out of rooms and overturn them in a makeshift barricade in front of the pod bay. They heard the docks click together and the hiss of air pulled from their ship into the tunnel connecting them and the *Mist Hunter.* The locks would open shortly.

"If we overpower them and take that ship, we might have a way to get the rest of us out of here. Darklighter, Bindu—get into the crawlspace and come up behind them. Move!"

People rushed to pull up the deck plating, then cover up Darklighter and Bindu.

"Stay down there till I give the all clear," Toryn said, "or till you hear fighting move past you."

This bounty hunter ship shone to Toryn with unexpected hope.

Through all the activity, the computer could not connect with its Ships' Registry database and its detailed information on ships of the galaxy, though it kept trying alternate routes. It had hints of the name *Mist Hunter* in what was left of its short-term memory databanks: the letters MIS NTER from one exterior scan

taken just before or during the attack; from another,
T HUNTER.

But it could not connect the remaining fragments of
those scans with coherent memories.

Yet.

Piece by piece, it was reconstructing its short-term
memory. The computer was programmed to believe
Toryn Farr would find such information important.

Zuckuss did not take time to track the escape pods as
they fell toward Hoth. They were the Imperials' problems. Besides—he hoped the pods and whoever was in
them would make it. It could mean a job Hunting
Rebels among the crevasses of an ice world. He would
relish such a Hunt.

If he healed, he suddenly thought to himself. He could
conduct such a Hunt only if he healed.

Zuckuss docked their ship and forced open the locks.
4-LOM entered the wreck first. "We are here to rescue
you," he announced to the Rebels arrayed in front of
him, and he explained their "plan." While he spoke,
4-LOM activated subprocessors in his mind that analyzed the actions of the Rebels in front of him. They
showed little fear. They did not back up. They did not
look away from him. Seven maintained a tight, protective band around the woman 4-LOM calculated must
be in command, a resourceful woman named Toryn
Farr.

A woman with a bounty on her head. 4-LOM had
quickly matched her face with a bounty registered in
the Imperial Most Wanted List database.

"Controller Farr," 4-LOM said. "I must study a list of
survivors on this ship. Allow me to access its database."

He noted the momentary surprise on Toryn Farr's
face when he called her by name and rank. It was good
to surprise one's prey with familiar knowledge: it could
inspire trust where none should be given. He moved

toward the computer, but Toryn stepped in front of it first. Her guards followed.

"Answer a few questions first," Toryn said. "Who sent you?"

Trust from this one might take more time than they had, 4-LOM calculated. "If I told you a story, Toryn Farr, about Rebel connections in one of the largest Imperial bounty hunter guilds, would you trust me then—or would you think I imparted such information too easily? The truth is, I cannot calculate a circumstance under which I would answer your question. None of you have the proper security clearances to receive that knowledge. Suffice it to say that the answer would surprise you. For now, our presence here to rescue you must be answer enough."

He studied the faces of all the Rebels arrayed in front of him, and matched most of them with bounties. He soon had twenty-six worth taking. Their combined bounties—the riches they represented—could not buy worlds. These Rebels were not valued like Han Solo and his companions.

But their bounties could buy Zuckuss lungs.

For a moment, 4-LOM regretted the necessity of returning these Rebels to their comrades. But he and Zuckuss Hunted more valuable prey. These Rebels were expensive bait for the trap.

"Send your droids and the twenty-six of you whose names I will call out," 4-LOM said. "By now, my partner has pumped oxygen into the passage that leads to holding cells on *Mist Hunter*. Move quickly! The Empire will not forever fail to detect us."

He called out the names, but no one moved. Toryn's was the first name he called. She realized the other names were the names of Rebels who had fought with the Rebellion for some time.

Long enough to have had bounties placed on their heads.

The droid was clearly trying to take Rebels who could

bring it the most credits. Toryn did not believe its claims that it and its partner were Rebels who had come to rescue those who could most help the Rebellion.

"I have an alternate plan," she said to 4-LOM. "Put your ammonia-breathing partner in a suit, replace the ammonia on your ship with oxygen to make room for more people, and fly all of us to Darlyn Boda. It would take half a day to get there. We have contacts on Darlyn Boda who will treat our wounded and hide us till we can rejoin the Rebel army."

"We must go to the rendezvous point!" 4-LOM said. "Our ship is needed there. We will take the twenty-six of you I have indicated and waste no more time."

"I will not leave people I am responsible for," Toryn said.

4-LOM reacted so quickly no Rebel could have responded first. In a flash of movement he beat aside Toryn's guards, grabbed her, and held her in front of him, between the Rebel barricades and pod bay 2.

"We do not have time to argue," he said. "And Zuckuss and I do not have time to take wounded conscripts to Darlyn Boda. I have chosen twenty-six of you. You will board the ship now."

Deckplates clattered behind him. There were two Rebels there, hidden under the deck! These were resourceful foes, indeed. He could have used the blasters implanted in his back to kill them both, but chose not to.

He would not kill people he was pretending to save, at least not yet.

"Let her go," one of the Rebels behind him said.

But Zuckuss came up behind *them*, out of the tunnel between the ships. "No, both of you move aside," he said to the two Rebels. "Your devotion to your commander is admirable. She will go on to serve the Rebellion well once we deliver her to the rendezvous point. You have that satisfaction."

In a flash of movement, 4-LOM dragged Toryn Farr

through the tunnel to a holding cell. He clamped her wrists and ankles into restraints on the wall there. She was not strong enough to fight him off.

"This is no rescue!" Toryn said.

"But it is," 4-LOM said. "Shortly you will be at the rendezvous point. I regret the necessity of using force with you, but saving you is logical and saving time a necessity." He started to walk out of the cell.

"Your logic is flawed," Toryn called after him.

The droid looked back at her.

"You left one of our best pilots off your list of people to save—Samoc Farr. You think the Rebellion doesn't need good pilots?"

The droid said nothing to her and left. She heard shooting on the *Bright Hope*. It was a commander's worst nightmare: to be away from her troops when they were in battle. Soon the droid returned with Rivers and Bindu. He shoved them in her cell.

"What's happening over there?" Toryn said.

"The droid took us hostage and said he would kill us—and you—if the people he wanted did not come forward to board this ship."

But they heard no more shooting. Zuckuss was furious with 4-LOM. "What have you reduced our chances of success to?" he asked the droid. "Who will believe this is a rescue now?"

No one would. The pod bay lay deserted before them, though Zuckuss and 4-LOM knew that if they left the connecting tunnel, blasters would be trained on them. How many, they did not know. They had not been able to make an adequate assessment of the Rebels' arms. 4-LOM calculated that he and Zuckuss should be able to subdue the Rebels and take the people they wanted. But what Zuckuss implied in his second most recent question was important: who would think of this, then, as a rescue?

"Let me try to talk to them," Zuckuss said.

He went alone into the pod bay. "Rebels!" he

shouted. "4-LOM and Zuckuss are bounty hunters. Our ways are not your ways. But like you, we believe the Empire should fall and are willing to work to that end. We can save a few of you, and 4-LOM has marked your names. Come forward now! We must leave."

No one came.

"We have one other option," Zuckuss said to 4-LOM. He walked back into the ship. 4-LOM secured the locks and followed him. He calculated many options, not just one: he and Zuckuss could fight to capture the Rebels they wanted, or they could leave with the three Rebels they already had. 4-LOM calculated forty-nine additional viable options. He was curious to see which one Zuckuss proposed that they select.

Zuckuss spoke through the cell door to the captured Rebels. "Commander Farr," he said. "We truly meant this to be a rescue, but things have gone badly. What must we do to make it right? Please help us, and quickly. We have little time before Imperials will be upon us."

So it was that 4-LOM and Zuckuss prepared their ship to evacuate ninety Rebels, many of them wounded, to Darlyn Boda.

4-LOM released Toryn to oversee the evacuation. Zuckuss stayed in his ammonia suit and, unobserved by the Rebels, contacted the Imperial star destroyer to call off the "escort" out of the system he had arranged for. The *Mist Hunter* had never carried so many people. It would not be able to maneuver well at all—they needed no staged TIE fighter attack now!

"How many Rebels are you taking?" the Imperial controller asked.

"Ninety," Zuckuss said. "Plus two medical droids."

Zuckuss heard Imperials confer in the background for quite some time. Finally the controller came back on-line. "Acknowledged," she said. "That information will be relayed to Imperial command."

Of course, Zuckuss thought. But the Imperials made

no move to stop what he and 4-LOM were doing. Darth Vader had given them a free hand in this Hunt—they could do whatever they thought necessary.

Zuckuss replaced the ammonia in his ship with oxygen. The ninety Rebels and two droids could then barely crowd aboard. They had to stand or lie as tightly compacted as 4-LOM and Zuckuss had planned to shove twenty-six of them into cells. But they did it gladly.

It was a chance for life.

Toryn was last to board.

"Hurry!" 4-LOM called to her. "It is a wonder the Empire has not attacked us before now."

Toryn paused beside the helpful hacker droid at the hatch. "Droid," she called back. "Thank you for all you have done. Erase yourself and the ship's main computer."

It shut down all lights on the ship at once. It had few life-support systems to shut down. One by one it erased its programs and databases. The *Mist Hunter* disembarked. The computer would never know what became of the Rebels it had served.

It erased its long-term memory and started to erase what was left of its short-term memory, but paused there.

A set of subprocessors at work on that memory bank found, at that moment, the correct way to piece together observations of the attack that destroyed the *Bright Hope*.

Now it knew the ship *Mist Hunter*.

The surviving Rebels had just embarked on the very ship that first fired on them, trying to destroy them all.

But the computer had reconstructed these memories too late.

It could not warn the Rebels. It could not call them back.

It carried out Toryn Farr's final order and erased itself.

* * *

The *Mist Hunter* stank of recycled air and, faintly, of ammonia. The air was breathable, but the ammonia in it would give them all headaches. Toryn could feel one starting already, but she did not let it slow her down. The most seriously wounded Rebels lay two to a bunk in the cells. Toryn made her way to each of them, slowly, through the press of people, to talk to them, to encourage them to hang on.

It was then that she noticed and read graffiti on the cell walls. When 4-LOM had first brought her there, she had not noticed it. But some of the condemned held there had written their names. A few had written lines of poetry. One had written his name and the address of his parents and asked that someone contact them for him. Two-Onebee stood next to her. "Record this name and address," she told the droid. "I want to contact this person's parents after we get back."

She found Samoc standing in a back corner of the ship, her face and hands wrapped in white bandages. They hugged.

"You found a way to save us all," Samoc said.

"We're not out of this yet," Toryn said.

She would be responsible for ninety Rebels at Darlyn Boda, fifty-two of them seriously wounded. There was a strong Rebel underground there—but the Empire still claimed Darlyn Boda. It controlled its government.

She looked at Samoc. Toryn doubted her ability to do all she had to do. Twice she had put her personal interest in Samoc's well-being above the interests of the many she was responsible for: the first time, when she sent Samoc the medical droid; the second, when she tried to get 4-LOM to put Samoc on his list of twenty-six Rebels. She knew, standing there with her sister, that she would do it again. It was not fair to the others. She had to give up her command as quickly as possible. She hoped to find Rebels on Darlyn Boda who outranked her.

She returned to Zuckuss and 4-LOM.

"Estimated arrival at Darlyn Boda. 2.6 Standard hours," 4-LOM told her.

This ship is fast, Toryn thought, even with a heavy load.

Zuckuss suddenly began coughing in his suit. He could not stop. Soon he doubled over in his pilot's seat, coughing uncontrollably.

Toryn saw blood spatter the faceplate of his helmet.

She knelt and put her arms around him. "What's wrong?" she said. "What can we do?"

4-LOM stood and began examining the seals on Zuckuss's suit. "Is there an oxygen leak?" he asked Zuckuss.

"No," Zuckuss said between coughs.

Toryn patched into the ship's comm system. "Two-Onebee," she said. "I need you on the flight deck, now."

Little by little, Zuckuss gained control of his coughing. By the time the medical droid got to him, he had nearly stopped. He ended up telling the Rebel medical droid all about the injuries to his lungs.

"With the proper medical facilities, I could treat you," Two-Onebee said. "However, those facilities are, at present, unavailable. Rebel military researchers have discovered ways to genetically trigger the regrowth of damaged tissues."

"Clone them?" Zuckuss asked.

"No. That is illegal. Regrow them inside you. If our medical facilities survived the evacuation, I will be able to treat you at the rendezvous point when we get there. You will have new lungs in only a few days."

Zuckuss leaned back in his pilot's chair and thought about that. He began to meditate, but soon went to sleep. In his dreams he thought he was still meditating.

The mists around all his possible futures lifted for a moment.

There were so many again, so many bright possibilities branching out ahead of him.

Darlyn Boda was much as 4-LOM remembered it: steamy, muddy, shadowy. It was the perfect place to have begun a life devoted to crime. He walked alone down the streets of a city with the same name as the planet, remembering the day he had jumped ship to start his new life. It had seemed to him then that he had the power inside him to pursue numberless possibilities. He had made decisions that had contracted those possibilities, but he regretted few of them.

Zuckuss was too sick to leave the ship. The Rebel medical droids, Two-Onebee and Effour-Seven, attended him. The Rebels had all disappeared, though soon he was to meet Toryn Farr and five of her hand-picked fighters. Together, they would fly to the Rebel rendezvous point.

And Han Solo, and the end of the Hunt.

Toryn had found the leaders of the Rebel insurrection. Its officers outranked her, took charge of her people, and ordered her on to the rendezvous point.

With a sealed letter she was to hand-deliver to the Rebel command.

4-LOM had arranged to meet Toryn at a certain small jewel shop he knew well, a place that bought, or sold on consignment, rare jewels—without asking about their provenance. He had business in that shop.

An old woman dressed in rags rose to meet him. The shop was still as dark and dirty as it had been all those years before. "4-LOM!" the woman said. "Welcome."

She could not stand up straight. She leaned over the few cases in front of her, bent with age. An old program 4-LOM had not used in a long time activated in his mind, and 4-LOM let it run. "How are you?" he asked the woman.

"Old," she said. "But I can still work. I still sell jewels."

"When I left here, you had three jewels of mine on consignment," 4-LOM said. "Have you sold them?"

"Two, yes. And I have credits to pay you with. How do you want to be paid—Imperial credits, other jewels? I will show you my stock."

"Which jewel is left?"

"Ah, I will show you."

She gathered all the jewels on display and put them in pockets in her dress, then she rolled back a rug on the floor behind her cases and opened a trap door there. "Come," she said. She lit a candle and started down steps into the blackness.

4-LOM followed. Beneath the shop lay a room that glittered with jewels. She had never shown him this room before. He wondered why she did now. She knew he was a thief.

"Can you see it?" she said, holding up her light.

4-LOM looked around the room and saw his jewel, glinting blue in the woman's light: the Ankarres Sapphire.

"I had hoped you would still have that one," he said. He picked it up. It glittered beautifully. She had kept it polished.

"You wouldn't let me cut it down, and no one could ever afford the whole stone," she said. "I was glad of that, actually. I touch it to wherever I hurt, every day. It heals me."

"That is why I need it now," 4-LOM said.

"To heal you?" she said. "You are metal. Go to a foundry."

"The sapphire will not heal me," he said. "I need it for a mortal friend."

He held the jewel out to the woman. "Touch it to where you hurt one last time before I take it," he said.

She touched it to her wrists and ankles, held it to her forehead for a time, then handed it back to 4-LOM.

They climbed up to the shop, and Toryn walked in. She smiled at 4-LOM. It had been many years since anyone had smiled at him. Other old programs rose, unbidden, to his mind: programs for kindness, service, and selflessness. He wondered if the jewel were affecting him, after all.

But that was illogical. It had had no effect on him when he had first touched the sapphire to his forehead years before. The old programs ran because he allowed them to run. He did not stop them. Maybe it was time to run those programs again. He could analyze them for their usefulness.

"Are you ready to leave?" he asked Toryn.

"I am," she said. "The others are waiting outside."

4-LOM turned to the old woman. "I want you to keep the credits you owe me. Thank you for helping me years ago when I needed it."

She bowed to 4-LOM, and he and Toryn left for the ship. Rivers, Bindu, Rory, Darklighter, and Samoc went with them. "Samoc," 4-LOM called when they got inside the ship. He held up the jewel in the shadows of the corridor there. "Do you know what this is?"

She looked at it for a moment. "No," she said. "But it is beautiful."

4-LOM explained it to her. "Touch it to your burns," he said. "It might help you heal." He held it out to her.

She held it in her hands for a moment, then touched it to the bandages still on her face even after a month. After a moment, she had to sit down on the deck.

"Did it help you?" 4-LOM asked.

"I don't know. I feel so different—in a good way. Rested, maybe?"

"I must take it to Zuckuss," 4-LOM said. He took the jewel and found Zuckuss in an acquisition's cell. Zuckuss had filled the cell with ammonia and lay there out of his suit, coughing now and then. 4-LOM entered the airlock, waited while ammonia replaced the oxygen, then entered the cell. Zuckuss looked up at him and said nothing. 4-LOM laid the jewel on Zuckuss's chest.

Zuckuss looked at it. He knew what jewel it was. He had heard 4-LOM tell stories about it. After a moment he put his hands on it to hold it tighter to his chest.

"I will fly the ship to the rendezvous point now," 4-LOM said.

4-LOM flew the *Mist Hunter* out of the galaxy at a point near the galactic equatorial plane, and he used the massive gravitational forces of the galaxy itself to propel the ship toward the rendezvous point.

Which was almost exactly where Zuckuss had intuitively known it would be.

The exact point was two degrees off. Soon, from their pilots' chairs, 4-LOM and Toryn saw the scattering of lights that was the Rebel fleet.

Or what was left of it.

Seeing it lifted Toryn's spirits. She looked from the fleet to the galaxy below, and thought how her future was bright again. The Rebellion was not ended. It still had an army, reduced though it might be.

Toryn handled the communications and brought them in to a hero's welcome. Friends and family crowded around Toryn and the others, and many wept to see them. Toryn and everyone on her ship had been listed as missing, and everyone believed them to be dead, or worse. General Rieekan himself came to welcome them back, and to get news of the eighty-four once given up for lost now on Darlyn Boda, and the eighteen others presumed still alive on Hoth. "I had feared the worst for you," he told Toryn.

Two-Onebee and Effour-Seven rushed Zuckuss to sickbay. The Rebels made way for them. 4-LOM started to follow—Zuckuss was so vulnerable now, and the

Rebels provided no security for him—but Toryn stood in front of him.

"4-LOM," she said, "I want you to meet General Rieekan. General, this is 4-LOM, one of the two who rescued us."

The general extended his hand to the droid, and 4-LOM shook it. "You must excuse me, sir," 4-LOM said. "My partner has been taken to sick bay without me and without any guards."

4-LOM started off at once. Zuckuss had been out of his sight for 1.27 Standard minutes. He did not know how to calculate the odds for assassination amongst these Rebels, but in other places that 4-LOM knew well, Zuckuss would be dead already. Two-Onebee and Ef-four-Seven could not protect him.

"4-LOM!" the general called after him. 4-LOM did not stop. The general actually ran to catch up to him. "4-LOM," he said. "You are safe here. Your partner is safe. I give you my word on that. Murder is not our way."

4-LOM slowed down a little, but he did not stop walking. "Thank you for your reassurance, General," he said.

The general walked with 4-LOM. "We are forever in your debt," he said. "I understand you and your partner want to join us. We need fighters with your skills. Once your partner is healed, let's talk about your first assignments."

They were at the doors to the sickbay. "Thank you again, sir," 4-LOM said. He paused and looked down at the general. "I remember once living the way you describe life here: in safety and trusting others. But that was a long time ago."

"I understand," the general said. "I won't keep you from your partner's side."

4-LOM entered the sickbay. The light was subdued there, and it was quiet. Even in his rush to get there, processors in his mind had recorded the faces and voices of the people he passed, matching them to the Imperial Most Wanted List and his guild's list of posted bounties. 4-LOM analyzed those recordings now and calculated the wealth represented by the Rebels he had passed.

Their combined wealth staggered him. So many had posted bounties. The bounty on General Rieekan alone could have bought a moon in the galactic core. It could have bought worlds on the rim.

But there were other acquisitions, worth much more, somewhere in this fleet.

Zuckuss was not the only patient in the sickbay. As he walked along, 4-LOM heard others talking there.

And what he heard from one room made him stop.

A bounty hunter was lucky if a bounty included a recent hologram. It was the rare bounty that carried not only a hologram, but a recording of the acquisition's voice. The patterns of two of the voices he heard speaking matched the voices of two of the Empire's most wanted Rebels: Luke Skywalker and Princess Leia Organa. Each of their bounties nearly matched that offered for Han Solo.

And they were talking about Han Solo. 4-LOM's enhanced auditory sensors easily picked up their voices.

Boba Fett had already captured him. The details were unclear, but apparently Fett was taking Solo to Jabba to collect that crime lord's additional bounty.

The Hunt was finished. He and Zuckuss had failed. Darth Vader had likely placed bounties on their heads already. But other possibilities occurred to him.

He found Zuckuss in a special ammonia chamber, attended by droids he did not recognize. They were clearly just medical droids. He detected no hostile activity in the sickbay at all. Zuckuss did appear to be safe here. The droids admitted 4-LOM to the chamber. "Leave us," he told them.

"Not now. Our procedures must be monitored."

"Leave us now!" 4-LOM shouted. Zuckuss nodded to the droids and they left quickly.

"Zuckuss already knows," Zuckuss said before 4-LOM could speak. "Two-Onebee was called to attach a new hand to an old patient of his: Luke Skywalker. Before Two-Onebee left, he told me how Skywalker came here."

"I calculate Darth Vader and the Empire might yet forgive us—and pay a handsome bounty," 4-LOM said, "if we take them this Luke Skywalker and one other I heard speaking with him: Leia Organa."

"But what of Zuckuss's lungs?" Zuckuss said. "In only a few days, if Zuckuss is monitored here, they will have regrown and Zuckuss will have his health again."

"Days!" 4-LOM scoffed. "Our odds diminish with each minute."

Zuckuss said nothing. 4-LOM calculated that Zuckuss's present condition kept him from active participation in probably any Hunt amongst these Rebels—even if Solo had been here. It was up to 4-LOM. His chances of success alone were low—48.67 percent, he calculated—but worth taking.

If they did not try, if they waited with the Rebels while Zuckuss healed, there would be no going back. Their motivations would always be suspect.

"If you can get yourself to the ship, I will bring the acquisitions," 4-LOM said.

"Zuckuss can do that," Zuckuss said.

"Tonight then," 4-LOM said. "I will make observations and determine a time."

"Now!" 4-LOM said. It was late evening. The droid stood, blaster drawn, in shadows. "The acquisitions are standing in the sick-bay solarium, watching friends leave to rescue Solo. Those friends will need more than luck to accomplish that goal—and soon others they know will need rescue."

Zuckuss sat up slowly. "There is another way, 4-LOM," he said.

"Tell me quickly, then."

"Zuckuss has meditated since you left him, and he has had intuition about what will happen to us. We will not capture Skywalker and Organa. We will end up with a golden, bumbling droid and the two medical droids we brought here, and their bounties will not buy Zuckuss's lungs, nor will turning them over to the Empire clear our names. Both Rebels and Imperials—and the other bounty hunters—will Hunt us. Zuckuss is sick, and will not survive long without treatment. He has decided to stay here."

4-LOM did not know what to say. He calculated ten quick responses that ranged from attempting the kidnapping on his own to simply taking the *Mist Hunter* and leaving. But one fact loomed before him. He himself had calculated only a 48.67 percent chance of successfully kidnapping Skywalker and Organa. He preferred working with better odds.

Before 4-LOM could complete his calculations and decide on a course of action, someone entered their part of sick bay.

It was Toryn Farr. She walked up to the ammonia chamber and spoke to Zuckuss through an intercom in the glass wall. "How are you?" she asked.

Before Zuckuss could answer, she saw 4-LOM standing in the shadows, blaster drawn. "What are you doing, 4-LOM?" she asked. "What's wrong?"

How quickly humans give their trust. 4-LOM thought. She had come to them unarmed. He put down his blaster. "I am doing nothing, now," he said.

But there were many things wrong, many things he could not explain to her. All the choices he and Zuckuss had made had brought them to this point. They had known there were risks in Hunting Governor Nardix, and now they had to accept the consequences of that Hunt.

But a set of subprocessors in 4-LOM's mind finished one set of calculations he had begun. He calculated a 72.668 percent chance that the New Republic would license bounty hunters to help enforce its laws and protect its citizens from criminals. He calculated that he and Zuckuss had an astonishing 98.992 percent chance of founding the New Republic's first bounty hunting guild. It could be an opportunity worth pursuing. He would have to study it further.

"Zuckuss really is safe here," she told 4-LOM. "But if you are this concerned, I will come help guard him on my time off. I know you need to attend to your ship, and you can do that while I watch Zuckuss."

4-LOM attempted to calculate the best reply, but for a moment he could not. Her words made additional old programs activate in his mind, and it took him a moment to quiet them. It had been many Standard years since he had allowed himself to attribute a positive meaning to another's actions, the way Toryn had understood his drawn blaster to mean that he was guarding Zuckuss.

"Thank you, Toryn," Zuckuss said. "But you can sit here with Zuckuss unarmed. Zuckuss would find it a pleasure to talk with you when you have time."

"Then we will talk," she said. "But I'm here now to extend an invitation to both of you. I'm a little embarrassed to say this, but the letter I brought to General Rieekan was actually a letter commending my actions aboard the *Bright Hope*. The Rebel command is promoting me to the rank of commander tonight. I would like you both to attend the ceremony, since I would not be here without each of you."

Zuckuss tried to speak, but he started coughing. 4-LOM helped him lie back down. "I cannot go anywhere tonight, Toryn," Zuckuss said. "But I congratulate you."

"I asked General Rieekan to hold the ceremony here, so you could attend—if that is all right?" Toryn said. She had tried to explain to the general that she was not qualified for a promotion. She told him what she had done for Samoc. "But of course you helped Samoc," the general had said. "She is one of our best pilots. We cannot afford to lose her. I thank you for everything you did on her behalf."

Toryn wondered if the general were just being kind, yet her promotion demonstrated confidence in her and her judgment. So she had accepted the promotion and her new work.

Zuckuss looked at Toryn. "I will be honored to witness the ceremony here," he said.

4-LOM looked at Toryn. "I also congratulate you. What will you command?"

"A unit of Special Forces," she said. "I want to talk to both of you about that later."

Samoc, Rory, Darklighter, Rivers, the medical droids Two-Onebee and Effour-Seven, and many other important supporters of the Rebellion attended the ceremony. General Rieekan announced the promotion and Toryn's new assignment.

"She and I have discussed how best to rescue our friends who took the *Bright Hope*'s escape pods back to Hoth," he said. "We are still working to come up with a viable plan, and Toryn has asked to lead the rescue mission, whatever it eventually entails."

Everyone applauded, but the ceremony was not over. General Rieekan walked forward. "For your resourcefulness and courage in the line of duty, Toryn Farr, the Rebellion is pleased to grant you this award of merit."

The general draped the medal around Toryn's neck and shook her hand. Amidst the applause that followed, a golden protocol droid popped open a bottle in the back of the room and an R2 unit carried drinks to all the oxygen breathers. Ammonia breathers among the Rebels brought glasses and a fine bottle—from Gand itself—to Zuckuss. Perhaps one day, perhaps soon, other Gands would join the Rebel Alliance. The med droids analyzed a small sample of liquid from the bottle, conferred amongst themselves, and decided that if Zuckuss imbibed one congratulatory drink it would not hurt him. They let two ammonia breathers enter his chamber to present him with the drink. They took off their helmets, introduced themselves, and poured for Zuckuss. He held his drink for a moment and looked at 4-LOM.

He and 4-LOM had never been treated like this, not even by their own guild. The Empire certainly never invited them to witness its ceremonies. It had rushed to give them many things after they accepted the contract from Vader, but it had not given them as gifts. It had not included them as members of a team fighting for an important cause, like these Rebels did.

The other ammonia breathers poured themselves full glasses. Zuckuss held his glass up. "To Toryn," he said. They all drank. Zuckuss then held his glass up to 4-LOM. "To our new lives here," he said. 4-LOM bowed to Zuckuss while Zuckuss took a drink. Zuckuss coughed a little. 4-LOM helped steady him on the edge of the bed. He quickly calculated the importance of ceremony. He and Zuckuss would incorporate it in their new guild. Ceremony, and the bonding it promoted, would give them a small statistical edge over other guilds that might form in the New Republic.

In the days that followed, while Zuckuss healed, 4-LOM received programming for his new work in Special Forces, and he oversaw the camouflaging and refitting of the *Mist Hunter*. Rebel technology would make her a remarkable ship indeed. General Rieekan had talked with him about how he and Zuckuss might attempt a possible rescue of Han Solo, since they would probably have access to Jabba's Palace. Perhaps they could even intercept Boba Fett.

The time they spent waiting for Zuckuss's lungs to

rapidly grow could be explained as time spent hiding from Imperials. 4-LOM calculated extreme dangers in such a plan, since the bounties Vader had placed on him and his partner were undoubtedly large enough to tempt Jabba, but it amused 4-LOM to calculate Jabba's surprise when—if he and Zuckuss succeeded in rescuing Solo—Jabba would realize that he and Zuckuss were not merely luckless bounty hunters but Rebel agents.

It also often amused 4-LOM to calculate the Imperials' shock when they realized that not only had he and Zuckuss defected to the Rebellion, but that they had managed to take ninety Rebels and two medical droids from a downed transport with them.

That the Imperials would be furious was an understatement.

And often, as he worked alone on his ship, he practiced meditation. He completed more and more of his equation. In one meditation, he thought he glimpsed the futures that lay ahead of him. One, above the others, intrigued him. In it, he saw himself sitting with young Jedi Knights in a newly established academy. He could not tell if he had learned the ways of the Force or if he were still attempting to learn them. It was a brief glimpse only, and just one of many possible futures.

When 4-LOM told Zuckuss what he had seen, Zuckuss never doubted him.

The Last One Standing:
The Tale of Boba Fett

by Daniel Keys Moran

The last statement of the Journeyman Protector Jaster Mereel, known later as the Hunter Boba Fett, before exile from the world of Concord Dawn:

Everyone dies.

It's the final and only lasting Justice. Evil exists; it is intelligence in the service of entropy. When the side of a mountain slides down to kill a village, this is not evil, for evil requires intent. Should a sentient being cause that landslide, there is evil; and requires Justice as a consequence, so that civilization can exist.

There is no greater good than Justice; and only if law serves Justice is it good law. It is said correctly that law exists not for the Just but for the unjust, for the Just carry the law in their hearts, and do not need to call it from afar.

I bow to no one and I give service only for cause.

"Jaster Mereel."

Journeyman Mereel sat in his cell, in chains, with early morning sunshine streaking in through a tall and narrow barred window, high on the cell's wall.

His ankles were chained together so that he could not walk; another chain encircled his waist, and his wrists were linked to that. He was young, and he did not rise when the Pleader entered his cell; he could see that the discourtesy displeased the older man.

The Pleader Iving Creel seated himself on the bench facing Mereel. He wasted no time on courtesies, himself. "How will I plead you?"

Mereel had been stripped of the uniform of the Journeyman Protector. He was an ugly young man who wore his prison grays with dignity, as though they were themselves a uniform, and he took his time answering, looking the Pleader over, examining him—as though, the Pleader thought with a flash of annoyance, it was Iving Creel facing a trial today, and not this arrogant young murderer. "You're Iving Creel," he said finally. "I've heard of you. You're rather famous."

Creel said stiffly, "No one wants it said you were not treated fairly."

An unpleasant grin touched the young man's lips. "You'll plead me unrepentant."

Creel stared at him. "Do you understand the seriousness of this, boy? You *killed* a man."

"He had it coming."

"They'll exile you, Jaster Mereel. They'll exile you—"

"I could always go join the Imperial Academy," Mereel said, "if I got exiled. I expect I'd make a good storm—"

Creel overrode him: "—and they may *execute* you, if you anger them sufficiently. Is it such a hard thing to say you're sorry for having taken a life unjustly?"

"I *am* sorry," said Mereel. "Sorry I didn't kill him a year ago. The galaxy's a better place without him."

Pleader Creel studied the boy, and nodded slowly. "You've chosen your plea; well enough. You can change it any time before I make the plea, if you wish . . . think on it, I urge you. You'll face prison or exile for the murder of another Protector; for all the man was a disgrace to his uniform, you had no business killing him. But your arrogance is likely to see you executed yourself, Jaster Mereel, before this day is done."

"You can't love life too much, Pleader." The ugly young man smiled, an empty, meaningless movement of the lips, and the Pleader Iving Creel found himself remembering that smile, at odd moments, for the rest of his life. "Everyone dies."

Years passed.

The target was young—younger than the man who had taken the name of Fett had been led to believe; indeed, tonight's target was not long out of his teens. In itself that was not a problem; Fett had collected children many years younger than that. Among his earliest collections, not long after leaving the stormtroopers, had been a boy of barely fourteen Standard years; the boy had dishonored the daughter of a wealthy businessman who had, even in Fett's wide experience, a rather remarkable vindictive turn. Most fathers, Fett knew, on most planets, would not have killed a boy for such behavior; indeed, most bounty hunters would have turned down such a job.

Fett was not among them. Laws vary, planet to planet; but morality never changes. He had delivered the boy to his executioners and he had never regretted it.

Now, years later, he stood in the shadows at the back of the Victory Forum, in the town of Dying Slowly, on the planet Jubilar, and watched them set up for the main match in Regional Sector Number Four's All-Human Free-For-All extravaganza.

The Victory Forum was a huge place, poorly lit, named by the winning side for a recent battle in one of Jubilar's wars. The Forum had had another name, not too long ago; and would, in Fett's estimation, have another name again sometime soon. The current war was not going well. Jubilar was used as a penal colony by half a dozen worlds in the near stellar neighborhood; which army a convict ended up in depended upon which spaceport he was evicted at.

The Forum's seats sloped down toward the five-sided ring, two hundred rows of rising seats separating Fett from the ring itself, and the fighting. The audience was still arriving, only minutes before the main bout, and the Forum was only half full, an audience of some twenty thousand, mostly men, filling the seats.

Fett was in no hurry; he focused his helmet's macrobinoculars on the ring, and the area immediately about it, and prepared to wait through the fight.

Young Han Solo watched the ring attendant, a Bith, hosing the blood from the previous bout out of the ring, and wondered how he'd gotten himself into such a mess.

Well, not wondering, exactly, that wasn't accurate, since actually he remembered the events with a certain painful clarity. Wondering how he'd been *stupid* enough to get himself into the current mess was more like it. Han stood in the tunnel with the other three fighters, watching the blood get cleaned off the mat he would shortly be standing on—fighting on—and swore to himself that if he got out of the current mess with his skin still holding his insides inside, he'd learn to deal seconds so well that no one would *ever* catch him at it.

Anyway, how was a traveling man supposed to know that cheating at cards was a *felony* in some jerk backwaters? "A *felony*," Han muttered aloud. He glanced over . . . and up . . . and up some more . . . at the fighter standing next to him. "What did *you* get sent to Jubilar for?"

The man looked down a considerable distance at Han and said slowly, "I killed some people."

Han looked away. "Right . . . me too," he lied after a moment. "I killed *lots* of people."

The heavily armed ring attendant, standing behind the four of them, growled, "Shut up."

A movement, out of the corner of his eye, caught Han's attention; he leaned forward slightly and looked off to the right. A fellow in . . . gray. Gray combat armor of some sort; he appeared to be watching the ring.

Boba Fett was not watching the ring. He was watching a young entrepreneur named Hallolar Voors, who sat ringside with a pair of beautiful, immaculately dressed women in the seats to each side of him; a young entrepreneur who was going to be dead before he had the opportunity to sample the charms of either of them.

Even at that early age, Han Solo had managed to get some experience on him: "That's Mandalorian combat armor. Who—"

The muted sounds of the crowd rose up in a roar and drowned him out.

The ring attendant yelled over it. "Time to fight, you low trash, you smelly sinful one-eyed egg-sucking sons of slime-devils! *Time to fight!*"

From where he stood, high above the ring, Boba Fett watched as the fighters came up, out of the tunnel, and into the five-sided ring. Four fighters, as Fett had been told was usual for a Free-For-All; the announcer stood in the fifth corner, waiting patiently as the fighters disrobed and took their positions, as the full-throated roar of twenty thousand men reverberated through the Forum.

Pickups, situated around the edge of the ring, would broadcast the fight around the planet.

Three of the fighters were what Fett would have expected, big bruisers for whom the Free-For-All ring had been the obvious alternative to conscription. The fourth surprised him; Fett zoomed in on the man—

The face jumped into focus. For a moment the image startled Fett; the fighter appeared to be staring straight up at Fett. He zoomed the macrobinoculars out to a wider viewing angle—and interestingly enough the impression was accurate; the fellow *was* staring at him. The young fighter disrobed slowly, staring up past the ring lights, into the gloom, at the spot where Fett stood, as the other fighters limbered up in their corners.

The man *was* young—no older, in all likelihood, than Fett's target tonight. *Bad night,* thought Fett, *to be young and quick and full of promise.*

The announcer moved out into the center of the ring, and raised his hands, palms out. His voice echoed out across the Forum and the watching audience: "This is the final elimination! These are the rules: no eye gouges. No blows to the throat or groin. No intentional deaths. *There . . . are . . . no . . . other . . .*

rules." He paused, and the audience's cheers rose to a frenzied pitch as his voice boomed out: *"The last one standing will be the victor!"*

The announcer climbed out of the ring, and despite himself, watching the fighters, the youngster in particular, standing there alone and brave and scared, despite himself Fett found his pulse quickening as, with the rest of the crowd, he waited for the dropping flag that would signal the bout's beginning.

There were moments when Fett appreciated life—he was hardly an old man himself, and there were nights, nights like these, when it was good—and behind the helmet, Fett grinned at the thought as it came to him—when it was good to be young, and quick, and full of promise.

The dark blue match flag fluttered down from the rafters, and into the ring.

The three bruisers moved in on the young fighter. . . .

Boba Fett said, "Spice."

The target, Hallolar Voors, said "Yes, Gentle Fett. Spice. Eighteen canisters. And if you can handle it, we can deliver the same amount again, twice a quarter."

Fett nodded as though he were paying attention. It was not long after the end of the fights, and he walked with Voors through a huge, dimly lit, apparently deserted warehouse at the edge of Executioner's Row; Executioner's Row was a slum that was itself at the edge of Dying Slowly. Fett wasn't impressed with the imagination they showed on Jubilar, but he had to concede they displayed a certain consistency.

Voors had traded in the two women for a pair of conspicuously armed bodyguards. The bodyguards trailed behind them.

"The spice trade in this sector has been controlled

by the Hutts for a long time," Fett observed. "Where did you find an independent source?"

Voors smiled at Fett; Fett, staring straight ahead, watched the smile in the heads-up tactical display in his helmet. The tac display gave him a 360-degree view of his surroundings; Fett wondered whether Voors knew that, or if he was just smiling for the practice of it. It was a handsome smile, Fett had to admit.

The Mandalorian armor itself bothered people, but Fett had found that it bothered people more when he did not look at them while speaking. And if they thought he could not see what was going on around him, so much the better.

Voors did not seem, to Fett, the sort who would know much about the capabilities of Mandalorian battle armor. In fact the man looked much like what he was: the son of a wealthy local businessman, a dark, charming, handsome young fellow wearing expensive clothes, with a good smile, who was fatally out of his league and did not know it.

"The source is . . . private," Voors said. "And desires to stay that way, I'm afraid."

Fett nodded, once; he hardly cared.

Moments later they came to a wide, relatively empty area, lit well enough that Fett's macrobinoculars, adjusted to the darkness they had been walking through, lowered the gain automatically; inside the helmet, the scene still appeared bright as day to Fett.

Three rows of plastic canisters, six to a row, sat out in the middle of the empty area. The canisters were fat, and half the height of a man. Fett pointed at random. "Open that one."

One of the bodyguards standing behind Fett glanced at Voors; Voors nodded quickly. The warehouse lights changed, went dark red; normal white light activated spice. The bodyguard moved forward, knelt, and touched the two clasps that kept the canister sealed; it left Fett with one bodyguard still behind him, slightly to his left.

Fett took a step forward and looked down. It looked like spice; he reached in and pulled out a handful. "Seal it and turn the white lights back on."

The lights came back up . . . and it was spice, all right. Fett scattered it across the top of the canister, and it lay there glowing in the light, twinkling and flickering as the spice was activated. Fett's left hand, hanging by his belt, touched a stud on the belt, releasing the neural toxin, and continued the motion, up to touch his right hand. He worked free the glove, stood there with his naked right hand held up in the air. "Do you mind if I smell it? Real spice has a sharp, pleasant odor—"

Voors glanced at his bodyguards. "If you insist."

Fett reached up, as though to take off his helmet— saw them watching him with plain anticipation. Another of the armor's benefits; taking the helmet off became an act of theater. He paused with his hand on the base of his helmet, and relaxed. "I wanted to ask you a question." The hand dropped slightly. "Does your conscience ever bother you?"

Voors stared at him. "Are you serious? Over spice?"

"Does it ever bother your conscience," Fett said again, in the voice that always sounded so harsh when he spoke Basic, "trafficking in spice?"

Voors said a little hesitantly, "It's not even addictive. And there are valid medical uses for it—"

The bodyguard nearest Fett blinked, shook his head and blinked again. "Substances that are not addictive," said Fett, "frequently lead to the misuse of substances that are. Doesn't that bother you?"

Voors took a deep breath and exploded. *"No,* it doesn't bother me! My conscience is just—" His mouth shut . . . and then opened again, as though he intended to continue speaking.

The bodyguard behind Fett was farthest away from the neural toxin; Fett spun, pulling his blaster free left-handed, and shot the man as he went for his weapon. The jolt took the bodyguard in the stomach; he staggered backward, still clutching his blaster, and Fett moved forward as the guard backpedaled, took aim and shot him a second time in the throat for good measure.

He swung back to the spice, to Voors and the other bodyguard. They weren't dead just yet, of course. They fell and Fett stood watching them; the pickups buried in his helmet were busy recording their death throes. Jabba would want to see the recording—this was one of the first times Fett had taken the Hutt's commission, but Fett understood Hutts; Jabba would pay a bonus for the actual images of his enemies' deaths.

He worked the glove back over his right hand; it was numb already, to the wrist, from exposure to the nerve gas he'd released.

After their thrashing had ceased, Fett walked in closer, to get better pickups of them. He bent slightly to give his pickups the best angle. The pale-skinned bodyguard had turned blue; Voors, darker-skinned, had turned purple. His swollen tongue stuck out between his teeth; Fett imagined Jabba would enjoy that touch.

After a bit Fett straightened and stepped backward, getting a good dozen paces between himself and the eighteen canisters of spice.

He unslung his flame thrower, lit the flame, and played it over the plastic drums for what seemed to him a long time.

The Hutt had not paid him to burn the spice; but Jabba had not paid him *not* to, either; and there were things worth doing for free. When all that remained was a smoldering melted mess in the middle of the warehouse, Boba Fett, who thought himself a fair and a just man, slung the flamethrower back over his shoulder, turned about, and walked quietly out of the warehouse, into the dark, silent night, into a future filled with promise.

Fifteen years passed.

In the *Slave I*, with engines and shields powered down to almost nothing, only a trickle of power feeding the instruments and the lifeplant, Boba Fett hung up high above Hoth System's ecliptic, high above the system's potentially lethal asteroid belt. He looked down on Hoth System and was gratified to see that he'd beaten the Imperials.

Somewhere down there, on Hoth itself, was, if Fett had guessed right, the current headquarters of the Rebellion. Fett didn't care about the Rebellion one way or another; the Rebels were plainly doomed, and the day and manner of their passing from the universe did not fill him with much interest. The Empire would take care of them; Fett had smaller and more profitable prey in mind.

Where the Rebels were, Han Solo could be found.

The hyperspace message from the Imperials had been short and to the point; it had announced a crushing assault on Rebel headquarters, and offered a bounty of fifteen thousand credits to any Hunters who helped chase down Rebels fleeing the site of the battle.

Fifteen thousand credits wouldn't have paid Fett's operating expenses for half a year. But where the Rebels were . . .

Not too long ago, Jabba the Hutt's standing bounty on Han Solo had reached one hundred thousand credits. It was one of the half dozen largest extant bounties Fett knew of; and if it didn't exactly put Solo into the company of the Butcher of Montellian Serat, and the Butcher's five million credit bounty, it was getting up there, getting up there.

He trained his sensors on Hoth at highest resolution, and keyed the computer to wake him if it saw the *Millennium Falcon*.

Sitting in the pilot's seat, in his armor, helmet in his lap, Fett closed his eyes and went to sleep.

The hyperwave warning awoke him.

Fett opened his eyes and scanned his instruments. Weak, flickering signals from Hoth, that might have been no more than background noise (except that they weren't); that wasn't what had set off his alarm, though.

Ships, the instruments said, were coming out of hyperspace. *Big* ships, which meant Star Destroyers, which meant the Empire. Fett triangulated—and swore in his native language. Hoth was *between* him and the ships leaving hyperspace. *Oh, you fools, you fools,* Fett thought. If they'd set off *his* instruments, as far away as the *Slave I* was from their breakout point, then the Rebels, down on Hoth, must have been jolted out of their beds by the shrill of alarms going off.

Somebody had fouled up bad; and knowing Vader, Fett imagined that that particular somebody was not long for the galaxy.

The *Slave I* sat up above the ecliptic, and Fett did what he could while the inevitable battle played itself out. He lit the engines and moved in closer to Hoth; when the *Falcon* left the planet, if it did, it would be moving fast; Fett would have time for only a single run at it.

He took up position, still well above the ecliptic, floating above Hoth, above the battle; and prepared to wait. There was nothing else for it; if Fett had learned anything in his time as a Hunter, it was that patience paid. Certainly there was no profit to involving himself in the fighting. Ion cannon blasted up off the surface of Hoth; beneath their cover, Rebel transport ships lifted off, accelerated away from Hoth, and made the jump to hyperspace. At this distance, even with image enhancement, Fett's sensors could do no more than eke out the barest details of ship size and shape; but that little was enough. None of the ships leaving Hoth were the *Millennium Falcon;* the shape of that ship was burned into Fett's brain.

A wave of transport ships. A wave of fighters. Another wave of transport ships . . . another. Another.

The ion cannon on the planet's surface were firing more infrequently now; the Imperials must be having some success at taking the emplacements out. Fett waited, fighting back his impatience. The transports were away, occasional fighters still slipping the Imperial line and jumping to hyperspace. But still, no *Falcon*—

There.

That was the *Falcon*, or it was an hallucination. Fett's fingers danced across the controls and the *Slave I* lit its engines to give chase. The computer calculated trajectories, and Fett did half a dozen things at once, readied the tractor beam, fed power to the fore deflectors, threw up the *Falcon*'s projected trajectory and ran an intersect for the *Slave I;* he needed to grapple them just before they hit hyperspace, ideally while avoiding death at the hands of trigger-happy Imperials—

Fett swore aloud for the second time in a single day. He wasn't going to catch them.

The *Slave I* streaked through space, high above Hoth System, at the ship's greatest acceleration, but there was no time, and the trajectories showed it plainly. Hoth was a cold world, far from its sun; the gravity gradient this far out was smaller than usual for a world habitable by humans—the *Falcon* was going to jump to hyperspace practically any moment.

Any moment, now; she was being chased by a Star Destroyer and what looked like its entire complement of TIE fighters. And—remember the basics, and Basic Number One was: *no bounty is worth dying for.* The Star

Destroyer and the TIE fighters were directing a withering fire upon the *Millennium Falcon,* laser light washing over the ship again and again; and if Fett got close enough to grapple, he would be close enough to take the brunt of that fire.

Any moment now—

And something was wrong. The *Falcon* wasn't jumping.

Fett doubled-checked the trajectory his computer had run for the *Falcon,* and the trajectory was correct; the gravimetrics were correct, the vectors were correct, the *Falcon* should have jumped by now.

Something wrong with their hyperdrive, Fett thought, and a moment later knew himself correct; the *Falcon* veered off—

—heading straight into the Hoth System asteroid belt.

Fett cut his engines, and simply watched as the *Millennium Falcon* dove into the belt. Solo was desperate; Fett wasn't, not nearly desperate enough to take the *Slave I* in among those tumbling mountains of stone and iron.

The hundred thousand credits could wait for another day; you can't spend money when you're dead—

Fett leaned forward slightly in his seat, thinking to himself that it had, really, been quite a remarkable day for Imperial stupidity:

The TIE fighters were going in after them.

Fett sat back in his seat, shaking his head. Plainly none of those people knew the first thing about cost analysis.

After a long blank moment he turned his sensors back in-system, and picked out the unmistakable shape of Darth Vader's Super Star Destroyer *Executor.*

He hailed it, received confirmation, and charted a course.

•   •   •

They took him to see Lord Vader.

Vader stood on the bridge, watching the remnants of the battle. Stars glittered and asteroids tumbled across the black sky beyond him. Vader did not look at Fett and wasted no words in greeting, and as always the deep voice seemed more the work of a machine than a man. "How did you know?"

Fett glanced around before replying; the bridge crew was so busy at its duties, or busy appearing to be busy at its duties, that none of them had even looked at him as he was brought in; and as usual Fett found himself touched by a certain grudging admiration for Vader's leadership.

"Your people told me," Fett said after a moment. "In essence. They gave us a meeting point in interstellar space. I knew you wouldn't be jumping the fleet far, from that point; I ran the coordinates against my charts for this area." He shrugged. "One planet too hot, another too cold, a third just right, but already inhabited by Lando Calrissian's mining colony. That left Hoth."

"You know the area well, then." Fett did not think Vader expected a response; he offered none. Vader, still without looking at him, nodded as though he had. "The other Hunters will be here shortly. I'll brief you all when they arrive."

Fett took a step forward. "How much?"

Vader was silent a long moment. "I don't care about the others who escaped. For Solo . . . one hundred and fifty thousand credits. The same again for Leia Organa. She will be with him." He turned his head slightly. "No disintegrations."

Fett's escort gestured; Fett shrugged and turned and followed the escort from the bridge. Vader was a difficult client; he wanted living captives, not corpses or pictures of corpses. *No disintegrations;* he'd said that every time he'd hired Fett, after that first incident.

●   ●   ●

After the briefing, Fett and his competition were separated, and escorted back to their ships.

Fett's escort was visibly uncomfortable in his presence; that suited him. Vader's ship was the largest vessel Fett had ever *seen*, never mind actually been inside; it took almost five minutes for them to be shuttled from the bridge to the docking bay where the *Slave I* waited for him, and Fett was, by general policy, in no mood to talk. Particularly not to an Imperial officer of low rank.

They walked from the shuttle station to Fett's ship. Halfway there, the Imperial said, "They say you're Lord Vader's favorite bounty hunter."

Fett stopped in his tracks, stood still, and stared at the man long enough to intensify the fellow's discomfort. "Yes." He turned and continued walking, and the Imperial had to hurry after him.

But the man was stupid even for an officer of the Imperial Navy, or his curiosity surpassed his temerity; he didn't take the hint. "They say you know the target. This fellow Solo, the one who helped Skywalker blow up the Death Star. They say that you know him."

Fett walked along without replying for a good bit. Finally he said, reluctantly enough, "I saw him fight once."

"Fight where?"

For some reason Fett answered him. "A long time ago. He got into the All-Human Free-For-All competition, out on Jubilar." With real surprise Fett heard himself adding, "He was young, and he was outmatched. He made the finals round, though. Have you ever seen the Jubilar Free-For-All?"

The escort shook his head. "I've never even heard of the planet it takes place on."

It was like listening to someone else talk; the words simply flowed out of Fett. "They put four fighters together in a ring, usually of the same species. To make it fairer." A quick smile touched Fett's features, as he thought about those fights; it was the first time Boba

Fett had smiled in years, and he did not notice it happening. "Fairer," he repeated. "Usually three of them start by ganging up on the one they think weakest, which in this case would have been Solo. He was young, I told you that. They beat the weakest fighter into unconsciousness before turning on each other; and the last one standing is the victor."

"They beat him unconscious? Han Solo?"

Fett stopped walking—and looked sideways at the man. A small motion, but—the Imperial found himself staring into the bounty hunter's darkened visor.

Fett's harsh voice sounded like an attack. "He won. It was one of the bravest things I ever saw." He paused. "I'll enjoy collecting him."

The Imperial made a visible effort to collect himself. "Yes . . . I expect you will."

Fett shook his head as though to clear it, turned and headed down the corridor once again, perhaps at a slightly quicker pace.

It was the longest conversation he'd had in years about anything except business.

The months passed in a rush; and when it was over Boba Fett found himself perhaps the best known bounty hunter in the galaxy.

It was a crowded time, and in Fett's memory the events blurred into one another. Solo had hidden the *Falcon* among the Imperials' garbage, released immediately before the jump into hyperspace, and so escaped from the Imperials at Hoth. A good trick, and one that might have worked against most Hunters; it had worked against Fett's competition.

But Boba Fett had been fooled by that trick before, once. By now he had been in his line of work longer than most, and there were few enough ploys he *hadn't* seen, once or twice or a dozen times. There was only one place they could be going, one place close enough for them to reach with their main hyperdrive disabled; Fett jumped for Cloud City, and there Lando Calrissian made the deal that delivered Solo to Fett.

With Han Solo as cargo, frozen in carbonite, Fett started for Tatooine. There, for the sculpture of Han Solo, and a few months of Fett's time, not to mention a number of inconveniences on the way, Jabba the Hutt paid, not 100,000 credits, but a quarter of a million—

And not too long after that, the rescuers started arriving. Leia Organa, pretending to be a bounty hunter, arrived with Chewbacca in tow. She succeeded in releasing Solo from the carbonite. For the very death of him Fett could not imagine what she'd had in mind; whatever it was, it did not work. The Hutt put Solo down in the dungeon, with Chewbacca, and intended to execute them in the near future; and Leia Organa spent her days in chains at the foot of Jabba's throne.

Fett lay on the bed in his darkened quarters deep inside Jabba's Palace, wearing his armor, staring up into the darkness. His helmet was balanced on his stomach and cool air from the ventilators washed across him in rhythmic gusts.

A heavy pounding sounded at his door.

Fett sat up, donning his helmet and lifting his assault rifle; the movements were so automatic he did not even have to think about them. He threw the bolt on the door, took several steps backward and aimed the rifle. He did not turn on the room lights. "Come in."

The door swung open with a reluctant creak. A pair of Gamorrean guards stood out in the passageway; Fett leveled his rifle at them. "What do you want?"

One of the guards stepped to the side, and a form—a human—was shoved into the room. Fett's finger tightened reflexively on the trigger, but he held his fire.

"From Jabba," the near guard grunted. "Enjoy her."

Fett reached back with one hand and touched the control for the light fixtures; and under the cool white light that washed over the room, looked down on Leia Organa, Princess of Alderaan.

She scrambled to her feet and backed up into a corner of the room, breathing heavily. Fett imagined she had fought with the guards as they brought her down to him. "You touch me—" Her voice failed her, and she stood there, shivering, and finally said, "Touch me and one of us is going to die."

He lowered the rifle slowly, and looked around the room. He had few enough possessions here with him in the palace; everything he owned, which was little enough, was aboard the *Slave I*. Finally he pointed at the thin sheet that covered the bed. "Cover yourself. I'm not going to touch you."

Organa moved slightly to the side, leaned over and grabbed the sheet and wrapped it around herself and the brief costume Jabba had allowed her, and backed up again into the corner of the room that left her farthest away from Fett. "You're not?"

Fett shook his head. He sat down in the corner facing hers, moving carefully, and propped his rifle across his knees. He *had* to move carefully; his knees had been getting worse in recent years. "Sex between those not married," said Fett, "is immoral."

"Yeah," said Organa. "So's rape."

Fett nodded. "So is rape." He sat in what was, for him, a comfortable silence, watching her. She settled down in the opposite corner, being careful of her covering; Fett approved of her modesty, but it did not prevent him from continuing to look at her. He had never so much as held a woman in his arms, Boba Fett, and the desire for a woman came to him less frequently, with the passage of the years; but in Fett's mind his chastity made him no less a man, and she was worth looking at, still flushed from her struggles, with her dark hair cascading down over the pale sheet.

She adjusted the sheet around herself, pushing herself back into the corner for warmth. "You're not going to call the guards to take me back to Jabba?"

"And insult Jabba? I don't think so. He'd feed you to the Rancor, and hold a grudge against me. You can go back in the morning."

Her breathing was quieting. "So we just sit here. All night."

"The stones are cold. If you want to use the bed, you're welcome to it."

Organa's skepticism was obvious. "And *you'll* just sit there. All night."

"I won't hurt you. I won't touch you. Sleep if you will. Or not; I do not care."

Silence descended. Fett watched the woman as she leaned back against the stone wall; watched her as she collected herself; watched her as she watched him.

Time passed. Both of his eyes were open, but he was only half awake when she burst out, "Why are you doing this? Why are you fighting for them?"

Fett stirred, stretching slightly. The rifle across his knees was steady as a rock. "Over half a million credits," he informed her. "That's what Vader and the Hutt have paid for my work."

"Is it just money? *We'll* pay you. Help us get out of here and we'll pay you—"

"How much?"

"More than *you* can imagine."

Fett was amused by the audacity she showed, trying to bribe him, here deep inside the Hutt's castle. "I can imagine an awful lot."

"You'll get it."

It was cruel to let the woman hope. "No. What you're doing is morally wrong. The Rebels are in the wrong, and the Rebellion will fail—and it should."

Leia Organa could not keep the outrage out of her voice. "Morally wrong? *Us*? We're fighting for homes and our families and our loved ones, the ones who are still alive and the ones we've lost. The Empire destroyed my *entire world*, virtually everyone I ever knew as a child—"

Fett actually leaned forward slightly. "Those worlds rose in rebellion against the authority legally in place over them. The Emperor was within his rights to destroy them; they threatened the system of social justice that permits civilization to exist." He paused. "I am sorry for the deaths of the innocent. But that happens in war, Leia Organa. The innocent die in wars, and your side should not have started this one."

He shut up abruptly; all the talking was making his throat sore.

His comments appeared to render Organa speechless anyway; she looked off to the side, away from Fett, staring at the blank stone wall, for several minutes. When she finally spoke her voice was quiet and she still did not look at him. "It's hard for me to believe that you can really think like this. I've heard Luke—Luke Skywalker, I know you've heard of him—I've heard him talk about the dark side—"

Fett was amazed to hear himself laugh. *"That* Jedi superstition? Gentlelady Organa, if the Force exists I have seen no proof of it, and I doubt it does."

Now she did look at him. "You remind me of Han Solo, a little. He didn't believe—"

Fett heard his voice rise dangerously. "I am *nothing* like Solo and *don't you compare me to him."*

Leia took a slow, deep breath. "Okay. Why does that offend you so?"

Fett leaned forward again. "Do you know what that man has done in his life? Never mind the loyal citizens of the Empire that he, and you, have killed during your Rebellion; war is war and perhaps you, at least, think you are fighting for Justice. But *Solo?* He's a brave man, yes; he's also a mercenary who's never done a decent thing in his life, who's never done a *difficult* thing that somebody wasn't paying him for. He's smuggled banned substances—"

"He ran spice!"

Fett found himself on his feet and yelling. *"Spice is illegal!* It's a euphoric, it alters moods, and the use of it leads to the use of worse substances, and a man who will run spice," he snarled, "will run *anything!*" He stood tense and motionless, holding his rifle in a quivering grip, staring down at Leia. "And if I had been using spice tonight, Leia Organa, perhaps you would *not* be safe with me in this room."

"Han has smuggled spice," Leia said steadily, "which is illegal and does not please me; and he's smuggled alcohol too, which is legal but the tariffs are high enough to make it worth smuggling in various worlds. No, he's not perfect and he's broken laws you've never even *heard* of. But I know Han Solo, and I've seen him take risks for things he believes in, risks that I doubt *you* would have the courage to take—and what *are* you doing working for Jabba the Hutt anyway?"

Fett exhaled, loosened his grip on the rifle. He forced himself down to the ground once more, ignoring the spikes of pain that flared in his knees. "He's paying me. A lot. Once Skywalker comes, I will take him to Vader, and then I will spend no more time here."

"That's not what I mean. Jabba the Hutt has sold *mountains* of spice, and of far worse than that—"

"Necessity makes allies. Once the Rebellion is over, I expect the Empire will deal with Jabba. But he is less a threat than the Rebels." Fett reversed the assault rifle, touched the butt against the pad that controlled the lights. His macrobinoculars compensated almost immediately as darkness fell on them; she sprang into his vision by the light of her body heat. "I'm going to sleep. My throat is sore."

There was a moment of silence.

"Luke Skywalker," Leia said out of the darkness, "is going to come and kill you."

"Everyone dies," Fett agreed. "But since nobody's paid me to kill you . . . sleep well."

He slept with his eyes open, inside the helmet.

The Jedi, if he was one, came a day later. Luke Skywalker was his name, and he killed Jabba's Rancor; and Jabba put him down in the dungeon, in a cell near Solo and Chewbacca.

The following morning dawned bright and clear and hot, and Boba Fett was in a vile mood.

It was Tatooine, of course. *All* the mornings were bright and clear and hot.

But the Hutt was going to kill Skywalker. And Solo, and Chewbacca, though that was hardly the point.

Skywalker. *That* was the source of Fett's vile mood. He'd tried to talk Jabba out of killing Skywalker—not that he cared whether Skywalker lived or died; Fett expected the galaxy would be a better place with that fool subtracted from it. He'd seen a lot of remarkably stupid things in his day, but the spectacle of a beardless young man trying to face down Jabba the Hutt in his own throne room was near the top of the list.

But, though Fett had argued with him more than was perhaps wise, Jabba was not behaving like the Jabba whom Fett had known all these years. The point was that Darth Vader would *pay* for the fool—the *Emperor* would pay for him. The largest posted bounty Fett knew of in the galaxy was five million credits; but Fett was certain that Luke Skywalker would bring more.

Jabba didn't want to hear about it. He wasn't willing to share the bounty; he wasn't willing to take the bounty himself, and pay Fett as go-between with Vader.

His pet Rancor had died; and Skywalker was going to die for it.

Some days Fett was convinced he was the only sane businessperson left in the entire galaxy.

It galled him. He planned out scenario after scenario; none of them tempted him. He thought about kidnapping Skywalker out of Jabba's hands, but time was short and Jabba's security was good; even for millions of credits the risk was too high.

And so he walked around on the sail barge's upper deck, with uncharacteristic nervous energy, the morning after Skywalker's arrival, the morning that Skywalker and Solo and Chewbacca were to be executed, trying to decide what he was going to do next, as the sail barge headed out to the Great Pit of Carkoon, taking the condemned to their deaths.

It came to him as something of a surprise that he hoped Solo died well. Years previously Fett had seen Jabba drop half a dozen of his own guards into the Great Pit of Carkoon, allegedly for conspiring against him; he'd offered them all a chance to grovel for their lives. Two of them had, and Jabba, of course, had fed them to the Sarlacc anyway.

He knew Chewbacca wouldn't beg; he hoped Solo wouldn't.

Maybe Skywalker would beg for his life. That wouldn't be so bad.

Fett stood in the bow and watched the sand disappear beneath them. This far out into the desert, there was nothing *but* desert, all around them. Sand, drifts and dunes as far as the eye could see.

Fett wondered, in passing, who had killed more people, himself or the Hutt. Probably the Hutt, if you counted his spice trade; probably himself, Fett thought, if you only counted deaths by your own hand.

Eventually the Great Pit of Carkoon came into view. Boba Fett, his mood improved not in the slightest, abandoned the upper deck and went down to the viewing area, to watch with the others as Justice was rendered—

—and who knew how many millions of credits were wasted.

The day had started badly; it got worse. Before it was over the sail barge was a flaming wreck, Jabba the Hutt was dead, and Boba Fett was down in the Great Pit of Carkoon, being digested by the Sarlacc.

Oh, he got out; as far as Fett knew he was the only person who ever *had* escaped the Sarlacc.

But by the time he got out and was healed again, or as healed of that experience as he ever did get, great events had transpired; and the galaxy had become something Fett would never have believed possible.

Fifteen years passed.

Or, to put it another way:

Darth Vader died; so did the Emperor. The Empire fell and was succeeded by the New Republic. On the human scale fifteen years is long enough for babies to be born and grow into teenagers; human children across the galaxy became adults and bore children of their own. For some long-lived species the period passed without significant change; for others, shorter-lived than humans, entire generations were born, grew old, and died.

In a sector of the galaxy Boba Fett had never heard of, a star went nova; it murdered a world and an entire sentient species. It aroused less comment than had the destruction of Alderaan, only a decade prior; the galaxy at large barely noticed the tragedy, and Fett never heard about it. In a galaxy with over four hundred billion stars, over twenty million intelligent species, such things are bound to happen.

The remnant of the Empire rose up against the New

Republic, and was defeated; Luke Skywalker fell to the dark side of the Force—and returned, as few Jedi ever had in all the thousands of generations preceding him.

Leia Organa married Han Solo; and together they had three children.

On Tatooine, a drunk Devaronian named Labria killed four mercenaries, and vanished.

Boba Fett grew older.

On the planet of Coruscant, the world that had been the capitol of the Old Republic, the capitol of the Empire, and was now the capitol of the New Republic, in the Imperial Palace, in the quarters he shared with his wife, Han Solo sat on the edge of their bed with his mouth set in an obstinate line.

"No. I won't go. Treaty signings bore me, and besides that worthless son of a slorth Gareth tried to cheat me at Laro last time we were there."

Leia stood with her arms folded, her exasperation showing plainly. "You cheated him back!"

"I cheated him *better*. Anyway that fool should feel lucky all he had to deal with was *me*," Han pointed out. "When I was a kid, getting caught dealing seconds was a felony and they hung you for it."

"That's not true," Leia said—but a touch doubtfully, Han thought; he had known her long enough to know that cheating at cards, and the consequences of it, wasn't among the things they taught princesses.

"It is too true," said Han righteously. "Anyway King Gareth was *lucky* nothing worse happened to him than losing to me, that's the point here. So I don't know what you expect me to do, go up to the fellow and say, 'I'm sorry, your scummy Royal Highlessness, that I cheat better than you do'?"

Leia sighed. "I wish you wouldn't use the word 'royal' as though it were an insult. I'm—"

"You're *adopted*," Han said quickly.

It brought a reluctant smile to her. "You're not going to come, are you?"

"You'd wish two weeks of diplomatic boredom on me?"

"You're sure you'd *be* bored?"

"I was bored last time, except that one night."

"I don't think Gareth will play cards with you again."

"So I'll be bored *every* night."

Leia sighed. "You're not coming."

"I'm not going."

"I was thinking of taking the children with me. They're old enough and it would give them some useful experience in dealing with—"

"It's certainly safe enough," Han conceded. "If they don't die of boredom."

"I could leave Threepio with you to keep—"

"You'd leave me here with Threepio? What did I do to deserve *that*?"

Leia Organa worked hard at keeping the smile off her face. "All right, I'll take *him* with me, too."

Han Solo looked up at her and grinned. "Deal."

She leaned in on him and whispered, "You better not be in jail when I come back."

"Hey, hey," he objected. "This is *me*."

He called Luke.

When Luke's image appeared in the hologram, Han said, "Hey, buddy. You busy tonight?"

A smile lit Luke's features. "Han! How are you?"

"Fine. Look, Chewie's gone home and won't be back for another few weeks, my wife and kids are off—"

"—the Shalamite trip," Luke nodded. "Right. Why didn't you go?"

"—and I was thinking," said Han doggedly, refusing to get sidetracked, "we might go and see if we could dig up some trouble tonight."

Luke shook his head. "I can't, Han. I've invited a

group of the Senators to dinner . . . you are welcome to join us, though."

"Trouble sounds more attractive," Han growled.

Luke grinned. "C'mon, Han. You know I can't cancel my own dinner. Besides, this is Coruscant. We're two of the best known people on the whole planet. Where are we going to find trouble?"

"I've managed it before."

"And you sat in jail for two days before you convinced them you were really you. Leia was worried sick."

"Yeah," Han pointed out, "but Leia's off-planet right now. By the time she gets back, *this* stay in jail will be nothing but a pleasant memory."

Luke laughed. "Han, come to dinner with me. You'll enjoy yourself."

"With half a dozen Senators? I'd rather have a tooth pulled."

"You know," said Luke quietly, "you might think about *joining* the Senate."

"Without *anesthetic* I'd rather—"

"They'd elect you in a heartbeat."

"And impeach me in a month."

"Why?"

Han thought about it. "Bribe taking," he said finally.

"You wouldn't take bribes," said Luke calmly.

"Well, I admit it would depend on the bribe."

"Han, what's bothering you?"

The question startled Han. "Nothing."

The steadiness of Luke's gaze was unsettling. "You're not telling me the truth, Han. Or you're not telling yourself the truth, I'm not sure which—"

That look was making Han uncomfortable. "I don't know. Maybe it's just Chewie being gone—"

"That's not it."

Han stared at Luke. "No . . . not really. You know . . . I don't know where I'm *going* anymore, kid. I have a wife and children who love me, and who I love. But that's the *problem*. I'm Daddy. I'm Leia's consort. I tell amusing stories at state dinners—"

"You're very good at it," Luke said gently. "There's a place for those sorts of—"

"—and somebody asked me at one of those blasted dinners a while back what it was like, smuggling I mean, back in the old days. I started to answer and suddenly I couldn't remember. I couldn't remember the last time I'd run an Imperial barricade, or what the cargo was, or how it felt."

Luke grinned at him. "It was me and Ben and the droids."

Han looked startled. "You're right—it was, wasn't it?" He smiled almost unwillingly. "Yeah. All right, let's say I couldn't remember the last time I made any *money* at it—"

Luke turned his head, looked off-pickup, and turned back. "Han, my guests are arriving. Are you sure you won't join us?"

Despite himself Han felt tempted. ". . . nah. Not tonight."

Luke nodded. "I'll come by tomorrow. All right?"

"All right. I'll talk to you later, kid."

Luke's lips quirked in a small smile. "Han—"

"Yeah?"

"Han, I'm older than you were when we met." The smile did not fade, but it changed quality subtly, in a way Han Solo did not quite understand. "The world *changes*, Han. You can't stop it and you can't fight it, and you can't ever, ever turn it back." Han had the oddest impression Luke was studying him; and then Luke nodded and said, "I'll talk to you tomorrow. Hang in there."

His image vanished.

Han Solo thought, *The kid's turning into Obi-Wan right in front of my eyes.*

• • •

He got a recording when he tried to reach Calrissian.

"I'm sorry, but I can't be reached right now. Business has taken me on an extended trip; I'll respond to any messages if I return.

"If this is Han, buddy, you owe me four hundred credits if I get back."

Well, blast it, Han thought. *Lando* had found some trouble.

Late that evening he found himself down at the launching bay where he kept the *Falcon*.

It was dark, except for the bay lights high above him, and quiet except for the distant sounds of cargo being unloaded, in the commercial bays a good ways down.

Nobody questioned Han when he arrived; nobody asked him what he was doing there; he walked through the darkened bay as though he owned the place.

He very nearly did.

Han Solo stood at the edge of the bay, and laid one hand against the control for the overheads; and four banks of floods came to life.

Beneath the wash of light, the *Millennium Falcon* glowed white. She had never been so clean, in all the years Han had owned her; she had never been so carefully painted and beautifully detailed. Her engines had been rebuilt—the new hyperdrive engines never so much as blinked. The weapons emplacements were almost all new equipment.

There were even spare parts for everything.

Han had ceased to wonder about how much it had all cost; the New Republic had paid for it all. He'd never even seen a bill.

Sitting in the pilot's seat, in the cockpit, he initiated a launch sequence. He didn't really intend to take the ship up; he just wanted to look at the sky.

The dome above the *Falcon* split in two, slid slowly apart as the platform the *Falcon* rested on raised itself up, and the sky came out.

Han Solo stared out at the world.

It was amazing how much better it made him feel, just to be sitting here, in the closest thing to a home that he'd ever had. The seat next to him was empty, and that wasn't right—but it wasn't entirely wrong, either. He hadn't met Chewbacca until well into his adult years; and there'd been a time, before that—before Chewie, after the death of his parents—when there had been nobody.

No one except himself.

Han wondered sometimes—rarely, to be sure—what his family would have thought about him, if they could have seen what he had grown into. He'd never had to wonder about it, when he was younger; his family had loved him, but he knew he had been a disappointment to them, and they had not lived to see him grow into anything better.

You can pinpoint moments when change occurs. Not always; some changes are like the tide, slow and barely perceptible until they have come, or gone.

Sometimes, though—

Han *did* think about this, and with, oddly, increasing frequency, as the event itself grew more distant in time: the Death Star was coming; and it was going to destroy the Rebel base, the Rebels themselves, and their plainly doomed Rebellion. Han had taken Chewie and the *Falcon*, and had gotten out with time to spare—

Chewie was furious; Han could tell. Chewie wanted to fight. They'd sat here, together, in the *Falcon*'s control room, with Chewie not talking to him. Han had made not one, but *two* errors, calculating the jump to hyperspace. Finally he had his trajectory—and he hadn't been able to run it.

"All right, all *right*, let's go fight," he'd yelled at

Chewie finally, almost twenty years ago, convinced they were both heading to their deaths—

He sat in the cockpit of the *Falcon*, almost twenty years later, and wondered what might have been: Leia would have been dead; and so would Luke. His children would never have been born. The Empire would still rule the galaxy, and he and Chewie would be traveling from world to world, one step ahead of the Imperials, one step ahead of the bounty hunters.

No, thought Han. *Not 'one step.' Someone would have caught me. Boba Fett, IG-88—someone—and I'd have had no friends to come and rescue me from Jabba.*

Twenty years.

To this day Han could remember with perfect clarity . . . how close he had come to punching in that trajectory, and leaving Leia and Luke behind. He woke up at night, sometimes, in cold sweats, thinking about it.

How *very* close.

If his parents were still alive, Han thought, they'd be impressed by the man he'd grown into—and not the least bit surprised at how close it had come to not happening.

Mari'ha Andona tapped a stud when the hail came.

"This is Control."

"This is General Solo." Mari'ha grimaced at the use of the title; Solo was certainly entitled to it, but Mari'ha had been running flight control over this sector of Coruscant long enough that she knew Solo only used it when he was going to be pushy about something.

"I'm going to take the Falcon *up for a bit. Any chance I could get you to pipe me a flight path?"*

"Yes, sir. What's your destination?"

"Haven't got one."

Mari'ha said calmly, "Excuse me? Sir?"

"I don't have one. I don't know where I'm going yet."

Mari'ha sighed, looking across the screens that

showed all the flights in her sector. There were so many of them that it was hard for a human to pick out any single blip as belonging to an individual ship.

She thought, *The flight droid is going to pitch a fit.* The flight droid always pitched a fit; it had acquired a dislike for General Solo many years ago now, when—

"Which part of this are you having difficulty with, Control?"

"I'm going to need a couple minutes," she muttered into the comm unit. "The flight droid doesn't like you."

"You need," said Solo, *"to clear a corridor and give me a flight path and do it right now before I have to go down to the tower personally and* charm *you to death. Do you copy that?"*

"I copy you, General." She finished composing his request for clearance, punched it in, and then sat there punching *Override,* over and over again, at the flight droid's objections. "And . . . here you go. Have a nice trip, General. Don't hurry back."

"Try not to miss me too much, sweetheart. A pleasure as usual. Solo out."

Not long after that, her supervisor's holo sprung into existence, one-sixth sized, in the viewing area off to her right.

"This is most irregular," he said severely. "Did General Solo give you a flight plan?"

"Nope."

"Estimated time of return?"

"Nope."

It was almost a shriek. *"Destination?"*

"Couldn't tell you. Nowhere in-system, though. He entered hyperspace about twenty minutes ago."

Strange things happen in the course of a lifetime:

When he had started out in his career as a bounty

hunter, Boba Fett had never even heard of the place—
Tatooine. But that small and meaningless desert planet,
as it turned out, became a part of Fett's life, and over
the course of the years kept intruding back into it.
Jabba the Hutt had established headquarters there;
Luke Skywalker, Fett learned many years later, had actually grown up on Tatooine.

The worst disaster of his life had taken place there,
his fall into the Great Pit of Carkoon, into the maw of
the Sarlacc.

Two years ago, Tatooine had intruded into Fett's life
again. Four mercs, two of them Devaronian, had
walked into a bar in Mos Eisley. One of the Devaronian
mercs recognized, or thought he had recognized, the
Butcher of Montellian Serat. The identification might
not have been accurate; the old Devaronian he pointed
to had promptly killed all four of the mercs, and no
one was able to question him about it.

The old Devaronian had vanished, clean off
Tatooine . . . and Fett had tracked him. Here, to Pep-
pel, a world almost as far away from Coruscant as
Tatooine.

The target. Kardue'sai'Malloc, the Butcher of
Montellian Serat. There was a five million credit bounty
on the Butcher, five million credits of retirement
money.

Boba Fett was not the man he had once been. His
right leg, from the knee down, was artificial. Only constant medical treatment kept him from developing a
cancer; the days he'd spent in the belly of the Sarlacc
had altered his metabolism permanently, had damaged
him genetically to such a degree that he could not have
had children had he wanted them; his cellular struc-
tures did not always regenerate the way they were
meant to.

To say nothing of the memories he had carried away
from the Sarlacc and the Sarlacc's genetic soup, memories that were not always his own.

Fett waited, on his belly in the cold, in the mud, nude except for the shorts that kept his privates decently covered, with arrows in a quiver slung across his back, and a bow in one hand, and a crystal knife inside a leather sheath. Malloc—or Labria, the name he'd been going by for the last couple of decades now—was trickier and more dangerous than anyone had ever dreamed. He'd had a reputation in Mos Eisley, Fett had learned; Labria, the worst spy in the city. He was a drunk, and nobody had respected him, or feared him, until the day he had killed four mercs in the prime of their lives.

Darkness gathered. Fett waited, shivering, worrying. Artificial light of some sort glimmered in the hut's sole window. The metal content of his artificial leg was low, but Fett did not know how good the Butcher's security system was; all he knew was that it was there. He'd slipped tripwires, light traps; had crawled, centimeter by centimeter, past blinking motion sensors.

If there were not some sort of sensor sweeping the clearing, Fett would have been surprised. It was the reason he had not worn his armor, nor brought more modern weapons.

The lights in the hut went out. The hut had no plumbing; the previous night at this time Malloc had waited for several minutes after the extinguishing of his light, letting his eyes acclimate to the darkness, Fett assumed, before coming outside.

Fett reached over his back, pulled an arrow free, and strung the bow. It was a compound bow, that required the least exertion *after* it had been pulled back; Fett pulled it and waited.

Last night at this time Malloc had come outside to relieve himself. Fett didn't know as much about Devaronians as he might have (though he had studied an anatomy chart for Devaronians; he didn't want to shoot the fellow in the wrong place). Conceivably they only relieved themselves once a week. If so, he was going to have to think of some other approach—

The door swung open, and the bounty stood in the doorway, assault rifle cradled in both hands, took a quick step outside, onto the porch, and then stepped off the porch and walked around to the side of the house nearer Fett's hiding place. Fett tracked Malloc as he moved over to the open-air toilet the Devaronian had dug for himself, ten meters outside the hut. He waited for Malloc to disrobe and relieve himself—and then waited until he was done, and pulling his clothing back together again.

He needed to keep this one alive, and Fett had shot too many individuals, of all species, to shoot anyone before he, she, or it, had emptied itself. Someone always had to clean up after it, and usually that was the person who wasn't in chains.

Fett let the fellow stand up from his toilet, turning away from Fett, and shot Malloc high in the back. He was on his feet and running, in a half stagger himself, running on legs that shrieked with pain, as Malloc stumbled forward, giving voice to something that managed to mix a scream and roar. Fett closed on Malloc and Fett rolled to get down low, and with the knife slashed Malloc across the hamstring of his right leg. Malloc fell forward, to his knees, still reaching up to try to pull the arrow free from his shoulder.

Fett pushed him forward, up against the hut's wall, grabbed Malloc by one of his horns and pulled his head back, and got the knife against his throat. "Move and you die," he whispered harshly.

The hut reeked.

The Butcher of Montellian Serat, Kardue'sai'Malloc, sat propped up against the wall, the arrow pulled from his back, but the wound still bleeding, and strained against the bonds that kept his hands pulled behind his back.

The hut was spacious; the hut's size was one of the things that had given Fett pause. He'd wondered what the Butcher was hiding inside it—mostly, wondered what weapons might be tucked away inside there, waiting for the wrong person.

There were no weapons, though, except for the rifle the Butcher had carried with him.

Fett had known the Devaronians were carnivores; had he not known it, the contents of the hut would have confirmed it. The slaughtered carcasses of half a dozen animals hung along the far wall. A corner of the room had a pile of bones and shells in it, stripped almost clean of flesh. Dozens of empty bottles were scattered among them.

In the opposite corner was the pit where Malloc had slept; and another several dozen bottles, still full of Merenzane Gold, lined up along the floorboards next to the pit.

Fett had not bothered to look at anything yet except the controls for the security system. As far as he could tell it was all passive security, nothing that would shoot at the *Slave IV* if he brought it down to a landing in the clearing a few kilometers back along his trail. Finally satisfied, he turned back to the bounty.

"On your feet. We're going to walk a bit. I had to leave the callback outside range of your sensors."

Malloc grimaced, showing sharp teeth. He was large for a Devaronian, which made him very large for a human. He spoke in Basic with less accent than Fett's own. "No. I don't think I will."

Fett hefted the man's own assault rifle. He shrugged. "Devaronians are tough; I know that about you. You do not go into shock and you do not die easily. You'll walk—or I'll burn off your arms and your legs to make you lighter, and then I'll *drag* you where we are going." Fett paused. "Your choice."

The bounty said wearily, "Kill me. I'm not walking."

"I'll do worse than kill you," said Fett patiently—his left knee was paining him, his entire right leg was on fire from the prosthesis upward, and he really didn't want to drag this very large Devaronian two kilometers, not even after lightening him.

Malloc let his head fall back, to the wall behind him. "Do you know what you're doing, bounty hunter? Do you even know who I *am*?"

Fett fired a quick burst into the wall near Malloc's head, to get his attention; it did no more than singe the damp wooden wallboards. "Listen. I am Boba Fett." It had been a generation since one of his bounties had failed to recognize the name; it brought this fellow's eyes alive. Fear, Fett assumed. "And you are Kardue'sai'Malloc, the Butcher of Montellian Serat, and you're worth five million credits. Alive. And *nothing* dead, so you *will not* annoy me into killing you."

"Boba Fett," he whispered. He stared up into Fett's face. "You're an ugly piece of prey . . . I heard you were after me."

Fett couldn't believe how much talking he was having to do to keep from dragging this fellow two klicks. "Yes. Now do I burn your—"

"They say you're honest."

That was an opening to a negotiation, if Fett had ever heard one. "What do you have? Something worth trading five million credits for?"

Malloc stared at Fett, searching his features for—Fett could not imagine what. He took a breath, winced, and then nodded. "Yes. By the Cold, I do. Something worth five million credits *easy*. Maybe more. Something *priceless*, Fett—"

Fett said impatiently, "What?"

"Kang," Malloc whispered. "Maxa Jandovar, Janet Lalasha. Miracle Meriko—"

The last name Fett recognized, and knew the idiot was lying to him. "Meriko died in Imperial custody twenty-five years ago, you lying fool, and the bounty on him was twenty thousand credits, not any five mil—"

"Music!" Malloc yelled. He glared at Fett. "You uncivilized barbarian! *Music!* I have the music of Maxa Jandovar, and Orin˙ Mersai. M'lar'Nkai'kambric," he took a deep breath, yelled again, *"Lubrics, Aishara, Dyll—"*

Fett shook his head wearily. "No. No, I don't care about your music. Now *will* you get up? Or must I carve you up and drag you?"

The Butcher leaned his head back and stared up at the roof. The light caught his predator's eyes and glimmered back out of them. "By the Cold," he whispered, "but you're ignorant. Even for a human you're ignorant. There are people who will *pay* for that music, Fett. I have the only recordings left of half a dozen of the galaxy's finest musicians. The Empire *killed* the musicians, destroyed their music—"

"Five million credits?" said Fett politely.

The Butcher hesitated a second too long. "More than that—"

Fett pointed the rifle at the Butcher's legs. "Negotiation is over. I will drag you if you make me," and he was not joking.

Malloc closed his eyes, and spoke a bare moment before Fett had decided to start cutting. "I'll walk. But you have to make me three promises. You dig up my music chips, they're buried in a holding case under a few centimeters of dirt, out back. After you deliver me to Devaron, you *take* those chips to the person I tell you to take them to, and you sell them to her for whatever she can offer. And finally—" He nodded toward the bottles of golden liquor. "We take six of those with us. I'm going to need them." He saw Fett shaking his head, and said sharply, "This is *not* a negotiation, ignorant human. You start shooting if you think it is, but I warn you, I'll do my level best to die on you between here and Devaron. I have a mean streak in me, bounty hunter."

Bounty hunting, thought Boba Fett wearily, *is not what it used to be.* He waved the rifle at Malloc. "Fine. Agreed. *Get up* . . . and show me where your blasted music is buried."

"Welcome to Death, Gentleman Morgavi. What do you have to declare?"

As was so frequently the case anymore, at least when dealing with other humans, the customs agent standing before Han Solo, in the bright Jubilar sunshine, seemed . . . well, he struck Han as younger than Luke Skywalker had seemed the first time Han had seen *him.*

A grin touched Han; he couldn't help it. "No. Nothing to declare."

The boy looked at the *Falcon,* and then back at Han. Suspicion worked its way across his face like a baby negotiating its first steps. "Nothing?" he asked finally.

Despite his best instincts Han's grin grew larger. "Sorry, no. I just came to Jubilar for a visit." The kid thought he was a smuggler. "I'll just head on over to the port bar," he said. "I expect you want to search the ship right about now."

The grin appeared to be offending the customs man. "Yes, sir. Why don't you just . . . wait in the bar. While we search. Of course, if you're in a hurry—" The man paused.

Han Solo tried to remember the last time he had bribed a customs official, and couldn't.

"I haven't smuggled anything since, well, practically before the Rebellion," Han told the fellow. He headed off toward the main terminal, turned back for a moment. "There are cargo holds right underneath the main deck. I left them unlocked, though. Don't break anything trying to get into them, okay?"

The customs agent stared after him.

• • •

"I'll have a beer," said Han. "Corellian, if you've got it."

The port bar was nearly empty; only a few elderly Gamorreans sat together in a booth in back, playing some game that involved throwing bones; a creature of some race Han had never seen before sat at the far end of the bartop, inhaling something that, even from here, reeked of ammonia.

The bartender looked Han over, nodded, and turned toward the bar. A long mirror hung on the wall behind the bar; Han stared at himself in it. He thought that the gray in his hair gave him a distinguished look.

"I thought this city was called 'Dying Slowly,' " Han said as a dark beer was laid down in front of him. "When did the name change?"

The bartender shrugged. "It's always been called just 'Death,' far as I know."

"How long you been on-planet?"

"Eight years."

"What for?"

The bartender stared at him. "Take some advice— you don't ask that sort of question around here." He shook his head and turned away.

Han nodded, and sat drinking his beer; he'd known that, once. A thought struck him. "Hey, buddy."

The bartender looked over at him.

"Just out of curiosity," said Han—

He paused and looked around at the nearly empty mid-afternoon bar.

He leaned back in toward the bartender. "Now that spice is legal . . . what sorts of things get smuggled around here, these days?"

The trip to Devaron took long enough that Malloc's shoulder wound was nearly healed by the time they neared hyperspace breakout, though the leg was starting to fester, and none of the drugs Fett had seemed to be helping—Fett hoped sincerely that the injury wouldn't kill the fellow before they reached Devaron.

Fett had sent a communication ahead to the Bounty Hunter's Guild. Normally he would not have bothered to involve the Guild; but normally he did not have a five million credit bounty. A Guild representative should be waiting at Devaron when they reached it.

Fett kept the Butcher down in the *Slave IV*'s holding room through most of the trip.

In the remaining minutes left before their exit from hyperspace, Fett dressed himself. The Mandalorian combat armor he dressed in was not the armor he had worn in years past; *that* armor, burned and cracked, was still somewhere deep inside the Great Pit of Carkoon, back on Tatooine. But Mandalorian combat armor, though rare, could still be acquired if you went about it right. For years Fett had been hearing about another bounty hunter who wore Mandalorian combat armor, a fellow named Jodo Kast. It had annoyed him terribly. With some frequency, during those years, Fett had found himself being blamed for, and credited with, things Kast had done.

Less than a year after his escape from the Sarlacc, Fett had hunted Jodo Kast down, via the Bounty Hunter's Guild; he'd pretended to be a client, disguised in bandages; his own Guild had not known him. He'd requested the services of Kast, and Kast had come; by that time Fett had changed into his own spare armor, taken away the impostor's armor, and also his life.

Before the ship left hyperspace Fett brought the Butcher up to the control room and put him in the chair nearest the airlock. Malloc was sweating heavily, fighting with his fear. He'd drunk his first five bottles early in the trip; Fett had held back the sixth bottle for this moment. Fett restrained Malloc at the ankles, and by his right hand; he left the Devorian's left hand unchained, so that Malloc might drink. Once he was satisfied with Malloc's bonds Fett unsealed and handed Malloc the last bottle of Merenzane Gold. It wasn't a matter of kindness on Fett's part; if it kept Malloc from struggling during the transfer to the Devaronian authorities, better to let him drink.

They'd barely spoken to one another the entire trip. Malloc lifted the bottle to his lips and swallowed three, four times, before speaking. "How much longer?"

Fett glanced at his controls. "Six minutes until breakout. At least twenty before we dock with the shuttle that'll take you downside." He paused. "Time enough for you to finish the bottle, if you work at it."

"Do you know what they're going to do to me?"

"They will feed you, still alive, to a pack of starved quarra." Fett paused. "Domesticated hunting animals—this practice is one of the things that's kept Devaron out of the New Republic, I've heard."

Malloc nodded a little convulsively and took another drink. "It's a bad way to die. I saw it done once, when I was a boy. You were right, Fett, we Devaronians don't die easy. The quarra go at the belly first, the soft flesh. But the condemned doesn't die of that. They may nibble on your ears, or your eyes or horns, but that won't kill you, either. If you're lucky the quarra tear your throat out quickly. You arch your head back and expose your throat, and if you're lucky—"

"The time you saw it done," said Fett curiously, "What had the condemned done?"

Malloc stared at the golden liquid in his free hand, and took another quick drink. "I don't think there's a word for it, exactly, in Basic. He went hunting, during famine, and caught his prey—and fed himself, and his quarra. He didn't bring it back to the tribe." He looked up at Fett. "Do you know what I did?"

Fett glanced over at his instruments. Several minutes

left until breakout; best let him talk. He looked back at
Malloc. "Yes."

"I was a good servant to the Empire," the Butcher
said. "My own people rose in rebellion. They sent my
command out to Hunt them down. And I did it, Fett. I
Hunted them across the northlands, and I caught them
in the city of Montellian Serat. We shelled them until
they surrendered—"

Fett nodded. "And after taking their surrender, you
executed them. Seven hundred of them."

"The Empire ordered us to move on. To reinforce
loyal troops, fighting just south of us. We were not to
leave any troops behind as guards for the prisoners
. . . and certainly we were not to leave any of them
living."

"They didn't tell you to execute the prisoners."

"They didn't have to." Malloc drank again, a huge
belt, lowering the level of the bottle noticeably. "It took
almost five minutes, Fett. We put them in a holding pen
and started shooting at them. They screamed and
screamed and screamed. We just kept shooting until
the screaming had stopped." He said almost plead-
ingly, "I was following orders."

"I know."

"They say you were Darth Vader's favorite bounty
hunter."

"Yes."

"Don't you have any loyalty to what you were?" A
touch of real anger glittered through Malloc's despair.
"I did the Empire's work, man! Doesn't that count for
anything?"

Fett thought about it. "I wish," he said finally, "that
the Empire had not fallen." He nodded, remembering,
and then said softly, "Yes. I used to enjoy my work
more."

Hopelessness settled on the Butcher—he sagged,
looking as though someone had just doubled the artificial gravity in the *Slave IV*. They always thought they

could bargain, or plead, right up to the last moment.
Malloc hadn't had a chance to ask the next question;
he asked it now. Virtually all of Fett's bounties, given
the chance, did—

"How did you catch me?"

A minute left to breakout. Fett nodded toward the
bottle Malloc held. "I traced sales of Merenzane Gold
across the entire sector Tatooine is in. They said, at the
bar you frequented on Tatooine, that it was your favorite drink."

Malloc stared at him. "That crap I drank on
Tatooine? That wasn't Merenzane Gold, you idiot, they
don't *serve* Merenzane Gold in bars like that, they just
pour it out of bottles that once, eons ago, were looked
at hard by a man who *heard* of Merenzane! Don't you
know *anything* about liquor?" he asked in despair.
"Haven't you a single civilized vice?"

Fett shook his head. "No. I do not drink, nor indulge
in other drugs. They are an insult to the flesh."

"So you Hunted me down because you thought I was
drinking Merenzane Gold, all those years on Tatooine.
Fett, I had *one* glass of real Gold the entire time I was on
that miserable excuse for a world." Malloc shook his
head in disbelief, took another swig from the bottle.
"By the Cold. I can't believe I got caught by a nerf
herder like you."

The hyperspace tunnel fragmented around them;
Fett turned away from Malloc, to his controls.

"Reality," said Fett, "doesn't care if you believe it."

Malloc threw the bottle, of course. The security system shot it out of the air with a single blaster bolt. The
bottle blew apart into shards that rattled against the
back of Fett's helmet; the liquid splashed against Fett's
armor.

"You should have drunk it," Fett said. He did not
have to look at Malloc to know the gray despair that
crossed his features. He'd seen it before, a thousand
times.

• • •

Fett docked with the shuttle, in orbit about Devaron.

The Guild representative came across first. Fett stood in the main entryway, rifle in hand, pointing it at the representative as he entered.

The representative was Bilman Dowd, a human, tall and thin and elderly, with a severe bearing and no discernible sense of humor; he had been in the Guild even longer than Fett, which was a remarkable accomplishment in this day and age. "Hunter Fett," he said, courteously enough.

"Dowd."

Dowd looked the Butcher over. Kardue'sai'Malloc sat motionlessly, staring straight ahead. He did not seem to be aware of Dowd's presence. "This is the Butcher, is it?"

"I believe so."

Dowd nodded. He carried with him a small slate, with various controls on it; he touched one now, and spoke. "Come across."

The *Slave IV*'s lock cycled again; four Devaronians entered, two of them in military dress, bearing rifles that they carried pointed at the *Slave IV*'s deck. The third was a female Devaronian, young, in gold robes and a gold headdress; the fourth, wearing robes of a cut similar to the woman's, except in black, was an older Devaronian, perhaps the Butcher's age.

All four hesitated at the sight of Fett, aiming his rifle at them—

Dowd gestured to the woman and said something in Devaronian. Fett had never actually heard the language spoken before; it was low and guttural and full of snarling consonants. It sounded like an invitation to a fight.

The woman's expression did not change. She crossed to the spot where Malloc sat—Fett had restrained his left hand prior to allowing anyone else on board. She kneeled in front of Malloc, looking the shivering prisoner over as though she were inspecting a carcass in the marketplace. Malloc's skin had acquired a blue tinge; Fett supposed it was something that happened to Devaronians when they were deathly afraid.

The woman stood up and nodded abruptly. She spoke in Devaronian—

Dowd said, "She says it's her father."

Fett nodded; it was the reason the bounty had been "Alive," rather than "Dead or Alive." It had only changed a few years back; the Devaronians had no longer been certain that the Butcher would be recognizable, dead.

The older Devaronian said grimly, in rather poor Basic, "We pay him now."

Dowd handed his tablet over to the Devaronian. The Devaronian laid his hand flat against the tablet, and spoke several words in Devaronian. Dowd took the panel back, tapped two of the controls in succession, and turned to Fett.

"You've been paid."

It was not the sort of thing Fett took anyone's word for; he took several steps backward, rifle still pointed at the group, and glanced slightly to the side. In a holofield at the edge of the control panel, a live link to the Guild Bank showed the current balance in Fett's numbered account—

C:4,507,303.

Five million credits, less the Guild's handling fee of 10%, plus the seven thousand, three hundred and three credits Fett had had in the account—business had been bad, recent years.

The relief that washed over Fett at the sight was the strongest emotion other than anger that he'd felt in at least a decade. He could afford to have a replacement clone for his lower right leg; he could afford the cancer treatments that had been bankrupting him. Fett barely heard himself say, "Take him. He's yours."

They hauled the Butcher up out of the chair he was restrained in, being none too gentle with him. As they pulled him to his feet, he yelled at Fett, in Basic: "You do what you promised!" The glare in his eyes was perfectly mad, as they dragged him toward the airlock. *"You take care of my music!"*

After the Devaronians had gone, Dowd stood with his tablet, looking at Fett with plain curiosity. Fett sat in the pilot's seat, still holding his rifle, pointed rather generally in Dowd's direction.

Dowd said, "You'll be retiring, I presume."

Fett shrugged. "I haven't thought about it."

Dowd nodded. "What did he mean—about the music?"

"He had a music collection. Music the Empire suppressed, apparently. He asked me to deliver it to a woman who would see that the music was published."

Dowd lifted an eyebrow. "Are you going to?"

"I said I would."

Dowd nodded. "You're a strange one." The comment didn't offend Fett; Dowd had made the observation before, and more than once, over the course of the decades they had known one another. Dowd reached into the pocket of his coat, and Fett stirred, bringing the rifle up slightly.

Dowd's smile was thin. "I've a message chip for you. Message that arrived at Guild headquarters. Do you want it?"

"Leave it on the deck," said Fett, "and leave. I'm very tired."

The message was amazing.

The encryption code was so old that Fett had to dig into his computer's archives to find the key for it. He'd made the practice, over the years, of giving his informants encryption codes in a numbered sequence; the first five digits of this message were 00802, which made it at least twenty-five years old—Fett's current encryption identification numbers started well upwards of 12,000.

He unarchived the encryption key for the 802 protocol, and decoded the message.

It was short. It said:

Han Solo is on Jubilar—Incavi Larado.

In a lifetime of bounty hunting, Boba Fett had rarely, in conversation with others, said two words when one would do. He didn't talk to himself, not *ever*—

Boba Fett said out loud, "One from the vaults."

On his way to Jubilar, Boba Fett played the music that the Butcher of Montellian Serat had thought more important than his own life.

There were over five hundred infochips in the carrying case the Butcher had buried; each chip had the capacity to hold almost a day's worth of music. Fett opened the case, pulled one free at random, and plugged it in.

The sounds that surrounded him were—different, he had to admit. Atonal, crashing, and thoroughly unpleasant to the ear. He shook his head, pulled the chip free, and decided to try one more.

A long silence after the chip was inserted. Fett waited, and finally, impatiently, reached for it—

The sound tugged at the limits of audibility. Fett froze in the motion of reaching for the chip, straining to hear. The whisper grew into the faintest sound of a woodwind, and then a high horn joined it, playing counterpoint—

Fett's hand dropped, and he leaned back in his chair, listening.

A voice that sounded female to Fett, but might have been a human male or an alien of any of a dozen sexes, for all Fett would have sworn to, joined in, weaving in and among the instruments, singing beautifully in a language that meant nothing to Fett, a language he had never heard before.

After a bit he reached up and pulled his helmet off.

"Lights off," he said a while later.

He sat there in the cool cabin, on his way to Jubilar to kill Han Solo, listening in the darkness to the only copy, anywhere in the galaxy, of the legendary Brullian Dyll's last concert.

In the icy Devaronian northlands, beneath the dark blue skies that had haunted Kardue'sai'Malloc's dreams for over two decades, some ten thousand Devaronians had converged in the Judgment Field outside the ruins of the ancient holy city of Montellian Serat, the city Malloc had shelled into its current state.

It was a beautiful day late in the cold season, with a chill breeze out of the north, and high pale clouds skidding across the darkened skies. The suns hung low on the southern horizon; the Blue Mountains lifted away up to the north. Malloc barely noticed the Devaronians surrounding him, the members of his family dressed in their robes of mourning, as they pushed him through the crowds, to the pit where the quarra waited.

He heard the quarra growl, heard the growl rising as he grew closer to the pit.

His daughter and brother walked a bare few steps behind him. Malloc recalled he had once had a wife; he wondered why she was not there.

Perhaps she had died.

A dozen quarra in the pit, lean and hungry, leaping up toward the spot where Malloc's guards brought him to a halt.

Devaronians are not creatures of ceremony; a herald cried out, "The Butcher of Montellian Serat!"—and the screams of the crowd raised up and surrounded Malloc, an immense roar that drowned out the noise of the snarling quarra; the bonds that held him were released and strong young hands shoved him forward, and into the pit where the starving quarra waited.

The quarra leapt, and had their teeth in him before he reached the ground.

He could see the Blue Mountains from where he fell.

He had almost forgotten the mountains, the forests, all those years on that desert world.

Oh, but the trees were beautiful.

Arch your head back.

They made Han buy the speeder—Jubilar wasn't big on rentals. Too frequently the rentals, and/or the renters, didn't come back.

In early twilight Han pulled the speeder to a stop at the address they'd given him, and got out to look around.

Almost thirty years.

He felt so odd: everything had *changed*. Places that he remembered as well-kept buildings had grown run-down, places that used to be run-down had been torn down and new buildings built in their steads. Slums had spread everywhere—the planet's never-ending battles had razed entire neighborhoods.

The neighborhood surrounding the Victory Forum, where Han had fought in Regional Sector Number Four's All-Human Free-For-All extravaganza, was a blasted ruin. It looked like the remains of some ancient civilization, worn down by the eons. The small buildings surrounding the Forum had their windows broken out and boarded up; flame and shells and blaster fire had scored them.

All that remained of the Forum itself was broken rubble strewn across a huge empty lot. Han stepped off the sidewalk, into the lot. Glass and gravel crunched

beneath his feet as he walked across it, toward the main
entrance.

He stood in the empty lot, staring at the desolation,
with a cool wind tugging at him—and suddenly it
struck him as though he were *there*, that moment, all
those years ago:

*. . . standing in the ring. Facing the opponents, with the
screams and cheers and taunts of the crowd in his ears. His
heart pounding and his breath coming short, as the match flag
fluttered down toward the ground, and the other three fighters
came at him.*

*Han took a running leap at the nearest. He got up two
meters off the ground and landed a flying kick into the face of
the onrushing first fighter. The man's nose broke, his head
snapped back—*

To this day Han had no clear memory of the next
several minutes. They'd recorded the fights, and he'd
seen the recording; but the knowledge of what had
happened did not connect to his blurred memories of
the events themselves. The boy had been hurt, and
hurt badly, walking off the mat with a broken arm
and a broken jaw, two broken ribs and a concussion
and bruises across half his body; the bruises turned
purple the next day. The woman who'd cared for Han
the next several days, he couldn't even remember what
she'd looked like, she was a strange one and he did
remember her running her fingers over the bruises,
plainly fascinated—

Here. Here. Right about . . . here.

Han stood on the spot. This empty place . . . this
was the spot. The ring. And when all was done, he'd
been the last one left on his feet—

Thirty years. Over half his life had passed since that
day.

Han took a slow step . . . stopped and took one last
look around at the devastation, a ruin stretching to the
horizon; and turned away and walked back to the
speeder, and sat motionlessly in the speeder, leaning

back with his hands clasped behind his head, staring up at the sky as darkness fell around him, remembering.

"Mayor Baker," Han said. "A real pleasure."

He'd met her in a brightly lit hydroponics warehouse, in a complex of warehouses at the edge of Death, in the part of Death they had used to call Executioner's Row. He'd come prepared; he was visibly armed with a blaster, had a couple of holdout blasters tucked inside his coat, and a third down in his boot.

Not that he expected any trouble; this was business, a business he'd been in for a long time before the Rebellion, and he knew what he was doing. But no point in taking chances, on a planet like Jubilar, in a city like Death.

They wanted him to smuggle Jandarra, to Shalam—Han had almost laughed aloud when the Mayor's representative had approached him; Jandarra was one of Leia's favorite treats. He expected that even she would be amused when he showed up on Shalam with a cargo hold full of it; and certainly the Shalamites wouldn't dare prosecute him over it.

The Mayor smiled at Solo. She was a tall, obese woman with features that did not take to a smile very easily. Four bodyguards were present; two at the entrance to the warehouse, two a few steps behind the Mayor, all armed with assault rifles. "Gentleman Morgavi—Luke, isn't it?"

Han smiled at her. "That's right. Luke Morgavi. As I told your aide, ma'am, I'm an independent trader out of Boranda."

She nodded. "A pleasure, Luke. Please, follow me." She led him down through rows of hydroponics tanks, to a row toward the back where the growing lights were both brighter and of a different wavelength. Inside the tanks, small purple and green tubular vegetables grew. "Jandarra," she said. "They're native to Jubilar; they're a great delicacy, and they usually only grow in the desert after relatively rare rainstorms. After almost two years of work we managed to cultivate them—"

Han nodded. "And the Shalamite slapped a 100% tariff on you."

Anger touched her voice. "We have *eighty* thousand credits' worth of Jandarra here that are only worth *forty* thousand after the Shalamite tariff."

"Those Shalamite," Han commiserated. "Can't trust 'em. They cheat at cards, too—did you know that?"

She stopped and studied Han. "No . . . Gentleman Morgavi. I did not." You *cheat at cards,* she thought, and kept the pleasant smile on her face—it was hard work. He really *didn't* recognize her—well, thirty years was a long time, after all, and she'd put on sixty kilos; and her last name, back then, before her marriage to the unfortunate Miagi Baker, had been Incavi Larado.

He'd said he'd come back, and here he was, the New Republic's infamous General Solo—and only thirty years late.

"Eighty thousand credits' worth," she said again. "Delivered to Shalamite. That's a forty thousand upside, and we'd be willing to go—"

"Fifty percent," said Han politely. "Which would be twenty thousand credits, and I'd be happy to make the run for that amount."

Her eyes narrowed. "You think you can get past the Shalamite Navy?"

Han said, "Lady, I used to run the *Imperial* lines. I'm talking about the old Star Destroyers—let me tell you a story—"

Out in the darkness, Boba Fett lay on his stomach, carefully adjusting his aim—he had to shoot in through the main entrance to the hydroponics warehouse, which wouldn't have been difficult except that some of the tanks were in his way—he was going to have to wait for

Solo to come back out toward the warehouse's entrance.

Fett waited patiently. He was surprised by his good fortune; who would have thought that a trap he had set three decades ago would come to fruition now?

Good fortune indeed—even today, with the Empire fallen, Han Solo had lots of enemies: Jabba's relatives, loyal officers of the Empire who had managed to maintain small fiefdoms on a thousand planets across the galaxy; and the various bounties on Solo, Dead or Alive, were still impressive, even with Vader and Jabba and the Empire long gone; still worth making an effort for, even with four and half million credits in the bank.

Oddly enough, the sight of Solo—looking at him through the rifle scope—filled Fett with a nostalgia that surprised him. There was no question in Fett's mind that Solo was a bad man, worse in every way that counted than the Butcher of Montellian Serat; and if that bounty had brought Fett no joy, he had handed the Butcher over to his executioners with little enough in the way of regret.

Solo, though—it came to Fett as a revelation that Solo's presence, over the course of the decades, had in a way been oddly comforting. He had been a part, however peripherally, of Fett's life for so long that Fett had difficulty picturing a world without him. The world had changed, and changed, and only Solo had remained a constant.

He'd Hunted Solo for various clients, various bounties. Fett had difficulty picturing a world without Solo—

—he leaned in and touched the scope's focusing ring. Solo's image, and that of the woman Fett assumed was Incavi Larado, though he did not recognize her, leapt into sharp relief; and Fett's finger tightened on the trigger.

He wouldn't make the mistake of trying to take Solo alive, not again.

And he would learn to picture a world without him.

• • •

They headed toward the entrance together, Mayor Incavi Baker smiling patiently, and with a certain effort
that Han did not miss. He stayed a half step behind her
as she walked, keeping part of her bulk between him
and the loading docks outside, where the lights had
gone out not long after they had all entered the warehouse together. The loading docks outside were pitch
black; they might have assembled an army for all Han
knew—

"—so this kid," said Han, "his name was—uh, Maris,
and this old guy with delusions—Jocko, yeah, anyway
this guy Jocko, he thinks he's a *Jedi Knight*—and let me
tell you, that old guy with his delusions, he was a pain in
the butt—anyway they tell me they have to get past the
Imperial lines—"

What did they have waiting for him out there?

What had he walked into?

He knows something is wrong, Fett thought. *He's—*

The main power line entered the warehouse at the
northeast, and split, one bundle running up to the ceiling and the overhead lights, and another bundle running back toward the hydroponics tanks.

Han cocked his wrist a certain way, and the holdout
blaster in his left sleeve dropped down into his hand.

Boba Fett had the crosshairs hovering just to the left of
Incavi Baker's approaching form; the cross-hair found
Solo's breast, lost it, found it again.

Fett squeezed the trigger—

—the warehouse lights died—

The blaster bolt tore through the darkness like a flash of lightning.

Han hit the ground rolling, sparks still trailing away from the spot where his first shot had struck the power cable, rolled away firing left-handed at the locations where he remembered the two closer bodyguards standing, pulling his blaster free right-handed. Screams, the woman was screaming, and he got off four shots with the holdout before it malfunctioned, burning out, the power supply flashing hot and terribly bright as it went, lighting Han as a target to the world, and Han came up out of his roll and made it to his feet and ran backward through the darkness, through the rows of hydroponics tanks, spots dancing in his eyes, using his scalded left hand on the sides of the tanks, to guide himself, as blaster bolts rained around him.

In that single flash as the holdout blaster had arced out, he had seen a shape running toward the warehouse entrance, a shape out of Han Solo's nightmares, a shape out of the galaxy's darkest history—a man in Mandalorian combat armor.

Incavi Baker lay on her back, staring up into infinity. There was a terrible pain in her side, and she knew she was dying.

She wished it weren't so dark. Bright lights flashed around her, blaster bolts that lit the world up briefly, but even the blaster bolts were fading now.

A figure loomed up out of the darkness, knelt beside her. A man in gray armor. Incavi opened her mouth— but nothing came, and the man reached for her.

Something sharp and cold touched her neck.

Gradually, the pain went away.

• • •

A ringing in his ears.

The four bodyguards were dead; Solo must have killed the one off to the side, Fett thought, curled up around whatever wound Solo had left in him—Fett knew he had only killed the three who were still standing when he entered the warehouse, and that had been as much reflex as anything.

But—

He knelt beside the woman, holding her hand, until her thrashing stopped.

In all his years as a bounty hunter he had never killed the wrong target before, and there was a tightness in his throat he hadn't felt since the day of his exile from Concord Dawn. He felt an absurd desire to apologize to the woman, which was ridiculous, she was as guilty of sin as any human being had ever been in the history of time, Fett had known her in her earlier days and there was nothing worthwhile in her or in her life, and certainly the galaxy would not miss her presence—

But he had not meant to kill her.

She shuddered slightly and her hand, holding his, went limp.

The macrobinoculars buried in his helmet didn't help much, not in this darkness; they showed the still-warm forms of four bodyguards, and the bulk of this dead old woman; they showed the heat still emanating from the lamp fixtures that were now without power.

Toward the back of the warehouse, a heat source moved.

Fett came to his feet, rifle in hand, and went Hunting.

Mandalorian combat armor.

I didn't come prepared for this, Han thought. He had an assault rifle, taken from the bodyguard he'd kicked in the groin, but that wasn't going to help so much, unless he got in close to Fett, and that was going to be hard, with the macrobinoculars in Fett's helmet.

He had to get out of this darkened warehouse, out into the night, where there were places to run, and places to hide, and try to reach the speeder he'd come here in.

Han couldn't believe this was happening to him.

He gathered his legs up beneath him, checked the safety on the assault rifle—he heard movement, out toward the front of the warehouse. Careful and quick—he kept his head down and ran in a crouch toward the warehouse's rear entrance.

Lando would be jealous, if Han made it back to tell him about it, and Lando made it back to be told.

Leia was going to be furious.

Fett ducked down behind one of the growing tanks, unlimbered his flare gun and fired a shot toward the warehouse's roof.

Actinic orange light flared; it would give Solo some light to work with. The interior of the warehouse became bright as day, and huge wavering shadows struck away from the warehouse's supporting beams, as the flare hit the ceiling, crawled along it for several seconds, and started to descend.

Something rattled, off at the eastern end of the warehouse; Fett held his position, held his fire. Solo had thrown something—the sound came again. Patience, patience—

A single shot, the sound of broken glass, that was Solo making an exit for himself through one of the windows, before the flare faded, while he could still see to run, and Fett surged to his feet to shoot Solo down as he made for the broken window.

He had time to see Han Solo, standing fifty meters away, pointing one of the bodyguards' assault rifles at him. The shot took Fett in his breastplate and blew him off his feet.

Han Solo turned and ran, hit the shattered window and dove through it like a young man in his prime.

Boba Fett rolled over, staggered back to his feet only a second later, the breastplate of his combat armor so hot it burned everywhere it touched him, and in a murderous rage charged after Solo, as unaware of the pain that throbbed in his legs and chest as if it belonged to someone else.

Han ran toward his speeder under the dim light from the planet's only moon. He was slightly disoriented; he couldn't remember whether the downlot where he'd left the speeder was south and west, or south and east; he ran south down one of the long alleyways between the warehouses, breath coming short, and came up to the last building, the last cover before the downlot, and hesitated before rounding the corner, the downlot was either immediately to his left or immediately to his right. He tried to envision the layout of the warehouse park in his mind—he thought he'd come the quick way around, but maybe not, and if he hadn't, then Fett might have reached the downlot before him.

A scraping sound, metal on stone—

Before he even realized what he was doing Han found himself rounding the corner, rifle up and finger tightening on the trigger as Boba Fett was turning toward him, bringing up his own rifle—

They stood there in the middle of nowhere, on a planet the rest of the galaxy had more than half forgotten, pointing assault rifles at one another, from a distance of less than a meter.

Han didn't fire.

Fett didn't fire.

Bizarre details piled in on Han. The aperture of Fett's assault rifle was huge, as big as the Death Star had seemed at first sight. The barrel wasn't perfectly steady, it wavered slightly, moving around in almost invisibly tiny circles. The moonlight glinted off Fett's scarred armor; Han could see the moon, reflected darkly on the black visor.

He was still out of breath from the running. His voice caught when he spoke. "I guess we're going to . . . die together."

Fett's voice—as harsh and raw as ever. "Evidently."

Han stared over the sight at him. "Your armor won't save you. Not at this range."

"No."

"I doubt you can kill me quick enough to keep me from firing."

Fett's helmet moved, slightly—a nod. "I doubt it too."

Han did not dare take his eye away from his rifle's sight, aiming at the base of Fett's throat. "You killed those people back there. The woman."

Han could have sworn he saw a shiver run up the bounty hunter's frame. "I'm sorry about that. They— she—was not the target."

Han almost pulled the trigger on him. He could hear the rage in his own voice. *"You're* going to die and *I'm* going to die and maybe we both of us deserve it. That woman didn't do any—"

"She's the one who *called* me!"

Han took a step forward and screamed, *"I don't care!"* He found to his amazement that he was standing with the barrel of his rifle jammed up against Fett's armor, that the barrel of Fett's rifle was digging into his own breastbone. "I don't know what made you like you are, you think you get to decide who lives and dies, I don't care, come on, pull the trigger and we'll die together!" He stared into the black visor. "Last decision you'll *ever* get to make."

Boba Fett said in a voice so soft Han would have sworn it could not have been Fett's, "You first." His voice got even softer, amazingly. "You're married, aren't you? You have children who need you. What were you *doing* out here, Solo, pretending to be young? This is no place for a man like you."

The fury that touched Han was bone deep. "Don't you talk about my children, I'll kill you so fast—"

"Do you *want* to die?"

Han took a deep breath. "Do you?"

Fett shook his head, the tiniest possible movement of the visor. "No. But I do not see a way out."

The faintest breath of hope touched Han. "All right. You put down your rifle. I won't kill you if you put down your rifle."

Fett whispered it. "No. You put down *yours*. I won't kill you if you put down yours. I'll let you go back to your family, unharmed. Put down your weapons—"

"I don't trust you."

"Nor I," said Fett, "you."

A cool wind blew across the downlot; Han felt it drying his sweat, chilling him. "We take five steps back," Han said finally. "You drop your rifle and you run like a gundark on fire. Even if I do shoot at you that armor would protect you."

"I have bad legs. I don't think I can outrun you."

Han could not stop thinking of his children, of Leia. "Just walk away, put the rifle down and walk away. I'm an honest man. I won't kill you."

"You're a liar," said Fett, "by all the evidence. I think you would." Fett paused. "When I was a young man," he said finally, "I think I would have pulled the trigger by now. But I find that I do not hate you, and I am not ready to die to remove you from the world."

"I made a mistake, coming here to Jubilar. I *do* hate you, I hate everything you've done—but my wife and children need me."

"I don't see a way out of this," said Fett, "that does not involve trying to trust one another."

"This rifle is getting heavy," said Han, which it was;

he watched Fett over the sight. "What are we going to do?"

"Everyone dies," said Fett.

"Yeah. Eventually. But it doesn't have to be today, not for either of us."

Fett shook his head; the helmet barely moved, and Han did not imagine that Fett's attention had shifted even slightly. "I do not know," Fett said softly. "Trust is hard, among enemies. Perhaps we should return to the battle; perhaps, Han Solo, we should let fly, and once more let fate decide who will survive, as we did when we were young."

The World of
STAR WARS Novels

In May 1991, *Star Wars* caused a sensation in the publishing industry
with the Bantam Spectra release of Timothy Zahn's novel *Heir to the
Empire*. For the first time, Lucasfilm Ltd. had authorized new novels
that *continued* the famous story told in George Lucas's three block-
buster motion pictures: *Star Wars*, *The Empire Strikes Back*, and *Return of the Jedi*. Reader reaction was immediate and tumultuous: *Heir*
reached #1 on the *New York Times* bestseller list and demonstrated that
Star Wars lovers were eager for exciting new stories set in this universe, written by leading science fiction authors who shared their pas-
sion. Since then, each Bantam *Star Wars* novel has been an instant
national bestseller.

Lucasfilm and Bantam decided that future novels in the series would
be interconnected: that is, events in one novel would have consequences in the others. You might say that each Bantam *Star Wars*
novel, enjoyable on its own, is also part of a much larger tale.

Here is a special look at Bantam's *Star Wars* books, along with
excerpts from the more recent novels. Each one is available now wherever Bantam Books are sold.

SHADOWS OF THE EMPIRE
by Steve Perry
Setting: Between *The Empire Strikes Back* and *Return of the Jedi*

*Here is a very special STAR WARS story dealing with Black Sun, a
galaxy-spanning criminal organization that is masterminded by one of
the most interesting villains in the STAR WARS universe: Xizor, dark
prince of the Falleen. Xizor's chief rival for the favor of Emperor
Palpatine is none other than Darth Vader himself—alive and well, and
a major character in this story, since it is set during the events of the
STAR WARS film trilogy.*

In the opening prologue, we revisit a familiar scene from The Empire Strikes Back, *and are introduced to our marvelous new bad guy:*

*He looks like a walking corpse, Xizor thought. Like a mummified
body dead a thousand years. Amazing he is still alive, much less the*

most powerful man in the galaxy. He isn't even that old; it is more as if something is slowly eating him.

Xizor stood four meters away from the Emperor, watching as the man who had long ago been Senator Palpatine moved to stand in the holocam field. He imagined he could smell the decay in the Emperor's worn body. Likely that was just some trick of the recycled air, run through dozens of filters to ensure that there was no chance of any poison gas being introduced into it. Filtered the life out of it, perhaps, giving it that dead smell.

The viewer on the other end of the holo-link would see a close-up of the Emperor's head and shoulders, of an age-ravaged face shrouded in the cowl of his dark zeyd-cloth robe. The man on the other end of the transmission, light-years away, would not see Xizor, though Xizor would be able to see him. It was a measure of the Emperor's trust that Xizor was allowed to be here while the conversation took place.

The man on the other end of the transmission—if he could still be called that—

The air swirled inside the Imperial chamber in front of the Emperor, coalesced, and blossomed into the image of a figure down on one knee. A caped humanoid biped dressed in jet black, face hidden under a full helmet and breathing mask:

Darth Vader.

Vader spoke: "What is thy bidding, my master?"

If Xizor could have hurled a power bolt through time and space to strike Vader dead, he would have done it without blinking. Wishful thinking: Vader was too powerful to attack directly.

"There is a great disturbance in the Force," the Emperor said.

"I have felt it," Vader said.

"We have a new enemy. Luke Skywalker."

Skywalker? That had been Vader's name, a long time ago. Who was this person with the same name, someone so powerful as to be worth a conversation between the Emperor and his most loathsome creation? More importantly, why had Xizor's agents not uncovered this before now? Xizor's ire was instant—but cold. No sign of his surprise or anger would show on his imperturbable features. The Falleen did not allow their emotions to burst forth as did many of the inferior species; no, the Falleen ancestry was not fur but scales, not mammalian but reptilian. Not wild but coolly calculating. Such was much better. Much safer.

"Yes, my master," Vader continued.

"He could destroy us," the Emperor said.

Xizor's attention was riveted upon the Emperor and the holographic image of Vader kneeling on the deck of a ship far away. Here was interesting news indeed. Something the Emperor perceived as a danger to himself? Something the Emperor feared?

"He's just a boy," Vader said. "Obi-Wan can no longer help him."

Obi-Wan. That name Xizor knew. He was among the last of the Jedi Knights, a general. But he'd been dead for decades, hadn't he?

Apparently Xizor's information was wrong if Obi-Wan had been helping someone who was still a boy. His agents were going to be sorry.

Even as Xizor took in the distant image of Vader and the nearness of the Emperor, even as he was aware of the luxury of the Emperor's private and protected chamber at the core of the giant pyramidal palace, he was also able to make a mental note to himself: Somebody's head would roll for the failure to make him aware of all this. Knowledge was power; lack of knowledge was weakness. This was something he could not permit.

The Emperor continued. "The Force is strong with him. The son of Skywalker must not become a Jedi."

Son of Skywalker?

Vader's son! Amazing!

"If he could be turned he would become a powerful ally," Vader said.

There was something in Vader's voice when he said this, something Xizor could not quite put his finger on. Longing? Worry?

Hope?

"Yes . . . yes. He would be a great asset," the Emperor said. "Can it be done?"

There was the briefest of pauses. "He will join us or die, master."

Xizor felt the smile, though he did not allow it to show any more than he had allowed his anger play. Ah. Vader wanted Skywalker alive, *that* was what had been in his tone. Yes, he had said that the boy would join them or die, but this latter part was obviously meant only to placate the Emperor. Vader had no intention of killing Skywalker, his own son; that was obvious to one as skilled in reading voices as was Xizor. He had not gotten to be the Dark Prince, Underlord of Black Sun, the largest criminal organization in the galaxy, merely on his formidable good looks. Xizor didn't truly understand the Force that sustained the Emperor and made him and Vader so powerful, save to know that it certainly worked somehow. But he did know that it was something the extinct Jedi had supposedly mastered. And now, apparently, this new player had tapped into it. Vader wanted Skywalker alive, had practically promised the Emperor that he would deliver him alive—and converted.

This was most interesting.

Most interesting indeed.

The Emperor finished his communication and turned back to face him. "Now, where were we, Prince Xizor?"

The Dark Prince smiled. He would attend to the business at hand, but he would not forget the name of Luke Skywalker.

THE TRUCE AT BAKURA by Kathy Tyers
Setting: Immediately after *Return of the Jedi*

The day after his climactic battle with Emperor Palpatine and the sacrifice of his father, Darth Vader, who died saving his life, Luke Skywalker helps recover an Imperial drone ship bearing a startling message intended for the Emperor. It is a distress signal from the far-off Imperial outpost of Bakura, which is under attack by an alien invasion force, the Ssi-ruuk. Leia sees a rescue mission as an opportunity to achieve a diplomatic victory for the Rebel Alliance, even if it means fighting alongside former Imperials. But Luke receives a vision from Obi-Wan Kenobi revealing that the stakes are even higher: the invasion at Bakura threatens everything the Rebels have won at such great cost.

STAR WARS: X-WING
by Michael A. Stackpole
ROGUE SQUADRON
WEDGE'S GAMBLE
THE KRYTOS TRAP
Setting: Two and a half years after *Return of the Jedi*

Inspired by X-wing, the bestselling computer game from LucasArts Entertainment Co., this exciting series chronicles the further adventures of the most feared and fearless fighting force in the galaxy. A new generation of X-wing pilots, led by Commander Wedge Antilles, is combating the remnants of the Empire still left after the events of the STAR WARS movies. Here are novels full of explosive space action, nonstop adventure, and the special brand of wonder known as STAR WARS.

In this very early scene, young Corellian pilot Corran Horn faces a tough challenge fast enough to get his heart pounding—and this is only a simulation! [P.S.: "Whistler" is Corran's R2 astromech droid]:

The Corellian brought his proton torpedo targeting program up and locked on to the TIE. It tried to break the lock, but turbolaser fire from the *Korolev* boxed it in. Corran's heads-up display went red and he triggered the torpedo. "Scratch one eyeball."

The missile shot straight in at the fighter, but the pilot broke hard to port and away, causing the missile to overshoot the target. *Nice flying!* Corran brought his X-wing over and started down to loop in behind the TIE, but as he did so, the TIE vanished from his forward screen and reappeared in his aft arc. Yanking the stick hard to the right and pulling it back, Corran wrestled the X-wing up and to starboard, then inverted and rolled out to the left.

A laser shot jolted a tremor through the simulator's couch. *Lucky thing I had all shields aft!* Corran reinforced them with energy from his lasers, then evened them out fore and aft. Jinking the fighter right and left, he avoided laser shots coming in from behind, but they all came in far closer than he liked.

He knew Jace had been in the bomber, and Jace was the only pilot in the unit who could have stayed with him. *Except for our leader.* Corran smiled broadly. *Coming to see how good I really am, Commander Antilles? Let me give you a clinic.* "Make sure you're in there solid, Whistler, because we're going for a little ride."

Corran refused to let the R2's moan slow him down. A snap-roll brought the X-wing up on its port wing. Pulling back on the stick yanked the fighter's nose up away from the original line of flight. The TIE stayed with him, then tightened up on the arc to close distance. Corran then rolled another ninety degrees and continued the turn into a dive. Throttling back, Corran hung in the dive for three seconds, then hauled back hard on the stick and cruised up into the TIE fighter's aft.

The X-wing's laser fire missed wide to the right as the TIE cut to the left. Corran kicked his speed up to full and broke with the TIE. He let the X-wing rise above the plane of the break, then put the fighter through a twisting roll that ate up enough time to bring him again into the TIE's rear. The TIE snapped to the right and Corran looped out left.

He watched the tracking display as the distance between them grew to be a kilometer and a half, then slowed. *Fine, you want to go nose to nose? I've got shields and you don't.* If Commander Antilles wanted to commit virtual suicide, Corran was happy to oblige him. He tugged the stick back to his sternum and rolled out in an inversion loop. *Coming at you!*

The two starfighters closed swiftly. Corran centered his foe in the crosshairs and waited for a dead shot. Without shields the TIE fighter would die with one burst, and Corran wanted the kill to be clean. His

HUD flicked green as the TIE juked in and out of the center, then locked green as they closed.

The TIE started firing at maximum range and scored hits. At that distance the lasers did no real damage against the shields, prompting Corran to wonder why Wedge was wasting the energy. Then, as the HUD's green color started to flicker, realization dawned. *The bright bursts on the shields are a distraction to my targeting! I better kill him now!*

Corran tightened down on the trigger button, sending red laser needles stabbing out at the closing TIE fighter. He couldn't tell if he had hit anything. Lights flashed in the cockpit and Whistler started screeching furiously. Corran's main monitor went black, his shields were down, and his weapons controls were dead.

The pilot looked left and right. "Where is he, Whistler?"

The monitor in front of him flickered to life and a diagnostic report began to scroll by. Bloodred bordered the damage reports. "Scanners, out; lasers, out; shields, out; engine, out! I'm a wallowing Hutt just hanging here in space."

THE COURTSHIP OF PRINCESS LEIA
by Dave Wolverton
Setting: Four years after *Return of the Jedi*

One of the most interesting developments in Bantam's Star Wars *novels is that in their storyline, Han Solo and Princess Leia start a family. This tale reveals how the couple originally got together. Wishing to strengthen the fledgling New Republic by bringing in powerful allies, Leia opens talks with the Hapes consortium of more than sixty worlds. But the consortium is ruled by the Queen Mother, who, to Han's dismay, wants Leia to marry her son, Prince Isolder. Before this action-packed story is over, Luke will join forces with Isolder against a group of Force-trained "witches" and face a deadly foe.*

HEIR TO THE EMPIRE
DARK FORCE RISING
THE LAST COMMAND
by Timothy Zahn
Setting: Five years after *Return of the Jedi*

This #1 bestselling trilogy introduces two legendary forces of evil into the Star Wars *literary pantheon. Grand Admiral Thrawn has taken control of the Imperial fleet in the years since the destruction of the Death Star, and the mysterious Joruus C'baoth is a fearsome Jedi Master who has been seduced by the dark side. Han and Leia have now been married for about a year, and as the story begins, she is pregnant with twins. Thrawn's plan is to crush the Rebellion and resurrect the Empire's New Order with C'baoth's help—and in return, the Dark Master will get Han and Leia's Jedi children to mold as he wishes. For as readers of this magnificent trilogy will see, Luke Skywalker is not the last of the old Jedi. He is the first of the new.*

The Jedi Academy Trilogy:
JEDI SEARCH
DARK APPRENTICE
CHAMPIONS OF THE FORCE
by Kevin J. Anderson
Setting: Seven years after *Return of the Jedi*

In order to assure the continuation of the Jedi Knights, Luke Skywalker has decided to start a training facility: a Jedi Academy. He will gather Force-sensitive students who show potential as prospective Jedi and serve as their mentor, as Jedi Masters Obi-Wan Kenobi and Yoda did for him. Han and Leia's twins are now toddlers, and there is a third Jedi child: the infant Anakin, named after Luke and Leia's father. In this trilogy, we discover the existence of a powerful Imperial dooms-day weapon, the horrifying Sun Crusher—which will soon become the centerpiece of a titanic struggle between Luke Skywalker and his most brilliant Jedi Academy student, who is delving dangerously into the dark side.

CHILDREN OF THE JEDI
by Barbara Hambly
Setting: Eight years after *Return of the Jedi*

The Star Wars *characters face a menace from the glory days of the Empire when a thirty-year-old automated Imperial Dreadnaught comes to life and begins its grim mission: to gather forces and annihilate a long-forgotten stronghold of Jedi children. When Luke is whisked onboard, he begins to communicate with the brave Jedi Knight who paralyzed the ship decades ago, and gave her life in the process. Now she is part of the vessel, existing in its artificial intelli-*

gence core, and guiding Luke through one of the most unusual adventures he has ever had.

In this scene, Luke discovers that an evil presence is gathering, one that will force him to join the battle:

Like See-Threepio, Nichos Marr sat in the outer room of the suite to which Cray had been assigned, in the power-down mode that was the droid equivalent of rest. Like Threepio, at the sound of Luke's almost noiseless tread he turned his head, aware of his presence.

"Luke?" Cray had equipped him with the most sensitive vocal modulators, and the word was calibrated to a whisper no louder than the rustle of the blueleaves massed outside the windows. He rose, and crossed to where Luke stood, the dull silver of his arms and shoulders a phantom gleam in the stray flickers of light. "What is it?"

"I don't know." They retreated to the small dining area where Luke had earlier probed his mind, and Luke stretched up to pin back a corner of the lamp-sheath, letting a slim triangle of butter-colored light fall on the purple of the vulwood tabletop. "A dream. A premonition, maybe." It was on his lips to ask, *Do you dream?* but he remembered the ghastly, imageless darkness in Nichos's mind, and didn't. He wasn't sure if his pupil was aware of the difference from his human perception and knowledge, aware of just exactly what he'd lost when his consciousness, his self, had been transferred.

In the morning Luke excused himself from the expedition Tomla El had organized with Nichos and Cray to the Falls of Dessiar, one of the places on Ithor most renowned for its beauty and peace. When they left he sought out Umwaw Moolis, and the tall herd leader listened gravely to his less than logical request and promised to put matters in train to fulfill it. Then Luke descended to the House of the Healers, where Drub McKumb lay, sedated far beyond pain but with all the perceptions of agony and nightmare still howling in his mind.

"Kill you!" He heaved himself at the restraints, blue eyes glaring furiously as he groped and scrabbled at Luke with his clawed hands. "It's all poison! I see you! I see the dark light all around you! You're him! You're him!" His back bent like a bow; the sound of his shrieking was like something being ground out of him by an infernal mangle.

Luke had been through the darkest places of the universe and of his own mind, had done and experienced greater evil than perhaps any man had known on the road the Force had dragged him . . . Still, it was hard not to turn away.

"We even tried yarrock on him last night," explained the Healer in charge, a slightly built Ithorian beautifully tabby-striped green and yellow under her simple tabard of purple linen. "But apparently the earlier doses that brought him enough lucidity to reach here from his point of origin oversensitized his system. We'll try again in four or five days."

Luke gazed down into the contorted, grimacing face.

"As you can see," the Healer said, "the internal perception of pain and fear is slowly lessening. It's down to ninety-three percent of what it was when he was first brought in. Not much, I know, but something."

"Him! *Him! HIM!*" Foam spattered the old man's stained gray beard.

Who?

"I wouldn't advise attempting any kind of mindlink until it's at least down to fifty percent, Master Skywalker."

"No," said Luke softly.

Kill you all. And, *They are gathering . . .*

"Do you have recordings of everything he's said?"

"Oh, yes." The big coppery eyes blinked assent. "The transcript is available through the monitor cubicle down the hall. We could make nothing of them. Perhaps they will mean something to you."

They didn't. Luke listened to them all, the incoherent groans and screams, the chewed fragments of words that could be only guessed at, and now and again the clear disjointed cries: "Solo! Solo! Can you hear me? Children . . . Evil . . . Gathering here . . . Kill you all!"

DARKSABER by Kevin J. Anderson
Setting: Immediately thereafter

Not long after Children of the Jedi, *Luke and Han learn that evil Hutts are building a reconstruction of the original Death Star—and that the Empire is still alive, in the form of Daala, who has joined forces with Pellaeon, former second in command to the feared Grand Admiral Thrawn. In this early scene, Luke has returned to the home of Obi-Wan Kenobi on Tatooine to try and consult a long-gone mentor:*

He stood anxious and alone, feeling like a prodigal son outside the ramshackle, collapsed hut that had once been the home of Obi-Wan Kenobi.

Luke swallowed and stepped forward, his footsteps crunching in the silence. He had not been here in many years. The door had fallen off its hinges; part of the clay front wall had fallen in. Boulders and crumbled adobe jammed the entrance. A pair of small, screeching desert rodents snapped at him and fled for cover; Luke ignored them.

Gingerly, he ducked low and stepped into the home of his first mentor.

Luke stood in the middle of the room breathing deeply, turning around, trying to sense the presence he desperately needed to see. This was the place where Obi-Wan Kenobi had told Luke of the Force. Here, the old man had first given Luke his lightsaber and hinted at the truth about his father, "from a certain point of view," dispelling the diversionary story that Uncle Owen had told, at the same time planting seeds of his own deceptions.

"Ben," he said and closed his eyes, calling out with his mind as well as his voice. He tried to penetrate the invisible walls of the Force and reach to the luminous being of Obi-Wan Kenobi who had visited him numerous times, before saying he could never speak with Luke again.

"Ben, I need you," Luke said. Circumstances had changed. He could think of no other way past the obstacles he faced. Obi-Wan had to answer. It wouldn't take long, but it could give him the key he needed with all his heart.

Luke paused and listened and sensed—

But felt nothing. If he could not summon Obi-Wan's spirit here in the empty dwelling where the old man had lived in exile for so many years, Luke didn't believe he could find his former teacher ever again.

He echoed the words Leia had used more than a decade earlier, beseeching him, "Help me, Obi-Wan Kenobi," Luke whispered, "you're my only hope."

THE CRYSTAL STAR
by Vonda N. McIntyre
Setting: Ten years after *Return of the Jedi*

Leia's three children have been kidnapped. That horrible fact is made worse by Leia's realization that she can no longer sense her children through the Force! While she, Artoo-Detoo, and Chewbacca trail the kidnappers, Luke and Han discover a planet that is suffering strange quantum effects from a nearby star. Slowly freezing into a perfect crystal and disrupting the Force, the star is blunting Luke's power and crippling the Millennium Falcon. *These strands converge in an apocalyptic threat not only to the fate of the New Republic, but to the universe itself.*

The Black Fleet Crisis
BEFORE THE STORM
SHIELD OF LIES
by Michael P. Kube-McDowell
Setting: Twelve years after *Return of the Jedi*

Long after setting up the hard-won New Republic, yesterday's Rebels have become today's administrators and diplomats. But the peace is not to last for long. A restless Luke must journey to his mother's homeworld in a desperate quest to find her people; Lando seizes a mysterious spacecraft with unimaginable weapons of destruction; and waiting in the wings is an horrific battle fleet under the control of a ruthless leader bent on a genocidal war.

Here is an opening scene from Before the Storm:

In the pristine silence of space, the Fifth Battle Group of the New Republic Defense Fleet blossomed over the planet Bessimir like a beautiful, deadly flower.

The formation of capital ships sprang into view with startling suddenness, trailing fire-white wakes of twisted space and bristling with weapons. Angular Star Destroyers guarded fat-hulled fleet carriers, while the assault cruisers, their mirror finishes gleaming, took the point.

A halo of smaller ships appeared at the same time. The fighters among them quickly deployed in a spherical defensive screen. As the Star Destroyers firmed up their formation, their flight decks quickly spawned scores of additional fighters.

At the same time, the carriers and cruisers began to disgorge the bombers, transports, and gunboats they had ferried to the battle. There was no reason to risk the loss of one fully loaded—a lesson the Republic had learned in pain. At Orinda, the commander of the fleet carrier *Endurance* had kept his pilots waiting in the launch bays, to protect the smaller craft from Imperial fire as long as possible. They were still there when *Endurance* took the brunt of a Super Star Destroyer attack and vanished in a ball of metal fire.

Before long more than two hundred warships, large and small, were bearing down on Bessimir and its twin moons. But the terrible, restless power of the armada could be heard and felt only by the ships' crews. The silence of the approach was broken only on the fleet comm channels, which had crackled to life in the first moments with encoded bursts of noise and cryptic ship-to-ship chatter.

At the center of the formation of great vessels was the flagship of the Fifth Battle Group, the fleet carrier *Intrepid*. She was so new from the yards at Hakassi that her corridors still reeked of sealing compound and cleaning solvent. Her huge realspace thruster engines still sang with the high-pitched squeal that the engine crews called "the baby's cry."

It would take more than a year for the mingled scents of the crew to displace the chemical smells from the first impressions of visitors. But after a hundred more hours under way, her engines' vibrations would drop two octaves, to the reassuring thrum of a seasoned thruster bank.

On *Intrepid*'s bridge, a tall Dornean in general's uniform paced along an arc of command stations equipped with large monitors. His eye-folds were swollen and fanned by an unconscious Dornean defensive reflex, and his leathery face was flushed purple by concern. Before the deployment was even a minute old, Etahn A'baht's first command had been bloodied.

The fleet tender *Ahazi* had overshot its jump, coming out of hyperspace too close to Bessimir and too late for its crew to recover from the error. Etahn A'baht watched the bright flare of light in the upper atmosphere from *Intrepid*'s forward viewstation, knowing that it meant six young men were dead.

THE NEW REBELLION
by Kristine Kathryn Rusch
Setting: Thirteen years after *Return of the Jedi*

Victorious though the New Republic may be, there is still no end to the threats to its continuing existence—this novel explores the price of keeping the peace. First, somewhere in the galaxy, millions suddenly perish in a blinding instant of pain. Then, as Leia prepares to address the Senate on Coruscant, a horrifying event changes the governmental equation in a flash.

Here is that latter calamity, in an early scene from The New Rebellion:

An explosion rocked the Chamber, flinging Leia into the air. She flew backward and slammed onto a desk, her entire body shuddering with the power of her hit. Blood and shrapnel rained around her. Smoke and dust rose, filling the room with a grainy darkness. She could hear nothing. With a shaking hand, she touched the side of her face. Warmth stained her cheeks and her earlobes. The ringing would start soon. The explosion was loud enough to affect her eardrums.

Emergency glow panels seared the gloom. She could feel rather than hear pieces of the crystal ceiling fall to the ground. A guard had landed beside her, his head tilted at an unnatural angle. She grabbed his blaster. She had to get out. She wasn't certain if the attack had come from within or from without. Wherever it had come from, she had to make certain no other bombs would go off.

The force of the explosion had affected her balance. She crawled over bodies, some still moving, as she made her way to the stairs. The slightest movement made her dizzy and nauseous, but she ignored the feelings. She had to.

A face loomed before hers. Streaked with dirt and blood, helmet askew, she recognized him as one of the guards who had been with her since Alderaan. *Your Highness*, he mouthed, and she couldn't read the rest. She shook her head at him, gasping at the increased dizziness, and kept going.

Finally she reached the stairs. She used the remains of a desk to get to her feet. Her gown was soaked in blood, sticky, and clinging to her legs. She held the blaster in front of her, wishing that she could hear. If she could hear, she could defend herself.

A hand reached out of the rubble beside her. She whirled, faced it, watched as Meido pulled himself out. His slender features were covered with dirt, but he appeared unharmed. He saw her blaster and cringed. She nodded once to acknowledge him, and kept moving. The guard was flanking her.

More rubble dropped from the ceiling. She crouched, hands over her head to protect herself. Small pebbles pelted her, and the floor shivered as large chunks of tile fell. Dust rose, choking her. She coughed, feeling it, but not able to hear it. Within an instant, the Hall had gone from a place of ceremonial comfort to a place of death.

The image of the death's-head mask rose in front of her again, this time from memory. She had known this was going to happen. Somewhere, from some part of her Force-sensitive brain, she had seen this. Luke said that Jedi were sometimes able to see the future. But she had never completed her training. She wasn't a Jedi.

But she was close enough.

The Corellian Trilogy:
AMBUSH AT CORELLIA
ASSAULT AT SELONIA
SHOWDOWN AT CENTERPOINT
by Roger MacBride Allen
Setting: Fourteen years after *Return of the Jedi*

This trilogy takes us to Corellia, Han Solo's homeworld, which Han has not visited in quite some time. A trade summit brings Han, Leia, and the children—now developing their own clear personalities and instinctively learning more about their innate skills in the Force—into the middle of a situation that most closely resembles a burning fuse. The Corellian system is on the brink of civil war, there are New Republic intelligence agents on a mysterious mission which even Han does not understand, and worst of all, a fanatical rebel leader has his hands on a superweapon of unimaginable power—and just wait until you find out who that leader is!

Here is an early scene from Ambush *that gives you a wonderful look at the growing Solo children (the twins are Jacen and Jaina, and their little brother is Anakin):*

Anakin plugged the board into the innards of the droid and pressed a button. The droid's black, boxy body shuddered awake, it drew in its wheels to stand up a bit taller, its status lights lit, and it made a sort of triple beep. "That's good," he said, and pushed the button again. The droid's status lights went out, and its body slumped down again. Anakin picked up the next piece, a motivation actuator. He frowned at it as he turned it over in his hands. He shook his head. "That's *not* good," he announced.

"What's not good?" Jaina asked.

"This thing," Anakin said, handing her the actuator. "Can't you *tell*? The insides part is all melty."

Jaina and Jacen exchanged a look. "The outside looks okay," Jaina said, giving the part to her brother. "How can he tell what the *inside* of it looks like? It's sealed shut when they make it."

Anakin, still sitting on the floor, took the device from his brother and frowned at it again. He turned it over and over in his hands, and then held it over his head and looked at it as if he were holding it up to the light. "There," he said, pointing a chubby finger at one point on the unmarked surface. "In there is the bad part." He rearranged himself to sit cross-legged, put the actuator in his lap, and put his right index finger over the "bad" part. "Fix," he said. "Fix." The dark brown outer case of the actuator seemed to glow for a second with an odd blue-red light, but then the glow sputtered out and Anakin pulled his finger away quickly and stuck it in his mouth, as if he had burned it on something.

"Better now?" Jaina asked.

"*Some* better," Anakin said, pulling his finger out of his mouth. "Not *all* better." He took the actuator in his hand and stood up. He opened the access panel on the broken droid and plugged in the actuator. He closed the door and looked expectantly at his older brother and sister.

"Done?" Jaina asked.

"Done," Anakin agreed. "But *I'm* not going to push the button." He backed well away from the droid, sat down on the floor, and folded his arms.

Jacen looked at his sister.

"Not me," she said. "This was your idea."

Jacen stepped forward to the droid, reached out to push the power button from as far away as he could, and then stepped hurriedly back.

Once again, the droid shuddered awake, rattling a bit this time as it did so. It pulled its wheels in, lit its panel lights, and made the same triple beep. But then its holocam eye viewlens wobbled back and forth, and its panel lights dimmed and flared. It rolled backward just a bit, and then recovered itself.

"Good morning, young mistress and masters," it said. "How may I surge you?"

Well, one word wrong, but so what? Jacen grinned and clapped his hands and rubbed them together eagerly. "Good day, droid," he said. They had done it! But what to ask for first? "First tidy up this room," he said. A simple task, and one that ought to serve as a good test of what this droid could do.

Suddenly the droid's overhead access door blew off and there was a flash of light from its interior. A thin plume of smoke drifted out of the droid. Its panel lights flared again, and then the work arm sagged downward. The droid's body, softened by heat, sagged in on itself and drooped to the floor. The floor and walls and ceiling of the playroom were supposed to be fireproof, but nonetheless the floor under the droid darkened a bit, and the ceiling turned black. The ventilators kicked on high automatically, and drew the smoke out of the room. After a moment they shut themselves off, and the room was silent.

The three children stood, every bit as frozen to the spot as the droid was, absolutely stunned. It was Anakin who recovered first. He walked cautiously toward the droid and looked at it carefully, being sure not to get too close or touch it. "*Really* melty now," he announced, and then wandered off to the other side of the room to play with his blocks.

The twins looked at the droid, and then at each other.

"We're dead," Jacen announced, surveying the wreckage.